"I think there is a strong new voice in crime fiction and it comes from Eva Montealegre. I really liked *Body on the Backlot*. Montealegre knows the secret, the best crime novels are not only about how a cop works on a case, but how a case works on a cop. Detective Joan Lambert is a refreshing new character and I'd like to see more."

—Michael Connelly, author of the Harry Bosch Series

"Detective Lambert bears little resemblance to Sue Grafton's Kinsey Milhone or Robert B. Parker's Sunny Randall. She's rougher around the edges, lives in the gritty world of Michael Connelly's Harry Bosch, and suffers even greater angst than Connelly's more famous LAPD detective. But give the lady time; Montealegre may equal Bosch's popularity…"

—Ken Fermoyle, *The Topanga Messenger*

"Montealegre has crafted a gripping spellbinder that draws the reader into the tale from the outset, holds reader interest, and keeps the pages turning….Settings are nicely detailed to bring the reader right into the scene. Characters are fully developed. Joan is believable, the scoundrels are suitably ill-famed, the tale itself is well written by a novelist having a fine grasp of language, situation, and stratagem."

—Molly Martin, *Reviewer's Bookwatch*

"…Eva [Montealegre]'s *Body on the Backlot*, casts a bright light on LA's dark side, where blind ambition rules and beauty is no more than skin deep. An absolute page-turner."

—Kris Neri, author of the Agatha, Anthony,
and Macavity Award-Nominated *Tracy*

"Wow! Eva [Montealegre] has certainly hit one out of the ballpark… Highly recommended."   —Janie Franz, MyShelf.com

BODY ON THE BACK LOT

EVA MONTEALEGRE

BODY ON THE BACK LOT

A VIREO BOOK | RARE BIRD BOOKS

LOS ANGELES, CALIF.

THIS IS A GENUINE VIREO BOOK

A Vireo Book | Rare Bird Books
453 South Spring Street, Suite 302
Los Angeles, CA 90013
rarebirdbooks.com

FIRST TRADE PAPERBACK ORIGINAL EDITION

Set in Dante
Printed in the United States

10 9 8 7 6 5 4 3 2 1

Publisher's Cataloging-in-Publication data
Names: Montealegre, Eva, author.
Title: Body on the backlot / Eva Montealegre.
Description: First Trade Paperback Original Edition | A Vireo Book | New York,
NY; Los Angeles, CA: Rare Bird Books, 2018.
Identifiers: ISBN 9781945572883
Subjects: LCSH Women detectives—California—Los Angeles—Fiction. |
Murder—Investigation—California—Los Angeles—Fiction. | Los Angeles (Calif.).
Police Department—Fiction. | Police—California—Los Angeles—Fiction. |
Suspense fiction. | Mystery fiction. | BISAC FICTION / Mystery & Detective /
Police Procedural | FICTION / Mystery & Detective / Women Sleuths
Classification: LCC PS3613.O547 B64 2018 | DDC 813.6—dc23

This book is dedicated to my husband, David,
the one who believes in me and champions my every endeavor.
In our love, I become joy.

"All we see or seem is but a dream within a dream."

—Edgar Allen Poe

"The most potent energy in the cosmos is dark matter.
We can't see it and we can't measure it.
We only know that it exists and that it powers the universe."

—Anthony Laurence, astronomer

CHAPTER ONE

IDRANK STRAIGHT FROM the bottle that night, just like my father. Plymouth gin, a trusted favorite. Driven from my bed by bad dreams and the insomnia that followed, I'd ended up outside my small home, sitting with my back against the old oak tree. Fact is, it's the only actual oak in the Oakwood area of Venice, California, and the reason I rented the place. Its distant relatives shaded the property I grew up on in the Ozark Mountains. A dream of that grand manor still clung to me like the scream that had set me upright in bed, bug-eyed and gasping for breath. When I was a kid, my grandmother told me that if you got killed in your dream, it means your old self's dying to make room for a new life. I wonder how she knew that. My mom had told me that Gramma was an elder, but it was the sort of thing you said in a whisper, like it was a secret you should keep. There were times that I would see Gramma dancing very exact steps—four steps, I remember—back and forth, and she'd sort of sing under her breath, as if she were whispering a chant. It was always gentle. A gentle secret. I was halfway through the bottle when it dawned on me that I should have asked my grandmother more questions about that.

My ears perked to attention as a muscle car prowled down the alley behind my house. The clamor of its muffler bounced off cinder-block walls and rattled chain-link fences. Headlights swept through the branches of the old oak above me. By that time, my butt was tucked into the roots of the tree, and my back was well pressed into the bark of the trunk. As the car approached, light poured through the fence, striping my face. Neighboring pit bulls barked in angry protest to the muffler's assault. Seventies funk music blasted from the car windows, vibrating a rhythm through the alley and permeating even the bones of my chest.

Carl had played that exact music tirelessly throughout the different phases of our romance. He worshipped those custom-built car engines from the same era. Could be he was paying me a "surprise" visit. I saw myself hitting him over the head with the bottle and thought what a terrible waste of good gin that'd be. As if catching me in the act, or maybe hearing my thoughts, the car picked up speed with a screech and roared down the alley. Yep, I decided, that was Carl.

Exhaust fumes, tinged with crumbled asphalt and alley dust, rose with toxic abandon and wafted through the night air. After the rumble of the car's muffler had faded into the night, what goes for a 3:00 a.m. silence settled. The moon shone from directly above me, shards of illumination pouring through the branches of the tree. The quiet was broken when glass shattered in the street followed by a drunken shout of curses. I listened, attentive to the unfolding drama, but all was calm again.

I watched a huge rat lazily make its way across the roof of my house toward the tree. One of the branches arched over toward the roof and the big rodent, apparently familiar with this route, lifted itself up onto the branch and continued coming toward the center of the tree. It seemed the oak gave sanctuary not only to the likes of me but also to the biggest rat God ever created. In a ray of moonshine, the truth of the creature came to me. The rat turned out not to be a rat at all. It was an opossum. I hadn't seen one of those for a while. The white opossum stopped halfway across the branch, still as stone, nose sniffing. Red eyes peered down at me. I took another swig of my gin to let him know I wasn't going anywhere.

"My father ate one of your kind," I informed him.

And it was true. Back in the Ozarks, our neighbors had offered opossum stew and Daddy thought it would prove we were "just folks," so he ate it. But this little guy trespassing in my yard was safe.

"Not to worry," I assured the opossum.

He didn't move. Opossums can stay extremely still for the longest time. That's how they convince you that they're dead. I could relate to that. It's not like I generally down a bottle of gin every night. But I do keep one handy. Just in case one of those long nights of the soul thangs jumps outta da swamp and bites my ass. Not that there are many swamps in the LA area. I sloshed down a little more Plymouth gin and held the bottle up to the moonlight. Two-thirds gone.

"Last one," I told myself.

A numbing peace came over me, like a raven turning smoothly in descent. I saw myself running after my mother through a green field of corn. I was trying to catch hold of her coal-black hair. She turned around laughing, then stooped down to catch me in her arms. Her hair, a silken mane, floated around and enfolded me like wings.

"Oh, Mama. I wish...I could have saved you." Darkness embraced me.

It seemed that I had just laid my head back when the auto-grind coffeemaker sounded from inside my house.

Morning's first light. A marine layer seeped in from the ocean and covered everything with a blanket of blue mist. A formidable stabbing pain in my head made standing up an iffy proposition. I held the tree trunk to steady myself, kicked the empty bottle of gin, then slipped back on my ass. Luckily, it was numb from its night in the roots. I noticed that I'd cleverly left the door to my house open all night. For all I knew, the opossum, plus any variety of characters, was inside there right now. I imagined a party of opossums using their little hands to open the big package from my aunt. In my mind, they unwrapped each item and devoured everything within the tall and commanding box and that was a good thing, because then I would never have to address the contents. I badly needed a shower, coffee, and a painkiller, in no particular order, so I forced myself to my feet. I stood there a moment, in the morning mist, a newly risen ghost. The pungent aroma of brewing chicory coffee drew me to the open door of my little home.

I managed to bang into a wall, a little self-punishment, no doubt, as I made my way to the bathroom. After a desperate search, I found a bottle of Motrin. There were only three left so I took all three and made a mental note to pick up some more, splashed water on my face, brushed my teeth, and peered at the pallor of my skin in the bathroom light.

After a scalding bath, I finished off with a cold shower. I was inching toward full humanity as I stumbled into the bedroom I had abandoned the night before for the oak tree. I slipped into clothes I'd already laid out for the day ahead: a men's blue shirt, black pants, black socks, and polished black shoes. I wrapped my small holster around my waist, reached for my Smith & Wesson .38, dropped it in, and snapped the strap.

As I walked through the kitchen, I eyed the hugeness of the delivered box leaning against the wall in the living room. I tried to guess what might be in it. A hangover has the strange power of taking one out of one's emotional trauma and landing one smack in the middle of being simply pissed off and irritable. What items would Auntee Trish deign to be delivered to me at this late date? And why now? Maybe to assuage her guilt. Perhaps she had finally decided that there were some personal items of my mother's that she could live without. Would have been nice if she had written me just once in the last eighteen years. Or as proper for a lady of her stature, minimally, she might have, first, sent me a note on some fancy stationery saying, *Hey, Joan, I'm going to send you a big carton of...*whatever the hell it was.

My eyes burned against the morning glare coming into the kitchen window, so I grabbed dark sunglasses and put them on even though I was inside my house. Carl liked to say I was going incognito whenever I wore those glasses. My mind often filtered my life through what Carl used to say or think and I resented that. It's hard to kick a bad habit when it's the only one you've ever had. My mother used to wear big sunglasses to the doctor's office after a particularly bad beating from my father. In an effort to change the tracks in my mind, I thought of the photos I'd seen in old *LIFE* magazines at that same doctor's office when I was a kid. I pulled up before my eyes tabloid snapshots of Maria Callas in dark sunglasses when she was happy and in love on a big yacht in the Mediterranean. How could she know that she would lose her love, her voice, become a pariah, and kill herself? I sipped the hot chicory coffee. I'd bought this particular brand for myself while in New Orleans. It was my habit to always drink coffee from an old-fashioned white diner mug. Used to have two mugs, bought them from my favorite breakfast place, but Carl broke one in a jealous fit. Whoops, there I was back on Carl again. Damn. Okay. So, what if I met a nice guy and wanted to share a cup of coffee with him? I'd only have one good diner cup. I was thinking

I'd replace it when the phone chirped an insistent "good morning." I looked back out the kitchen window in hopes of spotting the opossum asleep somewhere in the tree before I picked up the phone.

"This is Joan," I answered in what felt more like a confession.

"How's it hangin', Detective?"

"Hey, Satch."

Satch is my captain, downtown in Homicide, Special Section. He's a big Irishman with a lot of soul. Everybody calls him Satch because he has a raspy voice and he's also, absolutely, a New Orleans jazz and blues man. A guitar chord of longing sounded somewhere in my heart. I so wanted to be back in New Orleans still on vacation.

"We've got you busy this morning right there in your neck of the woods. Down at the beach a piece. The canal area. It's a young woman from St. Louis, apparently a young transplant. Dead in her home. There's a couple guys at the crime scene from Pacific Division."

"Anybody I know?"

"Can't say, but we're taking it from them in any case. When St. Louis Police Department notified the parents, turned out they own the St. Louis Muni opera house and they're tight with those beer people, the Anheuser-Busch family. So, that's front-page news, figure the case is ours now. Everything ASAP. You know the drill. Gus will meet you there."

"Okay, boss. What's the address?"

My stomach wrenched when I noticed the box cutter, still on the coffee table where I had left it last night. The tall package looked down at me accusingly, unopened. I wasn't ready, though. Not quite yet.

I locked up my house and, address in hand, split for the crime scene. My car was a late-model dark blue Crown Victoria, well recognizable as a cop car to just about everyone but especially criminals. I adjusted the rearview mirror and, for vanity's sake, ran my hands through my short black curls, grateful that I didn't have to fix my hair. I put the keys in the car ignition; underneath the seventy-six-trombone headache there sounded the morning chorus of barking pit bulls. I turned the corner onto Abbot Kinney Boulevard where a long line of drunks supported a brick wall while they waited for the door to open at The Brig, the only bar in this area with early hours.

The sun lit up the morning mist, and as I got closer to the ocean, the real estate improved. I'd forgotten to put on lip gloss and my lips were so dry they hurt. My destination was the canals. The canals run into the beach and they are also part of Venice, but much different, because when you hit the canals, the area abruptly transforms into an exclusive community of stars, studio execs, and others employed in the entertainment industry. As I got closer, the homes got bigger and the windows had leaded and stained glass in them instead of the black security bars of my neighborhood. When I dropped over a small hill I was greeted by the canals, full of ducks and sunshine-reflecting bridges.

I pulled past a rowboat on the last canal into a long driveway of a small palace and followed a row of pepper trees toward the beach. I took in a deep breath. A clump of palm and banana trees concealed what turned out to be a bungalow built on rocks and stilts out over the surf line. The front door faced the water where the sun shone through the fog and glimmered golden on ocean blue.

I parked. Praying for ChapStick, I groped around in my glove compartment, found some, and swiped it across my lips with a measure of relief. Getting out, I adjusted my gun in its holster and closed the car door of my "unmarked" with extra care not to slam it. I was feeling delicate. I pressed my lips together, making sure the ChapStick had covered the whole lip area, and took a moment to take in the scene while I put on my game face.

"Hey, Joan!"

Even with my sunglasses, the glare made it hard to make out anything more than a large, indistinct form. The voice was vaguely familiar, vaguely annoying. I figured it was Trevor Krantz. Trevor, yeah, he was working Pacific Homicide. That made sense. Had to be him. We were rivals years ago at the police academy. We had this competition thing going, always looking to knock each other out of the top spot and now, here we were. He lumbered toward me.

I refused to answer, as it would only add more pain to my aching head. The waves pounding against the rocks and pilings of the house were relentless. I caught peripheral movement that turned out to be a big black dog. It was sad-faced and furtive and immediately slinked behind a rock. Dogs aren't the best creatures to have around a crime scene. They like to carry things off and bury them. I fast-stepped my way toward Trevor, hoping to shorten the drama of my approach. He was all teeth, grinning at me like I was an old war buddy or something. I smiled back even though it hurt my face.

"How long you been back?" he asked.

"Today's my first day."

"You look good."

"Thanks, I feel like shit. It's nice to see you, though."

"I knew they couldn't keep you away," he added. "Well, if you knew that, you knew more than I did." That old sheepish look spread across his face.

"To tell you the truth, I have to thank you because today I collect fifty bucks. I told them you didn't crack. You're a tough guy."

It wasn't the first time I'd had odds laid on me. I was beginning to feel like a racehorse. When I went on board with Pacific Homicide, everybody in my unit said I wouldn't last long, that I cared too much. Bets were laid down that I wouldn't make it six months. But here I was, higher in the ranks than many of those who'd wagered against me.

"I appreciate your vote of confidence, but tough ain't always the answer," I said.

"Yeah, well, tell that to the bad guys."

"Really, huh." I agreed. "What do we got today, anyway?"

"Dead girl. Not from around here. St. Louis. Looks like a sex fest in there."

"What do you mean?" I asked. "Gadgets, dungeon stuff?"

"No, cozy. A real love nest."

"Like you would know."

A pained expression shot across his face but then he recovered, back to business.

"This one don't even seem dead. It's like lookin' at a big doll. A big pretty doll, no kiddin'."

"Who does that black dog belong to?" I asked.

"What black dog?"

I looked around, but the dog was out of sight. I shrugged and gave him a feeble smile.

"It doesn't even look like a homicide to me," he continued.

"No? Then what is it?"

"Recreational drug overdose, some lethal cocktail. Kids these days are into ecstasy and all that designer shit. It's not like we need Specials to come crashing in to figure it out."

"Maybe they just decided to give me an easy one. You know, my first day back and all, and maybe it didn't hurt that I'm from St. Louis. Her parents are heavy hitters, so don't take it personal. We'll make a big deal over the tragic death of their daughter and everybody can go home with a job well done."

"Okay. Right. Make your stats look good."

"Later," I said, immediately unhappy about how I had framed it. Why was I so quick to respond to his peevish complaints? Why did I feel I had to care for his precious ego? I made my move away from him and toward the crime scene.

"You've heard that there's three types of female detective?"

I turned back to him with exaggerated reluctance, or maybe it wasn't exaggerated.

"Your morning joke?"

"Nope, no joke."

"Okay, I'll bite. What's the three types of female detective?"

"Nympho, lesbo, and psycho."

"Very clever."

"Which one are you?"

I snorted and considered. "I think I'll have to go with psycho."

"It's not as interesting as the other two, but I see your point." He grinned his big teeth at me. "Welcome back," he said.

"Yeah. Is Van Chek in there?"

He nodded. "We already filled him in on all the details."

A breeze blew off the ocean as I followed a stone path through the sand to the front of the house and breathed in the smell of sea air. Once in front of the house, I stopped for a moment and took in the expanse of ocean. I spotted the black dog making its way down the beach. A wave slammed against a big rock beside the house and sprayed me in the face and shoulder. It was oddly invigorating.

Another one of LAPD's finest was putting up the yellow crime tape. Heavy in the middle, with rosy red cheeks, he looked like a young

W. C. Fields. The tape slipped out of his grip and the yellow ribbon blew up in the air. It flew and dipped, snapping over my head. I grabbed it and handed the plastic strip back to the detective and held up my badge, and he waved me in.

"McKenna," he said.

"Joan Lambert," I answered.

I wiped my sunglasses dry on my shirt and pressed sea-wet curls behind my ear as I pushed open the front door. It was a golden wood, carved in geometric shapes that fit together. One of a kind, custom living. You see it a lot in Special Section.

I entered the foyer and immediately got the "love nest" feeling Trevor conveyed. The place had a pleasant smell of incense. The decor was hip, sexy, with textured satins and silks amid jungle patterns and tropical plants. The constant crashing of the surf against the foundation pilings was unnerving. Yet the overall feeling of the place was "hideaway."

My partner, Gus Van Chek, Detective, third level, was tall and not a bad looker. I'd known him for a good ten years. In his late forties, the women were still major crazy for him. He strode toward me into the foyer from the living room on long legs like a big gray panther.

"You ready?" he asked.

I nodded, glad to see his thin rugged face and pepper-gray hair.

"What I want to know," he said, "is how can people live with that water slapping back and forth all day and night."

"I guess they must have a thing for the ocean."

My eyes were drawn to an African mask on the wall. I liked it. Gus followed my gaze.

"It's a Moon Goddess dance mask," he offered. "Probably from Upper Volta."

"Moon Goddess?" There were several carved circles and white paint around brown and black saucer eyes. "Who told you that?"

"Nobody told me, Joan. I know. Maybe you should go to a museum sometime."

"You mean one of those world culture digs you frequent?"

"Couldn't hurt. I'll invite you next time I go."

He gestured toward the living room as if he were the host in his own home.

My eyes took in a clean hardwood floor and came up the side of a maroon velvet couch and settled on the pale flesh of a young woman. The short skirt of her green cocktail dress was hiked up around her hips. She wore no underpants. The position of her body was sensual, one arm above her, beckoning. Her long red hair triggered a reaction in me. I almost hesitated to approach. It was as though I might disturb and awaken her. Gus was right behind me.

"'He saw therein a maiden of the greatest beauty. She lay as if asleep and was wrapped in her long hair as in a precious mantle.'"

"Brothers Grimm," I said. "Never known you to quote fairy tales."

"I still have a few in me."

We shared a moment of remorse for the girl we didn't know.

A dead body usually looks dead, the life energy gone. In this case, like Gus had said, it was as though this one would wake up with the right kiss. Maybe she'd been dreaming and had stretched her arm up above her. Except for her dress being hiked up, it was the pose of a glamorous forties film star. "Looks like she'll wake up, sashay out to the sand, and take a stroll," said Gus. "Her name is Autumn Riley."

Even dead, Autumn Riley was a breathtaking woman. I bent over and gently opened one of Autumn's eyes. She was wearing colored contact lenses and her bright emerald gaze stared back at me.

"Paramedics pronounce her?" I asked.

"Yes, a young guy. He just left, got another call, an accident on PCH."

"Did he seem pretty sure about that?" I asked.

"About what?"

"About her being dead, Gus."

"Oh, yeah. She's dead, all right. The coroner will be here any moment."

There was still sand on her bare feet from her last walk on the beach. I did a cursory survey of the room, too peaceful for a crime scene.

"So, who called it in?" I asked.

Gus sighed. "Pacific got an anonymous call. Somebody screaming Autumn Riley's been murdered, then they gave this address."

"Did you find a goodbye note?" I asked.

"Nope. No drug paraphernalia, no alcohol, no pills, no weapon, no sign of forced entry, no indication of robbery or struggle."

"Hmmph, curious." I moved toward the kitchen as Gus continued his report. The garage door that connected to the kitchen was open and I could see a brand-new silver Audi T. It looked like a high-tech bug.

"Anything in the car?" I asked.

"Nothing," said Gus. "She just bought it a week ago. Maybe she didn't like it and was so upset she committed suicide."

I shot him a disapproving glance. "How much mileage on the car?" I asked.

"Eight hundred miles."

"Was there any indication that she was emotionally distraught about anything?"

"Nope. She was one lucky little girl from the looks of things. There was an empty bottle of wine and two recently used wineglasses. No food whatsoever in the icebox, just condiments, diet soda, and nail polish."

Gus held out a box of latex gloves and I pulled on a pair as I browsed the kitchen, noticed the red sediment of the wine still in the wineglasses, opened several cabinet doors, and looked for dog food but found none. No bowls on the kitchen floor for water or food either, so the black dog was definitely not hers. The sink, icebox, and dishwasher were all stainless steel. A matching blue designer microwave, toaster, and blender accented the blue tile.

In the bathroom, a package of NoDoze was opened on the counter, but there were no other drugs or prescriptions. A still-damp green bikini was draped on a towel rack. A makeup bag had a powder compact, blood-red lipstick, liquid eyeliner, and mascara. Autumn Riley must have had a charmed life because she didn't even have aspirins.

The bedroom was decorated in reds and purples, in the middle of which there was a tussled bed but nothing to imply foul play. Her pillow was scrunched on the side, which might mean she liked to hug it when she slept. I do. Or maybe she had clutched the pillow during an ecstatic moment of lovemaking, which seemed more likely somehow. A large round mirror was framed in the same golden wood as the front door. A fierce dragon was carved into the top, a forked tongue licked through long teeth, its eyes huge, round, and all-seeing. A matching wooden dresser with a similar carved dragon had several stacks of eight-by-ten glossies on it, each a different professional photo of the vic. Most of the shots were sensual and elegant images, except for one in which Autumn posed in leather and wore dark makeup.

A primitive doll constructed of cloth and wood sat beside the stack of photos. Hand sewn, the eyes were blue buttons from an old peacoat and a red ribbon was tied around the doll's waist like a belt. The black-and-white fabric of the doll's dress was an African print. I'd always heard that people stuck pins in voodoo dolls, but I didn't find any.

Next to the doll was a jewelry box carved out of soapstone. When I opened it, I found a wide assortment of different styles of jewelry: an elephant hair bracelet from Africa, an antique ring with a large square ruby, a necklace with a symbol scratched in pewter, and an ankle bracelet of wooden beads.

An address book on the dresser still had the price sticker on it. There were only a few numbers in it. I bagged it and checked the shelves of the closet, reaching into the corners, then searched through the dresser drawers. In the bra drawer, I came across a flyer promoting what I assumed were musical bands. **DE SADE'S CAGE** was printed in bold red across the top, but there was no address or phone number. Finally, I went back in the front room to find Gus.

"Why are we calling this a murder, exactly?" I asked.

"Because of the nine-one-one call, that's it. That's why," he said.

"I want to hear the tape," I said.

"It's being sent over to Parker Center. By the time we get back it should be on my desk."

"Male or female?"

"The caller? Male, at least as far as they could tell."

"I want to go out on the roof."

"You still do that?" asked Gus.

"Why not? Doesn't hurt anything."

On the roof, you have a perspective you can't get inside. You can see a layout of the area, escape routes. Once, I spotted a system of paths created by neighborhood kids over the years. We followed the path and found traces from our crime scene. Turned out, our main witness was a thirteen-year-old girl who grew up in the neighborhood. "You go ahead," said Gus.

I didn't know if a designer put the big rock right next to the house or if the architect had planned the house to sit beside it that way, but I was grateful in either case. I scrambled up the rock and carefully stepped onto the Spanish tile roof. I stood there looking out over the tops of the houses in the Venice Canals and considered all the other people in the neighborhood inside their homes, drinking coffee, eating breakfast, untouched by murder. Even up here, the surf pounded, insistent, right up through my feet.

The image of Autumn Riley's fairy-tale face, pale white skin, and vibrant red hair stayed in my mind's eye as I looked toward downtown and saw the city skyscrapers emerging from a blue-gray fog. It was one of those days when the city of Los Angeles was a mirage. There were no earth-shattering clues on the roof, but, up here, I made a pact with Autumn Riley that I'd solve this crime wherever it took me. Commitment is an important aspect of Special Section because often the obstacles seem insurmountable. I made my way down the big rock.

Once inside, I went directly to the body. I took Autumn's outstretched hand in mine for a moment and regretted it immediately. Her cool fingers evoked a long-unforgotten sorrow within me. My mind wandered back to my mother and an antique hand-wringer washing machine.

I held the dead girl's hand tenderly, as if I could comfort her. But it was too late. The beast had got her. Like it had got Mama. I shook it off, forcing myself to focus on where I was and the specifics of this crime.

I decided that she could have done hand commercials. Or more likely hair commercials. That would explain my feeling that I had seen her before but couldn't really place her. I noted the green color of her nail polish. There were no needle marks between the delicate fingers or between her toes. Trevor and McKenna came into the room and stood in the back, careful not to get in the way. Their presence annoyed me and I found myself consumed with a protective feeling toward the body. I lifted Autumn's long hair away from her face and checked behind her ears.

"That hair alone could drive a man gonzo," Trevor said hoarsely.

Since he was standing there like a big goon, he might as well be useful.

"What was the temperature?" I asked.

"Excuse me?" said Trevor.

"The temperature of the body?"

"Paramedic said ninety-two degrees," said Trevor. "She's been dead for an hour, maybe."

"And what time did the call come in?"

"Five forty-five a.m."

I checked my watch, but since I forgot to strap it on that morning, I merely glanced at three beauty marks that dance upon my wrist. I cursed myself.

"And what time is it, Gus?"

"Seven."

"So, the call came in before she died?"

Trevor gave me a look and said, "The tests can be off by a half hour or so. You know that."

I didn't reply.

"We're going to have quite a few visitors," Gus said to Trevor and McKenna. "Since Media Relations hasn't shown, we'll need you both to handle the front line, okay?"

Trevor turned and walked out. McKenna mock saluted us and followed suit.

A police photographer entered the room. Craig Jones. He's a black guy, slight of build, kinda shy and quiet. He nodded at Gus and me, saw the body, and started snapping pictures.

Rose Torres, a Filipino woman from the crime lab, showed up just then as well. I was so happy to see her I could have given her a big hug, but touchy-feely emotions are frowned on in my position. After a quick handshake and a hello, she gazed at Autumn for a moment, then turned her inscrutable face to me. I'm used to being taller than most women, but I tower over Rose.

"Make sure we get the wineglasses in the kitchen," I said.

Her eyes went to the hardwood floor. Rose doesn't waste much energy on words.

"Usual search for fibers," I said. "I need to know where the doll in the bedroom came from. Take it apart, whatever you find inside, I want to know all about it."

She nodded and moved her short thick body into efficiency mode.

Gus pulled out a cigarette but didn't light it.

"What do you think of that voodoo doll?" he asked.

"Maybe she's got a tourist's fascination with that culture. Could be she meant to take some sort of Shaman's trip, downed a bad mix of hallucinogens, and never made it back."

"A Shaman's trip?" asked Gus. "Like a spiritual quest?"

"Could be. I knew this guy who worked bunko squad. Arrested an urban shaman, a woman. She nearly killed four wealthy Brentwood babes with some sort of vision quest potion. They went into a collective coma, so to speak."

"You mean like a group thing."

"Yeah, when they found them they were conked out on the floor, holding hands. At first they thought it was a cult death exit."

Rose was in the kitchen inspecting the wineglasses, holding them up to the light. The bedroom lit up from the flash of Craig's camera. These morose activities of investigation were a strange kind of comfort and yet, something was different for me this time.

"What kind of drug?" asked Gus.

"I think...barbiturates mixed with peyote or something from South America."

"What happened?"

"When they finally woke up from their comas, their money market accounts were empty."

"Good con."

"At least they were still alive."

"This one is dead, Joan. It's a damn shame. But she's gone."

I went to the window and spotted the newly arrived news crews, all microphones, cameras, and notepads. Each team raced against the others to the crime scene yet landed ensemble, a small riot making its way toward the bungalow just as the blue Coroner's truck pulled up.

"And here comes her ride with the first group of mourners." Gus shook his head.

Outside, the wind had picked up, handing out bad hair days to the media birds that scrambled and buzzed around the Coroner's truck. McKenna and Trevor had to hold back the pressing crowd to allow the coroner's staff out of the truck. Looky-loos gathered on the beach and around the perimeter of the house. The tumult of the reporters as they fired questions was an aggravating sound-mix.

"Poor little rich girl, a Midwest innocent murdered in evil Los Angeles," said Gus. "All of America is going to want the dirty details, shake their heads and cry. You realize that, right?"

I nodded, the wrench in my stomach coming to a full-tied knot when I recognized the lean form of Jesse Cand, crime reporter from the *Times*. He stood at the edge of the crowd, staring back at me. The guy was stalking me but I couldn't accuse him of that. He'd say he was just doing his job. Journalists always say that as they purposefully impale your life with their favorite writing instrument. Jesse was so happy to see me, he waved. "Well, hell!" I said.

Gus joined me at the window and spotted Jesse. "Don't worry, when we leave we'll just run over that bag of bones."

"A few more details here and I'll be happy to take you up on that offer. So, date rape gone wrong?" I asked.

"No indication of foul play or violence, particularly," said Gus. "The time of death and the issue of the phone call is fairly shaky at this point. The lab guys should be able to say for sure."

"It's a long line down there at the morgue."

"You do the dance that hurries the autopsy. That'll let people know you're back on the job," said Gus. "Satch gave me the number of the Riley's family doctor, I think I'll give him a ring."

Gus went into the utility room to make the call.

I was standing there, settling into my receptive state, when Autumn let out a sigh. I jumped. It's not unusual for air to suddenly escape the lips of a body, but it's always startling. Most of the time it happens when you move the body, not when it's just lying there. I stared and half expected she'd continue to breathe. Then I found I was hoping, willing her to breathe. I had experienced her last breath.

I leaned over the body, put my ear by her slightly open mouth. No more breath came. And in that instant I decided that something was off with this crime scene. It struck me as staged for the benefit of an audience. The way the body was found, the fact that someone called. I stared down at Autumn as if I could read the truth in her serene face, in the alluring gesture of her arm.

Gus came back into the room. "Normal kid stuff like measles and mumps, no health problems. None."

"Are the parents coming to LA?" I asked.

"Tonight."

"Did we get everything out of the medicine chest?"

"Medicine chest? You mean medicine cabinet, Joan."

"Did we get it?"

"Yes. You're thinking drugs or poison, right?"

"Seems obvious. How 'bout the icebox?"

"You mean the fridge."

"Whatever."

"We got that, too," Gus said.

"What about the neighbors?" I asked.

"Nobody noticed a thing. Nada," said Gus. "You believe that?"

"It's a keep-to-yourself neighborhood." We stood there silently for a moment.

I noticed the DVD, zeroed in. Gus picked up on it and pressed the eject button. A disc popped from the black mouth. I carefully pulled it out to read the title. *"Blonde Venus.* You know it, Gus?"

"Old Marlene Dietrich film. Play it," he said. I popped it back in and hit play.

A line of opiated dancers in jungle costumes, complete with spears, painted shields, and feathers, synch-stepped to an African drumbeat. A convincing gorilla appeared and joined in center stage. The gorilla pulled off its furry hands to reveal the beautiful bejeweled hands of a woman, which then reached up to pull off its gorilla head. It was Marlene Dietrich in a blond Afro. She emerged from the gorilla suit in a sparkly costume singing lyrics that lamented being enslaved to the drums and the enticing sins of voodoo. The DVD stopped.

Gus nodded and I bagged it.

Standing in the bedroom doorway, Rose caught my eye and held up two bags.

"We're in luck."

"What is it?" I asked.

"Semen from the sheets, hair samples. And, as per your request, fibers, red ones."

"Check the vic's shoes?" I asked.

"You know I will," Rose said as she turned away to continue her work. It was then that I realized Rose has the uncanny ability to make her voice sound melodious and weary at the same time. A deep sorrow crept into my being, or maybe it had been there all along and something in her voice called it out of me. Yes, that was more likely.

I found Autumn's driver's license in an orange patent-leather handbag. She was only eighteen years old. She had credit cards—Saks Fifth Avenue, Neiman Marcus, and others.

"That's some heavy plastic," said Gus.

After a more thorough inspection of Autumn's purse, I discovered a laminated card with a drawing of the Goddess Aphrodite. On the back, someone had written, "Kunda, The Malibu Psychic." Plus, yesterday's date and a time: one o'clock.

I flashed the back of the card at Gus and said, "I feel the need for spiritual advice."

"Yeah," sighed Gus, "I bet you do, too."

CHAPTER TWO

AFTER A SHORT RIDE up the Pacific Coast Highway with the ocean and tightly packed bungalows on one side and green mountains on the other, the MALIBU PSYCHIC sign pointed down an asphalt driveway. Black tarmac wound 'round a Mexican fast-food joint and ended in front of a modest white structure that had a view of the beach. Gus and I got out of the car. It was the end of September, but the day was warming up like July, not unusual in Southern California. I looked out to the spectacular blue of the ocean and saw a well-built guy with a deep tan and long blond hair catch a colossal wave and ride it all the way until it dissipated into bubbly foam in the sand.

"Gus, did you know that there's three types of female detectives?"

"Yes, I did."

"What are they?"

"Nympho, lesbo, and psycho."

"Which one am I?"

"You're asking *me*?"

"I'm asking your opinion."

"Oh, heck. I guess I'd have to say you're a psycho."

"Thanks a lot."

"You asked. Hey, it's probably a compliment."

"Is that what people think of me, that I'm a psycho?"

"Whaddya care what people think?"

"I care, okay? Don't you?"

"Not really. Anyways, it's a joke. You mustn't internalize these things."

The thing about Gus is that he psychoanalyzes everything and everybody. There's no stopping him. The worse thing about it is he's often right.

The tarmac guided us to the front door with yet another sign that promised us the Malibu Psychic. There was virtually no landscaping, only determined dandelions sprouting through the holes in the parking lot and a statue of a man-sized cat that stood sentry-like at the doorway. The cat was poised to strike on some invisible prey.

"You seen Carl lately?" asked Gus.

Ah yes, Carl. Ex-lover and ex-partner. Once upon a time, I had been safe in his arms. And then, it felt dangerous to even think of him. "No, I haven't."

"Why not?"

"I don't know," I said with a lame shrug.

Gus had to bring that up. I'd always possessed the knowledge that I was alone in the world. I never questioned it. I accepted it, like breathing. For a while with Carl, that had changed. My partner, Gus, believes that all problems can be solved with talk. Carl was his close buddy. We were all pretty much inseparable until recently.

"I got a feeling about this," said Gus.

"Like what?"

"Like maybe we're about to get a heavy dose of woo-woo."

"Woo-woo? Is that anything like bullshit?"

"Oh, yeah. Only more glamorous and enigmatic," Gus said.

"Well, start the show," I said as I came face-to-face with the stone cat. Gus looked from the cat to me and back to the cat.

"What?" I asked.

"I was thinking: *You have a lot of cat energy.*"

"Aw, come on," I said. "Let's wait until we get inside for that, shall we?"

"You said start the show."

A tiny bell tingled above the door, announcing our arrival. Smoke curled up from a brass incense burner on a wooden desk in one corner. I could identify sandalwood, but the other fragrances eluded me. The walls featured at least twenty framed posters, dramatic depictions of goddesses: Aphrodite, Goddess of Love; Athena, Goddess of Wisdom; Pele, Hawaiian Goddess of the Volcano; some Goddess of Death.

Cards stuck in the frames indicated which was which. Chances were good that Autumn had picked up her Goddess of Love card here. Crystals dangled from the ceiling on lengths of fishing line. Back home, in the Ozarks, we have psychics, but there we call them spiritualists. They're old ladies who sit in rocking chairs on the porch. They don't have crystals or goddess pictures or bells, but when they tell you something, you listen.

There were a half-dozen candles burning on tables scattered about the room and several comfy puffed-up chairs. I didn't see any voodoo dolls. An attractive woman appeared from behind a curtain and floated into the incense-smoky room. The purple silks she wore matched her startling violet eyes. Her straight honey-blond hair fell long to her hips and her push-up bra created a healthy cleavage above all the flowing purple silk. When she came toward us, I picked up the fragrance of roses and thought of my Gramma, who often used rose water as a perfume. The woman smiled at Gus and offered her hand as if for a kiss, but Gus reached out and shook it. He introduced us, then asked for Kunda. Her smile dropped off her face and she looked directly at me for the first time.

"I'm Kunda," she said soberly. "It's about Autumn, right?"

"How'd you know that?" Gus asked.

"I felt it here," she said, laying her bejeweled and manicured hands upon her heart. "She's dead, isn't she?"

I jumped right in. "Who told you that she was dead?"

"Like I said, I felt it."

"In what capacity did you know Autumn Riley?"

She looked confused.

"Was she a client?"

"Yes."

It was the kind of yes that passed through a lot of inner censors. My interest was piqued. I sat down on one of the comfy chairs, letting her know that I would not be leaving without some answers.

"Have a seat," she offered Gus as she herself sank into in a pink love seat. He passed.

"Can you tell us if Autumn was involved with drugs?" I asked.

Kunda appeared wounded at the very idea. "Never. Autumn was a health nut. Everything had to be natural." She bent her head for a moment, then raised it and continued. "She was wholesome and sweet. She had an incredible singing voice. She sang with great power."

"Did she sing professionally?"

"Yes. Autumn told me she performed opera at the Muni in St. Louis."

"Isn't she a little young to be an opera singer?" I asked.

"Yes."

I waited for Kunda to say more but she didn't.

"Autumn wasn't an actress?"

"She wanted to do modeling, be a film star." I heard a slight judgment in her voice.

Gus piped in, "In your relationship with Autumn, did you use the archetype of goddesses in your, uh, counseling? Did that signify something in particular?" Gus pulled out the goddess card we found in Autumn Riley's purse and showed it to Kunda.

"I don't think it's right for me to reveal private information about Autumn."

"We believe Autumn may have been a victim of foul play. We're conducting a murder investigation," I said. "We'd appreciate any information you could give us that would help us understand what happened."

Kunda bent her head down. She was beginning to annoy me and maybe she picked that up because when she spoke again she looked only at Gus.

"Aphrodite is a love goddess, the Sex Goddess. It's an appropriate archetype to guide one's life if your ambition is to have the masses adore you."

"Did she have any success as an actress?" Gus asked.

"Limited. Hardly made a dime. She used the money from her trust for most expenses."

"Like psychic readings," I added.

Kunda shot me her best affronted look.

"How about for art?" Gus asked.

"Oh, no," she said her eyes rolling back over to Gus in a knowing, familiar way.

"I happened to notice that she had some expensive African pieces at her place," Gus said.

"Glenn Addams paid for that bungalow and everything in it." Kunda's voice fell to a deep, foreboding tone.

"Glenn Addams?" I asked. "The producer?"

"Yes, he's a powerful force in the world of Hollywood."

She said the word "Hollywood" as if it were despicable.

"The landlord didn't mention a Glenn Addams," said Gus. "How is it you know what's in her bungalow and who paid for it?"

"Autumn told me much more than she told her landlord, I can assure you." She touched a lavender gemstone that hung from her neck. "I feel that Autumn Spirit must move on."

She accented this thought by gracefully lifting her hands like a magician freeing doves from a top hat.

"She is close, extremely close. I can hear Autumn Spirit breathing."

In my mind's eye, I saw Autumn Riley zipped up in a body bag, swaying back and forth in the coroner's truck, on her way to the LA County morgue.

"Autumn Spirit?" I asked. Kunda nodded.

"Can Autumn Spirit tell you how she died, who killed her?" I tried to hold down the sarcasm.

"No, no. You see things differently from that world. When Autumn was alive she was struggling with dark aspects. She was learning to embrace her shadow self. To answer your question, I'm not getting a killer per se. Betrayal—a betrayer, not a killer—comes through. You have to understand my work. I'm a healer. I heal lives."

The phone rang and Kunda floated to it, her purple silk fluttering around her like seaweed.

Gus leaned over to me and whispered, "Autumn Riley might argue that last point, if she could." I snorted.

Kunda cooed into the phone.

Gus picked up a book from the desk and read the title to me, "*A Guide for the Advanced Soul.*"

"Do they have one of those for dummies?" I asked. "Or for complete idiots?"

Gus grinned and said, "Hold a problem in your mind. Then open this book to any page and there will be your answer."

"Forget it, Gus. I'm not in the mood." I said.

"Okay?" asked Gus. "You got a problem in your mind?"

"That's not really a question. More like a statement, right?"

"Okay, now open this book and read what it says."

I opened the book to see a white page with a hand-drawn Asian symbol at the top. Below that, the words: EVERYONE AND EVERYTHING AROUND YOU IS YOUR TEACHER.

"Okay," I said. "I can agree with that."

Gus grinned and opened his arms to say, *See.*

Kunda came back into the room with an agenda. Or maybe her pixie dust was wearing off.

"I'd be willing to help your investigation free of charge," she said sitting back down in the pink love seat. "I see a damaged but still spiritually powerful man, one who has a lot to offer but who also has a lot of flaws."

I wasn't impressed. "How can one be damaged and still be spiritually powerful?" I asked.

"It depends on which spirits you call upon. Dark powers can be very strong."

"Is that well-aligned with your spiritual advice? The dark powers?"

"No, not at all." She paused. "I guess you're thinking I wasn't much help to Autumn."

I wondered if she might actually be psychic or just be stating the obvious.

"But I truly had a formidable foe," she continued. "It's as if he killed her, in an indirect way."

Gus and I shared a look. He bent over and leaned on the arm of Kunda's chair and jutted his chin toward her.

"Who's the *he*?" asked Gus. Kunda just looked at him. "Glenn Addams?" Gus prompted.

This caused her to fluster, or maybe her psychic channels were jammed.

Gus stood up straight and cleared his throat. "It's a serious crime to withhold information in a murder investigation."

Kunda lifted her hands and fluttered them as if to shoo away bad energy. "I don't always get the whole picture. I have blind spots just like anybody else. I'm only human."

"That's truthful of you," Gus said.

"It's hard to explain what I do for my clients." She stopped speaking and lowered her head again.

Gus leaned forward as if he were trying to see what she was doing exactly with her head down like that. I admit, I was curious, too.

Her head popped back up and she said, "You see, only you have the key to unlock the secrets of your soul. I can show you the door. But you must have the personal power, the courage to step through the portal."

Kunda drew in a deep breath and wrapped her fingers around the purple crystal that hung from her neck. She leaned back and her head sunk into the back of the love seat. Gus and I waited for more otherworldly insights.

"Glenn Addams points the way to unveiling the truth."

I'd had more than enough of the mumbo jumbo. I stood up.

"You say that this producer, Glenn Addams, may have killed Autumn in an indirect way? What's that supposed to mean exactly?" I asked.

Now, Kunda leaned forward to meet my confrontation and stared at me with her big purple eyes. I guess she was trying to see something in me. She looked searchingly over to Gus, then took his hand, clasping it in both of hers. His eyebrows shot straight up an inch on his forehead as he waited for her answer.

"People like Glenn Addams have a way of leading others down a dark, dark path and disappearing. And by then, death is already in your blood." She let go of his hand and opened her arms out as if she had lost something.

"You're abandoned there, wandering in the shadows, a ghost in your own life. By then, death is only a step, a thought in the wrong direction. Death is only as far away as the next deep breath of your own black potential."

I didn't think I had an answer to my question, but I accepted it. In spite of myself, and all the hooey, I had recognized a ring of truth to her words. I sometimes felt like a ghost wandering around in the shadows of my own life and I was familiar with the fact that a thought in the wrong direction can release a demon or two that you thought were strapped in. Then again, she may have just read that in one of those how-to books for mystics.

"Okay," I said. "Do us a favor and don't leave town." Gus gave Kunda his card and started toward the door.

"We'd appreciate a call if you think of anything that could help us," he said. "I'm sure Autumn in spirit would be grateful."

I hope to be of service," she said, having returned to her serene beingness.

As I followed Gus out, I glanced up at the poster of the Goddess of Death. Silvery and blue, with a young white colt in the distance and a huge horse skull in the foreground, there were swirls of prismatic light and smoke around a pale ghost of a woman's face.

A peculiar surge of electricity ran through me. I wouldn't describe it as pleasant.

"That's Epona," said Kunda.

I stopped in my tracks and turned to face her. She seemed to levitate toward me, her gaze a beam of fire.

"Epona," I repeated.

"Yes. Comfortable in both the realm of life and that of death."

I nodded and suddenly felt threatened by something. I couldn't get out of there fast enough as I continued toward the door.

"Epona is a strong symbol of nurturing, instinct, and vitality. She's a protector of women and children," said Kunda.

I turned back one last time.

"Did you have to go to some airy-fairy university to learn this goddess stuff?" I asked.

"Mythology is taught at the finest universities, detective. In fact, the first university, ever, was one of religious science. The Sorbonne? Perhaps you've heard of it."

"Sure, I've heard of it. It's in France, right? Paris. Though I think you might be thinking of Bologna. Do you actually have a goddess degree?"

"You kid me, but I see through your dismissal. You recognize yourself in Epona, don't you?"

"Maybe. But let me ask you a question on a different subject. What do you know about voodoo?"

Gus stood waiting beside the door during this exchange. "Nothing, really. I don't do spells and don't dabble in black magic. To be fair, voodoo is a whole culture of which I have no information."

"Did Autumn dabble?"

"Not to my knowledge. She never shared such interests with me. If she had, I would have counseled her against it."

"Okay," I said.

"I bet you have Jupiter in Leo," said Kunda.

"Say what?"

"She means in your astrological chart," offered Gus.

"I wouldn't know."

"I'm sure of it. Grace and poise in contact with the public, you act while others dream, you achieve your goals, but you must be careful not to become arrogant, and you have a tendency to overdo things." I looked at Gus. He shrugged.

"Thank you for that insight," I said.

"Feel free to call me."

"You can count on it," I said on the way out the door.

Outside, Gus put his hand on my shoulder. His tall form and gray eyes looked soft against the black asphalt and the occasional determined dandelion. Behind him, cars raced by on the Pacific Coast Highway. He squeezed my shoulder. "What's wrong?"

"I dunno. Do you think I'm arrogant?"

"That's a yes."

"And that I overdo?"

"There's no doubt."

"But I do achieve my goals."

"No one would deny that."

"And what's that got to do with Jupiter in what was it?"

"Jupiter in Leo. I couldn't tell you."

"She's invasive. It's creepy."

Gus chuckled and said, "Yeah, well. I get the feeling we're gonna drop through a few rabbit holes on this one."

"That a premonition?"

"You could say that. So..." he added, lighting up a cigarette with something that looked like a ray gun. "You in the mood for a Hollywood Movie Meister?"

"I dunno, sounds like a drink."

"No, Joan. A Movie Meister is a person, and they often get up in the wee hours of the morning to be on the set," said Gus.

"Oh. Okay. You think Glenn Addams might have made a breakfast call to Autumn Riley? That's kind of bright and early to be leading anybody down a dark path."

"Maybe he had to squeeze it into a busy schedule."

CHAPTER THREE

THE GLARE OF THE sun nearly blinded me as we ran into traffic on the drive downtown to Parker Center and were creeping along with every variation of the theme of SUV on the Santa Monica freeway when Gus's cell phone chirped awake. The conversation was one-sided. Whoever was on the other end was quite the talker. Gus didn't look too happy when he rang off.

"What's up?" I asked.

"The mayor is leaning hard on the captain about Autumn Riley."

"Why?" I knew *why*; I really meant *who*, as in, *Who was leaning on the mayor...?*

"Autumn's parents have been on the phone, and it seems their address book has the right numbers in it. The Manchesters, among others."

"Who're the Manchesters?"

"Manchester Theatre?"

"Never been. Whaddya know about Glenn Addams?"

"I think he's doing a film right now. He might even be on location."

"Oh yeah? Where?"

"I heard the film takes place in Spain."

"Spain? Always wanted to go there. Well, hey, you're the senior detective, don'cha think we should get a warrant to do a search on his pad in Spain?"

I smiled at Gus, enjoying the fantasy for moment.

"I'll make a few calls, run it by Satch. I suppose you want an expense account."

"Couldn't hurt."

I dropped Gus off on Spring Street. He wanted to check in with SIS and make sure they put the top guy on surveillance of Autumn's bungalow. It's just a couple blocks from Parker Center, so I headed over to Specials. I had just stepped into the building, pocketed my sunglasses, and was feeling sentimental about the big yellow brick walls. When you live your life in institutions long enough, the structure of it all becomes one with your psyche. I was thinking how pitiful that is when I spotted Jesse Cand, the reporter, coming down the hall toward me. He must have made a beeline here from the crime scene. Damn. Curses. Double damn, and damn again. The yellow bricks of the hallway closed in on me. I made my way toward the exit at the West end of the building to get the hell out of there. I was hoofin' it on out of there pretty good when the hallway was suddenly washed in the glare of a photographer's flashbulb. A brilliant flare of white bounced off the yellow brick. Ah, Jesse brought his photographer to get photos of me. I was blinded for a moment, then through blobs of black, purple, and blue I saw the round waddling form of Kip, the photographer. He came toward me, I guess to get another photo. This had to be the Joan-in-the-hallways-of-justice shot. It irked me to no end. I went for the exit, but Jesse came out in front of the photographer. This Jesse was fast on his feet, skinny enough to be a marathon runner. I made it out the glass door but not quick enough. Jesse came up on my right.

I'd made about three steps of descent down the stone steps and felt him gaining on me. What would he do? Chase me down? What if one of us tripped and we both went sprawling down to our deaths? At the bottom of the steps, traffic blew by on the street—Mercedes, Jaguars, BMWs, an old landscaping truck, a silver, oversized food truck selling coffee and egg sandwiches, more SUVs… God, I had to get out of Los Angeles, all these friggin' cars. I quickly resigned myself, stopped short, turned back, and Jesse nearly ran right into me. He had a combined look of shock and concern on his face.

"What is it, Jesse? What now?"

He put out his hand, but I didn't take it. Somehow, standing outside the building of Parker Center I felt even more intruded upon and vulnerable than I had when we were inside. My eyes were stung by the blustering wind; my short hair blew back from my face.

"You look stunning as ever," he said with a sticky smile.

I took in his stylish brown hair, thick on top, short on the sides, his thin neck and slight build in a suit that was too large for him. Maybe he was planning to grow into it. It gave him a fragile appearance. He probably used that to catch his victims off guard. I felt violated. I decided it was an appropriate reaction to some degree.

"Did you want to ask me something? Let's get to it. What?"

He dropped his smile and gave me a concerned look.

"Today you'll receive a great honor, the commendation from the community."

We were standing in the shadow of the Parker building. I looked back at the pair of columns that decorated the west entrance and a strange forlorn mood overtook me. I felt I would forever be standing in shadows, living in the great darkness of an imprecise despair.

"I don't want to talk about it. If you have something else to ask me, get to it."

"I need to inquire about the beautiful Autumn Riley."

"No comment, Jesse."

"Come off it, Joan. Cough up some information. It's all too mysterious. What's going on?"

"She's dead. That's all I can tell you."

"Joan. You have to give me something."

"No coroner's report, so there's nothing I can say at this point."

"You're holding up the investigation for the coroner's report?"

"No. And if you write that, I will kill you."

"I would never do anything like that. Listen, can I just say that you and I really need to have a better working relationship?"

"Why can't you wait for the press release like everyone else? It may be all of one hour."

"There's special pressure on me."

"You're breaking my heart."

"Joan, you need to get that I'm on your side. In fact, my boss liked the work I did on you last time so much, he wants me to do a special profile for the *LA Times Magazine*. Now, there's this commendation. The public loves you, Joan. And the Autumn Riley thing is big news, you can't avoid it."

The fabric of his pant legs flapped in the bluster of wind from the street, creating a bizarre percussion.

"You don't get it, Jesse. You want to make a big deal out of me. I don't want that. Why single me out? My partner, Gus, he's interesting, been on the job twenty-seven years. Do a profile on him. Do one on my old partner, Carl Erskin."

"We've done Carl."

"Yeah, and you about buried him."

"Joan, you're a woman, and that plays better with our readers. Besides, I feel like I know you."

"My friend, you are nothing if not mistaken. You know zero about me and I'll be keepin' it that way. So I'm a detective and I'm a woman, not sure why that makes me so special in the eyes of the *LA Times*. If anything, it's an insult and dishonors the work of my colleagues."

"Oh, that's a good statement, Joan. Very noble."

He pulled a small notebook out of his coat pocket and grinned at me. God, the guy had gall.

"But really, you have to get over the idea that it's insulting. The public wants to know about you. They want to understand what makes you tick, why you do this work."

"I do it for the same reasons the other detectives do it."

He wrote that down, too.

"Just give me one short comment about the commendation, okay?"

"You don't get it, you know that? You are completely off."

We held each other's gazes, locked in a standoff. His face softened. "You know this fight is not really between you and me. I'll wait for the press release on Autumn Riley, but you have to take me in Joan, really."

"I'll think about it."

"Since you mentioned Carl, I heard word he's leaving the force. Is it true he resigned?"

I took a deep breath to steady myself, but before I could stop it, a pressure came up my spine, and from nowhere a tear dropped over from the inside of my eye and down the edge of my nose to my lips. I tasted the saltiness.

Jesse gasped. A blinding flash whitened everything before me. I had forgotten about Kip. Jesse's photographer must have approached during the conversation. He'd held back, hiding behind the column maybe until the best photo opportunity had presented itself.

I put my hand to my face, covered the tear. I looked at Jesse. He held me in his gaze. I wiped the wetness off my face in one stroke and flew down the steps.

Jesse Cand didn't pursue me. Once I got to the bottom of the concrete steps and was on the sidewalk, well out of his reach, I looked back and saw Kip position himself for another photo, this one of my retreat, but Jesse reached out to stop him. They probably couldn't believe that they had been able to get a tear, such a revealing moment. Me neither. It was smooth, him asking me about Carl. I had shown him a different woman from the one he was familiar with. I knew he'd exploit that, draw a courageous profile of a vulnerable, caring woman in a raw, hard world. He would follow my career, never letting me out of his sights. I spotted Gus as he came around the corner and down the street. I dashed to his side, dread and foreboding coming off me like strong perfume.

"Jesse after you again?"

"Always, he follows me around like a bad mood."

"I think he likes you."

"Yeah, right. I like him, too."

We headed to the central entrance of Parker Center. The entrance hall is very grand, very Jungian. You feel like you're entering something that is going to decide your fate and chances are good that it's an accurate assumption. It's a threshold. I looked back once more toward Jesse and Kip on the west end of the building to be sure they weren't pursuing me, but they were nowhere in sight. Not that it's any guarantee.

"You going up to the third floor?" Gus asked.

"You guessed it. Gus, did you know that Carl had resigned?"

"Yeah, that's why I asked if you had talked to him."

"Why didn't you say something?"

"You should have been in touch with Carl yourself. You could have called him."

"Yeah, I know."

"One call wouldn't have killed you."

We rode up the elevator in silence to the Homicide Division and finally made it back to Specials. The office was quiet. I calmed a bit and settled in. The sun, filtered through smog, was a dirty haze that came in the window, hurting my eyes. I reached up to let down the blinds and made a phone call to get a list of released sex offenders in the Marina Del Rey and Venice area. It's standard protocol to do such a check. It shows that you've researched all possibilities for suspects other than just going for the husband, ex-boyfriend, or whomever. It was reassuring to sit at my old scratched-up desk. My calendar pad was exactly as I had left it. I was surprised by that and looked through the rest of my drawers in amazement that nothing was missing. I was sure I'd have to spend my first half hour back locating supplies. A sentimental flush came over me as I realized that my desk had been respected, saved for me to come back to work—like family that keeps your room ready for your return.

In seconds, the sex-offender list was provided. I recognized the name of Mason Jones. I checked the date of his release. I called his probation officer, and he told me that Mason was working at Costco, collecting carts in Marina Del Rey. Sex offenders like familiar areas, and often commit crimes repeatedly in the same neighborhood before they're caught.

I smelled designer men's cologne. The scent brought back a rush of warm memories combined with a primal sense of danger. I turned my head to see Carl Erskin, my ex-partner and ex-lover, standing at his old desk, straight across from mine, and I stopped still as a deer. Yep, it was the scent of Karl Lagerfeld. Funny, how a fragrance can have such a strong impact.

My throat constricted. When Carl and I were partners, we worked Special Section together. Let me say that everyone who works Special Section gets frustrated dealing with the media and celebrities. It gets to you. Carl had less tolerance than most. I thought that we did a good job of balancing each other out, but the last case we worked escalated in drama by the minute. It probably didn't help that we were romantically involved on top of everything else. We were trying to keep that under wraps, as it's frowned upon. Though no one had officially called us on it. Everybody knew. Of course, they didn't know that we broke up. Or maybe they did. Now was as good a time as any to confront him since I had been avoiding him for a month. In fact, this was ideal. He wouldn't make a scene here at work. Would he? I found it hard to swallow.

Carl glanced over and when he saw that I was looking at him, a light came to his face. He's a hard-ass, but those eyes told another story. He didn't greet me. Instead he picked up several items from his desk and put them into a milk crate. I noticed his beer belly was a little bigger since I'd seen him last, not that I mind that sort of thing. I had always found his body comforting, like a big strong teddy bear. I walked over and stood in front of him. He was waiting for me to say something and he looked up at me again.

"Hey, Carl."

"I'll be there. Front row center," he said. "You deserve it."

"No, I don't."

I was due a commendation in twenty minutes.

"Yes, you do. You're the one who broke the case when nobody else could."

He was talking about the case that did us in. He felt I was getting too close in, putting myself in danger. I felt I was doing my job. I changed the subject.

"Why are you cleaning out your desk?"

"I'm leaving, going to open my own investigating firm."

"Big demand for that these days." I bit my lip until it hurt. "Fastest growing industry besides computers and security."

Carl waited for me, begging me with those eyes, to say more.

I had to fight my instinct to hit him. At the same time, I wanted to go to him, hold him, comfort him. My chest could hardly contain my heart. I thought I was going to explode. People around us were politely ignoring our conversation while listening to every word. All eyes were averted, looking through files, anything but watching us.

"Joanie," Carl whispered, "I miss the curve of your waist, your voice, your laughter. I want to wake up with your ass to snuggle up against."

"Stop it, will you?" I whispered back.

"It's the truth. You were always big on us telling each other the truth. Being without you doesn't work for me."

I felt my stomach wrench. Did he have to do this here?

"I don't know what to say, Carl."

"Say you'll be with me."

I stepped back from him.

"Okay, that's too much," he said. "Listen, I could use a business partner, if you ever want to…make a change?"

"I don't know…I just can't think about that right now." I could no longer be his lover, and I couldn't be his partner, either.

"I got one question for you, Joan."

"What?"

"Do you love me?"

The answer to his question was, *Yes*. Maybe more than I had ever loved anybody, but I couldn't tell him that. Just because you love someone doesn't mean you want to be with them. Truth was, I hated him, too. I loathed and despised him. It wasn't just one thing that had happened between us, it was an attitude he had toward me. Like he owned me. Nobody owns me. There's pluses and minuses to that, but it's a true thing. I walked out without a word. I felt his eyes on me but I didn't look back.

I was grateful that the brown window shades were pulled down against the glaring sun in the squad room. The eggshell walls reflected a sepia tint that filled the scene, adding to the unreal feeling of the announcement.

The detectives of our division gathered before my eyes in a soft blur. The Carl thing had me off balance. That was the problem—the guy made me crazy. I wished I were a nice normal person who could have a pleasant reassuring love. For a moment, I fantasized that one day I would marry, that my husband and I would sit in front of the television together every night eating ice cream, getting fat.

How great that would be. I knew it was not my destiny. I was on another path. Though I *might* be able to pull off gaining weight, hanging around with my new partner, Gus. He loves chocolate. I spotted Gus in the room and he gave me an encouraging smile. He shared a joke with one of the other detectives and the two of them grinned at each other. I silently took it all in.

A flyer was circulated around the room of men. Another missing girl, eighteen years old. I held it in my hand and zoomed in on the location she was last seen—Marina Del Rey. Her name was Paige.

"How many does that make now?" I asked. Mark O'Malley, the one who circulated the flyer, was a detective that had turned away from a career in medicine to work in law enforcement. He was Irish and African American and had just the right amount of good looks. He also had an enormous amount of charm. People did things for him. But underneath all that I recognized the signs. If you got to know him well, you'd find that he was moody and temperamental, but mostly depressed.

"It makes ten since February," he said. "We're thinking that maybe these young women are dead. If you come across any information, hear of a Jane Doe, anything, call me."

It was rumored that the case was driving Mark crazy, that he was losing sleep and had broken up with his girlfriend over it.

"I've missed some of the previous flyers," I said.

"Don't worry, I got you covered," said Mark as he handed me several more flyers of missing young women, still girls really.

My eyes took in bright, happy-looking young women caught in different moments of their lives. Mark was convinced the missing girls, possibly murdered, were related, and I could see why. At first glance, you could immediately see a quality of sincerity, the life energy of each missing woman.

"I'll keep an eye out," I said. "There's this guy, Mason Jones, a sex offender, working at Costco in Marina Del Rey, collecting carts. Could be your guy."

"What kind of sex offender?" asked Mark.

"Violated little girls," I said.

"Ever kidnap one?"

"Long enough to do the damage, but never overnight." When I said it, I felt disconnected from my own voice. How callous, how glib. Murder investigation has made me hard.

For a nanosecond, I wondered how I would ever heal from my work. Maybe I would end up all out of balance like Mark.

"Yeah, we better check him out," said Mark, looking more depressed than ever. Not that you could blame him. "When did this Mason Jones get out?"

"February, the same month your first girl disappeared."

Satch, our captain, cleared his throat. "And we have a good job done, a commendation for Ms. Lambert. Welcome her back," said

Satch, his voice sounding just like Louie Armstrong. He handed me a beige piece of paper.

"Thank you," I said. "I'm not so sure I'm worthy of it."

I looked at the piece of paper with the signatures and my name in print. Everyone in the room was still. I looked into their expectant eyes and felt a responsibility to them. "In the face of much criticism," I added, "perhaps some of it warranted, remember there are those who believe in us."

I couldn't help it. I found myself searching the room for Carl during the applause and hoots. He nodded his approval. Satch, my boss, patted me on the back.

"You know what, you sound just like a politician."

Right, like *I* had a clue. God, I am so pompous and boorish sometimes. I think it comes with being a cop. Or maybe I think I really can rid the world of all its evil, or some of it, and maybe that's what draws one to Homicide.

"Anyway, you're back where you belong, doll." I didn't say anything more because I suddenly found I was so grateful to be there that no words would come out. Then everybody filed out, and I did the same. Carl caught me at the door.

"I'm not going to call you anymore," he said. "You want to talk, you call me."

"Okay."

"You promise?"

What promise? I nodded. It was a lie.

Satisfied with that, he left. I watched him walk out the door and away from me.

Relieved to be back at my desk with its oversize black phone and wise quotes fading under the plastic desk cover, Gus and I went to work on the murder book. We filled out the information on the interviews, added our notes and the strangely glamorous crime photos of Autumn Riley.

I signed receipts for the address book and a couple photos: one of Autumn, and one of the voodoo doll. The familiar rituals of routine procedure made for a comforting, soothing effect. "You gonna take a ride on the internet?" asked Gus.

"You bet," I said, and turned on the printer connected to my computer. In spite of what you see on television, we don't have all the latest newfangled devices. I was always grateful just to get online. I typed in my code and waited. It was a fine feeling, plunking away on my familiar keyboard. I was still in mild shock that no one had confiscated my stuff. Even the pale blue walls in bad need of a paint job were a comfort. It was good to be back. Now, if only I could prove myself, then I'd be okay. I have a little problem with thinking myself worthy. Nobody knows that, of course. Most are of the opinion that I'm arrogant. What they don't know is that the beast drives me. And the beast is everywhere, hiding in every crack, around every corner. The beast could be your own father, your lover, or a coworker. That's not just my personal take on it either. Of course, working homicide confirms it in a big way. Those closest to the victim are our strongest suspects.

The Carl thing was bugging me, and I couldn't shake it.

Back in the days Carl and I were partners, we were unbeatable. Then we became lovers and it seemed we became even better detectives. It started going screwy when I took a punch off a suspect. The guy was an exec, a big CEO at Meteor Air Group, a company that serviced all the airports, even Air Force One. I was interviewing the CEO, when out of nowhere he punched me and ran. Carl beat the crap out of the guy. The CEO's bruised and bloodied face made the front page of all the papers. Plus, after that, Carl fussed over me like a hen does a baby chick and everything thereafter was all terribly wrong. Finally, we solved the case—the guy had killed his wife and son by faking an accident on his yacht. But the downside was I had to do handstands to reassure Carl that I wasn't in constant need of his protection and, needless to say, nothing was ever right again. One little incident was all it took. As if I couldn't take a punch. Of course, it had been a bit riskier than a punch to get the goods on the CEO, and I had to do it all behind Carl's back. It's not an ideal situation to have to sneak around on your partner to get the job done. He felt betrayed, and maybe he was right. The worst of it was when Carl became jealous. It got to the point where he accused me of screwing my informant, some big mucketymuck. Everything else I forgave, but the jealousy, well, I couldn't handle that. I had a bad reaction to *his* bad reaction. That's when I decided to take some time off from the job until things cooled down. Now, I was back and Carl was leaving.

Probably all for the best.

I logged in online and typed in the word "voodoo" to see what came up. There was plenty of information on voodoo politics, and a case where a man claimed he was innocent because someone had put him under a curse. I didn't really know what I was looking for until I came upon a Dr. Sheffield at a local branch of the Institute of Organic Chemistry and Biochemistry who had some new analogues. I clicked on that. The institute was located in the Santa Monica mountains. I sent an email to set up a meeting.

I called the coroner's office to hurry up the autopsy, and the first run of defense gave me a sad song about it. Normal procedures meant Autumn Riley would have to wait in a long line of dead bodies due for toxicology exams.

I knew the guy who heads Public Information in the coroner's office. Ray Tanning. I decided to give him a ring. He's in his early fifties, energetic, rough around the edges. Don't get on his bad side. I dialed his number…

"Hey, Ray! It's me, Joan, calling about Autumn Riley."

"Oh, you're back, huh?"

"I'm back, Ray. Now, about the post for Riley…"

"Don't start with me, Joan," he said. "You people in S Section are always puttin' the hurt on me. Do you know how backed up we are here?"

"She just came in. You can't miss her. She's got red hair. Her name's Autumn Riley, I need the cut today."

"Today? You're crazy. And forget tomorrow, too. Why should she be more important than the cocaine whore who was murdered in South Central last Friday night? They were both somebody's daughter. First day, and you're already pulling this shit with me. Normally, we'd do her next week. Next week, ya hear me?"

He always did that, always made some statement regarding inequality among the dead. Like it's any different in death from when people are alive.

"I need you to think about who will be the one held responsible if her parents hire some big-time lawyers and sue us. Okay? 'Cuz that's what'll happen, Ray. They're angry and frustrated because there's nothing they can do. It's all out of their hands, but they have money."

"They'll lose because I am right about this."

"It doesn't matter if they lose, and you know that. Besides, what if it's a murder? Then we're all screwed. The Rileys will point at you and say you held up the investigation. Then you'll get to say that bit about her not being more important than a coke whore to a judge in court. See how that flies."

"I don't think I can cut her any sooner. I'm telling you we're backed up. I haven't even had lunch yet and I've been here since six-thirty this morning. Let me check it out, I'll see what I can do."

Ray hung up. He definitely needed me to take him out to lunch. Today. He'd brushed me off way too easily. How busy could it be over there?

"Hey, Gus. You wanna go with me, take Ray Tanning to lunch?" I looked at the clock on the wall since I'd forgotten my watch. It was one thirty. "He's giving me the blues, thought I'd chum him up."

"Okay, sounds good. Let's listen to the tape first, then we'll go."

Dispatch had sent over the 911 tape and we sat around the Homicide Special Section table, which is essentially my desk and Gus's desk lined up side by side. We listened to an overly twangy Southern accent. A couple of the other detectives stood around and listened in.

"Autumn Riley's been murdered! She's here at the beach house. That's all I can say."

The connection was broken before the dispatcher could ask anything further. Venice Police Station had located the address through the computer link-up of the phone system. Autumn's bungalow.

"Sound Texan to you?" asked Gus.

I shrugged. "More like Australian."

"Why would he try to make it sound Texan?" asked Gus.

"A person could have a million reasons for disguising their voice," I offered.

"But it's someone who knows her."

"They as much said so."

The other detectives peeled off, more interested in their own assignments.

"Record the voiceprint!" yelled Satch.

Nothing gets by the captain. I mean, the ears on that guy. He was right, of course. A voiceprint would be definitive in a court of law. It's similar to a fingerprint in that no two are exactly alike. That way we could absolutely verify identity should we come across someone we believed made the phone call.

The big LAPD machine got to work doing the paperwork for the voiceprint. Gus filled out the form, wrapped it around the tape, popped a rubber band on it, and dropped it in the basket on the voiceprint desk. Then he got on the phone, fast-talking one of his buddies in the film business.

I called Crime Lab and waited for Rose Torres to answer.

"Yes, detective?" said Rose Torres in an impatient voice. "Anything on the doll?"

"We're working on it now; let me finish and then I'll call you."

"Okay, you can call Gus on his cell phone. You got that number?"

"Memorized. Later."

The Women's and Children's Hospital houses the coroner's office. It's a sprawling piss-yellow building. You can get depressed just looking at the outside, never mind once you get a load of the tragedies within. For a homicide detective, it's a bittersweet relationship. Some of the worst truths are discovered here and some of the best clues as well. Gus and I parked, entered, and were buzzed through. We walked down the administrative hallway past glass and wood and serious-looking secretaries to knock on Ray Tanning's door. I couldn't hear him in there on the phone like I usually do. In fact, it was dead quiet in there.

Fast-moving steps came down the hall. It was a driver, Joseph Carrillo. I was surprised to see him. He's a close bud of some people I know, and I thought he'd quit to open a Cuban restaurant over on Washington Boulevard. His usually serene face looked frustrated.

"Hey, Joseph. *Que hondas?*" I asked, meaning *How are the waves?* in Cubanese.

"Hi, Joan, Gus. How're you?"

His manner was more serious than usual.

"What are you doing here?" asked Gus. "Thought you were in the restaurant business."

"That's right. This is my last week here and it's crazy as hell. Gotta go."

"Where's Ray?" asked Gus.

"Downstairs."

Downstairs is where they take care of real coroner business. "Where downstairs?" I asked.

"I couldn't tell you."

Joseph shot out the swinging doors at the end of the hall.

Every once in a while there's a strange incident in the world of the coroner. The most publicized fiasco was when the wrong body was sent to a grieving mother in Mexico.

Chaos in the morgue always throws them way behind, and I assumed that's why Ray was giving me the run around. I felt sure I could convince him to squeeze in Autumn's autopsy.

Gus and I took the elevator down to the basement to find Ray. They keep the bodies down there in a cold room. The temperature stays around forty-two degrees. They were bringing in a small elderly man on a gurney. He was naked, and I averted my eyes out of respect. Gus and I put paper baggies on our feet and paper masks over our faces. I glanced over at the other bodies, a bloated black man with half his head caved in, a tiny older lady and a heavyset Hispanic youth with tattoos and gunshot wounds. I didn't see Autumn anywhere. We looked for Ray in several rooms. He wasn't in Photos, not in Toxicology, and he wasn't out back with the drivers waiting to come in.

We entered the room that held the largest supply of corpses. They were wrapped in soft plastic, as if they were alien pods in some sci-fi movie. Ray Tanning hadn't lied when he said they were backed up. It was wall-to-wall bodies in there. When we found Ray, he was moving a body from a gurney. This is not usual for him. He's the guy on the phone schmoozing councilmen, stuff like that. He's a short spry older man with thin black hair and a thick mustache. He wore the same baggies and mask as me and Gus, but he also had on an apron and safety glasses. The body he was moving wasn't Autumn Riley, and I was disappointed. He saw us and gestured for us to grab some latex gloves from the dispenser and give him a hand.

I wanted to refuse, but we were trying to get on his good side. The gloves lined with talcum powder slipped on easily. The fragrance was a brief relief. Things had to be super bad if Ray was rustling bodies.

This one was a white male in his late thirties and had to have weighed in at 250 pounds. Couldn't blame Ray for having trouble with it. If the face is the landscape owned by the geology of the soul, this dead man had been wretched in life and mean as hell. I pulled in my stomach and centered my weight as I grabbed the feet, Gus supported the weight in the middle, and Ray took the shoulders.

"Thanks for helping out," Ray said through his mask.

We nearly had the dead man on the steel table when Ray pulled the upper body toward the table and misjudged. The head, which was hanging lower than the shoulders, got banged at the right temple, on the corner of the worktable. I winced. The dead feel no pain, I told myself.

Ray lifted the shoulders higher and up onto the steel table. The head hit first with a soft thud. I swore to myself that I would never be a body in the morgue. If I could help it.

"When do we get to Autumn Riley? Any information so far?" I asked.

"Uh, you're not going to believe this." Ray looked from me to Gus and then back to the body we had just moved. "I have, some...I have some bad news. She's gone."

Gus and I stood staring at him, so he continued.

"I went to go check out your Autumn Riley to see what we could do for you. I talked to the driver who brought her in, but when I got to her gurney it was empty. She wasn't there. It's never happened to me before, and I don't mind telling you, I don't know what to say."

"Excuse me?" I was hoping my ears weren't working right.

"Autumn Riley is gone, Joan. Her body has disappeared." The beast had come back for his prey.

"Have you looked for it?" I asked.

Without the autopsy, the investigation would be stalled. My eyes darted around the room really studying the bodies now. The coroner's is always creepy, you never really get used to it, but suddenly I felt especially leery.

"Yes, Joan. We searched the place up and down."

"Let's check your security tape, right now," said Gus.

"I did that already," said Ray. "Thing is, her body never really made it in. Like I said, we're backed up. The check-in is slower than usual. The driver brought her just inside the door for processing. So, there's really only one camera that had anything. It's a little fuzzy, the tape is old, you know we use them over and over. Okay, I admit, it's a lot fuzzy. You can't see shit."

"Don't worry, we can work with it," said Gus.

"You think someone would have reason to steal her body?" asked Ray.

"Maybe they don't want us to do the exam," I said. "Don't mention it to anybody else just yet, okay?"

"I have to report it, but I'll try to keep it quiet, believe me. You think I want to see it on the news? I'm shook up about it myself, you know?"

"Ray, Gus and I wanted to treat you to lunch…"

"Ah, no time for that. I'm ordering in. Let me go get you the tape."

Gus nodded, and I stood there like someone had just kicked me in the stomach as Ray split to get the tape.

Parker has access to a team of techno guys that can unravel computer codes and clear up any recordings. I'd never seen them fail. Gus and I would have to run the disc over to Tech Corp by the airport.

"The question is, who has the resources to get a body out of the morgue without being detected?" I said.

"Maybe somebody with a lot of friends and money, who wields a lot of power, and has a lot of favors owed them."

"Like a movie producer."

"I've heard stories before of investigations where bodies disappeared," said Gus.

"And?"

"None of them had happy endings."

CHAPTER FOUR

GLENN ADDAMS'S STUDIO WAS next to Oliver Stone's lot, off Electric Avenue, a funky but chic area in Venice. After we nearly ran over a jogger that sprinted out before the light changed, we pulled into the entrance up to a security shack. Gus knew the guard and convinced him to let us in without a big announcement to Addams. We parked in the visitor section. As we walked across the lot, Gus and I looked like a couple of hard-ons in our suits compared to most of the movie populace in their casual or hip clothes. I'd heard somewhere that Hollywood producers were migrating westward into the ever-increasing upscale Venice area.

"Addams kept his inamorata and his job site nice and close," said Gus.

I don't know this word *inamorata*, but I figured he meant Autumn Riley. Gus has a vast vocabulary of words for sex and all those issues around it.

"Just a few miles from each other," I said. "Could make for an alibi."

"Hmph. Maybe. Word is this Addams literally envisions the movie and then looks for a script or hires somebody to do what he dreamed up."

"Sounds like a nice job. Hey, I had a dream last night. Here's eighty million so I can see it again."

Actually, I wouldn't want to see a movie of my own dreams. They're strictly low-budget fare, a mix of hardboiled and noir with a dash of horror.

We walked into a lobby across black marble. The security was muscled-up bodyguards, not the retirees you'd might expect. They had walkie-talkies and vigilant eyes, looked like Secret Service guys. When they walked, their shoes made no noise on the marble floor.

A security guard dressed in dark blue pants and a white shirt seemed to recognize us before we even made it to the receptionist desk. Black glass rose up behind him. His pale skin against the dark shiny glass created a 3-D effect. "You here to see Glenn Addams?" he asked.

"Yes," I said. "How'd you guess?"

"Everybody's a psychic," Gus said in my ear.

"He's expecting you," the man answered.

We pulled out our IDs and said our names, and the man gestured to an elevator. I was annoyed because I wanted to catch the producer off guard before he could have someone write him a script for an alibi.

"And how is it that he is expecting us?" I asked as the three of us stepped into the elevator.

"Mr. Addams has his sources."

Gus and I shared a knowing look.

The elevator was silent as a tomb. We got out on the third floor, and the security guard led us down the hall like a proud school monitor. At the end of the hallway were two black doors, which the guard opened, allowing us entrance. They closed silently behind us. We were standing inside yet another reception area of marble and black glass.

An exuberant young man with glowing skin and blond wavy hair greeted us.

"Good morning. I'm Benton, Glenn Addams's assistant. He'll be with you in a moment."

Benton, tanned and fit, could have been a social director on a cruise ship. A young woman appeared beside him. She wore a short blue skirt and a blue-and-white-striped men's shirt. Her streaked blond hair was styled in a pageboy, flipped under like in the fifties "Connie, get these fine people some coffee, or would you prefer sparkling water, tea?"

I passed. Gus got black coffee. Benton smiled brilliantly and was gone. Connie brought Gus his coffee.

Her eyes were expectant like maybe we were going to arrest someone. "You're here because of Autumn, right?"

"News travels fast," I said.

"Mr. Addams said you'd be coming in."

I nodded. Gus swallowed coffee and studied a black-and-silver sculpture in the corner. "How well did you know Autumn?" I asked.

"I saw her a few times. She never spoke much, came into the office a couple times, sat down, hardly looked at me," Connie said.

I handed her my card.

"Oh, no. I'm just a secretary, more like a receptionist, really. I'm nothing."

I think she really believed that. Maybe it was part of her job description.

"Keep the card, anyway. Who knows? And since we're at it, how 'bout a home telephone number?"

Connie looked around to see if anyone was watching, then scribbled her name and number on a nearby pad, folded it, and handed it to me like a secret.

"Thanks," I said. I was definitely going to call her.

Benton reappeared and put out his hand like an angel guiding the way to paradise.

"Please be quiet when we enter. I'll let Glenn know that you're here."

We walked down a hallway and entered through a curtained wall to a darkened room that opened into a stage with a giant green screen, in front of which a team of fifteen people worked silently. A man I recognized as the famous director, Rob Siennes, paced the floor.

"How much longer?" Siennes asked.

Another man in a headset answered, "Five minutes."

"Okay, I want this in one shot. *One shot*, understand?"

The team of people nodded in agreement. A woman's voice rang out, "Should be no problem. We've already run through it twice without makeup." Siennes nodded.

A lanky, dark-haired woman appeared. I recognized her as the actress, Ginny Deaver, a well-known animal activist. She walked across the set dressed only in red body paint from head to toe.

"This is the film about Spain?" I asked Gus.

"Parts are set in Spain, but it's futuristic, sci-fi stuff."

A tall chair with the name GLENN ADDAMS printed across the back caught my eye. I didn't know they still did that. I watched as a man took a seat in it. He was small, had close-cropped hair, and was younger than I expected. He looked relaxed, bored even.

Benton went up to him and whispered in his ear and the man turned to look at us. He gave Benton a lazy wave of his hand. Benton scurried back over to us.

"He'll be with you as soon as this scene is shot, won't be long."

The crew went to work in quiet focus as they put straps around the waist of the actress and attached that to a long cord. A large crane was moved into position, and the cord hooked up to it. Then everyone took their positions, leaving only the red form of the actress in front of the green screen on the stage.

Two large cameras were rolled up to the edge of the stage. Someone snapped a board and said the title of the movie and a number. The director Siennes said, "Roll 'em and action!" The actress folded over backward until her fingers reached the floor behind her. She was essentially in a backbend position when the person operating the crane cranked it and the actress allowed her body to be pulled up into the air. She appeared lifeless as if she were supposed to be asleep or dead, I couldn't tell which. Then, suddenly her eyes shot open like she had just discovered what was happening to her. The crane continued pulling her slowly, ever so slowly, up and up. Her arms and legs writhed around like that of a helpless spider in a hysterical panic.

"Cut!" cried the famous director, and everyone applauded. Glenn came down off his throne and walked over to us. Behind him, they lowered the actress back down to the stage floor.

"How can I help you?" he asked, looking at me.

"I'm Detective Lambert, and this is Detective Van Chek." Either he already knew our names or didn't care to. "We're here about Autumn Riley." He looked sad right on cue.

"I figured I'd be first on your list."

"Why?" I asked.

"Isn't the lover always your number one suspect?"

"We received a nine-one-one call insisting that Autumn had been murdered by her producer boyfriend."

"Christ, you're kidding me."

Gus gave me a side-glance. That's not what was said on the nine-one-one call, but we are allowed to lie when questioning suspects. It's legal. There would be no way for Addams to know different unless he made the call himself.

"Let's have this conversation elsewhere," said Addams. "Follow me, will you?"

We followed Addams down a hallway to a small office with a desk, a phone, four chairs, and little else.

He invited us to sit. Gus took a seat, as did Addams, but I stayed standing.

"There was also mention of a drug," I said. Gus cut me another sideways glance.

"What do you mean, a drug?" asked Addams.

"That drugs may have been a factor in her death. Do you have any reason to believe that Autumn may have been experimenting with drugs and overdosed?"

Addams shook his head. "No way. That doesn't sound like the Autumn I know."

"Mr. Addams, did you kill Autumn Riley?" I asked.

"No."

I didn't really think I'd get a confession, but I was looking for that tick, an instant of body language. I got nothing.

"Why do you suppose someone would call the police department with such a claim?"

"I'm not a detective, but I'd venture a guess that they'd want to mislead you."

"Anybody you know have a grudge against Autumn?"

"Absolutely not."

"Maybe one of your old girlfriends, one you left behind for Autumn." I stepped toward him, hoping to have more impact.

"No. I'm not like that."

"When was the last time you saw her?" I asked.

Addams spun his chair away from me. "Look, I just got back in town a few hours ago."

Gus repeated my question, "When was the last time you saw her?" We waited for him to answer.

"Last night, at her place," Addams said finally.

"Did you make love last night?" Gus asked.

"Yes."

"We're going to need a sample of your semen," I said.

Addams jerked his head toward me but said nothing.

"Was she alive when you left?" I asked.

"Yes."

He answered the questions without a shred of emotion.

"Did you have a fight?" I asked.

Addams paused, looked at me, glanced over at Gus, then looked away again, back to the corner. "Not exactly. More like a disagreement."

"Explain that," I said softly.

He sighed and turned in his chair toward me.

"She wanted to go for a walk on the beach. I was tired. I had to catch a flight to Palm Springs. I couldn't stay. She got angry. Said she was going to find the kind of man who would take her for walks. I didn't bother to argue. I was exhausted." He looked at me as if I should understand these things.

"You weren't too tired to make love," I said.

He shook his head again.

"One might think it would be more appropriate for you to be at home grieving," I said. "But here you are on the set."

Addams slumped in his chair. He wore comfy, expensive clothes: a charcoal sweater and soft-looking black pleated pants.

"There's a lot of business to attend to. People depend on me. The show must go on, you know."

"Mr. Addams, I need to ask you, let me see, how can I put this?" He gave me that blank expression of his, so I dug in, "Was Autumn difficult to control?"

"This conversation makes me want to call my lawyer."

I leaned toward Addams. "Sure, go ahead and call him if you like. But this is not an interrogation, it's only an interview. Maybe there's something you can tell us about your friends."

"I don't have friends, I have associates."

"Yes, okay, associates. Any of them become friends with Autumn?" I asked. "Did she ever party with any of your associates? Do drugs, have kinky sex?"

"Autumn would have none of that, so it's not germane. I don't mind telling you that I find that question offensive."

"Perhaps one of these associates had a new high in their coat pocket, some new-fashioned mixed-up ecstasy, say, and Autumn came upon it. Maybe your friend is completely innocent of any wrongdoing, maybe he was in the bathroom taking a wee-wee and didn't know."

"That's an interesting story, but Autumn is not the sort of person that takes things from pockets and she doesn't do drugs."

Gus cut in, "Yes, but you do have some friends that might have drugs. Right? You sort of have that rep."

"Detective Van Chek, that journalist who wrote about me in *Premiere Magazine* saw me at a party. We never even talked. It doesn't mean anything."

"Did you love Autumn Riley?" I asked.

Addams put his elbows on the desk and dropped his forehead into his hands. "I cared for her, a lot. She was singular. It's a tragedy she's dead. But I had nothing to do with it."

I waited him out.

"I have my airplane ticket," he continued. "Stewards in first class who served me and witnesses as alibis in Palm Springs, the whole nine yards. Benton will get it all together for you. I'll have my lawyer contact you if there's anything further."

Gus stepped in. "Have Benton send over those details, but a lawyer's not necessary at this point, Mr. Addams. We're sorry for your loss. We merely wish to figure out what happened here."

Addams nodded numbly.

I didn't want to let him off the hook so easily. "Will you be attending her funeral?" I asked.

Addams blinked at me. "Of course."

He moved a stapler on the desk, then a paper weight.

"One last thing," I added.

He looked up at me without expression. He had probably practiced that in the mirror.

"It's important."

He waited for me to continue.

"Was Autumn naked or clothed when you left her last?"

He was silent for a moment. It was a struggle for him to keep his mask in place.

"Naked," he answered.

The dam broke; his face turned red and scrunched up in pain. A moaning, from deep within, rose in him and burst from his lips. A loud wail filled the room. I went to him but he jerked away. I put my hand on his back. He turned to me then.

"I neglected her. I'm a bastard. I should have held her hand more, hell! I should have taken her for a walk last night on the beach. She might still be alive if I had done that one thing! But I didn't kill her. I swear to you."

"Okay," I said. "We merely need to find out how things were between you."

He looked at me for the first time with what I took for genuine anguish.

"Autumn wanted me to make her a star. It's so common. Everybody always carries on about the evil producer preying on young women. But can you imagine how tedious it is that every woman you meet wants you to put them in a movie? Cynical is not even the word for it. I thought Autumn would be a different experience. I met her at an environmental rally, one of those Save the Bay things, and she so impressed me. She was brave and passionate."

Tears fell from his eyes and made big splatters on his desk calendar. I stared at them for a moment in a strange disbelief.

"When Autumn asked me to make her a film star, I was hurt, I admit, disappointed. I thought she was an opera singer. What was with this actress thing all of a sudden? For me it was a cold hard slap, and I reacted by being an ass. I was angry, I guess. But I didn't kill her. Did I love her? I don't know. I wanted to."

⑂ ⑂ ⑂

WE PULLED INTO THE Costco parking lot in Marina Del Rey. It didn't take long to spot Mason Jones helping a woman put several massive cases of Diet Pepsi in the trunk of her car. Everything at Costco comes in family-size or bigger.

"Will you look at that?" I said to Gus. "I bet that's not in his job description."

"Quite the gentleman, ain't he?"

After the female shopper pulled away, I approached Mason. He was six feet two, with jailhouse muscles and a blond crew cut. Mason was successful as a molester because, in spite of his formidable appearance, he's very charming and personable. He's from Alabama, and he plays on his backwoods appeal. His blue eyes are engaging and his manner is that of a Southern gentleman.

A tattoo of a voluptuous woman in baby-doll pajamas, her tits and the bottom of her ass peeking through, was inked across his right peck. The baby-doll tattoo was clearly visible as he was wearing a sleeveless tank. It had been that very tattoo that had led to his arrest and conviction. Several of the young victims described the baby-doll tattoo and later identified him in a lineup. Thank God most criminals are stupid. Apparently, Mason had been a model prisoner, and now he was, for all intents and purposes, a free man.

I slid up and walked in step with him. His white T-shirt was actually a dingy gray, and his light freckled skin was smeared with dirt and grime. The jeans he had on were worn and filthy. A thick chain was double-wrapped around his waist.

"Hey, Mason, what's going on?"

He turned to me with a smile on his face that dropped into a grimace as soon as he recognized me.

"Oh, shit. What do you want? I didn't do it."

"Didn't do what, Mason?"

"Leave me alone."

Gus got in step on the other side of Mason. Mason stopped walking.

"I don't know why you're here and I don't wanna know."

"Mason, what's the chain for?" I asked.

"I collect the shopping carts, okay? I have to string them together. I need this chain to do my job. This is not right what you're doing. I'm going to get fired 'cuz of you. Leave me alone."

He searched around making sure no one had spotted us.

"I got my eye on you Mason," I said. "You better not do wrong. You better not."

"Don't put your eye on me. I'm clean, sober, legal, okay?"

"Where do you live, Mason?"

"On Brooks, why?"

"In an apartment?"

"I rent a room."

"What's the address?"

"Seven-forty-two, but don't go there and fuck up my thing, okay?"

"Don't they know you're a sex offender there?"

"No, they don't."

"Any young girls in the household?"

"No, no girls."

"How 'bout on that block?"

"Not really, but check it out if you want. Just don't fuck me up. Do not fuck me up. I'm trying to do good here, and you... You're going to ruin my life, aren't you?"

"Why would we want to do that?" asked Gus. "You being an upstanding citizen now and all that. Let's see, how many little girls did you ruin before you went to jail and learned the consequences of your actions?"

"I did my time. I paid. Aw, man, this ain't even right. Shit."

We left Mason to his shopping carts and took a drive over to 742 Brooks, not far from there. It's an area that used to be known for drive-by shootings and drug trafficking. Now, it's quickly becoming a high-end real estate investment. Some of these bungalows are getting re-fabbed and going for four and six million. An older man sat on the front porch in an aluminum chair. He looked a little misplaced, like he was posing for an urban-style *American Gothic* portrait.

"The old man could be in it with him," said Gus.

I stepped up onto the porch. Gus walked around to the side of the house. The front door was open, but I didn't get the feeling that anyone was being held hostage inside. I showed the old man the flyers of the missing girls and asked him if he'd seen any of them. He hadn't, but said his eyes weren't that good. I asked him if anyone else lived with him, and he mentioned Mason but didn't seem to have any complaints. No, Mason had never brought any girls home, not to his knowledge anyway, but his hearing wasn't that good either. When I asked if Mason was home most nights, the old man said he believed that his tenant was taking classes.

"What kind of classes?" I asked.

"I don't rightly know. Never asked, to tell you the truth. Now that you mention it, I guess I'm curious, too. I get the feeling he's a serious boy, wants to make something of himself."

"Are there many kids in this neighborhood, sir?"

"Kids? Maybe, but you don't see them about much."

"Why not?"

"Well, you oughta know. You two are cops, aren't ya?"

"Yes, sir."

"Well, there used to be a lot of shootings in the area. Drugs and things. Kids don't run loose 'round here."

"Doesn't stop you from sitting on your front porch." I smiled at him.

"No, and nuthin' will, lessen they shoot me dead. Maybe I should git me one of those bulletproof vests like you all wear."

I called surveillance and put a stakeout on the Mason Jones residence and the Marina Del Rey Costco.

As we were driving away, Gus got a text from the office with a lead from an anonymous tip. The night before she died, Autumn had been seen at a strip club on Sunset Boulevard. Reportedly, it was amateur night, and Autumn had won the strip contest. "What's a nice little opera singer doing in a strip joint?" asked Gus.

"Winning money and making friends?"

We drove over to Hollywood. That address on Sunset Boulevard was the neighborhood known as the wet dream of the billboard artist. All the big blockbusters buy billboards, and even whole sides of buildings, to advertise in that section of town. Major studios pay big bucks for that sign space. Several elite hotels and restaurants are in the same block. We pulled up in front of the address. The place was called The Body Shop.

When we entered, the driving beat of Michael McDonald singing "Signed, Sealed, Delivered" greeted us. Always liked that song. A top-notch security guard nodded, allowing us entrance, and Sapphire, a petite brunette with bright blue eyes in a see-through harem outfit introduced herself after prancing over to us on what looked like high heels made out of glass. I noticed that her toenails were painted gold. She hooked her arm in mine and with her other hand squeezed my bicep, her golden fingernails catching the lights. Her manner was casual and inviting, making it hard to put up much of a fight. She was such a tiny thing. It brought out some sort of protective thing in me. The blue glitter on her eyelids created a hypnotic effect. You couldn't help but look at her. She pressed her breasts against me, and I felt my breath catch. Her nipples had been graced with the blue glitter as well. She ushered us deeper into the dark cave of the club. I was taken off guard when she asked me if I wanted a lap dance. Normally, I would straight-out refuse, but I found her immediate intimacy difficult to reject. I bet most men had the same response. Naked women seem so vulnerable. Gus grinned at me, enjoying my discomfort.

"Maybe later," I said.

She pulled away from me, and I started breathing a little easier. Her pretty blue eyes reproached me with hurt and rejection but then she broke into a smile.

"Okay, later."

She gave me a lascivious grin that held much promise and did a swooping gesture with her arm, indicating that we could sit anywhere we pleased.

"Do I look like I want a lap dance?" I whispered to Gus.

He chuckled. "Maybe she likes lady cops."

The place was small and dark with the most miniscule bar I had ever seen. Beveled mirrors were on all walls including the ceiling. There was a shadowed section with cubicles for lap dancing that struck me as more than a little perverse. A strut stage jutted out into the middle of closely packed chairs filled with men, their faces turned up looking at a dancer. On stage, a full-bodied, completely naked Latina shimmied her tits, then turned around to wiggle her butt. Then she bent over, reached back with her hands and opened her cheeks. She looked over her shoulder at us. Gus nodded at the woman, and she flashed him her pearly whites. I stood beside Gus in the dark room of men and dancing naked women feeling odd and vaguely angry.

From nowhere, Sapphire's golden fingertips lightly touched upon the arm of my jacket, then stroked my forearm as if I were a cat. "Have a seat, why don'cha?" she said.

"Hey genie," said Gus. "Can you direct us to the owner?"

The request caught the beautiful harem girl off guard. Her body language asked what it was we wanted with the owner, but she decided she'd be pleased to lead us to the office. It did give her an opportunity to show off her best asset. Her full buttocks rocked back and forth underneath the transparent harem pants. She peeked back at us to make sure we were following and, I guessed, to see if we liked her wares.

"Nice ass," said Gus.

"Oh, thank you. Remember, my name is Sapphire if you want to request me for a lap dance or anything."

"Sapphire," said Gus.

"Yes, Sapphire, like the precious gem. That's me. But if you really want to, you can call me Genie, I don't mind."

The owner, Don, was a plump Armenian man in his late forties. His office was a little larger than an outhouse. Pictures of naked women covered the walls. His voice was loud and boisterous as if he were used to having to speak over loud music. He recognized Autumn's picture immediately and told us that she had won the amateur dance contest Monday night. "What did she do to win?" I asked.

"She took off her clothes," he barked.

"But don't they all do that?"

"Oh, yeah, but she was something. She really knew how to work the crowd. She'd zero in on the guys, you know, with those green eyes. She had a way of taunting the men, challenging them, and they ate that shit up. When she won the thousand bucks she bought everybody drinks. I offered her a job but she refused. Said the crowd was too easy and cut out. Anything else?"

"When she left, did anyone go with her or follow her?"

"No men follow the girls from my club. We have high-tech security in this establishment. There are security cameras on the inside, and on the outside. We got top security personnel on the doors and in the parking lot. The girls don't ever have to worry, never, ever, you don't even need to go there."

"So she left by herself."

"She was with a friend, a skinny blond. The friend competed, too, but she didn't win."

"Can we see the videotape of that evening? Perhaps we could identify the blond."

"I said we had security cameras, not videotape. We keep it very confidential for our clients. We got top-notch businessmen here. Our patrons are famous actors, studio execs, investors, the whole Hollywood tamale, and they know we respect their privacy. If you got a picture of the blond, I'd be happy to ID her. If you need any further information, I suggest you get a subpoena."

Gus and I thanked Don and made to leave. Without our asking, Sapphire escorted us back to the door and invited us to come another time, promising me a very special lap dance. Gus said he'd be back. When she insisted on more of a commitment from me, I politely demurred.

Sapphire's spell vanished as we walked back into the bright of day. Although the sign indeed declared live nude girls, it didn't quite convey the experience. I must have had a dumbfounded expression on my face 'cuz Gus looked at me funny. It's not that I'd never been in a strip club; I'd been in plenty, but I'd never been "worked" like that. Usually, the strippers save that action for the male cops. Gus and I walked towards the car, the sun's glare warming our heads.

"She just wants your money," Gus advised me. "Always remember that."

"Aw jeez, I thought she really liked me," I said with a half grin. "You get the feeling that Don has been through this drill before?"

"He's got his ass covered."

"Can't say the same for the live nude girls."

⑈⑈⑈

IT WAS CLOSING IN on five o'clock and we hadn't eaten all day, so Gus and I drove over to Harry's, a cop bar, for a sandwich. The décor is heavy on department paraphernalia with about twenty tables and several booths in the joint. The bar runs down the wall of one side of the room with plenty of space to place your elbows. Above the bar is a display case with hundreds of badges. Several police batons hang on each end of the display case. Flyers are always posted around announcing retirement parties. It's a dive, but the food is good. We took a seat at the bar for quicker service. I slid my ass up on the red leather stool and planted my feet on a perfectly placed ledge under the bar. Some places just feel like home.

"So how was New Orleans?" asked Gus.

"It was nice. Great food, incredible music, nice people. I found it hard to leave."

"Meet anybody special?"

"There was a teacher's convention, lots of ladies in T-shirts drinking daiquiris. No, nobody special."

Gus gave me a knowing look. "For you, the world is full of nobody special."

"Oh, I don't know about that."

"Well, I do. You experience love, you're lucky."

"Maybe love is in the eyes of the beholder."

"That's deep coming from you."

"Yeah, well, you might not know me as well as you think."

"That's highly unlikely. Not to change the subject but, you pretty sure that was a voodoo doll in Autumn Riley's place this morning?"

"Yeah. But crime lab needs to find something in it to be sure," I said.

"Like what?"

"Oh, I don't know, frog's toenails, or blood, strange stuff tied together with needles or nails stuck through it on the inside or something like that."

"Where do you get this information?"

"The Cubans," I said like he ought to know that.

"Right, right."

"And the Internet."

"You didn't get any good gris-gris or mojo while you were in New Orleans?"

"Nope. I did get some free advice, though. No, I take that back, had to pay twenty bucks to get the old gypsy to leave me alone."

"What kind of advice?"

"It didn't make any sense. Something about my mother."

"What about her?"

"Anybody ever tell you that you're nosy?"

"Some. Most people just answer my questions, I don't know what's wrong with you. You're a hard nut to crack." He paused for a moment.

"You know, I think that Autumn Riley was into something the producer wasn't aware of."

"Yep. It feels like she wasn't completely on the up and up with him. What I don't get is why Addams wouldn't take her for a walk on the beach," I said.

"Autumn Riley was a hardhead, demanding. That's what he liked about her and that's what he wanted to resist." Gus was doing his style of profiling the victim and the suspect.

"Yeah, well, he's a cold bastard in my book," I said.

"You weren't touched by his show of emotion?"

"Not much."

"You believe what he said about Autumn?"

"Sure, why not? Autumn wanted a man who could make her a star. Otherwise, why not stay in St. Louis, sing opera, be adored, and marry the most eligible bachelor? That seems like a better choice to me, especially since all she got was dead. Addams had her all set up like a mistress, it probably went to her head. She was just a kid, for Chrissake."

"From St. Louis, Missouri, like you."

Our meatball sandwiches arrived. Gus and I ate in silence. Technically, I'm from the Ozarks, but St. Louis is my old stomping ground. My juvie officer, Donna Paynt, took me with her when she moved from the Ozarks to St. Louis. She was the first woman police officer in St. Louis. If not for her, I would have spent my youth in a quasi-prison for girls. Later, she made arrangements for me to be taken in by a Cuban family in Venice, California, while I studied at the police academy. I hadn't thought much about St. Louis lately, but with Autumn Riley being from there, it made me remember things.

In Officer Donna Paynt's blue and white, I came to know the ins and outs of St. Louis like my own soul. You could say that Donna started training me as an investigator way back then and you'd be right. It gave me an edge as a female investigator. Not many females worked Special Section and no one—man or woman—in Specials was as young. I turned thirty-three this year and I was pleased with my career, though admittedly I walked a thin line. I was known to take what I called calculated risks that paid off. The rest of my life was a shambles, but I was used to that, and besides, you have to be grateful for what you can hold onto. Gus says police training during my adolescence meant that my development as a human being was thwarted.

Maybe so, but it sure beat sitting in prison with a whippin' stick.

I thought of the sand on Autumn's bare feet and the young woman's hunger for a simple loving gesture. Perhaps in a desperate moment, Autumn had tried to return to a part of herself that was less worldly, more authentic. She must have misjudged something, someone, and somehow it had killed her.

"Who do you think took Autumn for a walk?" I asked. "Maybe she went by herself."

"And the strain was so great she had a coronary?"

"It's a quandary. Maybe Autumn died of a broken heart," I said.

"Yeah, sure. You know, I heard those Hollywood producers die of that a lot," Gus said, his voice dripping with irony. "And that," he added, "brings me to dessert."

He pointed to the chalkboard menu on the wall. Under dessert it read, HEART ATTACK CAKE.

"It's dusted with chocolate powder and laced with Kahlua," he explained.

His eyes grew large and happy with anticipation. I thought of the pin-wheeling spiral eyes of the mask in Autumn's bungalow. The hypnotic gaze bounced around in my mind. Who had worn the mask? What was its purpose? How had it ended up in Venice, looking down on the body of Autumn Riley? I recalled Kunda's explanation of the Goddess Epona being an expression of the life cycle, including death. "Gus, that mask this morning, the moon goddess. Do you know what it signifies?"

"The mask? It's a mask of harvest. One part of a ritualistic dance that celebrates the cycles of the moon and the seasons. Regeneration, rebirth, that sort of thing. Why do you ask?"

"Just curious."

"Do you want a piece of this heart attack cake or not?"

"I think I'll pass," I said.

Gus called the waitress and I took the time to look around. When we came in, the place wasn't so busy, but now it was packed to the rafters as it was a Wednesday and payday. It's a narrow room with baseball pennants and an old-fashioned jukebox in the corner. The bar had a full load of officers, detectives, firemen, 911 operators, court reporters, and others of the public service ilk. Gus got his heart attack cake and devoured it with a glass of milk.

Yet another of the incessant reports on the cop scandal came on the bar TV and the barmaid turned up the sound. The cops in Harry's bar were of every age, race, and class. The television showed a picture of one of the accused cops who had turned stooge in return for immunity. The reporter said the bad cop had finally been given a release date. The bar was a roar of boos and curses. After the newscast was finished, the barmaid turned the sound down and everyone was silent.

The door to the dark bar opened and sunlight filled the room. All you could really make out at the door was a pair of thick thighs. For a moment, it was as if the woman straddled the sun. More womanly shadows gathered at the entrance then came to life as they strolled in the door. Four cop groupies in full living color looked around with desperate, hungry eyes. I was embarrassed for them only because I heard how the guys talked about them. The four women looked like they belonged together. They ranged from thirties to forties, each dressed in their version of the uniform: short skirts, tight pants, and plunging necklines.

The one who came in first yelled out, "Has anybody seen Joe?"

Several cops yelled back. "I got what you need," and "Here, I am, honey," then, "Over here! I got your Joe."

At Harry's Bar, a single mother can at least be sure that the guy they pick up has got a job. They can only hope he'll be a decent role model for their kids. 'Course, some of the groupies just want to get laid and there were cops aplenty with hot hands.

A DJ appeared from some back room. He shouted and revved up the tunes, The Funkadelics, I think. It was right on time and a welcomed change of energy if incongruous. At least it took everyone's attention off the scandal.

I had been following the scandal, myself, because of my own work history on the force. I had managed to avoid a lot of trouble by taking a leave of absence under the guidance of my shrink, Dr. Mercuri. I came out okay.

Maybe there were some that considered me a risk. Not my captain.
Not Gus. They were in my corner. In my world, that's a lot. Now, if only
I could convince myself. The barmaid had stopped in front of Gus.

"What's your poison, tonight?" Gus asked me.

"A Cosmopolitan," I said to the barmaid.

She went to work on the drinks, pouring them with plenty of the
good stuff right before our eyes.

"Why would they be so stupid as to leave wineglasses if they're in on
it?" I asked Gus. "They gotta know their fingerprints are on those glasses."

"Fine," Gus said, "whoever drank the wine with her is probably
innocent. Unless, they fucked up. Maybe they're not a drinker and the
wine got to them and they screwed up on that one detail."

"You're dreaming."

"Let me dream. But...I'll bet money it's the producer's prints on
the wine glasses and his semen on the sheets."

"Sure, he already stated that he made a run to get some before
he left town."

"Don't be crude, Joan."

"Hey, I'm not the one who's crude. I guess he wanted to be all nice
and relaxed before his big money deal."

The barmaid placed our poison and quickly moved off. We clinked
glasses and drank.

"It's important to be cool and calm when you're talking high
investment," said Gus.

"Oh, yeah? You know about that?"

"I've lived a life, Joan. I've lived a life."

"That's more than Autumn Riley can say." I swallowed my
Cosmopolitan; it went down easy.

"No need to get all worked up. We don't even know she's been
murdered yet."

"Well, her body is gone. Something's definitely wrong. She was
ambitious, beautiful, had big plans for herself," I said. "Unless she walks
in and orders a drink, I'm callin' a foul."

"Maybe it's a necrophiliac."

"That stole the body?" I asked.

"Sure, why not?"

"They'd have to move fast. How quick do those necros fall in love?"

"At first sight, so I hear."

"Jesus, Gus. I never lost a body before."

The barmaid strolled by like she couldn't hear what we were saying and I wondered how many different conversations like this she'd listened to as nursemaid to the cops. I waved to get her attention.

"Keep it coming," I said.

She poured me another quick one. Gus eyed me, apparently judgmental about how fast I'd downed my first drink. I glanced away from him, not wanting to meet his gaze.

I saw my ex, Carl, enter with Debbie, the rather spectacularly beautiful Korean woman who worked in Missings. Carl spotted me immediately, of course, but I turned away, pointedly giving him my back, and I hoped he'd take the hint. Cop relationships have been known to get way out of hand. Guns, sex, and working the bad streets of LA make for crazy. More than a few cop love affairs have ended in murder and mayhem. That might be one reason why it's discouraged.

I was going to say something to Gus about Carl and how 'bout we get outta there but, just then, the prettiest of the cop groupies slinked up on the other side of Gus. She was blond and buxom, in the standard plunging neckline, short skirt, and high heels, not exactly his type but then, she wasn't aware of that.

"Hey," she said. "Don't I know you?"

As Gus swung on the barstool, turning his whole body toward the pretty female, his cell phone rang. He pulled it from his pocket and handed it off to me, not missing a beat. I saw him acknowledge Carl with a nod, then focus in on his newest fan.

"Homicide, Special Section," I said.

"Gus?"

"No, this is Joan." My voice is low but not that low.

"Oh, this is Rose Torres, crime lab. I got some info."

"Give it to me."

"On the voodoo doll: we found nine different types of fingernails in a pouch with nine strips of fabric soaked with menstrual blood, types: A, B, AB, and O. That means the blood could possibly be from nine different people. We're still running other tests."

"And those red fibers?" I asked.

"They most commonly exist in cheap red carpeting, one often used to decorate cut-rate motels. There were no red fibers on the vic's shoes or any of her other belongings."

"Thanks, Rose. Anything else?"

"We got the prints on the wineglasses. One set belongs to the victim. The other set has no match yet."

"Okay, and how 'bout those hairs?"

"Well, we found more black hair in the living room and it matched the hair in the bathroom."

"Okay, good. Keep us posted."

"Will do."

I said goodbye and pressed the button on the phone. Gus had politely gotten rid of the hot babe.

"Whadda we got?" asked Gus. He was a bloodhound on a trail.

"We got one bona fide voodoo doll, fingernails from nine different women, you can probably ditto that on nine strips of cloth soaked in menstrual blood. We got more black hairs in the living room. The red fibers are from a no-tell motel, and Autumn Riley wasn't the one who dragged them in."

"Well, all right."

Beyond Gus, I saw Carl making his way toward us, leaving Debbie behind in a booth. She didn't look pleased. Did he really think I was going to chat with him and Gus like old times?

"Gus, give me the keys, I'm going out the back. Carl's coming this way. Head him off, will ya? Tell him to go back and sit with his date. It's disrespectful for him to leave her and…"

"I got it, Joan. You don't have to write me a memo."

Gus handed me the keys. Before I ducked out the back door, I shot a discouraging glance toward Carl who was squeezing his big belly through the crowd.

I was sitting in the car, resting my eyes, as my grandma would say, when Carl knocked on the window and slid his big tummy in beside me.

"I can't miss you if you won't go away."

"Are you going to call me?"

"Not if you keep harassing me, no."

"I just want to talk."

I looked into his big brown eyes. "And I just don't. You see the problem?"

"Not really. I don't understand what happened. What happened?"

"Sometimes you have to give up the life you have to get the life that's waiting for you."

"Sounds like guru talk to me."

"You lost me, Carl. You did all the things that I despise. I know you're a good guy. I know you didn't mean it. But I just lost that lovin' feeling, okay? And I can't get it back for you."

"Just give me a chance."

He reached over to me and put his hand on my cheek and softly squeezed my earlobe. I could hardly breathe. I felt like I was suffocating.

"Carl, you see the way you're touching me now? I know you mean it to be loving but it doesn't feel like that to me. It feels like you're trying to control me."

He took his hand away.

"I don't want you to touch me, to...claim me. When you do that... something curls up inside me and I get...very...angry."

"But, why?"

"I don't know. Maybe because I need space and you're not giving me any. What do I have to do to be free of you? You're really tempting me to put a restraining order on you. I feel like I need to get it on record somewhere that I don't want your attention."

"Look, you're free. You don't have to leave town, put a restraining order on me, or any of that crap. I'll give you your space. Just promise that if you need anything. Anything at all. You'll call me. I'm here for you."

"Oh yeah? You're there for me? And what about Debbie? Poor girl is sitting in her booth all alone. Don't leave her there abandoned for too long, somebody else will snatch her up."

"Debbie will wait."

"You should respect that."

"I do. I respect her. I respect all women."

I gave him the most bored look I could muster.

"Call me. You promised me you would." He started to get out of the car.

"Okay, but don't hold your breath."

He stopped and settled back into the seat. "Such a tough bitch. You think I buy that for one second?"

"You should. You know why? Because Carl, if you don't get out of this car and go back to your booth, I'm going to shoot you and claim it was self-defense."

He got out of the car and walked back into the restaurant without another word. A couple minutes later, Gus slid into the car.

"How ya doin?"

"Not great. Thought you were gonna run defense for me."

"Yeah, well I was guarding for basketball and he was playing football." I snorted.

"Maybe you should give him a chance."

"Did he ask you to say that?"

"Okay, yes, of course he did."

"He had his chance."

CHAPTER FIVE

GUS AND I ENTERED Caroline Johnson Management at six thirty that evening. We were putting in overtime. The firm represented actors and models and was on the second floor of a brick building located on the corner of Hollywood Boulevard and Palms. It offered a plush gray carpet, soft lighting, and engaging contemporary artwork displayed on white walls. Voices murmured from behind the cubicles but no one came forward. I stopped at the entrance, not quite sure what the procedure is at a management company. There was no receptionist to greet us, just those gray cubicles with the voices. "She told me to come straight back to her office," said Gus.

I noticed an incredibly good-looking man in one of the cubicles as Gus and I walked by. He could have been an actor or a model himself. He gave me an insinuating look and I blushed. I picked up my pace and didn't look into any more cubicles.

Caroline Johnson was on the phone and put her hand up for us to wait while she finished her phone call. She wrapped it up quickly and motioned for us to come in and sit down in front of her desk. She was a trim woman in her fifties with brown chic-cut hair and a hip jersey knit ensemble of colorful triangles. We introduced ourselves and Ms. Johnson's back straightened. She seemed to get larger before our eyes.

"It's horrible. Horrible. How could such a thing happen?" She took a big sip from a huge takeout cup of coffee.

"That's exactly what we want to know, and we're hoping you'll be able to help," said Gus.

"Autumn sent me a few photos and I thought they were good. I called her in for an interview, but I hadn't even signed her yet, so I don't have much to say."

Ms. Johnson used her hands to punctuate her intensity. She wore heavy gold triangular earrings. Her wedding ring finger sported a thick gold band with yet another gold triangle.

"I just can't imagine Autumn being prey to a bad element. She didn't seem the type."

"What type is that?" I asked.

Ms. Johnson bounced her pencil on its eraser a few times then answered, "Well, you know, some girls are more prone to abusive situations. Autumn Riley wasn't one of those, I'm sure. She was different from the rest I'll tell you that. I could have done something with her."

"Like what?"

"Quite a few of our people are multitalented, and that Autumn was one of them. I've been developing the right connections to nurture the careers of people like Autumn. She had star quality. She could sing, she could act, and she could dance. That's what we call a triple threat."

"Was Autumn referred to you?" asked Gus.

"Yes. It was one of our other clients, Dani, who told Autumn to send her photos to us. They were close chums."

Ms. Johnson's heel bounced on the carpet. She was like a teenager with too much energy. Maybe she had overdosed on the caffeine.

"Can we speak to her?" I asked.

"Dani? We had to let her go."

"Why?" asked Gus.

"She had a drug problem and she slept with everyone. I think she must be a sex addict or something."

"Is that usually a problem, if a model sleeps around?" I asked.

"Well, no."

Ms. Johnson drummed her fingers on the phone as if to will it to ring, then said, "But, I'm telling you, Dani fucked everything that walked; she was trash. Though you're right, that's not really why we let her go. She was unreliable, and once she showed up at a photo shoot with a black eye and welts across her back. I think she was into some sick stuff."

"Do you have an address?" I asked.

"It's no good. She moved. Didn't pay her rent."

"What kind of drugs did Dani use?" I asked.

"Everything and anything, from what I understand."

"Do you have a picture of her?"

"Not anymore. That Dani was a loser, she doesn't work for us, and I won't ever take her back, so I pitched her glossies. I kept hoping Autumn might walk back in here, so I kept her photos and very impressive resume. She was an opera singer, you know." I nodded numbly.

"Yes, I wanted to represent that Autumn. She was driven, had a point to prove to her parents."

"What's that?" asked Gus.

"I overheard Autumn say as much to Dani," Ms. Johnson answered, "'I have to be successful,' she said. 'I have to show my mom and dad that I can do it.' It's a damn shame she's dead, because that little girl was going to go somewhere and I would have been pleased to take her there."

Her phone rang, finally responding to her drumming fingers.

"I have to get back," she said, picking up the phone.

◄◄◄

BACK IN THE CAR, we sped through a progressively upscale neighborhood on our way to the photographer's studio where Autumn Riley got her glam shots done. The sun was setting with hues of purple, orange, and red as I considered Caroline Johnson. We continued to sail down the winding river of cars, beautiful people and billboard signs on Sunset Boulevard. This part of Hollywood was more than appropriate to the thoughts I was meandering through. Often, the spots a person haunts in life reveal the nature of their murder. Without fail, a murder victim always has a life story that reveals a trail to their demise. Sunset Boulevard, its big money and bigger stakes, make it a dangerous place. The photos and resumes of beautiful and talented women were filed in the trash more than not. And then what? Where did these young women go with their disillusionment? Agents were like a crucial valve

in the heart of entertainment. I looked out the car window to see that
Taylor Swift was competing with Beyoncé, big-time.

All the images, in fact, were bigger than life, big as skyscrapers
in some cases. Once we snagged the address of the photo studio,
we lucked out on a parking spot and docked.

Evan Shore Photography was a gorgeously lit studio, utilitarian
simple with large-scale prints of men and women in photos everywhere.
The receptionist, an Asian girl with big pouty lips, was dressed in a
pink leather miniskirt, a tiny purple T-shirt, and spacey-looking moon
shoes on her feet. She flipped through her files, looking up at us ever so
often. I guess, just in case we did something she didn't think was right.
"She got her pictures done here, true."

"By who?" asked Gus.

"Frantz, but he left for Alaska two weeks ago. Won't be back till
who knows."

"How did she pay?" I asked.

She looked at me like I had way too many questions but finally
relented and looked through the file.

"Cash. You know, there was this guy she came in with, like,
a bodyguard? We all thought that was kinda weird."

"Describe him," said Gus.

"He had long black hair. Looked kinda like a thug, all dressed in tight
black clothes and he had to be taking some serious steroids. We were all
like, dude, why don't you try out for the Wide World of Wrestling or
something, ya know? 'Course nobody actually said that to his face."

"Why do you say he was a bodyguard?" I asked. "Did she introduce
him that way?"

"No, it just was, like, how they related, I guess. Oh, and he had this
Teenage Mutant Ninja Turtle tattoo on his bicep. I mean, what was that?"

⁂

We walked out of the photographer's studio and back to the gray
sedan. The sun was warm and each person we passed on Sunset was in
great shape, well-dressed, and wearing sunglasses. I do mean everyone.
"Scratch the photographer off the list," I said.

"He could have given her a slow-acting poison," said Gus.

"Sure, but where's the motive?"

"Maybe he's just a creep. What do you think about the bodyguard?" asked Gus.

"Who knows? Could have been a friend. A Teenage Ninja Turtle tattoo…"

"Teenage Mutant Ninja Turtle tattoo, you mean."

"Yes, but can you say that ten times fast?"

Gus lit a cigarette. Again. I should've been used to it, but I quit not so long ago and it was bugging me.

"Did you know that a doctor has made the statement that cigarette smoking shuts down the functions of the heart?" I asked.

"Oh, really? Where'd you hear that?" Gus blew several smoke rings in the air.

"It was on the news."

"That's not news, Joan, everybody knows that."

"Not only the physical heart, the emotional heart," I insisted. "Cigarette smoking stops a person from feeling."

"Let me just say for the record," Gus stopped walking to emphasize his point, "that I feel plenty. Too much, in fact."

⸎ ⸎ ⸎

THAT NIGHT, I TOOK home the voodoo information I'd printed out from the Internet with the intention of getting the 411 on all that stuff. When I entered my house, I was greeted by the big box from Aunt Trish. I put away the box cutter. It would have to wait. I decided I wasn't quite ready to unleash the past into my present reality. For me, the job always comes first, and this case promised to be challenging.

Or maybe that was an excuse, which was just fine with me. I figured whatever was in the big box had waited for all these years, could wait until I was good and ready.

I read over the printed-out news clippings that indicated that, in Haiti, there had been a Dr. Blanchard whose lab had caught on fire. Villagers were mourning the deaths of family members and friends who had been engulfed in the flames. Dr. Blanchard's journal had somehow escaped the flames, and I read over some excerpts hoping to find some sort of clue to what really happened. I kept reading a certain passage over and over:

> Subject A has begun walking round and round in a circle. Subject C seems almost normal, eating and nesting and participating in other activities as if never treated. Subject B shocked me the most. When I arrived for the daily examination, he was masturbating. How is it possible to have such extremely different reactions? I can only assume the individual chemistry of each brain processed the chemical in its own unique way.
>
> The heat threatens to undo me. Not only have the rats eaten into my supplies, the flies have become unbearable. My only hope is that a breakthrough is near.

I got a strong feeling that the so-called subjects were people. It wasn't long before I was convinced that Dr. Blanchard had, indeed, been doing his research on humans, probably the native Haitians. No wonder his place caught on fire. The Haitians had probably rebelled and set it. Dr. Blanchard's journal was offered for a fee and I ordered it to be sent to my home.

The Cubans, as I affectionately call them, are the members of the Marquez family. I stayed with them when I first came to Los Angeles to study at the police academy. They're French Cubans and they took me in at Donna's request. I guess she felt I needed a change of environment. Maybe she thought I'd fit in with them because of my dark looks. She knew my mother was Native American and French. Lots of Cubans have French in their DNA. Plus, Tony Marquez was an instructor at the police academy and had been a long-time buddy of my juvie officer. Family of sorts.

I moved out of the Marquez home as soon as possible because the emotions always ran high in that house and I found it a little too toxic or reminiscent or something, I dunno. But on this particular day, I thought it might be helpful to my investigation to reconnect. I decided to take a walk over to see them, make an unannounced visit, keep it simple. I hadn't moved far; they only lived a couple blocks from my place.

Tony's wife, CC, is nicknamed after the famous Cuban songstress, Celia Cruz. Other than that, there's no resemblance. CC's a big-busted girl with light brown hair and tanned skin. She's hard-edged and fairly sexy. It was eight o'clock in the evening and I knew CC would still be up and at a full roar.

I could hear Ruben Blades blaring from the stereo as I approached. I don't speak Spanish, but once Celia translated several songs for me as Ruben's words blasted from the speakers. Was it the music or the way Celia recited the words? I remember being deeply affected by the lyrics.

I crossed a courtyard of hibiscus and palm trees as I approached the front door. The pleasant fragrance of Cuban food brought back memories of culinary orgasms. Celia could whip up a gourmet meal like it was nuthin'. I was just getting the hang of cooking Cuban cuisine myself when I decided I had to move. I appeared outside her screen door and spotted Celia in the kitchen, she shouted, surprise.

"God a mercy damn!".

She learned that expression from me. Celia had a giant butcher knife in her hand when she came running, swung open the door with her foot and gave me a hug and a wet kiss on the cheek. I smiled like a big kid and took a seat on a leopard-print barstool in her kitchen. I peered over at her cuisine as she returned to her pots and pans on the stove. Any man who didn't fall for her feminine charms would surely lie down for her cooking skills. She chopped onion, garlic, and multicolored peppers, all varying degrees of hot, then threw the ingredients into a pot of tiger shrimps with yellow rice. She was a choreographed performance of ruthlessness and delicate measure.

Before I could say *"Que hondas?"* she launched into a rant.

"Tony, he's been actin' strange. I'm going to put a big spell on him."

She placed saffron strings in a Mandala configuration on the top of her creation.

"Funny, you should mention spells," I say, "cuz' that's what I wanted to talk to you about."

Celia strutted around in her apron, flicked a wooden spoon and waved her butcher knife to emphasize and punctuate certain statements.

"You? You, who closes her ears on every word I say?"

"I don't close my ears. I listen to you."

She was surprised because I've shunned her mystic advice in the past. "My spells have failed on Tony," she spouted angrily. "But not anymore! I met this man, very big in the craft."

"And then what?" I asked.

"You must obtain a bone of your most precious ancestor," she said. "I will get my grandmother's thighbone!"

"What do you need that for?" I asked. I would never desecrate my grandmother's grave like that.

"To have a spiritual connection with my ancestors that empowers and protects me. Makes sense, right?"

"Oh. I never thought of that. Hmmm, I guess. But, uh Celia, ever hear of the person continuing on inside you? You know, in your heart and in your thoughts?"

"They always say that at funerals," she said with disdain. "Intellectual crap!"

"That's not true. I believe in that."

"But I will have a spiritual divining rod. Human beings need ritual, honey. How many times I have to tell you. What, are you deaf?"

I'd been baptized in the Missouri River holding hands with a hundred others. I remembered that day as a turning point for my soul. It was as if there might be some chance for me. In spite of all that had gone before, I accepted the cleansing and yes, I even experienced the idea that I might be blessed and held in the bosom of Mother Mary. So truthfully, I had deep beliefs regarding the power of ritual and spirituality. I might even think there was something to Celia's divining rod, but it wasn't something I was taught.

"Hey, didn't you hear? The Dodgers!" she exclaimed.

"What about 'em?" I asked.

"They burned their uniforms, good gloves, and even new bats."

"Why?"

"Because they can't win! All of them did it, too. Not just the ones from the Dominican, even the white boys."

"They're not boys. They're grown men with families," I said.

"That's right!" CC declared. "Not only that, but they are the highest paid in the league. All a bunch of millionaires and even all of them are participating in a ritual to better their careers."

"Did it work?" I asked. "No. Right?"

"Whatever, they did a ritual, is my point. To get rid of the bad luck. And you know what the manager said?" she taunted.

"What?" I really wanted to know.

"He said he was glad they didn't put him on top of the pile and burn him, too!"

We both laughed and guffawed.

"Hey, you know what your problem is? You're a double Taurus. Double Taurus means very stubborn. You are very stubborn."

"That's true," I admitted with some reluctance. "Where are your grandmother's bones, anyway?" My grandmother's bones were on sacred ground on a Kickapoo reservation. There was a big furor over whether she qualified to be buried there. They said she didn't have a large enough percentage of Kickapoo blood to qualify. Other people said she had heart and spirit and had done deeds that qualified her more than others.

My mother fought, she wouldn't rest until they accepted Gramma for this designation. But, ironically, it was my mother who died first. They buried her with my father's family on Lambert land in the backwoods of Missouri. Later, they buried my father's body right next to hers. I guess he got what he wanted in the end. Strange how this conversation was digging up my past and all my own buried bones.

"New Jersey," answered CC. "I'm going to Jersey next week. I will keep her thighbone under my bed and this will protect my marriage, keep Tony and me safe. But first, this man I met, Cavo, is going to do something very special. What, I dunno."

"I'm pretty sure it's illegal, even in New Jersey, to just dig up a grave, even if it's your own grandmother's."

"Oh, shut up, you. What do you know?"

I almost asked how the hell she thought she was going to get that thighbone and what the rest of her family would feel about her plans for her grandmother's remains, but I let it go.

"Well, I'm sure you're the authority in that department. In fact, I was wondering, do you ever hear about anyone who works with dolls?"

Her eyes widened. "Dolls? Girl, where have you been hanging out? What do you know from dolls?"

I showed her the picture of Autumn's doll and she insisted on taking me directly to Cavo's Botanika. She put a lid on the pan of shrimp and rice and popped it into the refrigerator, grabbed her purse, and inspected her image in a mirror placed next to the front door.

"Aren't those places closed at this time of night?" I asked.

"Cavo lives in the back and honey, he will open up for me."

I took that to mean that Celia was a good-paying customer, but with Celia you couldn't be so sure. We drove over to Third and Kingsley, a mostly Korean neighborhood, and came to a storefront with a sign that read BOTANIKA. It had to be one of the last Latin businesses in the area. That meant the botanika had been located in that neighborhood since the seventies, before it became Koreatown. To me that was a good recommendation. In all that time, no unhappy customers had burned the place down and the bunko squad hadn't closed it.

Cavo was a small older man, Latin, in his early sixties, with a full head of wiry gray hair and a gray mustache. He answered the door in a casual manner and wasn't surprised to see us.

"Cavo, I want you to meet my friend, Joan." We smiled at each other. He invited us in.

The inside was lit by a gargantuan candle on a counter that provided the customer with every variety of oil and a short description of what it would accomplish. In one corner of the store, a white-haired old lady in a white dress gave advice to a plump young woman. A reading was taking place. The old lady tossed shells across a table. She spoke in a soft warning tone. Tears streamed down the plump woman's face. The light and shadows from the candles cast them in a dramatic portrait like an old painting.

I inspected the oils more closely. There were samples of "come back" oil, "go away" oil, "money" oil, and "career" oil. Some of the bottles indicated that they were samples. I tried the career oil. It smelled musky and sweet at the same time. Cavo stood behind the counter and eyed me as I dabbed the career oil behind my ears and on my wrists. He was dressed in white jeans and a white T-shirt. I peered over the counter to see his feet. He had on white sandals. "Show him your picture," Celia said.

I pulled out the picture of Autumn's voodoo doll and put it under his nose. He shook his head.

"Voodoo in America has evolved into something quite different over the years. This looks Haitian. Pure, straight from the devil's heart, so to speak."

"What's with the dolls? Why use dolls?" I asked.

"The doll is like a power point, a focus of the energy. Basically it's a vessel for the spiritual work to move through."

"Maybe someone brought this doll over from Haiti?"

"Could be, but it's more likely it was made here by someone who once practiced in Haiti."

"Why do you say that?"

"Because of the materials and the design on the dress. For one thing, it's new. Also because, well, Haiti is a long way to travel. You want it for your career?" asked Cavo.

"Is that what it's for?" I asked.

"Ambition, power, control," he said.

"Is that why there's no pins stuck in it?" I asked.

He laughed and said, "Maybe. But you don't have to go to Haiti for that. Just buy that oil you tried." He picked up a full bottle of the oil and handed it to me.

"How much is it?" I thought it might be helpful if I played along.

"Fifteen dollars."

I paid the money.

"Rub it on your chest and stomach and the soles of your feet."

I nodded. Celia clicked her tongue.

"You should have got love oil," said Celia. I shot her a withering look.

"Can you tell me why someone would put fingernails and blood inside a doll like this?"

"You can tell her, Cavo. She's like family to me."

I looked at Celia, touched by her declaration but not entirely sure it wasn't merely said for effect.

"I can't tell you anything exactly. I don't want to mislead you in any way. I'm not an authority on Haitian voodum but I tell you this, that shit is heavy."

"What do you mean?"

"I mean you can't mess around; it gets deep fast. We're not talking about a love spell put together by some young chick working at The Psychic Eye in Woodland Hills. We're talking some deep roots. That shit is from Haiti, okay?"

"Okay."

He gestured for me to come closer and I leaned in so he could whisper in my ear.

"Strong mojo in Haiti requires a sacrifice, big sacrifice."

"A big sacrifice," I said. "A goat or a chicken?"

"Really, I couldn't say what. I just don't know."

"Who knows the answers to these questions?" I demanded.

"Nobody who would tell you, that's for sure. Those sacred secrets are guarded, passed down to descendants, not reported to *Access Hollywood*. You see what I mean?"

"I guess," I said.

"Things are different in Haiti. So many trespassers on their souls; people have a different slant on life."

"It's in their history?"

"The slavery, the efforts for colonization over and over again by the Spanish, the French, the English. But no! The Tianos, slaves and free people of color, rose up and defeated their oppressors. But the scars, the interruption of their culture, have left its mark."

We nodded at each other. I love history, even the facts that are upsetting. I'm always interested in the truth. Cavo had just named all my European ancestors as the bad guys but I could feel that in that moment he decided that I was good people.

"Tianos?" I asked.

"The indigenous people of Haiti."

"Oh." I can't help but admire the fact that they refused to be enslaved.

He nodded. "They are a beautiful people. And they are strong in spirit. But, as you say, the history…terrible. The religious history of the intruders. It's a whole different thing there. You have no idea."

"What do you mean, exactly?" I asked, curious as all hell.

"Take my word. Over there in Haiti, they have ten different distinct kinds of zombies and a hundred different ways to turn you into one."

CHAPTER SIX

ONCE I ENTERED MY home, I went straight to the box cutter and carefully cut the full length of the package from top to bottom on both sides and then across the top. Like a foldout bed, the side of the box came down and revealed to me its contents. The smell of oil paint and linseed oil came at me with a flood of colors and images of my mother with paint on her apron, her cheek, and her forehead. I felt her hand wrapped around mine, her fingertips colored different shades of blue. Inside my tiny fist was a long, thick-bristled paintbrush. She made large swooshing and then short dabbing motions with my arm and that meant the paintbrush, heavy with blue oil pigment, left vibrant swirls of color that had meant something to my mother. I stayed with that memory. It was some time before I realized I was standing there in front of the opened box with a smile on my face.

My mother's easel, her palette, some oil paint, brushes, and several of her unfinished paintings were wrapped in paper. I pulled everything out, carefully unwrapped each piece and arranged them around my living room. Each object was aglow with her presence. The easel ended up in the corner and I placed the painting of a woman emerging from the earth on it. I could see a phantom of my mother standing before it working the paint with her brush to an exact effect. Her thick black hair would be piled on top of her head in such a way to make her look like a Dr. Seuss character. I remembered her working on this very piece and her explaining to me that she was going to use gold on the outline of the woman from head to toe in order to create a shining nimbus. I was only five at the time and my mother was already teaching me to oil paint. I had learned quite a lot, and now I marveled at my memory of each lesson. At the time, when she told me her artistic intention for this particular piece, I remembered thinking that it would look just like the saints depicted in the artwork she had shown me in those heavy art books she'd pull out for reference. I had not recalled those memories for many years. I could hear the gentle authority of her voice as if she were in the room with me. Her possessions were alive with her spirit and I was humbled by their strength.

My mother's style was different from my aunt's self-effacing charm, in that she carried herself like royalty even when she was standing barefoot in the mud of a cornfield. I often thought of her toes as roots that could sink into the mud and her hair as black coils that could reach up to the stars. It didn't hurt that she had once painted a self-portrait much like that. It had been sold at an auction in St. Louis, Missouri, and she had garnered a high price for a charity I no longer remembered. I had proudly attended the auction with my mother, but I remembered that my father had not been happy about it when we got back home. He never really understood my mother. He had tried to hold her captive. Unsuccessfully. She was nobody's possession. She belonged to the cosmos, maybe, but not to any earthly thing—not even to me.

I stood still in the living room. Everything was placed as if in reverence. What more could I do to honor this gift? My mother had been taken from me abruptly. That one event had shaped me. An uncanny desire to do something to complete my relationship with my mother overtook me. Something ritualistic, something profound. I had meant to spend the night evaluating the case, pulling it all together for a new attack the next day. I didn't know how to do that, not from where I was existing in that moment.

A blinking light on my answering machine called to me. The first message was from Carl. It was obvious that he'd been drinking. My heart went cold when he said he couldn't stop thinking of me, especially once he saw me at Harry's. He wanted me to understand that he didn't love Debbie the way he loved me. Lucky her. I had tried very hard to put an end to all "talks" with Carl, especially when he'd been drinking. Such conversations repeatedly ended with him threatening suicide or worse, clumsy efforts to seduce me that bordered on attempted rape.

These talks only made it impossible for me to be his friend. My feelings for Carl spiraled from discomfort to rage with an occasional dizzying spin of pity. I would have had a restraining order put on him, but it would have been detrimental to both our careers. Besides, I was pretty sure I could handle him for the most part and could take him if I had to. Shadows of my father, full up on Johnny Walker Red, haunted my thoughts, but I pushed them back into the recesses of my mind.

The second message was from Gus, saying that Autumn Riley's parents had arrived and were down at the station and that they wanted to meet with us this evening. A wave of relief overtook me. That sounded like a much better idea than having my evening interrupted by a visit from Carl. I could only guess that Carl would drive by my place several times during the night until he saw my car was parked in the alley and then make his appearance. I dialed Gus on his cell phone.

"Sling it!"

I don't know why Gus answers the phone like that. I guess he thinks it's funny.

"They want to meet with us tonight?" I asked.

"You got it. Plus, they want the body."

"Did the captain tell them it's gone?"

"Not yet."

"What's he waiting for?"

"Can you make it?" Gus asked.

"Sure, I can."

"The Rileys want us to meet them in Hollywood."

"Hollywood?"

Autumn's parents had picked the chapel on the same grounds where Marilyn Monroe and Valentino were buried in the heart of Hollywood for their daughter's memorial. They wanted Gus and I to meet them there while they made arrangements. I found this highly irregular. I could only guess that the captain was bending over backward for them.

Why were the Rileys in such a rush to throw a memorial for the friends who waylaid their daughter and put her in danger? I maneuvered through fast-moving traffic on Sunset, snaked down Franklin, and took Vine toward the cemetery.

Everyone and everything was out on the street. Transvestites in overt sexual display strolled down Santa Monica Boulevard. I recognized one of them: Gilda. She, as she liked to be referred to, truly bore a striking resemblance to Rita Hayworth. The image was enhanced by her costume of a strapless ankle-length dress and gloves that came up over the elbows. Three years earlier, Gilda had helped me out. Several transvestites had been murdered and Gilda had worked as bait for three weeks making it possible to catch the killer. I was disappointed but not surprised that she was still on the street.

I pulled up beside her and she purposely ignored me for a moment. I had learned, under Gilda's tutelage during the investigation, that the working girl initially ignores the driver; it's all part of the dance. I kept on riding alongside her and finally she acknowledged me. I stopped the car and waved her in. A strong but pleasant fragrance filled the car as she slid into the front seat. Her personality had a radiance, and you couldn't help but grin in her presence. "Oh my, it's been so long!" she exclaimed.

"Gilda, thought you'd be off the street by now." I didn't hide my disappointment.

"Oh, this is my last week. I'm outta here."

"How long you been sayin' that now, three years?"

"I know, but I mean it. I almost didn't come out tonight."

"How come?"

"There's some nasty people 'round these days."

"Always been nasty people Gilda, that's how we met."

"Yea, but its real bad now. I heard there's a man and woman, real predators. Story goes they're out here now and they got a whole graveyard full up of young girls, some boys too."

"How's that?"

"They go for the runaways, pick 'em up and torture them to death, even heard they set 'em on fire."

"That a fact?"

"I believe it. Some of these kids disappear quick. Runaways don't even have a chance."

"You got a line on that?"

"No, and I don't want one. No, no, I'm really getting out. I met a nice man. I'm going to move in with him."

"Where's he live?"

"Frasier Park."

"What's he do?"

"He's an astronomer."

It did sound like she had found a nice man. That's more than I could claim.

"He knows everything about you?"

"Everything. And he doesn't judge me, either."

"That's good."

"He's my dream man, honey, I swear. He says only thing that's wrong with the world is people can't see the stars and don't even take the time to look up."

"Sounds like he's got a philosophy going."

"That he does, that he does."

"Well, when you move in with him, invite me over for dinner. I wanna meet him." I scratched my phone number on the paper pad I keep on my dash.

"If you don't come, it will hurt my feelings," she said.

"I'll be there."

"With a date?" she asked, teasing me.

"Now that I can't promise."

We laughed together and she put the paper in her beaded purse. Then she gave me a kiss on the cheek, opened the car door, got out, waved, and strolled, deftly avoiding a broken beer bottle.

I pulled away from the curb and back into the traffic and considered, not for the first time, the realities of Gilda giving her body to strange men. It caused me distress and that was nothing compared to my distress when I pondered a graveyard of runaways. I found I was enraged. People always say that when you do police work for years you become inured to the atrocities. All I can say is, that's not been my experience.

Carl constantly warned me that my emotions were my fatal flaw. He said that if I weren't careful, I'd end up eating my gun. It's not uncommon. The suicide rate is high among cops, but suicide never held much attraction for me. Carl was probably talking more about himself than me. I always felt the eyes of my grandmother on me, and she would never approve of such behavior. That woman had the strength and the wisdom of a hundred oak trees. Plus, I owed it to my mother to live and thrive. If anything, my emotions were blown fuel and I was a fast car in a NASCAR competition. I had to be careful, though, had to control myself, couldn't work Special Section with flames shooting out my ass.

I drove in through wrought-iron gates and stone pillars into the grassy green and statuary-riddled Hollywood cemetery. I parked in a white gravel lot next to the small chapel. I paused and said a short prayer for my mother and grandmother before I entered and asked them both to help me with this case. Or any other way they saw fit. I was open.

The chapel had nice wood everywhere, including a large cross in the pulpit. There was one stained glass window plus rows and rows of wooden pews. For an instant I was reminded of the Mt. Zion Baptist church where we held both my mother's and my grandmother's services in the Ozarks. Gus was already talking with who I assumed were the parents. They were gathered around the podium.

Two men were conversing in quiet earnest in the corner. The coolness of the air-conditioning caressed me as I crossed toward Gus and the parents.

Mr. and Mrs. Riley stood close together, leaning on each other for support. My first impression was that they were of the "one can never be too rich or too thin" ilk. I could see where Autumn got her fine looks. Her mother had short curly auburn hair and green eyes. She didn't have a matronly bone in her body. One might have mistaken her for Autumn's sister. Mr. Riley appeared quite healthy and vibrant with thick white hair and dark piercing eyes. Gus stepped away from them and toward me when he saw me approach and pulled me to the side. The Rileys watched our transaction with intensity.

"How's homicide?" I asked.

"Mr. and Mrs. Riley have made a formal complaint with the city regarding the loss of their daughter's body. And how are you?"

"The voodoo doll is from Haiti, part of a spell having to do with ambition, power, and control. What're the parents like?"

"Hard to explain. You'll see."

Gus introduced me and I gave my condolences. Mrs. Riley's hand was hot. She definitely ran at a higher temperature than most folks.

"I understand Autumn sang opera," I said.

"She was a prodigy," said Mrs. Riley.

"Yes, I thought she was a little young to have performed at the Muni."

"She was fifteen the first time she performed. The critics were wowed."
The woman was a live electric wire. Her eyes burned with intensity.

"When did you first notice her talent?" I asked.

"She was five. But one doesn't sing opera naturally, it takes years
of training."

"I would think so, especially since many of the songs are in other
languages," I said.

"Autumn spoke Italian, French, and Spanish fluently."

"Fluently?"

I had never met anyone in St. Louis who spoke three foreign
languages fluently.

"Yes," said Mrs. Riley. "When a child's mind is forming, it is capable
of learning a great deal. We hired language tutors, professional opera
singers, and acting coaches as soon as we saw the bright flame of
Autumn's talent."

I gave Mrs. Riley a slow nod and tried to imagine the pressure that
the five-year-old Autumn Riley must have been under.

"You have to understand," said Mr. Riley. "Once you learn that your
child is a genius, you have a responsibility to nurture their gift. Autumn
learned languages and musical scores like other children learn the alphabet."

"I see," I said. "I wish I could have seen her perform."

I've had more than my share of experiences with the next of kin
but none were anything like this.

"It was something to behold," said Mrs. Riley. "Perhaps we spoiled
her a bit. Maybe her life was not like other children's." Her voice
quavered as she continued, "But she was not destined for normalcy. She
was an exception. She was beautiful and brilliant and she had presence.
Most adults never claim the dignity that Autumn had at ten." Tears
filled Mrs. Riley's eyes. Mr. Riley put his arm around her.

"In her teens," the father continued, "she became more impetuous
and less disciplined. We tried to give her free reign. Her senior year
she begged to have the exchange student at her school stay with us and
we agreed." He sighed a heavy sigh and shook his head.

"Where was the exchange student from?" asked Gus.

"Australia, Dani was her name. A bright girl but inappropriate. We still regret it, but there was no way to know."

"Know what?" asked Gus.

"Dani had deep psychological problems," said Mr. Riley. "In fact, I had to peel her off of me on several occasions."

"Don't think we didn't try to be compassionate," said Mrs. Riley. "We hired a psychiatrist. We even spoke with the school counselor, but there was no undoing what was wrong with that girl. And we couldn't persuade Autumn that Dani was anything other than her truest and best friend."

"Did you feel that Dani had undue influence over Autumn?" I asked.

Mr. Riley said, "Yes, I did feel that. And nothing Dani did was wrong in Autumn's eyes. It became impossible. Things went missing from our home. Dani stayed out all hours. Once, she disappeared for three days."

"Autumn was sick with worry for her friend," added Mrs. Riley. "Turned out Dani went on a weekend cruise with a married man."

"To make matters worse, Dani got it in her head that Autumn should try out for a pop star audition here in Los Angeles," said Mr. Riley. "We thought maybe if we were supportive, Autumn would go have an adventure and get it out of her system. We knew she wouldn't make it as a pop star, she didn't have that sort of voice. She was an opera singer, not one of these tarts that sell Pepsi Cola."

Gus slid his eyes over to me and then back to Mr. Riley. "Do you think Autumn enjoyed the adventure?" he asked.

"No. Not at all. Autumn has never had any real competition," said Mrs. Riley. "She has always been the only one, the complete focus of all attention. She was a phenomenon. It had to have been very painful for her not to be chosen. We didn't recognize her after that. It was as if an alien being took over her body and Autumn disappeared. I started noticing credit card bills for a psychic. I'm telling you, my daughter was a devout Catholic. She used to go to confession once a week. I don't know how she could possibly have had anything to confess, she worked so hard on her training. Thoughts, I guess. Next I noticed credit charges for some goddess workshop. It was all so unlike her."

"I believe the pop star audition absolutely destroyed her," said Mr. Riley.

"Yes, that was the turning point," agreed Mrs. Riley.

"She had her credit charges sent to you?" I asked.

"She never bothered to change the address," said Mrs. Riley. "I send all the financial documents to her accountant, our accountant. It's much easier that way."

We were distracted from our conversation when the producer Glenn Addams entered the chapel with an entourage of mourners in black. It was a couture group, admittedly a Hollywood crowd, but there was something over-the-top-glamorous about the Glenn Addams camp. An air of impropriety hung about them. Had the parents invited Addams to this impromptu meeting as well?

What I took to be a chapel attendant gestured to Mr. Riley, and the couple immediately excused themselves, leaving Gus and me to talk.

"Was it Dani or Addams that took Autumn Riley down a dark, dark path?" I asked.

"Either of them must have seemed cheery compared to those old passion plays in foreign tongues," said Gus.

"Why would anyone do that to their kid?"

"Ought to be against the law."

"Are there any roles that a fifteen-year-old can play in those things?" I asked.

"Carmen, maybe."

"Carmen? That's racy stuff. She gets stabbed in the end."

"By her jealous lover."

Mrs. Riley was speaking with a man in hushed tones. From the back, I could see the man's skin was tanned to a fine caramel color and he had dark curly hair, a strong upper body. Mrs. Riley's body language was deferring to the man. That could be her DNA responding to an alpha male, or possibly the man was giving her valuable information. The man and Mrs. Riley whispered back and forth and at one point Mrs. Riley looked over at Addams and asked the man a question. The guy nodded and she glared back at Addams.

I overheard snatches of the Addams crowd's conversation. They were chattering like old lady gossips. One of the women laughed loudly.

"Shh, La Crisia!" said another woman. "Control yourself."

La Crisia covered her mouth with her hand. She had a near white complexion and black hair. Wearing a black jacket over a long black skirt, she had the decided flair of a vampire.

"I'm so sorry, so sorry," Addams said as he crossed the room and addressed Mr. Riley.

Gus and I became attentive to the conversation.

"Who could have done this?" asked Mr. Riley. "You have to help us, surely you must have some idea."

"I don't know. I can't imagine. I don't understand it," said Addams.

"But you will help the investigation," insisted Mr. Riley.

"Any way I can," said Addams.

"Let me explain something to you, Mr. Addams. If I find out that you had anything, anything at all to do with Autumn's death, I will use all resources available to me to make sure you fry. If you're innocent as you claim, then I damn well expect you to help with the investigation in every respect."

"Of course. I will help."

Now I knew why the Rileys made a point of having this memorial planning rehearsal. It was in order to set the stage for this confrontation with Addams. Mr. Riley motioned for us to join him.

Glenn Addams said we could call on him any time of day or night; then he made for the exit door. Gus and I agreed to split up. I would continue to observe the Addams entourage while he took the memorial. I watched from the chapel lobby as Addams and friends piled into a limousine. I slipped out the chapel door and into the parking lot just as the limo pulled away. I dashed to my car, got in and turned the ignition, then waited a moment before I followed the limo out through the iron gates.

CHAPTER SEVEN

THE LIMO SNAILED DOWN La Brea, turned right on Melrose, then down an alleyway, and finally parked behind a concrete building painted a steel gray. It was the easiest vehicle in the world to tail. I searched around in my glove compartment and found a stale pack of cigs, then dug around in my purse, found some matches, and lit up. The doors to the limo opened and the Addams entourage got out one by one and gathered together for a moment.

I took the smoke into my lungs as I remembered what Kunda had said about death being as far away as the next deep breath of your own black potential. I decided that saying of hers could be my life theme. A familial affliction of melancholy came over me. I can't explain it except to say that it goes beyond depression. It's much more active than that. I brooded again, my thoughts running over what Gilda had said about a graveyard of runaway children that had been tortured and set on fire.

The building appeared to be a private club. In LA, they call them anonymous clubs. The gray concrete structure offered no signs or any other indication that it was open to the public. The lot was filled with Mercedes, Jaguars, and various 4x4s. There was only a back door, the frame of which was painted a vibrant red. A portly bald man stood guard at a formidable chain that crossed the entranceway. A red light spilled from the doorway over the doorman, making him look like the gatekeeper to hell.

I waited until all the Addams flock had entered. Addams hadn't paid to get in and I got the distinct impression that the doorman knew him. Maybe I wouldn't have to flash my badge and announce to everyone I was a cop.

I'd always wanted to do undercover work, but my foster mum, Donna, had advised me against it. Said it was too stressful, that I didn't have the stability or the stomach for it. I locked my car and strolled over to the entrance.

A group of four young women—girls, really—ran up as if in a hurry to get on a ride at Disneyland. They assembled, all giggles and nervous energy, at the doorway in front of me. Their fresh faces and expectant grins belied their daring attire. Their bodies were adorned with chains, leather, and handcuffs and they each wore bust-enhancing underwear as if it were acceptable as clothing. The doorman inspected their IDs and told them to come back on Thursday night. I had to resist my maternal urge. Where I come from, you don't have to know a kid to give them a switchin' if they're doing something wrong. If I hadn't been working and trying to slide in without making a scene, I'd have pulled those girls to the side and lectured them on self-respect. "If you're gonna let us in on Thursday, why not tonight?" demanded one of the girls.

"Thursday is under-twenty-one night," said the doorman.

They sulked away in a cloud of curses and disappointment.

"Glenn Addams," I said to the doorman with a nod down the hallway as if I knew it would allow me entrance. It did.

The red-lit hallway took a couple right angles. I arrived in a pitch-black room with a few tiny red lamps and recognized the music blasting from the speakers as Nine Pound Hammer—sort of a joke, referring to the one popular group, Nine Inch Nails. I only knew the music because of a case I worked previously involving a rock star of sorts. I looked around the room, spotted Glenn Addams in the light around a pool table, and moved toward him. Addams studied the green table, about to break. The white ball blasted into the triangle of colors and the numbered balls went scurrying.

La Crisia, and the other young women with Addams, slowly stripped off layers of clothes to reveal racy S&M outfits of leather, vinyl, and chains. Not exactly proper grieving attire, more like Satan's little helpers. I stayed well back, away from the red lamps, careful not to be spotted.

Finding my way in the dark, I leaned against a wall with a ledge on it. I figured it was probably for drinks. After a while, my eyes adjusted to the darkness.

A woman dressed in a black rubber mini-dress sat at a nearby table and puffed on a long cigarette holder. Her dark hair was short and spiky. She lifted one of her finely sculptured legs and rested a stiletto-heeled foot on the table.

Just then, Addams took a break from the game and whipped out a dog leash, and I forgot about the woman in rubber.

The producer demanded, "La Crisia!"

La Crisia dutifully stepped forward. She wore a crisscross of leather that barely covered her breasts and snatch. A thin thong of leather went up the crack of her white butt. She had on a pair of thigh-high black boots that had gone unnoticed at the memorial because of her long skirt.

Addams snapped a rhinestone collar on her neck, which he hooked onto a leash. La Crisia was prompt to heel, sit up, lie down, and so on at Addams's command. Their behavior had a tango aspect to it, all done in dramatic playfulness. If you go for that sort of thing.

A tall guy in a Calvin Klein suit broke out some white powder and shared it with members of the party.

I looked around for a payphone because I had lost my cell phone in New Orleans, spotted one near the restroom, and made my way over. I dialed Gus on his cell.

While Gus's cell phone rang on in my ear, a skinny black guy with long dreadlocks pulled out a giant joint and lit up. He had a big knot right in the middle of his forehead. It gave his face a magical quality as if he were a budding black unicorn. His eyes were startling blue pinwheels. His thin body and his nervous electric energy made me think he did more than smoke a little pot, and I had him pegged as a mainliner. Somebody needed to tell these folks there was a law against drugs. But then, in a sense, this was a different sort of chapel. A church of darkness. Gus didn't answer, so I left a message telling him my location. I figured the memorial must be wrapping up by now, which meant he could meet me here in case I got a line on something. Gus is good about checking his phone messages, so I hoped he would show before I left.

The black guy with the bump on his head was talking to a woman and I heard him speaking with an Island accent. "Oh, Dewey, you sweet!" exclaimed the woman as she grabbed the giant ganja roll from him and took a toke.

Dewey? More than a few people pressed forward around him. A blue-eyed black guy with an Island accent and a big knot on his head, named Dewey. Couldn't be too many of those around. I made my way back to the bar and found a seat, thinking that was as good a place as any to keep an eye on the scene.

As soon as I got settled in my chair, someone blocked my view. I could see nothing except the perfect specimen of the male physique before me, his hands on his hips. His look said, *I'm sizing you up.* I would have laughed at him, but his wide chest and washboard stomach were uncomfortably impressive. He was the type of man that women drool over and advertising execs exploit in diet drink commercials. His skin was tanned perfection. He wore black leather pants and no shirt, and a small gold cross hung from a gold chain around his neck. Dark body hair curled tightly around his belly button. His leather pants hung low on the hips where more body hair pointed the way to his manhood. His wavy hair was fashionably messy.

"Good evening," he growled.

I stared at him wondering how long it had been since I'd been with a man. Had it been six months? He was checking me out in a friendly way. I didn't want to care about how attractive he was. I realized when I looked up at him I had to gaze past his pecs to look into his face. I considered standing up but decided against it. I also noticed there was a small diamond stud in his left ear. The fragrant cologne and intense sexuality were pleasantly distracting. I found myself imagining what it might be like to kiss such perfect, full lips, to hold a neck like that in my hands.

"Can I get you anything?" he asked.

Was he asking me what kind of kink I was into? He stood close and waited patiently for my answer. Meanwhile, he inspected my neck, my hair, and my lips. His eyes danced all over my body.

"Well?" he said. "What will it be?"

Another possibility sped through my mind and I chose that one.

"Gin straight," I blurted.

He seemed amused at my momentary confusion. I felt naïve, maybe even stupid. "Be right back," he said and turned his back on me. He moved across the room like royalty, as if he weren't naked from the waist up, and then I lost him in the darkness.

The guy didn't really seem to belong in this crowd. Though his costume was very convincing, his demeanor said he was above such antics. Perhaps that was part of his act.

A wiry man with bleach-blond hair over by the Addams crowd jerked spastically to the music. From what I could see, he seemed to be buddy-buddy with the black guy with dreadlocks. It became increasingly apparent that the blond guy was irritating people. One of the Addams girls shooed him away, dismissing him with a flick of her bony wrist. The Addams bunch generally tried to ignore the guy as much as they could, turning away from him at the earliest opportunity. I thought I picked up an Australian accent off him but couldn't be sure. He snorted some coke and did a lewd rocking movement with his hips which wasn't even remotely sexy.

Everyone in the crowd near the pool table was still snorting white powder and smoking pot. I heard the wiry guy with bleach-blond hair yell a couple of obscenities at his reluctant companions. Why he was yelling and cursing wasn't clear. It was hard to tell if he was upset or just having a good time.

"Will someone get The Barb out of here?" said a voice nearby. The Barb?

"Ah, let him be," answered a dominatrix with a British accent, in shiny silver vinyl. She had a widow's peak like the evil stepmother queen in Snow White. Cleavage jutted out above shiny silver rocket-ship breasts. There was a decidedly camp atmosphere to the whole experience.

Where was my drink? I wasn't sure if I had guessed right about the underwear model. He didn't exactly have a tray for drinks or anything like that, but I hoped he would come back with the gin in any case. There was a bar right beside me so I was a little confused and then suspicious about where Studly went to get our drinks. I slipped my hips up on the barstool, swung my feet under me, pulled another stool toward me, hooking it with my toes. I planted my big feet on the bottom rung and tried to relax.

A strange couple was sitting at the bar, two big lumps dressed in rumpled clothes. They had to have five hundred pounds between the two of them. I thought it must be a man and a woman. They looked like they could be twins. They never spoke to each other—just sat like two boils, nursing their drinks. The big woman-lump chain-smoked, worse than Gus, lighting up one after another. The man-lump fidgeted, picking and biting at a red, raw thumb. Then the wiry blond guy, The Barb, came up and whispered to the man-lump who counted out some money.

I assumed it was for drugs, but here it could be for anything.

The woman-lump caught my eye and I instinctively looked away. Those two lumps were a team of sorts and I meant to keep them in my sights.

The woman-lump beady-eyed a young girl, who must have scored a fake ID because she didn't look a day over fifteen, as she made her way to the ladies' room.

Several other people were smoking cigarettes and I reached for my pack of stale Marlboros. I took a red box of matches from a glass bowl on the ledge and lit a cigarette. Black letters on the box said DE SADE'S CAGE in the same print as the flyer I'd found at Autumn Riley's. I took in the smoke with no small amount of pleasure. Addams continued to play pool. I tucked the matchbox in my pocket.

So this was De Sade's Cage.

I signaled to the bartender, a weary guy in his late thirties—you could tell that he'd just about had it with his drink-making career at De Sade's Cage. He wiped barstool seats and the counter in a rapid display of cleaning skills. His legs were muscular in his red spandex pants. One side of his head was shaved and the other side had long hair, brown and straight. He had several earrings in each lobe, which gave him the appearance of being much younger than his years, until you looked into his tired gray eyes. He came over to me and I flashed my badge as discreetly as possible.

"Answer my questions and answer them fast. I'm investigating a murder."

"A murder?" He shook his head as if to negate that reality somehow.

"I want to know about the blond guy over there acting like an ass."

"Oh, him? Sure, whaddya want to know? Can't stand him."

"Who is he?"

"The Barb, they call him."

"Why do they call him that?"

"That I don't know. He's tight with that Haitian guy, they go way back."

"What Haitian guy?" I asked.

"The one he's arguing with."

He pointed to where the Barb was rough-talking the guy with dreadlocks and the bump on his forehead.

"The black guy they call Dewey?" I asked. The bartender nodded. "They argue like that a lot?"

"All the time. Who's on top, that sort of thing. Don't worry, they'll make up."

"You mean they're lovers?"

"I don't know and don't want to."

"Why do you say they go way back?" I asked.

"One night they sat right here at the bar, talkin', bullshittin', you know. Then the Barb, he puts some lighter fluid in his mouth and then he, he uh, he takes the lighter to his mouth and man, it was a blowtorch! I don't know if he learned that in the Aussie circus or what."

"That it?"

"No. Thing is, they burned the seat on one of the stools, caught it on fire. I don't know how they did that. Must have been when I wasn't looking. I thought they were trying to scare me or something, I'm not sure. I threw a pitcher of water on it right away. But I didn't like that shit too much and the next time they stayed late, I kicked them out before I started closing up. Stupid fuckers is what they are."

"Aussie circus?" I asked.

"The Barb, he's Australian, and I think the two of them met in Haiti. They can go back there and stay as far as I'm concerned."

I watched for a moment as the woman-lump hefted her large mass up from the bar and shuffled across the room. She was huge and she looked strong. The man-lump became more animated, chewing on his thumb. The guy really needed some therapy. As did everyone else in the room. What an orgy of psychotherapy a good fifty shrinks could perform in this room. The woman-lump disappeared into the restroom door just beyond the payphone.

"Did they ever mention what they did back in Haiti?"

The bartender was wiping his bottles, making them shine, and stopped for a moment to consider the question. "Right, yeah. They said something about working for a doctor. The guy, Dewey, he was like a lab assistant? Or something like that."

"Would you say they supplied a lot of drugs to the group that hangs out here?" I asked.

"I would."

"Mostly pot or harder stuff?"

"Whatever you can dream up, really, from what I heard. You name it, they could get it for you, for a price."

"Did you ever buy any drugs from them?"

"Nah, I stay away from those fuckers."

The dominatrix with a whip in her talon circled me several times like some kind of silver falcon. I gave her a look that said, *Back off.* She must have decided that I was too formidable to be prey because she began circling in on a man who looked remarkably like an accountant.

"One more thing," I said as I pulled out Autumn's picture. "Ever see her here?"

The bartender inspected the picture.

"Sure, she came in once. I don't think she liked the place much."

"Why is that?"

"Just a vibe I got."

"Who was she with?"

"That guy over there," he said, nodding toward Addams.

"With Glenn Addams?"

"Right. It was a problem because she was underage and I refused to serve her, told her she had to leave. We can lose our license, you know. We have an official under-twenty-one night. I told her to come back then."

"And what happened?"

"She split."

"Did Addams go with her?"

"No. He stayed. I'm sure the limo took her home. I got the feeling they weren't getting along so good."

"Okay, thanks."

When the beautiful guy came back with my drink, there was no charge and he didn't leave. In fact, he didn't say a word. Instead, he settled in beside me with a drink of his own. I searched the place for

Gus, hoped he wouldn't have trouble finding the place and wondered if he'd wait for me outside or come in. "Where'd you have to go for this drink?" I asked.

"The bartender in the other room really knows how to make a drink. Nice and strong."

"What's in the other room?"

"Spanking."

I decided that I really needed to have more of an objective perspective, like maybe I should leave. I held the gin in my hand but didn't drink it.

"So, what are you doing here, Joan?" asked the underwear model.

I almost dropped my glass. I closed my mouth, opened it again. "Who the hell are you?" I demanded.

"Are you here because of Autumn Riley?" he asked.

A closing in came over me, as if I were playing some karmic video game where everything that moved was a threat. He leaned in toward me, as if to whisper in my ear. I put my drink down. When he put his arm around my waist, I snaked my hand around his forearm, twisted it hard, grabbed my gun, and stuck it in his ribs.

"Whoa, whoa, hold on there," he said with a grimace.

It required all the control I had not to take him down. It's a reaction I have to men who pounce on me.

"You're not invited, get it? I don't let strangers put their arms around me."

"Calm down," he said. "You're losing our cover here. You should act like we know each other."

"Don't worry, your cover's not blown. They probably think we do this all the time, that we're into it."

"Can I have my arm back?"

"Please."

"Please?" he said.

"Look," I said. "I don't know you and already I don't like you much." I released him and slipped the gun back into my holster.

"You are tense, babe, you need to relax," he said.

"What's your name?"

"You can call me Eduardo," he said. "But my friends call me Coastal."

"Coastal?" I asked. This was becoming the case of weird names.

He nodded and casually took a sip of his drink like women pull guns on him all the time.

"That's a name?"

"Coastal, as in Coastal Eddy."

I'd heard of him somewhere. My mind did a quick computer check and I recalled an article in the *LA Weekly*, a radical newspaper, declaring Coastal Eddy as a great environmental hero.

"You're the guy that organized those people and saved the whale that got stuck on Topanga beach?"

He nodded.

"You're not anything like what I had imagined."

"Oh, this." He looked at his own washboard stomach and his lower body clad in leather. "It's a disguise."

"Very convincing," I said. "You had me going."

"Did I?" he smiled at me.

I gave him a hard look. "What do you want? What is this?" I demanded.

"I want to know who killed Autumn Riley," he said.

I thought about that for a moment and took a stab. "Were you the one talking with the Rileys at the memorial chapel?"

"I was talking with them," he said.

"Are you working for them?" I asked.

"No, I'm not, as a matter of fact."

A vulnerable and pained energy stirred the atmosphere between us. His brown eyes were injured, accusatory. I thought it had been a fair question.

"I'm not working for anyone," he said regaining his composure. "You might say I'm an investigator."

"Oh, an investigator," I said.

He gave me a cool assessing look, then he downed his drink.

"Look, I have to go," he said. "It was not so nice to meet you. Good luck."

"Wait. Did you take a walk with Autumn the night she died?"

From his expression you'd think I had just slapped him in the face. His brown eyes were incensed.

"No. I wasn't there," he said, and then his voice became a wistful whisper. "I wish I had been, maybe she'd still be alive."

Then he moved away from me, into the crowd, his majesty among the thrall. I glanced over at Addams. He was patting La Crisia on the head. Jeez. How much of an advantage did the guy need in a relationship? When I looked back, Coastal Eddy was nowhere to be seen. I couldn't help but wonder where exactly he had slipped off to.

I had to take a pee.

When I entered the women's room, the huge woman-lump had the underage girl pinned down in a corner, her forearm pressed hard on the whimpering young thing's clavicle. The lump's other hand was snaking around in the girl's low-rise jeans. Without thinking, I kicked the fat woman in the ass—it was a knee-jerk response. The lump let the girl go and turned on me, getting a vice grip on my neck. I kneed her in the groin, giving her pubic bone a good crunch. The chick in the low-rise jeans dashed out the door.

I'm not exactly used to fighting women of any size, certainly not as large as this one. She smelled remarkably like rancid bacon. When she bent over to grab her crotch in pain, I gave her another knee to the nose which sent her backwards against the wall. Blood spurted out her nose. I pulled out my badge to settle the argument. She was holding her bleeding nose and leaning against the bathroom wall, which was covered with for-a-good-time-call graffiti. She held her hand up. I took that as a truce and went into one of the stalls because like I said, I had to pee. I heard the lump outside the stall, shuffle over to the sink, curse, run water, and pull out a number of paper towels. I figured she was cleaning up her bloody nose.

"Why didn't you say you were a cop?" she whined.

In my mind, I prepared a little speech for her on rape, and I wasn't going to mince my words. Not that I had time to arrest her right then. Who really could say what was acceptable behavior in what was apparently an S&M club? When I unlocked my stall door to exit, the lump rushed me, pushing the door into my breast and then knocking me back against the toilet with the palm of her huge hand. The back of my neck hit the corner of the porcelain tank cover and I remember worrying that I'd broken my neck when I blacked out.

When I came to, I was on the bathroom floor, still in the stall. I got to my feet fast and saw stars for a moment so I rested, my hands hanging on the bathroom stall door, and took several deep breaths. I had to admit that my self-defense was a little rusty. It's hard for me to forgive my mistakes. Besides, in police work it can be fatal. Some first day back this was turning out to be. Maybe I should have stayed in New Orleans. I looked around the bathroom stall, made sure I still had my badge and gun, and said a prayer of thanks for that—oh, and that my neck wasn't broken. When you wake up in a bathroom stall, you must be grateful for the small things.

As I moved through the club, I did a quick survey of the room and the bar, but the two lumps were nowhere to be seen. Nor was Gus. I moved fast toward the doorman at the end of the red hallway and he hastily undid the chain without a word. I got the feeling that maybe I was not the first person to walk out of that place in a hurry.

As I pulled out of the De Sade's Cage parking lot, someone flung their body in front of my car and I had to slam on my brakes. It was The Barb. He kicked the side of my car twice. So, I thought, okay, maybe the evening wouldn't be a complete loss. I pulled over to the side of the street and got out. The Barb was foaming at the mouth he was so mad, or maybe it was the recreational drugs. His hair shot out in short spikes. He was thin, extremely thin.

He ran away cursing and I gave chase, tackled him from behind. We rolled across the sidewalk and I could smell rum on his breath, coming out of his pores. I got his body pinned beneath me and held him there. "What the fuck?" he screamed. "Are you a cop?" I detected an Australian accent.

"Good guess. I want to ask you some questions. You know anybody by the name of Autumn Riley?"

"Never 'eard of her."

"Get up, we're gonna have a little chat."

He snarled and got up on his feet in one angry move. "Fuckin' dyke."

I dragged him to the side of my car, where he had kicked it. "Stand here and don't go anywhere."

I inspected the car. The Barb had left a short rubber skid, but there was no dent. I spotted Gus as he drove by in his gray sedan. He took in the scene in a blink, pulled past us, and parked. I grabbed The Barb by the arm and jerked him over to Gus, threw him in the back seat of the sedan. Gus was smoking a cigarette. He had a wry grin on his face. I got in and sat in the front seat beside him, took a deep breath. "Who's your friend?"

"Meet The Barb, he's from the Australian circus."

Gus turned around and gave him the once-over. "What he do?" he asked.

"Nothin' much, just kicked my car. He's friends with some Haitian guy named Dewey. And he had a little conversation that included money changing hands with two large lumps at the bar."

"Is that against the law?" asked The Barb.

"What was the money for?" I asked.

"They owed me some cash. Why do you ask?"

I looked at Gus in exasperation. I wasn't going to let on in front of the Barb that the woman-lump had kicked my ass in the women's room.

Gus turned to The Barb. "You give drugs to any nice young ladies lately?"

"Fuck off."

"What are you doing here?" asked Gus.

"What, at De Sade's Cage?"

"No, here in America."

"You the INS or what?"

"His friend, Dewey, used to work for a doctor in Haiti," I said. "They were dispensing a lot of drugs."

"Not me. No drugs on me. Go ahead, search. You cops? Go 'head, write me a misdemeanor for being drunk in public or something like that and I'll go my merry way."

"I think you need a ride home. Where to?" asked Gus.

"I don't need no fucking ride."

"I say you do," said Gus. "What's the address?"

Dewey came out of the club, craned his neck around. His dread-locks cast a shadow of gargantuan snakes against the concrete wall of the club.

"Your buddy is looking for you," I said.

"Naw, he ain't," said The Barb.

I got out of the car and walked over to Dewey, flashed my badge, and brought him to the car, sitting him next to his friend in back. The Barb relented and gave us an address on Pico and said, "You know, I'm a producer. You should be careful how you treat me."

"Oh, yeah?" I said. "What do you produce?"

"Nothing too big in this country. I've had a hard time going here. But back in Australia I did a few things."

"Like what?"

"Music videos, things like that."

"I'll keep an eye out for your rising star," I said.

"You do that. I'm not the first one to have a hard past. You know Madonna? She ate out of dumpsters before she got discovered."

"You going to get discovered?" asked Gus.

"No, not exactly. More like I'm gonna do the discovering."

The guy was talky, probably because of the high. "How did you and Dewey, here, meet?" I asked.

"Oh, wull...I was on a spiritual quest."

"A drug quest or a spiritual quest?"

"In some religions it's the same thing. But mine was spiritual, definitely spiritual."

"And?" I asked.

"I went to Haiti and met Dewey in this nice little village. His mother was a famous voodum. She taught Dewey everything she knew. Me and him just hit it off." Dewey looked uneasy with the conversation.

"So, you've been together ever since?" I asked.

"I'd say so, that's about it."

"What did you learn?" asked Gus.

"Eh, what?" said The Barb.

"What did you learn on your spiritual quest?"

"Oh, that. Wull, it's simple really. Evil begets evil."

"Shut up, mon. Don't run your mouf," said Dewey.

I looked over at Dewey. He became terribly fascinated by something outside the window and turned away from me.

"How come you decided to move to America, Dewey?" I asked.

"I ain't moved here. I'm jus' visitink."

We pulled up to a green motel with a hundred flags painted all over it. Gus and I walked The Barb and Dewey up to the motel room and invited ourselves in.

"No, you're not coming in," said The Barb.

"We're coming in," said Gus, "or we're taking you downtown, your choice. While we're booking you, we'll get a search warrant. Either way, we're coming in."

"Fuck! Come on in then. Shit."

We went into a filthy room with a double bed.

"Well, I'll be damned," I said looking at the carpet. "Gus, you see what I see?"

It was a red carpet, the cheap kind that you usually find in cut-rate motels. Gus looked at the dirty spotted carpeting and nodded.

"You guys gay?" I asked.

"Naw, man," said The Barb.

"You sleep in the same bed," I said.

"No way, we don't," said Dewey. "Not gay, no. We're like brothers."

"I'm touched," I said, continuing the search.

We checked it out thoroughly but got nothing but a bag of weed under the mattress. No pictures, no clothing, nothing to connect them to Autumn Riley. Gus leaned against the wall and smoked a cigarette. In the bathroom, a piece of barbed wire was on the sink. I got a bad feeling off it.

"What's this?" I asked as I waved it in The Barb's face.

"It's a gag. Someone gave it to me for a joke."

I bagged the barbed wire, then cut fibers from the carpet and bagged them, too. Dewey was resigned and got into the car quickly like he wanted to get on with it. On the other hand, I was about to put The Barb into the back for the ride downtown when he decided he didn't want to go. A struggle ensued.

"Get in the fuckink car, mon," said Dewey.

The Barb quit struggling as if Dewey had offered him profound spiritual advice, but not before I had grabbed him by the hair and got a handful of short blond stubbies. I bagged that, too. Once both suspects were secured inside the sedan, Gus and I stood there for a moment looking at our relatively easy quarry. I could hear a low rumbling of an argument between the two men inside the car even though the windows were closed.

"Australia, Haiti. Quite an international set we have here," Gus said.

"Oh, yeah, an Australian voice on the phone and a Haitian voodoo doll. Makes you think. Plus, they were mighty strung out in that private club. I had a little run-in with a mean fat lady. Though 'lady' might not be the right word to describe her."

"What kind of run-in?"

"Let's just say that if I ever see her again I'm going to arrest her for assault on a police officer. I gave her a chance but she came back for more, snuck up on me."

"All in a day's work. She doesn't sound too smart."

"Not exactly an intellectual crowd. I did have an interesting exchange with a whale saver concerned about our Autumn Riley."

"A little late for concern, I'd say. You say an environmental activist? In there?" Gus was incredulous.

I nodded. "Said his name was Coastal Eddy."

"You mean the wildlife hero?"

I nodded again. "He sort of came on to me. I'd seen him at the memorial talking to Mrs. Riley. And that producer, Addams, is a total freak."

"How so?" Gus asked.

"He had a girl on a leash. He was patting her head like a dog."

Gus chuckled and said, "Sounds like he must be in terrible mourning. I must say, you had a lot more fun than I did."

On the ride downtown, Dewey chanted a strange sort of mantra. His voice began as a low hum and gradually moved up to a higher pitch. The Barb hummed along in a sort of harmony. I listened for a while, trying to figure it out. It vaguely reminded me of my grandmother. I pulled down the visor and looked in the vanity mirror to see Dewey's eyes roll up in his head and tears stream down his face as he turned up the volume. The Barb's eyes were rolled up in his head as well. To say that I found it disturbing would be an understatement.

Finally, I couldn't take it anymore. I had to admit it got under my skin.

"Shut up," I said. "Open your eyes or I'm going to open them for you."

Dewey continued his mantra but The Barb had the wherewithal to open his eyes and look at me.

"Tell him to stop that now," I said.

The Barb punched Dewey in the arm. Dewey's eyes came down and he stopped his caterwaulin'.

"What? What is it?" he asked Barb.

"Lady cop doesn't like it."

Dewey's blue eyes calmly took me in. "It's my religion. Dis is still a free country, right?"

"Ain't nothin' free in this country," I said.

"I tink dis qualifies as police brutality."

"You know, you come here from somewhere else, usually from some really horrible shit, and the first thing you claim is free country. Like it's some kind of pass for your criminal activities. I bet there's a reason why you decided to leave your nice little village."

"Unless you a Native American, you a foreigner too," Dewey insisted.

"Yeah? It just so happens I am part Native American."

"Well, den pardon me Ms. Part Native American. But let me jus say dat quite a few Americans have come to my country and not all of dem were of high moral integrity."

"Is that supposed to be an excuse?"

"I'm jus' saying."

"You know how to make a voodoo doll?" I asked.

"Sure, no problem. You need one?"

"Yeah, I need one for a coupla assholes I know, they're really pissing me off and I'd like for them to pay for their deeds."

"What dey do to you?"

"Not me I'm worried about. It's a young lady by the name of Autumn Riley."

"Seems like I heard that name before."

"I bet."

"Why you worried about her?"

"Well, you see, Dewey, these two morons did something bad to her. What exactly, I don't know yet."

"You got it all wrong. I don't tink I can hep you."

I got it wrong, huh? I'd like to hear his correction. We booked The Barb and Dewey and they lawyered up immediately. Funny thing was, for a couple guys who didn't seem to have much money, their representation was top-notch.

I ran both Dewey and The Barb through Interpol. Gus brought me the printout.

"I didn't know you were Native American," he said.

"Yep, about one quarter."

"That must be why you're so good at tracking people down."

I just looked at him. I knew he meant it as a compliment. He didn't know how my mother had suffered with snide remarks and insults regarding her heritage.

"Well, you do sort of have that thing," he had to add.

"What thing?" I was starting to get pissed but I didn't let on, just acted like I was mildly interested in his stabbing around in my psyche and my ethnicity.

"That thing where you can catch a trail off the wind. I thought you told me you were English. Joan Lambert is an English name."

"My dad was English. My mom was French, Spanish, and Native American."

"And where was she from?"

"Her family traveled up the mighty Mississippi from New Orleans on a steamboat called *The River Queen*."

"Oh, so you're Native American on your mother's side."

"That's right."

"Never knew that."

"And now you do. Where I'm from, people don't brag about being Native American. You might as well write 'shoot me' across your forehead."

"The Ozarks? Thought there were plenty Injuns back there."

"Used to be."

"What happened?"

"They're mostly dead, Gus."

"Oh, right."

"You know, for a smart guy, you sure are dumb sometimes."

"So, you're like an English, Creole-Cajun, right?"

"I guess so. You could say I'm multiracial. They got a label for everything these days. Seems to me we all come from one source, Mother Eve. Which means we're all black under the skin."

Gus guffawed on that. "Right, Mother Africa."

"I figure I speak English, I'm an American, end of story."

"I don't think so."

"You don't think I'm American?"

"I don't think that's the end of the story."

"Gus, if I want to be pigeonholed, categorized, and psychoanalyzed, I'll go see my shrink, okay? What's the report say?"

"We got a hit."

It was a permit violation on The Barb for an S&M band performance he had produced in Australia. He was also arrested for assault with a tire iron. The Barb had claimed it was self-defense, as the man he had assaulted was twice his size. When they picked him up, The Barb was blue and holding. They had to rush him to the hospital for a drug overdose and when they searched him he had heroin, speed, and coke on him. The man he assaulted with the tire iron eventually regained consciousness, but he refused to press charges. Maybe it had something to do with the drugs. There was nothing else on Dewey as far as a criminal record and he wasn't even listed with DMV. It was like he didn't exist. I asked for a more in-depth search, for any report in Haiti that mentioned his name, but that could take as long as a week. We had to let them go. We couldn't hold them on the red fibers alone. It hurt to see them sprung so easy.

"I'll have Rose Torres do the check on the hairs I got off The Barb and see if there's a match to the Riley crime scene."

"That'd be good," said Gus. "Think The Barb wanted to produce Autumn Riley as an act?"

"Bartender at De Sade's Cage said Autumn didn't go for the S&M scene."

"Maybe he had to convince her," said Gus. "The Barb's not really a player, too rough around the edges. More of a bottom feeder," I said. "Nobody likes him."

"Nobody liked Bill Gates, either. Okay, so they're wannabes. But with that lawyer? I'm telling you, somewhere they're packing some power," said Gus.

"You wouldn't think it to look at 'em," I said.

"Who'd front the cash for those two losers?"

"Maybe they're blackmailing somebody."

"Or someone owes them a favor."

"They could even be working, doing the gritty stuff, like grave robbers, drugging young women, confiscating bodies from the morgue, doing whatever's necessary for a guy with the cash," said Gus as he pulled out a cigarette.

"For Dr. Frankenstein, you mean?"

Gus lit his cigarette and drew in the smoke.

"Yeah, something like that." He blew several oval-shaped smoke rings, then added, "Or for Dr. Moreau."

"The one with Val Kilmer and the big fat guy...what's his name..."

"Brando. No, not that one, the original, *Island of Lost Souls* with Charles Laughton and Bela Lugosi."

"Okay, whatever."

"By the way, Brando was not always fat."

"Neither was my cousin, Jenny."

CHAPTER EIGHT

M<small>Y BEDSHEETS WERE SWEAT-SOAKED.</small> In my dream I had done something wrong, I couldn't remember what exactly. Whatever it was, I had misjudged someone and made a terrible mistake. Because of my poor judgment, Carl had been shot and his blood had spurted, like a geyser, covering me in red. I was swimming, then drowning in his blood. A hand reached for me. I grabbed on for dear life.

The hand was creamy white with green-painted fingernails. The face of Autumn Riley loomed before me, serene in death. Then it was as if she had awakened just as I had hoped she would that day at the crime scene. She danced away from me like a spirit. I followed but couldn't keep up with her. She was fleeing me. The faster I ran after her, the more elusive she became and finally she disappeared into blackness and I was too frightened to follow. Everything became dark around me. When I awoke, my bedroom was as black as the dream.

I heard a click as the numbers changed on the clock, loud as a door slam in the quiet night. I glanced over to see the time. A green digital glow told me 2:03 a.m. I pressed my eyes closed in an effort to will myself back to sleep. I thought of my mother. The demons were upon me. It was no good.

I felt I was suffocating and opened the bedroom window, risky in Los Angeles. I recalled investigations where the murderer had climbed in through an open window. Eight of them. I laughed at my morbid mind. Most people count sheep.

A slight breeze afforded me a gentle caress, a small relief.

The Autumn Riley case pulled at me as if I had no boundary of protection. The beauty of her was so vivid. Was that it? Her beauty? My own mother, long dead now, had been exceptionally beautiful like that. It wasn't just that, though. I recognized the girl. I went through the massive inventory in my brain. All the people I had ever interrogated, all the commercials I had seen on television, all the gala affairs I had ever attended, but my memory failed me. Where had I seen that face, that hair before?

I'm a person who likes to be in the moment. I don't live in the past and good thing, too. But when I can't sleep, old memories, like ghosts, come to visit me.

I entered the kitchen, grabbed a glass, and reached for the filtered water at my sink. I thought of how I used to drink fresh spring water from an old hand pump and in that instant I was in the backwoods of Missouri. It was because of Gramma that we kept the hand pump fountain for water. She refused to give in to the new contraptions. She taught me to sew on an old sewing machine with the foot pump. Gramma could cut and measure out her own patterns and she instructed me to do the same. She could design and construct a fine high-collared Victorian dress or fashion a suit right off the front page of Vogue. I often think that was the beginnings of my evaluating and piecing things together so they fit. Gramma was especially enamored with the washing machine with the hand wringer. We could well afford the best and latest devices, but Gramma begged us to wait to acquire "those devices" until after she died. Since Mama considered it absurd, which it was, we hired a woman who came and cleaned the house and did the laundry. Mama kept busy with her painting and ladies groups and she entered a few of the artist contests. I was ten when Gramma and I received the news that Mama had won the Ozark Artiste contest.

When Daddy got the news, he snatched me out of my breakfast chair and threatened to cut off my hair. Somehow my grandmother had prevailed and he didn't cut it. He took his seat at the kitchen table in angry resignation and began drinking Johnny Walker Red straight from the bottle.

When Mama returned from Springfield, where she had to go to receive her Ozark Artiste award, she entered the kitchen where Daddy had sat waiting for hours. His fierce blue eyes inspected Mama for infidelity. He complained bitterly that the cleaning woman hadn't come, the laundry was undone. He said that it smelled, stank up the house. It seemed a senseless argument between my parents and I remember how badly I wanted to explain to them the solution. Their combined fury began in the kitchen and ended in the basement when my mother went down to do the laundry herself and my father followed.

I don't know where Gramma was. Maybe she felt somehow responsible for the argument and made herself scarce. My parents screamed at each other, their voices ringing up the basement stairs and I hid under the kitchen table crying to myself in fear. I became completely filled with dread when the hollering stopped. So quiet, it was. I strained to hear.

What I heard caused my heart to twist in my chest. My mother was whimpering. I went down the basement stairs, one step at a time; they were steep, carved out of the beautiful Ozark stone. My legs were stiff as sticks.

Mama was slumped over the old washing machine. Her mascara ran in black rivers across her face. I watched in horror as my father yanked her hair through the hand wringer. The silken hair that so many had admired was stringy wet with soap and dirty water. He cursed her and jerked her hair, then cranked the handle until her head was tight against the rollers. My mother's eyes caught mine in new alarm. I sensed that she was afraid for me so I stepped back into the shadows. Daddy's face loomed before me, distorted with rage. He had a shovel in his hand. I heard my mother whispering The Lord's Prayer. Then Daddy's body burst into an explosion of hatred. Mama's face smashed in when he struck her with the shovel and the blood spurted across my own face and body.

Red, everywhere, warm red all over my body. I fell backwards onto the laundry basket of dirty clothes as if my mother's blood had knocked me back, and I was there when my father stomped by and back up the stairs. He never saw me, never even knew I was there. I heard his steps as he crossed the kitchen floor upstairs and called my name. I didn't answer.

Mama's bloody arm stretched out from the side of the tub reaching to me. I crawled across the floor to her limp body, took her hand and held it, still warm, in my own. I don't know how much time passed but I remember my Gramma callin' me, her steps coming down the stairs, and the look on her face as she rushed toward me. She wanted me to let go of Mama's hand, but I refused.

The next thing I remember, Gramma was running water to give me a bath. There were bubbles, a huge cloud of bubbles. When I got in, Mama's blood turned the water and the bubbles pink. The water was too hot but I didn't cry and I didn't complain.

Gramma sang a hymn: "Abide with me: fast falls the eventide; The darkness deepens; Lord with me abide: When other helpers fail, and comforts flee, help of the helpless, Oh a-bide with me!"

Gramma explained it all to me. She said it was all a bad dream and that Mama wasn't in the basement, she was with God. She assured me that all those things that had happened in the basement were only a bad nightmare and not true. I shouldn't speak of them nor should I even think of them. If I did, the devil would rise from the river and grab me from my bed. She promised me that God had Mama in his arms just like a baby and God was singing a lullaby to her.

⽊⽊⽊

THE WATER WAS STILL running in the sink when I came back to real time. I was a homicide detective now and I had seen horrific scenes but nothing worse than the deaths of my most loved family members. Memories. I didn't want to recall so many memories. I drank my glass of water and searched my mother's paintings in the living room. Did they hold some unknown truth? Why had Trish sent them? Was it a guilt thing? My father had never been prosecuted.

My mother's murder was categorized as an accident. My uncle, Sheriff Robert Lambert, was in charge. Aunt Trish must have known better. Had everyone known? Was that why I got off so easily for the murder of my father? Was that why they called it justifiable? Was that why Uncle Robert and Aunt Trish wouldn't take me in? Were they advisers to Donna, my parole officer? Get lil' Joanie out of the state, put her on a plane to California, and everything will be forgotten. Was there anything I could have done differently to change the way it had all played out?

These questions have haunted me for many years. It wasn't the first time I had stayed awake pondering the meaning of my past. I knew all too well that I wasn't going to just lay my head back and fall asleep. It would be useless to lie in bed. I put on a pair of sweats and a T-shirt and slipped on my running shoes.

I ran down my alley and through small crooked streets to the beach. The night was purple-blue and there was no moon, only stars. When I got to the water, I continued south until I arrived at Autumn Riley's bungalow. It was about three and a half miles from my house. I checked on her street and found surveillance in a van.

I walked closer toward Autumn's house and went around on the beach side. There was the black dog, the one that had been slinking around the first day of the investigation. It was asleep on Autumn's porch steps. I recalled that Autumn had no dog food in her house, nor were there any bowls for food or water anywhere on the porch. Why was this dog sleeping on her steps? As I approached, the animal came to attention and the hairs raised on his back. I'm not afraid of dogs, though sometimes they are afraid of me. He came toward me in a suspicious crouch.

"What's your name? Huh, what's your name?"

I put my hand out for him to sniff and he rubbed his wet nose on my palm. I patted him a long time and that he enjoyed. I was surprised how long and soft his hair was. He was like a Labrador, but larger, thicker, and silkier. He became animated, loping away from and toward me, all big and friendly. I started walking down the beach and the dog came with me. He picked up a stick and brought it to me to throw, which I did, and he retrieved it, his big onyx eyes wanting more.

"Hey, are you the guy Autumn went for a walk with? Hmmm, handsome?"

I threw the stick. It slipped out of my hand and went out over the ocean and into the sea. The dog went in after it, as if he were saving the stick's life, and brought it back to me.

I laughed and praised him lavishly for his heroism. After much running and fetching, I had my fill. Where did the dog come from, anyway? Did it belong to a neighbor? I'd call surveillance tomorrow and ask about the dog. If they hadn't noticed me, I was going to be pissed.

When I got home, I went straight back to my bed where I keep my old Raggedy Ann on a pillow. I clutched it to my chest like I did when I was a girl. I sat in the front room on my leather couch with my doll. My father had given it to me. I had held onto it over the years, just as I'd held onto the many memories of love and tenderness my family shared before our world was shattered by jealousy and rage. Looking at my mother's paint things and holding onto my Raggedy Ann doll, I tried to reclaim the essence of that time before.

When I was quite young, before my mother's death, it had been my father who taught me to swim across treacherous waters. The Current River, in Missouri, was legendary as a killer. Its underwater currents had pulled down even the strongest of swimmers. Many a person had dove in to save somebody else only to add yet another to the number of drownings. Some folks said the devil was in that river and that he dragged innocent folks to their watery deaths. My father could read the ripples on the top of the water, and he taught me to avoid the devil that waited underneath. It had always been my father's way to teach me the secrets of the caliginous undercurrents of life. He took pride in tutoring me on these important things. I learned under his instruction to glide right into and yet still escape the devil's clasp. Somehow, I had taken that skill and turned it into a career. Would I ever fall prey to the devil as my father had? Could I lose my way on a dark street or in a public restroom? Would an unseen evil sneak up and take the negligible life I had created for myself?

Would I be able to read the waters?

I held the Raggedy Ann close to my chest. My thoughts returned to Carl and the bloody dream that had brought on this terrible meandering through my past. I was plagued with a terrible restlessness. I wondered what the hell darkness in my dream meant. Why was I drowning in Carl's blood? What was the darkness, the unknown? Death? Something inside of me? My shrink would say that I already knew the answer. That my subconscious was talking to me. You think? I had long ago decided that the blackness was rage to which there was no end. But since that gave me no relief, I was open to the idea that it might be something

else. There would be no sleep tonight. My eyes fell upon the wooden
liquor cabinet in the kitchen. I had a half bottle of gin left in there.
As I reached for it, I said a little prayer that it would relieve some small
part of my torment.

⊕⊕⊕

NOT SOON ENOUGH CAME thin morning light, bringing with it a fierce
headache. Though it was a cloudy morning, a pale blue sky peeked
through white puffs, a sweet promise of hope. My blues hung on the
bedroom door, newly arrived from the cleaners. I wanted the uniform to
be ready to go if I needed to wear it. For a brief instant, a sliver of light
illuminated my nameplate. It was as if I had been blessed or something.
I sure as hell needed some blessings. I hung the uniform back in my
closet and noticed that my every heartbeat throbbed in my right temple.
The phone rang, blasted into my head and joined the fierce lava flow of
blood. I turned to the digital clock. Who was calling at five thirty in the
morning? Gus, I hoped. I wanted to get to the phone before it rang again
but failed. The sound of it bounced around inside my skull.

"Joan! You sleepin'?"

"Hello, Gus. No, I'm awake."

"What's wrong?"

"I'm fine, just a headache." I pressed my hand flat across my
forehead hoping to hold the pain in place.

"I called to see if you wanted to have breakfast. You know where."

"Sounds great," I said.

Within a half hour, I had showered and combed my short wet hair
straight back from my forehead. Springy curls sprout from my skull
without my even touching it. My morning routine is simple as boot
camp. I dabbed a small amount of clear gloss on my lips.

I remembered to strap on my watch, a gold Gucci with a brown
leather band. The Cubans had given it to me when I graduated from the
police academy a million years ago. It was not an unpleasant memory.
I decided on a rich brown Dana Buchman suit for the day. It was about
half the price of an Armani and the fit caressed my body. I thought

of my grandmother, who would have appreciated the fine tailoring. She could sew anything I thought of. Once, she made me the most beautiful fringe skirt out of a soft suede. Loved that skirt, wonder where it went? Funny how things just disappear when your life changes. Gramma would have approved of the watch as well.

⁂

I PULLED UP TO the twenty-four-hour diner located in Beverly Hills and found a parking space right in front. The diner was painted barn-red and had large storefront windows so that you had a view of whoever was sitting at the counter and a number of the booths. Gus liked this joint. Probably because a large supply of pretty Beverly Hills hussies frequented it. They were the kind of women who enjoyed the aspect of exhibition that permeated the place, actresses and models. There weren't too many women on display this morning. It was a bit early for all that.

Heads turned as I entered the familiar diner, a small reassurance that I wasn't entirely a washout. Gus was sitting in a booth, surrounded by red leather. For a brief moment, the color sunk into me, rushing into my pupils, saturating my insides. Red stains slid and slipped all over my body. I swallowed and kept walking toward Gus and fought it off. The taste of salt filled my mouth. If I could just get to his gray form and hear his voice, I'd be okay.

Gus had his elbows set solidly on the thick wooden table and he held a coffee mug in one hand. His kind gray eyes looked up when I entered. Seated in his usual booth in the back, he was engulfed in the warm golden glow of an ornate hanging lamp above the table. He was wearing a gray suit. He always wore gray; had a suit in every shade of gray invented.

He gave me a knowing nod as usual. I focused on his eyes and moved toward his comfy warm image, slid across the red leather and basked in his sardonic smile.

"So, how do you like being back?" he asked.

I answered with a wan smile and a furrowed brow. Gus never greets me. He always acts as if we've never parted and so there's no need for "hellos" and "good-byes", "see ya laters" or "how ya doin's." He signaled to the waitress.

"Hey, somebody bring another cup of black water over here, huh?"

People usually did exactly what Gus asked of them and in a hurry. Coffee was steaming under my nose in nanoseconds. My head was still throbbing.

"Gus, you got any aspirins?"

He reached into his pocket, smooth as silk, and pulled out one of those tin holders with six aspirins in it. I took three of them, downed them with the hot coffee, nearly scalding my throat, and handed him back the tin. "Listen, I got you this for your birthday," he said.

He handed me a new cell phone. One of those fancy iPhones. It wasn't my birthday. He just said that so I wouldn't refuse it. Gus lit a cigarette.

"Thanks Gus," I said, a little overwhelmed. "This is good."

Gus was trying to tell me, in as many ways as he could, that he was there for me. Even if everyone else turned on me, he'd be behind me. I looked at him sitting before me, pulling another deep drag on his cigarette and giving me the eagle eye.

"Your work was excellent yesterday. I was proud of you," he said, blowing smoke up into the air.

I grabbed the big diner coffee cup just like the one I had at home and took a big gulp to avoid his gaze. I wanted to buy a couple more of these cups for my house. It'd be good to have a matching set and even one or two extra for guests. I glanced back up at Gus. He was taking another hard drag off the cigarette. Jesus, he was a chain-smoker. I watched the end of the cigarette spark up a bit. Then the curl of smoke, caught in a current from an air vent, did a fierce dance above his gray head. How had he convinced this diner to let him smoke? I smiled at him and spun the coffee cup round and round in nervous agitation.

"I need to use the head," he said. "Be right back."

He got up, took a couple of long-legged strides, and was gone.

Somewhere a busboy threw dishes into a sink. I winced with pain and kept my eyes closed for a moment. If I could get rid of this headache and get some protein in my system, I'd be okay. I pulled out one of the blue-and-white cards and reviewed the information. I made a point to memorize Gus's cell phone number. Three one oh, five six eight, three nine six seven. I have an excellent memory. It ain't photographic but damn close.

Gus had ordered for me. Kind brown hands set scrambled eggs, sausage links, hash potatoes, and a bagel with fluffy white cream cheese before me. The hands belonged to a light-skinned young black woman in a plain white uniform dress with two big pockets on the hips. She was charming and pert with expectant golden brown eyes. Her bronze-colored hair was styled in a wild cut that shot out like a small explosion on her head. I stared at the simple beauty of the meal for a moment before I plunged in, enjoying each bite, washing it down with the black coffee. The food was warm inside me and took some of the nervous edge off my thoughts.

The edgy-hot waitress wore a nametag that said "Tia." My eye was curiously drawn to her as she filled sugar containers, then pulled a small compact from her skirt pocket. She deftly applied a blood-red lipstick.

That was when I remembered where I had seen the dead beauty, Autumn Riley. It was here in this restaurant.

On that day, a few months ago, two high-spirited young women had entered the diner laughing. They were manicured, pedicured, puffed, and powdered. They brought with them high-octane energy. My nose recalled the vanilla fragrance as they slinked by and I smelled it with my mind.

I replayed their self-conscious insolence, how they had strutted and dazzled, then slinked into their booth. They sat in the one next to the window where their pretty thighs would be picture-window fare. Tia, the waitress, had talked with the girls as if she knew them.

I stared at the window booth where they had sat and saw each moment before me like a movie. Theirs had been the latest in gauche fashion: the blond in a red vinyl miniskirt and the redhead in yellow hot pants. They both wore pastel fishnets, high chunky heels, and bright neon colors of crushed velvet stretched across their breasts. Their haughtiness told you that they were not available even if they did look like demented street hookers.

The redhead, long full hair and creamy skin, was Autumn Riley. She had thrown her hair from side to side, having an impossible time deciding which she was comfortable with. The other, a reed-thin blond with short wispy hair and pointed, delicate features must have been Dani. Her fingernails were painted an electric blue. The young women were tropical birds—light, happy, talking about boyfriends. Autumn said hers was a "total control freak!" The women, girls actually, giggled nervously. Their lips moved nonstop. They both wore the bright red lipstick. It was as if they had gone shopping together and both liked the same color of blood red.

I waved to Tia and she came over. "You know an Autumn Riley?"

"Yeah, I do. She's an actress, used to come in a lot, we talked."

"Do you know her boyfriend? Any of her other friends?"

Tia was looking at me with apprehension now. "What's going on? Is she in trouble?"

"You could say that. She's dead."

"Oh, no! What happened?"

"That's what I'm trying to find out. When was the last time you saw her?"

"Oh, I don't know." Her freshly red lips pursed as she thought about it. "Maybe a month ago?" Gus slid into the booth. "You know anything about her friend, the blond?" I asked.

"A blond?"

"A blond with short hair, thin."

"Oh, yeah. Dani."

"Got an address for her?" I asked.

"She stays at the Villa Elaine on Vine. Number eleven."

⊪⊪⊪

I WAS NUMB AS I walked behind Gus and we made our way out the door of the diner. The dream from the night before was haunting me. In my mind, I was covered in hot red blood. Carl's blood, my mother's blood. I looked down at the floor avoiding eye contact. A pool of red was left by each step I took, exactly the same color of Tia's lipstick.

We took separate cars. I followed Gus. He drove straight down Wilshire Boulevard to Rossmore Boulevard, took a left, and sped through Hancock Park, a high-rent area of midtown Los Angeles that moved into a not-so-high-rent part of town. Hollywood, to be exact. Tia didn't have an address for Dani, only the name, Villa Elaine. Gus said he knew it well and said it was referred to as "The Villain," a haven for drug lords, porno stars, call girls, and a few aging actors.

The building was a leftover from the thirties. The architecture was extravagant, reminiscent of Art Deco and high glamour. It had been quite the place to live during the heyday of Hollywood. Though neglected to a great measure, it maintained its beauty and charm. It appeared to be the proper place to house the left-behinds with their broken dreams and crushed spirits. The gigantic wrought-iron gate had a damaged lock on it, so we went right in. Dry leaves crunched under our feet. We found apartment eleven without much trouble.

The door was askew with only a screen door as a barrier. I easily recognized Dani, the reed-thin blond, sitting in her front room smoking a joint. She was listening to punk music coming from a cheap plastic radio when we knocked. It was seven forty-five in the morning. She quickly put out the joint, lit some incense, and came out on her front landing. She didn't let us in. We talked to her on her front stoop. While Gus questioned her, I took a long peek through the screen door into her place. There wasn't much furniture, no television, a few clothes on the floor, empty fast-food containers, and a small array of cosmetics on the kitchen table.

Dani wasn't in the mood to give us much information. Her thin form indicated to me that she had health issues or wasn't getting proper nutrition. Maybe she had a drug problem. With her short hair and in the right clothes, she could have easily passed for a young boy. All eyes and legs, she reminded me of a sick white colt my uncle Robert had given me. It was skin and bones with huge sorrowful eyes. I had called the vet who promised to come the next day, but the colt had died in my arms before she even got there.

I can't tell you what despair I suffered over that poor colt or how angry I was at whoever it was that hadn't cared for it before it came to me. I had never been comfortable with my uncle again. Thereafter, I looked upon him with suspicion. Dani focused her big eyes on me and finally confided that she and Autumn were friends and had tried to get a big-paying modeling gig but they had heard nothing definite. She desperately needed the cash for rent, etc. When we told her Autumn was dead, she didn't believe it.

"Blow it out your ass. Don't give me that crap. Look, I don't have time for you fuckers, I got a very important appointment." Her strong Australian accent was suddenly pronounced.

"Let's see your visa," insisted Gus.

"Fine." She sullenly went inside, her skinny legs stomping around as she searched for her purse. Several neighbors peered out of windows, stepped out onto the balconies.

The couple next door came out on the stoop and stared blatantly at us. A different style of neighborhood watch.

"Can we come in?" Gus asked.

"Fuck no!" Dani shouted. She came back out and handed Gus a neon-green faux-alligator wallet. "Have at it," she said. "Then get the fuck out of here. Don't give me any more crap about anyone being dead."

"Why don't you believe us?" I asked, curious as all hell.

"Cuz," she said. "Autumn Riley ain't fuckin' dead. And that's all I got ta say 'bout that."

"We're investigating her death," I said.

"Wull, have a good time."

Gus quickly inspected the wallet. Inside was a California driver's license and Dani's green card. "You're good for a while longer," Gus said.

"That's right," she answered, "and I'm gettin' on the line to my lawyer. You can bet your ass on that!"

How come all these low-renters could afford all this top-notch legal advice?

"We've got your friend, The Barb, in a cell right now," I lied. "Maybe we can arrange one for you."

"You coppers are bleedin' liars. Wull, if you got The Barb in jail, I fuckin' wonder how I'll get any modeling gigs."

"What's The Barb got to do with you getting jobs?" I asked. "The Barb your new agent?"

"Manager. So what?"

"What kind of modeling jobs? You know, there's models and then there's *models*."

"The Barb is a professional. He used to be an independent music producer in Australia, he knows people. He gets us jobs that pay, okay?"

"Oh yeah?" I said. "He was a producer? Name some bands he produced, one song."

"Damned Demons, Lords of Excess, and Heavy Accessories."

"Heavy Accessories, that's funny."

"They did the song, 'Dysfunkshun,' it had a good beat."

"Never heard of it," I said. "I guess I just don't get what that has to do with modeling. Can you explain that to me? Just pretend I'm retarded. I mean, what do you model exactly? Clothes? Or more like heavy accessories?"

"Oh, wull, you're hilarious."

"Answer the question, will ya?"

"Wull, if you must know, he did get me a few intimate apparel jobs. But he gets some real class stuff sometimes. You know Hollywood sort of likes the rough trade. It gets attention."

"Yeah, I heard that."

"I know better but...I'm sure if you have The Barb in jail, like ya say, he won't be there long, so I'm not too worried about it. Like I said, I got somewhere to go. Is this fun conversation over now?"

"Does The Barb also get you drugs?" I asked.

"What is this?"

"It's a question."

"Wull, the answer is no."

"So, if we take that pot you were smoking when we arrived it wouldn't match up with the ganja that Dewey, The Barb's friend, smokes?"

"No, it wouldn't."

"How 'bout ecstasy, roofies, or more exotic stuff?" I asked.

"No. Nuthin. The Barb gets me gigs, that's it. Are you going to bust me?"

"We're kinda busy," I said. "Maybe some other time."

"Where's your meeting?" asked Gus. "Who's it with?"

"Nunya your fuckin' bidniz. If you want to know so bad, get a subpoena."

"We're concerned about you," I said. "We're trying to resolve your friend's death. Don't these things mean anything to you?"

"Yeah, okay. Thanks for your concern. Good luck with your investigation, officers. I gotta go."

"Here's my card," said Gus. "Call if anything comes to mind."

He carefully placed the card in her hand. She flicked the card away and it fluttered to the ground.

⫶ ⫶ ⫶

GUS AND I DROVE over to the airport to see the techno guys and check out the video before we went into Parker Center. I amused myself by imagining how glamorous the same scene would be depicted on television. I'd have slimmer hips and thighs and Gus would have bigger biceps. The inner workings of the tech department would be all hip and glossy with mood lighting and an amber glow. We parked our respective cars and walked up to the dingy-looking office building as an airplane roared by overhead. The air was thick with smog that burned my eyes. We knew exactly where we were going, having been there at least a hundred times, and we headed up the stairway because we knew the elevator was slow. Then we headed down the bleak hallway lit with long florescent bulbs toward the video suite. Gus followed me, breathing heavily, probably due to all that cigarette smoke. I desperately hoped the video from the morgue would offer up some kind, any kind of clue. The techno guys had helped us out a number of times before.

"How'd you know she was so damn close with The Barb?" asked Gus.

"I didn't," I said and used my new cell phone to call surveillance. Anthony Sauri answered. "Hey, this is Joan. Get anything off Autumn Riley's place?"

"Nope, just a jogger and a dog," said Tony.

"Where's that dog from, anyway?"

"The dog? I don't know. You want me to find out?"

"Exactly, thanks. Anything on Mason Jones?"

"The guy is clean as a whistle."

"No way."

"I never watched anyone so boring in my life."

"Keep on him. The guy was always slick."

"Will do."

"When we put him away last time, he was working as a janitor at a Sunday school. His alibi was the church deacon. We interviewed Mason's present landlord and he informed us Mason was taking a class. I want to know more about that."

"All eyes and ears are upon him."

"Thanks, Anthony."

I put my new cell phone away as Gus moved out ahead of me and opened the crooked door on the video department. Jonathan, a tall, lanky computer geek, stood and greeted us with a strange smile and indicated that we should have a seat in his room of computer monitors, video equipment, and television screens.

"That smile on your face tells me you have something for us," said Gus.

"Yeah, we got a look see." The guy was a full foot and a half taller than Gus.

"What is it?" I asked.

"Check it out for yourself."

I sat down in an old-fashioned wooden desk chair and waited for the screening. Gus stood behind me. Jonathan bent into a right angle and played with the knobs for a while. Finally, a picture came through crystal clear.

At first we were merely looking at an unobstructed view of the coroner's doorway. The driver of the coroner's truck from the Autumn Riley crime scene arrived. The back doors flew up and out came the gurney with the body wrapped in a white sheet. Business as usual. It looked probable that the body could be Autumn Riley's. The gurney was parked inside the driver's entrance just like Ray had said. The driver walked away. There was no action for a moment. Then the gurney came alive. Whoever was under the sheet was struggling like a butterfly fighting its way out of the cocoon. First one arm, then the other and then finally, Autumn Riley, still in her green cocktail dress, her red hair wild, squiggled out of the tightly wrapped sheet. She slipped off the gurney, slumped for a moment against it, then, with a dazed look, shuffled out of frame. I bolted straight up out of my chair.

"Ohmigod," said Gus.

"She's not dead," I said.

"Nope, she's not," said Jonathan.

"You think Dani has seen her, talked to her?" I asked Gus.

"Could be," Gus said and hit rewind to see it again. We sat there silently and watched once more as Autumn Riley was reborn and stumbled off screen. "We have to notify the parents," Gus said.

"That should be good. Sorry, Mr. and Mrs. Riley, didn't mean to upset you, know you filed complaints, had newspaper articles written and paid for a big fancy memorial, but your daughter is not dead. She's wandering around in Los Angeles somewhere in a wrinkled green cocktail dress."

CHAPTER NINE

WE FAST-TRACKED BACK TO the office. I had called the motel where The Barb was staying but he had skipped out on his bill. Gus had clout from his previous history working Hollywood division, so he'd made the call to have them pick Dani up and bring her in. When they went by Dani's place, she had already fled, taking her radio and all her clothes and make up, leaving nothing behind but empty fast-food containers.

"Everybody's in the wind," said Gus.

We conferred with Satch and did the paperwork to put an all-points bulletin out on Dani for Los Angeles county. I called surveillance for the second time that day and talked to Sauri. He said there had been no sign of anyone at Autumn's bungalow. And the dog was apparently a stray. I looked in on Satch. He was on the phone and from the look on his face I could tell he was speaking to the parents.

I called Dr. Sheffield, the scientist I found on the Internet, to confirm our appointment, hoping that he might be able to shed some light on what kind of drug would make a paramedic believe Autumn Riley was dead when she wasn't. Gus made calls to a couple of his drug snitches.

I sat down at my desk and stared up at the boar's head on the wall, the Special Section mascot. Just then my phone rang. I grabbed it so hard I hit myself in the head with the receiver.

"Joan? Is this Joan Lambert?" a voice asked.

"Yes, who is this?"

"This is Kunda, I need to talk to you."

"Talk right now, 'cause I'm kind of busy." Kunda, the Malibu Psychic. This oughta be good.

"I saw Autumn."

"What?"

"I saw her. I know it was her. She was standing in front of Wacko on Melrose. But she's disappeared now. Can't find her."

"When?"

"About an hour ago. I lost her in the crowd somehow."

"Was she with anyone?"

"I didn't see anybody, but maybe. I don't know for sure."

"Okay, Kunda. Thanks."

I hung up. It was two o'clock.

"Gus, I just got a call from Kunda, says she saw Autumn outside some store. Wacko, on Melrose."

"No shit?"

"Plus, I've got a meeting with a Dr. Sheffield," I said.

"Who's that?"

"He's an expert on botanical cures."

"Botanical cures? What's that got to do with…"

"I found him under voodoo drugs on the computer."

"Hmmph."

"You know, like they use in Haiti, to make zombies."

Gus looked at me like maybe I had something.

"You ready to go tell Satch that Autumn Riley has been seen on the street? That you're meeting with Dr. Livingston to flush out a zombie lead?"

"You're not going to say it like that, that it's a zombie lead, are you?" I asked.

"It's your lead, you explain it. It's not like we're making this shit up, you know. Don't look so apologetic."

I glanced over again at the wild boar's head mounted on the wall. There's a hat hung above it in deference to the Hat Squad, a bunch of detectives from the forties.

"You keep staring at the pig," whispered Gus.

"So?"

Gus headed for the captain's office. I followed. Satch was reading a report and shaking his head when we entered his office.

"Cap'n, we got a sighting of Autumn Riley," said Gus.

"What?" He looked from Gus to me to see if there was an explanation.

"She was seen on Melrose," I said.

"On her own two feet?"

"Yes, sir," I answered. "We put out an APB on her best friend, Dani, an Australian girl we just interviewed."

"The parents are going to call me back for an update. In my thirty years of service I have never had to do anything remotely like this. There's nothing in policy to address it."

"We'll get a team to canvas the area with her picture," said Gus.

"You damn right you will. I want a real lead, understand?"

"Yes, sir," Gus and I both said in unison.

"Okay, get out of here and get to work."

As we were heading out, Mark O'Malley asked me if I had come across anything on his missing girls.

"No, I checked in on Mason Jones, a sex offender in that area. And we put some surveillance on him but it looks like nothing. In a minute I'm going to add Autumn Riley to your list of missing."

"Except in her case, we know she's dead."

"Wrong," I said.

"What?"

"She's alive, woke up and walked out of the morgue."

"Where'd she go?"

"That's the question. I gotta run, but let me get a look at your missing files and I'll see what I can do."

"I'll make you a copy," he said.

"That'll be good. I'll study them when I get a chance."

"Thanks," said Mark. "You know one of the missing girls, Katrice, wrote a note in her diary. She said something about being dead and then waking up. I thought it was peculiar and made a note of it. What you just said about Autumn Riley reminded me."

"Do you think it happened to her?"

"I don't know. Maybe. Katrice, it seemed like she was fascinated by it, you know?"

"Get me that copy of the files, and leave it on my desk. I'll see if there's any connection. I gotta go."

Mark nodded in a distracted way and I couldn't help but think that maybe he oughta be taken off the case. Not that I would ever suggest such a thing. I know how it is. I was hoping that I'd be able to help him out. We do that for each other sometimes. Plus, Satch likes to mix up the partners every once in a while. But right then, I had my hands full. Gus and I sped down the freeway toward Melrose Avenue followed by two other sedans. The guys in Robbery and Homicide had joined us in an effort to fast-forward the canvas. Making a team of six experienced investigators, we entered restaurants, clothes shops, candy stores, cigar shops, ice cream stores, sex shops, and even Wacko. In Wacko, there were lots of what my grandmother would refer to as whatnots of Elvis and Jesus. Whatnots. Funny word. I was hoping they had voodoo dolls, but no luck. After two hours, we had nothing. I was late for my meeting with Dr. Sheffield. I'd have to leave the rest of the team to carry on the canvas. Just as Gus and I were about to get in the car, a guy who was completely done out in leather, including a leather baseball cap on his head, came running up behind me.

"Excuse me, excuse me."

I turned to face him. "Can I help you?"

"You were in the store where I work. The leather store. You were asking questions."

"Yes." I showed him the picture of Autumn. "Have you seen her?"

"Is she missing?" he asked.

"Yes, she's missing, did you see her?"

"I did. I saw her."

"Why didn't you say that when we were in your store?"

"It's like this, she was this beautiful girl, and she came in when I opened the store. She was shivering, her teeth were chattering like mad. She was obviously in some kind of distress. I gave her a leather jacket from our inventory. Plus, I gave her some change from the register for a phone call. She didn't have any money and I felt sorry for her and if my boss knew I did either of those things I'd be fired so fast!"

"Okay. Did she say anything?"

"Not a word. I didn't know if she'd been raped and just let out of a car, or if she had been doing some bad drugs, or what. She was a mess. Pitiful."

"Did you see which way she went?"

"No, she walked out the door just as my boss came in. I nearly pissed my pants. It was early, before the crowd, and I was sure he'd seen her and recognize the jacket, but he didn't. Hardly noticed her, thank God."

⫘ ⫘ ⫘

GUS DROVE AND I quietly organized my thoughts as we sped through Pacific Palisades.

It took a little getting used to, this concept that Autumn Riley was alive. I was ashamed of my strong sentiment when I recalled the crime scene and how I believed I had experienced her last breath, how I held her cold hand with such grief, how badly I wanted to save her. At the same time, a crazy surge of hope and the miracle of life mixed into my emotions. One moment she was dead and it seemed the whole world wanted to know why. The next, she was alive and walking around in a new leather jacket. A real-life resurrection. Still, she had to be horribly vulnerable in such a state and a new set of concerns besieged me. We drove past a well-to-do beach community on Sunset Boulevard, then up behind the old Getty Museum, until we came to the modest facilities of Dr. Sheffield's laboratory. Nestled in the foothills, surrounded by mountains, it was an idyllic place to do research.

A receptionist, an older woman who looked horribly bored, escorted us to Dr. Sheffield's office. A tiny round man with bifocals and a hawk-like nose greeted us and invited us to sit on two French chairs in front of his desk. My mother had brought a whole house of French furniture with her from New Orleans when she and my father married. It had filled our large Ozark home and had been an item of gossip in those hills for years. I sat on Dr. Sheffield's French furniture and decided that it was not as nice as my mum's.

I introduced Gus and I couldn't help but notice a colorful abstract painting on one wall. I looked at it closely; the painting had been done on goatskin. A white streak went through the colors of red, orange, and electric blue. I thought perhaps the jagged streak was representative of lightning. I don't really go for the abstract stuff but the colors were so vibrant that I was tempted to ask about it.

"We've never had homicide detectives come to see us before," said Dr. Sheffield.

"Yes, thanks for taking the time," I said. "I realize it is a bit unusual but I'm really hoping you can help us."

"How?"

He looked over his bifocals at me and his birdlike eyes looked amused.

"Can you name a drug that can induce a death-like state?"

"Of course, there are many drugs," he said warily. I said nothing, so he continued. "If you wish to paralyze, so that a conscious person will be trapped in a body that can't move, you'd need Anectine. It's short-acting, lasts only six to eight minutes, and is given by IV. It's often used during surgery to relax, or paralyze skeletal muscles, thus preventing the movement of arms, legs, even breathing and swallowing."

"Are there any similar drugs that last longer?"

"There are other drugs that are longer-acting: Tracum, lasts thirty minutes, Zemoron also lasts thirty minutes. Nuromax, lasts nearly ninety minutes. All of them are given by IV."

"I see," I said.

"May I inquire into the reason you want to know these things?"

"We have an important case we're trying to solve."

"Oh."

"We think the victim may have been drugged by someone unknowingly."

"I once knew a colleague who was doing some research in that area. He had some success with scopolamines using belladonna, a nightshade extract. Apparently, there had been some previous use of it as a truth serum. Persons under the influence of scopolamine can be ordered to release passwords, empty bank accounts, and engage in sexual acts without their consent or even full knowledge."

"Could that be what we're dealing with here?"

"It's difficult to manufacture. The problem was that it often caused retrograde amnesia and walking trances. The new research revealed that in certain doses it did create the effect of suspending the life force. There were some problems, however, with circulatory collapse—blood pressure dropped and respiration became inadequate. I believe some subjects died and those that lived were horribly traumatized. Needless to say, this doctor's research was dispensed with."

"Dr. Blanchard. He was doing research in Haiti."

"Why yes, him. You seem quite knowledgeable."

"I understand that Dr. Blanchard was killed in a fire set by Haitians. Was he doing something, uh, dishonorable perhaps? Maybe using Haitians in his experiments?"

"That is the story. One never really knows the truth in these things. It may have merely been an accident or a misunderstanding."

"Is there any possibility that this drug is available for a person who might want to use it for recreation?"

"No, I think not. Perhaps the CIA has a supply. I did hear something about a drug potentiated by the raw plant extract of the borrachio, referred to as the drunken tree. It causes a fugue state, a disassociated feeling, loss of ego, the sense of self is gone."

"But would that drug cause a person to be mistaken for dead?" asked Gus.

"Not in its pure state, but drugs can be altered, things added and such, and the results can be, well, deadly. The therapeutic efficacy, or not so therapeutic in some cases, depends on several factors including purity, potency, and correct dosage. As you might guess, standardized procedures are frequently lacking on the street."

"Did Dr. Blanchard ever pass on any of his findings to you?" asked Gus.

"Not to me in particular. His studies were published." He smiled at Gus.

"But you know so much about it," Gus insisted.

"Any doctor or student has access to those writings through the local university research library. His work was somewhat 'tabloid' and played on the knowledge or theory, depending on how you look at it, that zombies were the first slaves. There was a lot of talk in the medical research community, most of it speculative. The intriguing feature being that the individual lacked free will and, in theory, a soul. It was a source of great debate. He was working on creating a synthetic drug. I believe a trial potion was formulated but never published."

"A trial potion? Of what?" I asked.

"The original formula was a combination of poison accumulated from toad skin, poisonous plants, and puffer fish administered through the skin. The concoction brought a person to a near-death state and then later, less formidable doses kept them manageable but functioning. Oh, and there was even some mention of dolls. But that was just rumors and gossip, really. After the incident, its scientific popularity faded."

"Except for on the Internet," I said.

Dr. Sheffield frowned and gave me a disapproving look.

"I hope you don't believe everything you read on the Internet," he said.

"And what exactly are you working on?" asked Gus.

"I'm working on alkaloids, two of them. One found in a Cameroonian rainforest vine and another from an Australian chestnut tree. Both have shown beneficial activities against the AIDS virus. It's long laborious work and I should be getting back. I do sympathize with your problem. If you like, I can make some calls and see what we can do to provide the coroner's toxicology department with some samples of the newer, lesser known drugs, so they so you can include them in your official tests. It could be of help in your case about this woman."

A screeching siren filled my ears. It took me a moment to realize it was my new cell phone—Satch.

"Hold on, Satch, just a second. Thanks, Dr. Sheffield, that would be great," I said and shook his hand. "And thank you so much for your time."

Gus finished up the goodbye and I pressed the cell phone to my ear to continue the call from Satch. There was an edge to his voice and I knew that something was wrong. I took a few steps away from Gus and the doc.

"Joan, I need you and Gus to meet me at a crime scene here in North Hollywood. Your girl, Dani, is dead."

"Dani? Autumn's friend? How could she possibly get dead that fast?"

"Looks like some sick fuck got to her. Sex crimes is here."

"What's the address?" Satch gave me the directions. "We're on our way."

I gave the directions to Gus and tried to focus in on the interview with Dr. Sheffield before I lost anything. As we pulled away from the institute, I reviewed every word that Dr. Sheffield said. We drove down from the Santa Monica mountains and back into Pacific Palisades before it hit me.

"Gus, he said in your case about this woman."

"Huh?"

"He said 'like in your case about this woman,' remember? I never mentioned it was a woman."

"Oh, yeah, he did say woman. But women are always the victims of the date rape drug and situations like that. He probably just assumed."

"Maybe he's our Dr. Frankenstein."

"What, you think that old guy is hanging out in Hollywood, enticing girls to his car then drugging them so he can do zombie experiments on them?"

"No. Well, not exactly."

"The guy's busy looking for the cure for AIDS, he's making money, why would he do anything like that?"

"Dr. Blanchard did experiments on humans."

"The guy in Haiti? And now you think he's the one Dewey worked for?"

"Exactly. You must be psychic."

"It goes to follow. Now Dani's dead?"

"Yeah, strange, huh? One minute we're interviewing her, the next, she's a sex crime victim."

"She kept saying she had an appointment."

"Yeah, I remember. Too bad we didn't arrest her for the pot."

⊸⊱⊸

WE HEADED OUT THE 405 freeway. The traffic was long lines of cars, smog, heat, and brake lights—someone's fine idea of hell.

After forty-five teeth-gnashing minutes, we pulled up in front of what appeared to be an abandoned warehouse. Several police cars were parked on the street and the officers were putting up the all too familiar crime tape. A small crowd of looky-loos stood around waiting for whatever it is they wait for.

Inside, the place was lit up like a B-movie set, the stage design culminating into low-budget dungeon. Medieval, maybe. A renter's agreement had been located and was laid out on a table. It indicated that Dani had been renting there for two months.

Monica Sutton, from the coroner's office, was finishing up. Monica was tall, thin, and reminiscent of some Egyptian goddess. She could have been a supermodel but instead chose to be one of LA's top coroners. Her black skin had a velveteen aspect to it and though she was an incredible beauty, no one bothered her much because she was a lesbian. Her eyes were ablaze with fury at the scene as opposed to her ordinarily detached manner. Satch had probably requested her because of Dani's association with Autumn Riley and the media attention the case was sure to attract. Monica shook her head like a disappointed queen while she waited for the photographer to do his thing.

Dani was strapped in a chair with silver duct tape. Her head slumped to one side. Dried blood trailed from her mouth, down her neck, to her breasts. Her blond hair was matted with sweat, as if she had been held captive in the chair. She wore a pair of leather chaps and nothing else. There were cigarette burns on her thin white arms and a deep gash on her left cheekbone. It appeared that someone had swung a blunt object at her—what they call blunt force trauma. I imagined that Dani had dodged it and she got clipped on the cheekbone. It was probably not the death blow.

"At first look, I'd say the extensive bruises on her neck indicate she's been strangled to death," said Monica.

I checked the wire trash can in the corner and found several half-used rolls of the duct tape.

Monica opened Dani's mouth which was filled with coagulated blood. "She's got a tooth missing."

"What?" I asked.

"This victim is recently missing a wisdom tooth," Monica repeated with discernible anger.

"Must be a souvenir," said Gus.

"People who take souvenirs are often repeat offenders. Means there's more victims to come, or there have been already," I said.

Monica indicated that the photographer should take more photos while she held open Dani's jaw. Sadly, these pictures were not as pretty as last time and our beauty was not going to get up and walk away.

Monica carefully removed the tape from Dani's arms and we bagged it as evidence. Most coroners require a little assistance with the body. Without a grunt, or any other indication of effort, Monica lifted Dani from the chair and placed her on a gurney.

I couldn't quite believe she was dead. Dani, the sick colt I couldn't save. You know it's not your fault, but you can't help but think there was something you should have done. We didn't have a clue as to who was responsible.

The person who called it in was a blind woman who heard two unfamiliar pairs of footsteps and voices she couldn't recognize coming from the warehouse apartment. She said Dani had always been kind to her and she was concerned about the girl. After the strange voices had left, the blind woman cried out for Dani. There was no answer so she called the cops.

Somewhere in Sydney, Australia, a family was going to get the bad news. Brutal murders cause the most torment. Loved one's anguish over how the victim died and their last thoughts. Or maybe they wouldn't give a damn. Maybe there was no one to give a damn. Maybe we were the only ones who ever would: me, Gus, and Monica, the coroner. I took a photo with my new cell phone of the tortured Dani and slipped the phone in my pocket and prayed for trace evidence.

The crime lab was already well into the investigation. They were swarming over and searching the place like scout ants. I walked away from the scene and down a long dark hallway where I discovered a locked door.

"I'm gonna need the bull!" I called out.

We got a battering ram and busted in. Inside the room was a stained mattress on a grimy floor. Every kind of sex contraption known to man was piled in the corner. On one wall there were shelves, a small library of porno films. Several of the DVDs indicated, in black marker, that Dani was featured as lead. She had positioned herself as a producer/star in the S&M niche of the porno industry—much to her demise. Monica came into the dreary room looking for more bodies.

"Looks like there's only one victim," she said. "I'm clearing out unless there's anything else you need."

"No. Thanks a lot, Monica."

She shook my hand and gave me a meaningful look. "Good luck on this one," she said.

She shook with Gus as well and left, deftly pulling the gurney with Dani's body out the front door.

Next to the filthy mattress, I found a piece of paper with a telephone number on it. I dialed the phone number and a weak, mealy-mouthed voice answered, "Cocks and clits." I grimaced.

It was a not-so-elite porno distributor by the name of Mikey. Gus logged the number in on his cell.

After several hours of combing through every item in Dani's warehouse, a repulsive list of sexual depravity, we noticed that one important item was missing. The camera. We headed out the door to go question the distributor.

The address indicated the company was operating out of a motel room in Van Nuys. This particular motel was known in the law enforcement community for trafficking drugs: mostly crack, cocaine, and amphetamines. Downtrodden hookers worked the rooms offering both sex and drugs.

We arrived at the motel and knocked on the motel room door. The neon sign blinking NO VACANCY also indicated porno films as one of its attractions. A short man answered the door and let us into the dingy room. Mikey. If he had been any smaller, he'd have to be a dwarf. Mikey was a frightened man with a pink pockmarked face. Gus requested more light and Mikey obliged, getting a light bulb and screwing it into a lamp with no lampshade. The effect was to wash the room with a bright glare. Someone once said the only difference between erotic film and porno was the lighting. Now that the room was well lit, I could see rows and rows of wall-to-wall DVDs advertising what was apparently Mikey's inventory—a spectrum of porno available in his small motel room.

Men with gigantic cocks and women with huge tits each had their own section. As did the oral sex films, the vibrator films, and other contraption films. I noticed an anal sex film entitled, *The Butt Detective*.

You didn't really have to rent these DVDs to know the storylines because you could get the gist from the promo boxes. Women willingly offered their vaginas and assholes. Some of the women were not so attractive while others were gorgeous. Same with the men. I noticed there was a blond girl, who looked about fifteen, by the name of Meridian who starred in several of her own series of porno tapes. I wondered where her porno tapes would take her.

In one corner, magic marker designated B&D—bondage-dominance—and S&M—what I believe is referred to as sadomasochistic films. There was a bumper sticker above this section that read, "MIKEY LIKES IT." Finally, I located Dani's videos in the S&M section. She had on a full leather head-mask. She used her own name, Dani, on the promo, which helped, plus I recognized her small naked breasts and pale white skin. She was wearing the same pair of black leather chaps that she died in. I brought the box up to the desk where Mikey was sitting. He blinked several times at me. I must have worn an expression of distaste.

"Don't judge me," he said. "Some people need these films. They find them, uh, liberating."

"I don't judge you, Mikey. That's not really my job. Mostly, I'm an understanding person. If anything, I'm empathetic. I know what it's like to see the moon turn red." I pointed at the picture of Dani in the leather head-mask and chaps. "She's been murdered," I said.

"That's highly unusual. Nobody is supposed to die. I certainly didn't have anything to do with it."

"Okay," I said. "But she's definitely dead and we're investigating her homicide and you need to answer some questions."

"Fine, what do you want to know?"

Mikey's pink face flinched when Gus asked him questions as if he were afraid someone might hit him. How could anyone hit a little guy like Mikey and live with himself? Then again maybe he was into that, maybe he even paid someone to hit him.

"How did you get the tapes?" asked Gus.

"She delivered them to me herself, I'd pay her and then I'd mail them to the customers."

"How 'bout a copy of that list?"

"No problem, I got it right here."

Mikey continued to flinch, but he was cooperative. He was a little pimple, the nervous ringmaster, the center of elephantine sex parts and exaggerated sex acts. It surrounded him, the human circus freak show.

He handed over a hand-typed list with about two hundred names and addresses on it.

"Other than that, I knew nothing about her. Don't know where she lived or nothing. I made good money off her DVDs, always paid her in cash. I'm sorry to hear that she's dead."

I wasn't sure if he was sorry on a personal level or regretted that his income would suffer.

Most of the addresses on Mikey's list were out of state. Time would not be on our side. I gave Mikey my cell number and made him promise to call me immediately if he had anything, anything at all.

⊪⊪⊪

GUS AND I WERE back at Parker Center. We had to view all the DVDs, fifteen in all, to see exactly what happened in each one. We fast-forwarded, cutting down the viewing time to four hours. Porno films are much shorter than regular movies. None of the DVDs recorded Dani in the kind of acts that included strangulation or cigarette burning, nor getting hit in the face with a hammer, but she had participated in a plethora of S&M.

I took a moment to digest the aberration of the fifteen films. I came to the conclusion that the need to watch such disgraceful acts was a misfortunate ailment. Nobody was going to ever convince me that what I saw was "liberating." And now, amongst her other problems, Autumn Riley's best friend was dead.

"Autumn is hanging with a bad crowd," I said. "Maybe they're trafficking humans, making snuff films, who knows. It could be anything."

It was 10:00 p.m. and Gus was looking tired. We ordered another computer search and then a summary of each person on Mikey's S&M mailing list. One was a prisoner in an Illinois penitentiary. None of the others had previous sexual or violent records.

"Okay, you're probably right," Gus said. "Figure it's somebody dealing with the peddling of human flesh. Go home and get some rest and we'll get back on it tomorrow."

I picked up the stack of porn promo photos collected from the Dani crime scene.

"I'll look these over tonight," I said.

On the drive home, I remembered a piece of paper I had slipped into my wallet. It needed to be put into the murder book. I decided to call a young woman who was just a receptionist, nobody really— Connie, from Glenn Addams's office.

The new iPhone Gus had given me was getting to be real handy. I punched in the number.

"Connie, this is Detective Lambert," I said.

"Yes?"

My mind raced. "I'm interested in anything you've got to say to me at this point."

Her voice quavered with nervousness. "I'm a… I just need to keep my job. You know?"

"Sure, I understand. Nobody needs to know you said anything."

"I'm not sure really what it means."

"What what means? Spit it out, will ya?"

"Before Autumn died?"

"Yes?"

"She planned this huge elaborate party and there was a big deal about the invitations. I have the database and all that and I had to help Autumn with it because she doesn't know anything about computers. I had an argument with Mr. Addams because I didn't feel it was part of my job description to help Autumn plan her ego parties."

"Okay."

"And well, tonight is the party and people have been calling all day, saying they'll be at the party and so on and that's sort of weird, right? I mean, Autumn planned this party and now Mr. Addams is having the party and I don't know."

"What time is this ego party?"

"Oh, it started an hour ago."

"How come you're not there?"

"Oh, I wasn't invited. Not that I would go."

"Why not?"

"Well, some of those people are wacked. Out there, strange, you know?"

"I'm beginning to. Where is this party, anyway?"

"At Glenn's house in Bel Air."

I called Gus and asked him to pick me up. We were going to crash a party. He agreed with a modicum of reluctance.

CHAPTER TEN

THE SKY WAS CLEAR, one of those nights when LA sparkles like a diamond. Glenn Addams's estate was near UCLA, up in the hills. There had to be at least twenty cars, mostly European sports sedans and 4x4s, lined up in front of the palatial Mediterranean-styled sprawling estate. Gus and I parked next to a Rolls Royce. My eyes took in the posies, tulips, and gardenias in full bloom. I looked down on the city and marveled at its seeming beauty.

"Addams has some view. Not a bad spot to throw an ego party."

Gus took a moment to stand at my side. "If your view captures even a segment of what they call the diamond necklace, it ups your property value by a million dollars."

I studied my partner's face. "How come you know all the inside details of big money deals?"

"I'm a little older than you, been around a few more places."

African drums and cries of celebration punctuated the night air. We were far away from corpses stored in a cold room. The grass was perfectly manicured and large graceful willow trees lined the walkway as Gus and I approached the imposing entrance.

A butler answered the door and showed us in. We passed through the foyer decorated with a large and eclectic collection of erotic art. The party sounds were coming from somewhere within. A flourish of drumming ended. There was applause, and the hum of the crowd became more animated.

We didn't have a warrant. I reminded myself of this fact as we entered the high-ceilinged room of the party. The dress code of the evening was casual elegance. There was a noteworthy amount of cleavage and perfect faces; thighs were elegantly prominent. Gus and I were dark, muted, appearing staid in comparison to the bright colors, jewels, and skin.

Addams stood in the center of the room surrounded by his entourage. They were listening intently to Addams. I feigned a smile and stood aloof, my famous eavesdropping disguise. Addams caught sight of us and stopped midsentence to walk over and address us. He didn't look too friendly. Myself, I wasn't really in a party mood.

"Hello," I said.

"You must be having problems with the case, otherwise you wouldn't be here. Not without a warrant."

He sure hit that one on the head. I didn't really expect to get anything on him. I only wanted to check it out, see what there was to see. Make him nervous.

An effeminate elderly man nearly tittered, "Oh, LAPD party crashers. Do you think I could get her to arrest me?"

"That can be arranged," I said. "What would you like to be arrested for?"

"Lewd behavior." Crazy old coot.

"Have a few more drinks," I said. "We'll see how the party progresses."

"Just shoot him," said a woman. "Do us all a favor."

It was crucial that Gus and I handle this situation correctly. We could easily compromise the investigation. No doubt any number of people in this crowd had their finger on the speed dial to the press, publicity people, and tabloid papers. It's no accident that the paparazzi types are informed of what the celebrities do. We were walking a thin line. Then again, Addams had told the Rileys that he would help the investigation in every way imaginable, or something to that effect.

I widened my Mona Lisa smile and whispered in Addams's ear, "What can you tell me about The Barb?"

He drew back from me as if I had a disease. "Who?"

"One of your pals from De Sade's Cage. The Barb. C'mon, you know who I'm talking about."

"He's a creep, a hanger-on. There's lots of those parasites around and they're hard to shake."

"Did you ever buy drugs from him or his friend, Dewey?"

"You think you learned a lot from your visit at De Sade's Cage, don't you? Let me be first to tell you that you don't know shit."

"Answer the question. Please. I thirst for enlightenment," I said as I flushed with a red anger.

"You'll notice that there are no drugs at this party. No, I didn't buy any drugs from The Barb or Dewey. And I certainly hope you don't have some theory that Autumn took a walk on the beach with The Barb. You don't, do you?" His expression was incredulous.

"Mr. Addams, in my line of work, people often do things that are considered unlikely."

People began to gather around, sensing the drama. Bodies crowded nearer and a few came in close behind me. I just kept smiling as I realized my reaction to the sudden surrounding and closing in was to draw my gun. I couldn't get a handle on why I was so angry. I could hear people whispering. Addams watched the rising tide.

"I'm glad you joined us, Joan," said Addams, changing his tone. "Next time I'll send you an invitation. You're off duty, right?"

"No, I'm working."

I surveyed the faces around us but didn't see anybody I recognized.

"In any case, I insist you and your partner…"

"Detective Gus Van Chek."

"The two of you must stay for the unveiling."

"I love unveilings," I said. "You could say they're my passion."

It was a duel now and I would play it out. Besides, legally he had invited us. Anything I learned from this visit would be admissible in court. A woman had engaged Gus in conversation. He nodded politely at her, still keeping an eye out on me. I wanted to scream at these people, to let them know that Dani was dead. Surely, one of them had information that could help our investigation. The question was, did any of them care? Odds were good that the answer was no.

"It's a new piece of artwork for my collection," Addams continued. "Music and drama are all part of the presentation. It's quite entertaining if a bit spooky.

"What kind of artwork?" I asked.

To say I felt self-conscious would be an understatement. My conservative nature and reserve were like a naked canvas for their wild-colored theatrics. I had learned from a young age to make a face a blank screen. As I had this thought, I spotted an ornate African mask on the wall across from me. It was red and black with nails for eyebrows.

"You'll like it, Detective Lambert, don't worry. You'll find it actually relates to your own line of work. It's an ancient tribal instrument used to tell the truth. It has the ability to point," and then he pointed from person to person, "to the guilty party."

He ended with his finger in my face. The crowd laughed and sniggered. They were good at it.

I heard one of the guests say, "What do you think she's guilty of?" and then another, "She sure looks guilty to me."

"Sounds like it's right up my alley," I said.

Addams bowed dramatically and turned away from me. Our little scene was over, I guessed. I hadn't even heard anyone call out, "Cut."

I sighed, and since I saw several people smoking, I pulled out one of the last of my stale Marlboros. I was looking for a match when a strong masculine hand sparked up a military-gear-like lighter in front of my nose. I glanced up into the serious brown eyes of Eduardo, aka Coastal Eddy.

"Hello, Joan."

He was wearing loose-fit jeans and a burgundy sweater. He looked casual, enticing. I was sure I looked grim, unyielding.

"Yeah, hi," I said. "You were rude last time we met."

"I'm afraid we got off on the wrong foot," he said.

"Let me say right now that if you so much as look like you're going to put your arm around me, I'm taking you down and I'll put my foot on your neck." As soon as I said it, I wished I hadn't.

"Forgive me." He seemed to mean it. "You're a lady," he continued, "I had a few too many that night. I behaved inappropriately." He turned away from me and looked at the crowd which had begun to stir. "The show is about to begin."

I turned around as well, trying to remember the last time anyone had ever described me as a lady.

The distinct sound of conga drums and a Latin beat, accented with African rhythm, fused into a percussive explosion. A procession began of stately black women dressed in traditional fabrics and head wraps. They each held a staff with flames burning at the end. Good thing the place had high ceilings or it would've caught on fire. The drumming was accompaniment to their sensual, hypnotic movements. I was reminded of the Marlene Dietrich scene that Autumn had in the DVD player in her bungalow. Connie, the receptionist, nobody really, had said that this party had been planned extensively by Autumn. It was a thought-provoking connection, to say the least.

A striking woman, dressed in ceremonial spectacle which could only be described as African empress, presented an artifact to the room. It was about three feet high and made of wood, fabric, and some kind of animal or human hair. It was ancient, according to the woman's announcement, and handed down from many previous owners. It was the depiction of a small man with a cruel, amazingly cruel, expression on his face. He had long arms and especially long fingers. It was infused with evil, embodied with malice. This was evident even before the regal woman explained its ritual use.

The woman spoke with a French accent. She explained that the man doll, as she called it, was used in ceremonies to reveal the truth and to point to the guilty party whenever there was a dispute in the Congo. The power of the ceremony was often abused. Innocent people were pointed out. Villagers feared the ceremony and of alienating the appointed personalities involved, to the point of distraction and sometimes insanity. The vile ritual created a paranoia that empowered the whole process even more.

The African empress took a deep breath, made a dramatic gesture of presenting the man doll for a demonstration, and pointed first at me. I swallowed. The doll's long finger stayed on me unwavering. I knew that the woman was controlling it. Still, it unnerved me. The women then pointed the doll's finger at Addams and he began to cry. The guy was something. La Crisia was there with a handkerchief. The doll moved on. One by one, the woman continued to point the doll at each person at the party. It caused quite a stir.

Everyone had a different reaction, mostly of aversion.

I understood this whole presentation to be therapeutic, cathartic for Addams. I was sure he felt guilty for not loving Autumn the way she needed to be loved. The man certainly had pulled Autumn Riley into a subterranean crowd. I thought maybe he overestimated his influence. The Autumn that was emerging for me was of a bold and defiant character, not a dog on a leash and not a victim. Not Addams's victim, anyway. Maybe I was wrong. I'd have to wait until I met her. I had every intention of doing that, and soon, too. Thing was, I needed to find her first. I didn't want to get to her too late.

Dani's death had set off a bit of a panic in my chest. I looked at Coastal Eddy who was thoughtfully watching the demonstration. His gaze settled on the weeping Glenn Addams.

In that instant, I understood an incredible irony. I knew it was true that I was guilty. That Addams was guilty, but not of murder. I also understood that in some strange way, I belonged with these people and their dark, perverse ways. I didn't want to belong. I wanted to be better than them, but I wasn't. I was in the black snake pit right beside them and time would tell who was stronger, or smarter, or meaner. But regardless, I was a slithering life form squiggling in the primordial slime just like them. I knew it and they knew it, too. They accepted me and now, albeit uncomfortably, I accepted them.

Percussionists entered from another room, playing their drums that hung from leather straps over their shoulders. The party was moving into full roar.

A tall, overly muscular man moved away from the gathering. I hadn't noticed him before.

"Excuse me," I said to Coastal as I put down my drink and stood up.

"Be careful. You're vulnerable," he said.

I've been accused of a lot of things. Being vulnerable ain't even on the list. Why would he say that? A vulnerable lady?

"You don't know anything. I'm hardly even human," I said.

"You're funny."

"Do you always hang with this crowd?"

"When can I see you again?" he asked.

"No telling. Everywhere I go, you magically appear," I said. "Truth is, I'd like for us to have a chat so I can find out more about you." I gave him my card. He looked at it.

"No fair," he said, "no home number."

"And you claim to be an investigator," I said and crossed the room, not waiting for another comeback.

I was following the trail of what I assumed was a steroid-fed man, all dressed in black. His muscles bulged unnaturally against the confines of his black T-shirt, jeans, and combat boots. He had a tattoo of a Teenage Mutant Ninja Turtle that glistened on the recently oiled skin of his forearm. The bodyguard that had escorted Autumn to the photo shoot appeared out of my imagination and was walking down a hallway.

I wanted to get to Steroid Boy before he got away. He ducked into a bathroom and closed the door. I waited for a moment, then knocked. I heard him cursing. I kicked in the door. He was leaning over the sink, shooting up in a vein of his armpit.

"I want to talk to you," I said simply.

He finished shooting the drug into the vein, "So talk. Shit! What is it?"

I closed the door behind me. His eyes bulged.

"What the fuck?"

He put his paraphernalia into a slick-looking black leather container. His look was deranged. His forehead broke with sweat.

"I'm Detective Lambert." I flashed him the badge. "You know an Autumn Riley?"

He looked like a kid who'd just been told that his mother was outside and wanted to see him. "Sure, she's the producer's main squeeze."

"You ever give her any drugs?"

"Not to my recollection."

"You're sounding very presidential; you know that?"

"What is the problem? I heard this morning she was shopping for new clothes on Melrose. What's all the fuss?" I felt like dragging Steroid Boy out to my car for a more intense interrogation.

"Who told you Autumn was shopping for clothes on Melrose?"

"Aw, man, everybody is talking 'bout it, I don't know who."

"You got a friend from Haiti named Dewey, right?"

"Why are you asking my life history?"

"Answer the question."

"I may have met the guy somewheres."

I pulled out the photo of Dani from the murder scene. "Maybe you recognize Autumn's best friend from Australia."

Hector looked at the photo, took it in. "Never seen her."

"Where'd you meet The Barb?"

"The Barb?" he laughed. "I don't really know him."

"I heard you were close."

"You heard wrong. Man, you know, this is a private party."

"And man, you know, you're under arrest."

I could sense that the guests took our leaving at that particular moment as having some sort of significance. I got a lot of party pooper attitude. Even though Steroid Boy came willingly, I insisted on the cuffs. Gus broke off his conversation and fell in behind me and I waved a goodbye to Addams on the way out. He didn't wave back.

CHAPTER ELEVEN

ONCE WE HAD STEROID Boy back at Parker Center and cooling it in the interview room, we did a background check on him. Turned out, his name was Hector Cardona and he was on our records as being on probation for burglary with a previous history as a runaway foster kid. He was clearly of age now, having grown up on the streets of Hollywood. I called his old Juvie officer, Freda Dietz, a personal friend of mine who gave me more information than was the normal policy.

My purpose for doing that was to get a handle on young Hector Cardona's head. Freda explained that at one point, while still a juvenile, Hector was suspected of killing his foster mother, Grace Cardona. I got goose bumps over my scalp.

"What was Grace like?"

"The woman was a saint," said Freda. "Grace was known for taking in foster kids, forty-three in all. Hector, her last foster kid, stayed with her the longest. She had a reputation for turning kids around. She treated them like her own and her style was to inform them of the realities of crime, of the statistics. She told it like it was. Grace didn't coddle her foster kids, she held them accountable, taught them to take responsibility for their lives, showed them a future."

There weren't too many like Grace in the world. Freda's description of Grace reminded me of Donna Paynt, my own foster mom. Foster homes have notorious reps for conditions worse than the child's original home. Horror stories about foster homes tell a lot about why runaways prefer the streets.

"So, what happened?" I asked.

"Grace had officially adopted Hector and had even changed his last name to hers. But then Grace and her husband were both murdered within the same week."

"By Hector?"

"Who knows. We couldn't prove anything and Hector disappeared into the streets after that."

We let Hector wait in the interrogation room for an hour, then Gus decided I should work him.

"Okay," I said, "Let's go get lied to."

The small room had one table and two chairs. Hector sat in one and I took off his cuffs, handed him a cold Diet Pepsi, and sat down across from him. I noticed he wore one of those international watches that indicate the time in Japan and other parts of the world. He drank the soda down in one long gulping action, then crunched the can. It sat between us like a statement. Seeing him up close, he didn't look so tough, more like a teddy bear with a scowl on his face. One of his brown eyes was slightly smaller and the color was darker, almost black. Gus leaned against the wall but didn't say anything.

"Okay, Hector. I'd like this to go smoothly. You cool with that? You need a smoke?"

"Don't smoke."

"That's great. Wish I could say the same. I quit but got back started again."

"Sorry to hear that, Detective Lambert."

"Call me Joan. When you think of me, always think of me as Joan. Okay?"

"You want me to call you Joan? Not officer or detective?"

"That's right. Just Joan."

"That's an outdated name. You look too young for a name like Joan. Sounds so Beaver Cleaver."

"I'm from the Ozarks, Hector. They're kind of old-fashioned back there. 'Course, Hector is not exactly a cutting-edge name, either. Gus, where's that name come from? I tell you what, Hector, Gus knows everything. I got the smartest goddamn partner on the planet."

"Hector," Gus obliged. "Hecuba's son, hero of Troy. Hector was killed by Achilles in retribution for murdering Achilles's lover, Patroculus."

"Oh, not such a good ending," I said.

Hector deadpanned me.

"Which ninja turtle is that?" I asked.

A crooked smile flickered across Hector's face. "It's Rafael," he said, then covered it with his hand as if to protect it from me.

"Oh, is that the one that eats a lot of pizza?" I asked.

"Yeah, it is."

All the Teenage Mutant Ninja Turtles ate pizza. But Rafael was the smart ninja turtle, the one who always figured out the game plan.

"Hector, you sure know a lot of different kinds of people, you move in a lot of different social strata for a runaway foster kid who came to age in the streets of Hollywood. Movie directors, music producers, et cetera."

"Does that impress you, Joan?"

"In fact, it does. I have to wonder… What is the common thread between all these people? What's the connection? You know us detectives think like that."

"Fascinating."

"What happened to Grace?" I asked.

"Wha? Why you bring that up?"

"Did you kill her?"

"No." There was a long pause before he spoke again. "Everybody said I did."

"Why did they say that?"

"I don't know."

"Who killed her?"

"I think it was George."

"George?"

"Her husband, but they couldn't prove it."

"Why not?"

"Why not? Because George died."

"How did he die?"

"How did he die? Somebody mugged him or something, I was a kid. I don't remember."

"I think you do remember. I think you could recall certain details. You killed him, right?"

"I had an alibi, and you must know that, you know everything else, so don't even start with that shit."

"Good thing you had an alibi. Boy, you had to learn the ins and outs of the justice system early, didn't you? I bet you're an intelligent and clever person. I mean, how else could you survive all those years on the streets, just a kid?"

"I'm not dumb. I can survive. Not too many make it."

"No, that's right. What's the average survival period for a kid on the streets?" I waited for him to answer.

"Two years."

"Where'd you learn that?" I asked.

"Read it somewheres."

"When?"

"I don't know. When I was a kid."

"I bet you read that in the *National Institute of Justice Journal*."

"Maybe that was it. I don't remember."

"Who gave you that to read?"

"Grace."

"She cared about you, didn't she? She wanted to help you, make you understand things."

He nodded and closed his eyes for a moment. When he opened them he gave me a look of deep resentment and looked pointedly at the international watch wrapped around his wrist.

"She the only one?"

"Only one what?"

"That cared about you."

He closed his eyes again, took a deep breath then answered, "Yes."

"See there, I know that, Hector. I know you, I got it down. I say that because I just want you to understand that I got you all figured out. That's all I'm trying to say here. You're grown up now, got yourself all buffed up and nobody can touch you. But I know you, okay? You don't fool me. You're strong, I'll give you that, but I know your weaknesses. I don't care about George, or who killed him. He's long dead and he sounds like a bastard anyway. If I had been in your situation I might have done the same. I'm not here to talk to you about George except to say I understand certain things. Maybe you fooled some folks along the way, and maybe some other people got the wrong idea about you. But I don't belong in either of those categories."

He looked at me like he was seeing me for the first time. The smaller, darker eye squinted.

"Okay, sure, whatever you say," he said and twisted in his chair.

"Where do you get your steroids?" I asked.

"I'm not giving anybody up so you can forget that."

"Did I ask you to give anybody up? I'm a homicide detective, Hector. Why would I be interested in your doctor friend?"

"I don't have no doctor friend." Hector looked over at Gus then down at the table.

"I'm sorry, I mean your pharmaceutical friend. Is that better?"

Hector looked at Gus and back at the table again but didn't say anything.

"You got this guy who puts this stuff together for you, don't you? Makes it himself, I bet. Thing is, you think I care about that? I don't. I just used your drug supply and your friends Dewey and The Barb as a reason for you and me to have this sit-down. It's the other stuff I'm concerned about. The secret potion that gets slipped to an innocent young woman and knocks her out so bad she's dead. Oh, wait a minute, she not dead. Funny, that. A drug brings you down so low, everybody, even the paramedic, thinks you're dead."

"I don't know about that," he said to the table.

"I think you do."

He sat up straight in the chair and gave me a slight smile. "This psych game you been playing has been interesting. You think I'm a mouse and you're a big cat. You want something from me, tell me now. You gonna charge me with something, do it. I'd like to call my lawyer before I answer any more questions."

"Fine. You don't want to help me. You know all the right things to say and not say. You know not to talk, to call your lawyer. Let me tell you something. I'm going to find out everything. Everything, you understand? If you know something about Autumn Riley and some strange drugs and who gave them to her or maybe just where she got her voodoo doll, you need to tell me."

"I don't know about that girl, okay? I don't know about drugs she took or who she took them with, who slipped them to her or what. I sure don't know about any voodoo."

"You're lying to me, Hector. Why would you do that? I've got witnesses that can refute everything you just said."

He closed his eyes again and sat silent. I tried another tactic.

"You know, Hector, it's the voodoo that really has me concerned. Some people believe that if you make a sacrifice it intensifies the magic, you know, like a spell. You ever heard of that?"

"Sure, everybody's heard of that."

"But you don't know anyone who practices voodoo, who makes sacrifices?"

"Fuck no. Now, let me go. I'm not enjoying this conversation."

"Your friends, Dewey and The Barb, practice voodoo. Didn't you know that?" I stayed with the gentle tone.

"They aren't my friends and what they do is not my problem."

"You got a raw deal but I want you to listen to me. You weren't meant to do evil, Hector. That wasn't your destiny."

"Not everybody who practices voodoo is evil, you know."

"No, of course not."

"Some don't even sacrifice animals. Not every voodum believes in sacrificing animals."

"That's right. I've heard that somewhere. Seems you know more about it than I thought."

"I'd like to call my lawyer now," he said, looking at Gus.

"You're not like those kids that torture the neighborhood kitten. Are you?"

The room was heavy with silence—then—"No."

"You like animals, right?"

"More than people."

"Can't say that I blame you there." I smiled at him but he looked away from me. "Life gave you some bad breaks and you made some decisions along the way. You want to know how I know? Not from a file, Hector. I had some bad breaks, too. I made some decisions just like you."

He laughed. "Sure," he said. "I bet you were cute when you were a kid. I can just see you on the street, begging for spare change." He sneered and added, "I bet I could have got you a lot of cash. Woulda made bank with you, fo' sho'. Stop with the psych shit, okay?"

"So you pimped runaways? That's what you're telling me?"

"I want my lawyer now."

"You know what? You don't need to call your lawyer, Hector. I'm going to let you walk out of here, no charge. I'm not even gonna mention your little drug habit to your probation officer. But let me say first, I gave you a chance. This was your best chance ever and you blew it. It's going to go down hard and heavy after this. If you don't believe me, that's okay, just watch and you'll see. Here's my card. You think about what I've said to you. Prove to me you're not the worse slime on the planet, why don'cha?"

"Can I go, now?" he asked Gus.

Gus stood up and opened the door.

"Before you go, Hector, I got a question for you," I said and stood before him.

"Really, a question? You got a lot of those."

"When Grace looks down on you, wherever she is, do you think she likes what she sees?"

He closed his eyes for a brief moment, put his head down, and lifted his heavily muscled body out of the chair. He was the same height as me. We stood there for a moment, face to face. His smaller eye squinted at me.

"No answer," I said. "Seems like you got a lot of those."

"Bye, Joan."

"Bye," I said and stood aside giving him room to exit. "You call me if you want to talk."

Hector walked out of the tiny room. Gus and I followed. To Hector's back, "I'm on the trail, Hector. I'm a mad mama bear and you'll be seeing me again. You know that game hide and seek? I always won at that game when I was a kid."

Hector stopped in his tracks. For a moment he just stood there, then he turned around and said, "Me, too. That's another thing we got in common, you and me. Hide and seek. I'll see you around, Joan."

Gus and I watched as he trudged out the door.

"He knows plenty," said Gus.

"We can't let him walk out this building without a tail," I said as I called surveillance.

CHAPTER TWELVE

I WENT HOME, TIRED from not getting any sleep the night before, and I was determined to get some rest, but my mind was racing. They say that yoga is good to calm the mind but to relax, I threw on some sweats, went out to my little yard, and practiced my karate moves. I stood in the middle of my small patch of grass and prepared to release some endorphins. After that, I meant to take a hot bath and work on my relaxation pose. I took several deep breaths, releasing my day, relaxing my mind, calming the chatter.

Outside the door of my house, a wild rose bush trained up the old oak tree and overhung the street. Several dancing banana plants and a big elephant ear philodendron offered a cooling shade on hot afternoons. Morning glories covered the chain-link fence and entwined with the bamboo that surrounded my yard and afforded me privacy.

My gate was an old wooden thing that I'd painted white. The yard was a sliver of Eden that I claimed in the world. A flock of wild parrots had escaped from a neighborhood pet shop and liked to terrorize the neighborhood with their loud squawking. They seemed to especially enjoy my yard and came to visit every so often. They were loud and rowdy and caused quite a commotion whenever they appeared. They hadn't been by for a while and I missed them.

I bent over and stretched out my back, allowing air to flow freely out my lungs. I went through my karate drills, performing each kata with mind, body, and spirit. I started with basic blocks and strikes and evolved to kicks and eye-plucking moves. The katas transformed into a series of combinations, all finely memorized, systematically executed. A precise rhythm, gaining in momentum, created an explosive, dominating choreography until fight cries and deadly blows sang simultaneously. There was a body-sized bag in the corner of the yard that I gave several hard kicks. Low kicks are the most devastating, not those high fancy things you see on television and in the movies. A hundred quick low kicks on the bag did the trick for me every time. As my lungs worked harder I found myself relaxing, I felt the fury draining from me.

A thin film of perspiration covered me from head to toe. My concentration was so intense that I didn't hear the neighborhood dogs barking until I stopped for a moment, exhausted. In that pause of my warrior dance, I listened to the barking and rapidly approaching footfalls in the alley. I ran and hefted my body up the oak tree like a bear.

What looked like a chubby gangbanger in baggy jeans and a flannel shirt cowered in fear when he saw me. I merely stared at him as he continued down the alley, walking faster now. He was probably late getting home and his mother was going to give him hell. He glanced back over his shoulder at me, several times, just in case I decided to attack.

The moon came up that night big and yellow. I sat in my yard and pondered my life, considered what the future held for me. If I'd ever marry. That big moon peeked over the oak tree and I could almost feel it on my face. Before Gramma died, she told me that every time the moon looked down on me that it would be her, no matter what shape it was. And even when it wasn't there I should know that she was always in the sky watching over me.

"Well, Gramma," I said to the moon. "I could use a little tenderness, don'cha think?"

The moon kissed my face in sympathy at my foolishness but she was not in a talkative mood. I asked her to please, send me an appropriate lover. I told her that she could choose someone for me since I was so bad at it myself.

"Send me somebody that will make me a better person. Send me someone that will help me heal. I can't live the rest of my life like this."

Grandmother Moon knew me all too well. The galaxies that I would have to travel before I'd ever land on a planet where the words "I do" ever came out of my mouth were daunting. Not even the opossum came to visit me on any kind of regular basis. She told me she would send me my "appropriate lover" but I would have to be able to recognize him. And you know, that was just like something my own grandmother would say. Once, I asked her how to find a good man and she said it was simple, that the way was to be a good woman. Everything was always a riddle with her. And she knew my heart better than anyone.

I shook my head at my wild imaginings and went inside, fixed a tuna sandwich, and polished it off with some orange juice. What was the most important quality a man could have? Gentleness seemed like a good quality to ask for. You'd think I'd be capable of recognizing that. Laziness overtook me and instead of carrying my dishes into the kitchen, I placed them on the coffee table. I gazed for a while at the moon now peeking into the window of my living room.

As I was settling in on the couch, my eyes fell on Dr. Blanchard's journal. I picked up the pages and leafed through a few until I came across something that caught my eye.

> Victory! After months of frustration and refiguring of the formula, I have finally attained my first goal. Three subjects have remained in a suspended state for ten days. I will call my colleagues to report and initiate the next phase of the experiment. The Haitians are beginning to trust me. I have become an accepted member of this small community though they still test me constantly.

I imagined three people in a suspended state for ten days. Who were they and what did it mean to them? What did it mean to their families? Did they have families? Why had the Haitians come to trust the doctor and how was it that they accepted him into their community? It was clear to me that there was some connection between Dr. Blanchard's studies, the Autumn Riley case, and Dani's death, but what was it exactly? How could I prove it? A drug test on Autumn Riley might be illuminating, for one. Dewey had to be the connecting link. Maybe Hector would lead me to something. I took a deep breath and planned to make a new attack on locating Autumn tomorrow.

I flipped on the television and sat back, relaxing on the couch, preparing myself for a state of vegetation. I fell asleep watching a bad dating game show where the couples either pawed each other or spewed insults at each other. I woke up to percussive music and for a second thought I was back at Addams's party. On the television, basketball players dribbled and did amusing basketball stunts then commanded me to obey my thirst.

The news came on and a weather report was followed by a newscast about Autumn Riley. Somebody had gotten a copy of the videotape from the morgue. During the report, they flashed photos of both Gus and me as the investigating detectives. The newscaster made no attempt to disguise the report as anything other than high entertainment. He was smirking and carrying on like it was the joke of the century. I knew that the coroner's office didn't leak the story and it wasn't the tech guys.

I called the captain because I knew he had to make certain reports on an official level. Satch answered the phone.

"Sir, this is Joan. I need to know if you gave Autumn's parents a copy of the tape."

"Yes, as a matter of fact."

I told him about the news cast.

"We're going to burn on this one," he said. "That's all there is to it."

I hung up the phone and stared in dejection at the television and what was now a report of a missing child, Tommy, a ten-year-old boy. The missing boy's family was Mexican, owners of a Los Angeles fast-food chain. There was some speculation that it was a kidnapping, but there had been no contact regarding ransom. The mother and father made tearstained statements and a photo of the kid was shown. I looked away, uneasy with the exploitation of the parents' grief, and took my plate and glass to the sink to wash them.

I heard the reporter say the kid was last seen with his dog, Pancho. I know such news reports are necessary and often have helped to find kids, but I can't handle the pain of the loved ones. I turned back to the television to see yet another photo of the boy with a big black dog. The reporter said that the breed of the dog was a Newfoundland. I thought the resemblance to the black dog that was hanging around the Autumn Riley crime scene was more than an interesting coincidence. I called Anthony Sauri, the guy on surveillance.

"Anthony, this is Joan Lambert, has anyone come by Autumn's bungalow?"

"No, nobody."

"Anything interesting on Hector?"

"Not much. He was in a Venice coffee shop chatting up the customers all day, then walked over to The Gold's Gym and that's about it."

"Which coffee shop?"

"Abbot's Habit."

I knew the coffee shop, had been there myself plenty of times. It's walking distance from my house.

"What'd you find on the dog?" I asked.

"I checked it out. The neighbors said it was a stray. Showed up around there a few days ago. Animal Control picked it up yesterday and took it to the pound."

"Which pound?"

"Santa Monica, why? You going to adopt it?"

╫ ╫ ╫

ON THE WAY TO the animal shelter, if you can call them that, I dialed Rose Torres on my cell phone.

"Rose, this is Detective Lambert."

"Yes?"

"Those black hairs you found at the Autumn Riley crime scene? Are they dog hairs?"

"Yes, Detective. How did you know that?"

"Just a wild guess. And how about those blond hairs that I bagged off The Barb, they dog hairs, too?"

"Uh, no, but I'm going to see if they match any hairs from the Autumn Riley crime scene. We will know by the time we go home tonight."

"Call me immediately either way," I said.

"Will do."

"Thank you."

I pulled into the driveway of the animal shelter. It was after hours and I had to convince the person on the speaker, who sounded sort of young but was the only person left in charge, that the dog was essential to my investigation. When he came out to greet me, sporting a Dodger baseball cap and a matching jersey in a size extra-large, he looked to be about fourteen. He assured me that they hadn't put the dog to sleep and insisted I wait while he called his supervisor to get the okay to let me in. Finally, after giving my badge number to his supervisor, we walked into the area where they keep the dogs, all concrete and little jail cells. It hit me strange that these creatures were being held for the crime of being unloved and unattached or just lost. I saw at least five dogs that I wanted to take home. The kid had no mercy and was giving me the hard sell on every dog I even glanced at. In one of these cages was the dog I believed to be Pancho, that I hoped was Pancho, so I could have a lead that would help find Tommy and who knows, maybe even Autumn Riley.

"You seem a little young for this gig, kid."

"I'm fifteen. I have a social security card and the legal right to work."

"Okay, then. You ever get any bloodhounds?" I asked.

"Nope, not really. The kind of people who buy bloodhounds don't usually lose or abandon them."

"Right. That figures."

"But we have so many other dogs. Does a dog have to have a pedigree to deserve a good home?"

"No," I said rather somberly.

"No, in fact, mixed breeds are healthier both physically and mentally."

"I'm sure you're right about that. But at this moment, I just need the big black dog."

"It's a Newfoundland. It's right here."

And sure enough, there he was in all his big black glory. The dog from the Autumn Riley crime scene was looking at me through a wire cage like I was the love of his life. His big ole fluffy tail wagged like he recognized me and had been waiting for me to come.

"He knows you."

"Not that well."

"You'll have to pay the fees," said the kid.

"I'm a homicide detective, kid, I'm not paying any fees."

"It takes money to run this place, you know."

"Well, your boss should give you a raise. Don't worry, the owners will pay the fees, I'm sure."

"Oh yeah? Where are the owners, anyway?"

I paid the fifty-five bucks and the kid released the dog to me. I had just got the dog I was guessing might be Pancho into the car when my cell phone rang.

It was Gus. He wanted me to come to his place.

"You gotta see this," he said.

There was a strange note in his voice that told me that something was up.

"What is it, Gus?"

"You have to see it in person."

"Okay, but I'm bringing a guest."

On the way there, I called Missing Persons and told them I had a dog that looked a lot like the one that was with the boy. They asked me to check his back leg for a scar.

⁂

GUS HAS A SMALL house on Palms and Centinela, a better neighborhood than mine. He's got this cool architectural catwalk-looking thing that approaches his front door. He told me once it was Japanese and that there was supposed to be water on either side filled with Koi fish. How cool would that be? I wondered when he'd ever fill it with water as I walked across it with the dog. Gus opened the door and greeted us as we approached.

"Who's that?"

"There were dog hairs at the Autumn Riley crime scene," I said.

"And this is the dog?"

"Right. Plus, I think this is the same dog that went missing with the Mexican kid. The one that's all over the television right now."

"You're kidding me."

"I don't know for sure, Missings told me to see if the dog had a scar on its back leg."

Gus checked the back legs of the dog and sure enough, there was a scar going up his right leg to his haunch.

"Looks like this is the dog," said Gus. "So, what the heck…"

"His name is Pancho."

"That dog was inside Autumn's place? What does that mean?"

"Could mean she took pity on him and let him in the house."

"Or if not, maybe someone else brought him in," said Gus. "So, now we have a dog, a missing kid, a woman who has come back alive, and a dead porno star, all on one case."

"Nobody ever reported that they saw the kid with the dog anywhere around Venice canals," I said. "So, what if the dog was brought to the canals without the kid?"

"By who?"

"By whoever visited Autumn Riley," I said. "The Barb, for one."

"Okay, I'll go for that, but hairs won't prove it."

"Fine."

"You're doing a good job, Joan."

"Yeah, I'm just the greatest."

"Stop that. Listen, I have to testify in court day after tomorrow. Move ahead on the case but make sure you get everything in the reports and keep me informed."

"Sure, of course. What did you want to show me?"

"Oh, wait 'til you see this. Take a look."

We walked into his super cool living room and sat down on some famous designer's leather and wood chairs. Gus gave me an imported beer in a designer glass and showed me a professional photo of Dani feeding Autumn Riley fresh raspberries. Obviously a commercial print for a magazine, the scene was erotic and suggestive. The photo had a recent date printed on the back. Gus pointed at the date and said, "Day before yesterday."

"Where'd you get that?"

"Tia."

"The waitress?"

"The Barb came by the diner with Autumn and Dani and gave her the picture, promising Tia some modeling work."

"Tia's not going to do the modeling work is she?"

"I don't know. I doubt it. He must have scooped Autumn off Melrose and taken her straight to the photo shoot. No wonder Dani didn't believe Autumn was dead. She had just done a photo shoot with her the day before."

"Guess now he needs a black chick," I said.

"Tia, yeah. He can sure pick some lookers, I give him that," said Gus.

I put my glass down on an ebony black coffee table and stared for a moment at his arrangement of chopsticks in a glass tube surrounding a gorgeous green orchid. For the briefest moment, I wondered if Gus might be gay. He is always so perfectly stylish in every aspect of his life, every moment.

"So, what's going on?" I asked. "You think the Barb set Dani up with a bad gig?"

"It's a strong possibility."

"We could use Tia as bait."

"No, forget that."

"You know they're ridiculing us on television."

"What now?"

"Somebody got a copy of the videotape from the coroner's office and they made a big joke about us investigating the murder of Autumn Riley who isn't dead."

"Ah, who cares?"

"I do. Why does every move I make have to be on the eight o'clock news? If they're not making me out to be a whore, they're pointing out what a clown I am. It pisses me off."

"When did they make you out to be a whore?"

"On the last case with Carl."

"How so?"

"They made innuendos about me and Carl being involved when he beat up the CEO. In the public's eye I became a whore."

"I don't remember that."

"Good, don't let me remind you."

"That might have been just in your own mind. All that whore stuff. A woman can be involved with a man, doesn't make her a whore. You have issues."

"Don't analyze me right now, all right?"

"Myself, I think I'd prefer to be a clown."

"Well, you got your wish."

"Don't get all riled up over nothing. Go home and get some sleep, okay? Talk to you tomorrow."

As I walked out across the catwalk to my car, he called out, "Nice dog you got there."

I stopped by the pet store on the way home. Pancho whined when I left the car and I had to go back to give him a pat and reassure him.

"What's wrong? You got abandonment issues? Separation anxiety? Join the club, kid."

I was cruising the chew toys in the pet store when my cell phone rang.

"Hey, you fine thang."

It was Carl. Dammit. Gus must have given him my cell phone number already.

"Hi."

"Are you still going to go to the fundraiser with me? I raised a lot of money last year with the Mach One. Don't you want to ride and wave your hand like a homecoming queen?"

"Oh, Carl. That's sweet but…no, I don't think…"

"Come on, babe. We're raising money for kids, babies here. Can't you suffer me for one afternoon?"

"Did Gus give you this number?"

"How'd ja guess?"

"I want you to lose it, Carl. Don't call me anymore, okay? Please? I'm begging you, now. Don't call me."

"Well, you said you were going to call me and you didn't so, I just wanted to help things along here. You know, get our communication lines back open, that sort of thing, is all."

"What do I have to do to get rid of you, Carl?"

"Agree to see me."

"Nope. It's not going to happen. It's not really a good idea for you, either, you know. You need to move on. You have something good going on with Debbie, don't mess it up. I ride in your car at the fundraiser? That would ruin everything for you. Debbie would really appreciate having that honor more than me so get a grip, Carl. Ask Deb to the fundraiser event. I'm history, babe."

"You're my history."

"New era, Carl. Get with it. What do I have to do?"

"Shoot me like you said. You'd be doing me a favor. Like that dude in Casablanca."

"I'm hanging up the phone, Carl."

"Joanie, baby…"

"Don't call me anymore."

I pressed the end button. If only it were that easy.

I bought some dog food, two doggie bowls, a collar, and a brush. The cell phone rang but I didn't answer it.

When I got home, I brushed Pancho and bagged quite a few hairs for comparison.

CHAPTER THIRTEEN

I WOKE UP EARLY the next morning to a loud pounding on my front door and Pancho's ferocious barks. I bolted from the bed and peeked through the peephole of the front door. Jesse Cand was standing on my porch with a microphone in his hand. A video camera loomed up large over his shoulder. The guy was merciless. It was 6:00 a.m. for Chrissakes. "Okay, hold on!" I yelled through the door.

I gave Pancho another good boy pat. "You can bite this one if you want," I told him and darted back into the bedroom.

I slipped on a pair of black jeans, searched around for a comfortable bra, got that on, and then grabbed a T-shirt. Sunshine poured in through the bedroom window, the warmth of the rays soft on my face. I sat on the bed, paused for a moment, and decided to try a different strategy today. Maybe I could work an angle with the press instead of them always working me. For one day I would be open to what Jesse had to say. I opened the door and allowed Jesse and his camera guy, Kip, inside.

"Why are you here?" I asked.

"The dog is big news."

"How do you know about the dog?"

"We heard about it on the police radio last night."

"I didn't mention it over the radio."

"You're not the only cop who has one, you know. Cops talk to each other just like anybody."

"Cripes. Okay, fine."

I gestured for them to have a seat on the leather sofa, which they did. Pancho jumped up on the couch and settled in next to Jesse.

Apparently, Pancho was allowed on the furniture at his home. I could smell coffee brewing and thanked God I had one of those automatic things. I left Jesse, Kip, and Pancho alone so they could all get to know each other while I poured the java.

When I came back in the front room, I realized with some distress that my mother's artwork would certainly be a promising source for questions. I carried a tray of three mismatched cups of coffee which I presented with apologies but nobody seemed to mind. Jesse took a sip off the coffee and smiled back at me, obviously thinking it was a great coup to be sitting on my couch. He eyed my mother's artwork but didn't say anything.

"What do you need?" I asked.

"How about a shot of you with the dog?" he asked.

"Just the dog," I said.

He wrote something on his pad.

"When did you find the dog?" asked Jesse.

"I noticed the dog the day we were investigating the Autumn Riley case."

He wrote more, picking up the scent.

"I understand that investigation was officially terminated?" he prodded.

"No."

He scowled and scribbled more notes. Exciting stuff.

"But, Joan, she's alive."

"Jesse, could you stop scribbling for a moment and allow me to say something off record?"

"Could I? You bet." He put down his pad but hung onto the pen and angled himself on the couch to promote more eye contact, as if that were possible. He was super attentive, panting for a treat. I had to be careful what biscuit I gave him.

I handed the leash to Kip. I was still kinda pissed at him for that surprise photo he snapped of me at City Hall.

"Would you mind taking Pancho for a short walk? He hasn't been out this morning."

Kip took the leash and his cup of coffee and headed for the door; Pancho followed him.

"Guard that dog with your life," I said.

"Isn't he supposed to guard me?" Kip asked.

Once they were safely attached to each other and out the door, I turned back to Jesse.

"Go ahead, shoot," he said.

"Promise me you won't write about it."

"Promise." Jesse put his hand on his heart.

"Autumn Riley is not dead, true, but there are other concerns here."

"Like what?"

"We have reason to believe that the situation is more complicated than it looks."

"What do you mean, exactly?"

"I can't tell you right now. I couldn't speculate at this time. Believe me, in this case, the truth may be way more bizarre than fiction. I'm concerned that Autumn's in trouble, maybe under the influence of bad people."

"Who?"

"I'm not sure, yet. But last night, her best friend turned up dead."

"Who's her best friend?"

"A S&M porno star from Australia by the name of Dani."

"This just gets better and better." I scowled at him. "I mean, sorry, but you don't want me to write about that?"

"No."

"Okay, I understand that you don't want to talk about your investigation at this point and really I don't blame you. So don't tell me anything more, just promise me I get first story."

"Promise."

"Okay, we'll just do some videotape of you and the dog."

"Why do I have to be in it?"

"Joan, you could stand some good PR. Don't be an ass. I can get a picture of you from archives anyway. You might as well give us some different footage from what they've been using."

"What about all those photos you took last time at Parker Center?"

"Oh, well, those are for the *LA Times Magazine*."

"I want you to know that I think you're stalking me."

"Come on, Joan. I'm a professional. It's time you became more so."

"You took a picture of me when I was crying."

"And it came out wonderful, let me show it to you."

I said nothing, so he pulled out a file folder from his briefcase and handed me the photo. It was as I expected: a big tear dropping down the side of my cheek, wind blowing through my short hair, a tormented cast to my eyes. I had to give Kip credit for his composition, as he had managed to get the entrance of the Parker Center building in the background, but I didn't consider it a professional portrayal. It was a dramatic, narrative thing that made me uneasy.

"I know you're not comfortable with it, but it gives a face to the LAPD, a face that is far and away from the shooting of a homeless woman with a screwdriver in her hand."

I sighed and Jesse gave me his best "I'm a good guy" look.

"Okay. I'll have to put on a suit."

"So, do it. In fact, how about your uniform?"

"No, I'm not putting on my blues. That's too hokey."

"Whatever you say."

Kip came back with Pancho. A quick walk in anybody's world, but Pancho did look relieved.

"Why don't you set up, Kip?" I said. "I'll go get dressed."

Pancho came into the bedroom to check on me while I changed clothes. I found it hard to believe that dog ever let the kid out of his sight. I slipped into a black suit. When I reentered the room, both men gave me appreciative looks that I was not entirely comfortable with. Pancho was right behind me.

"Okay, no fancy stuff, just shoot," I said.

Kip took shots of me with the dog. It was a matter of seconds. He was quick, that guy. "Thanks, Joan. It's good to work together," Kip said as he packed up his equipment.

Jesse reluctantly rose from the couch. "Yes, thank you," he said with a meaningful look.

I guess he thought we were close now. He'd caught me last week on camera crying and this week I was serving him his morning coffee and posing for his news stories. I could just see him and Kip in a dark room blowing up all the shots of me and gloating. Now, they had a video of "Joan and the big black dog" to add to their collection.

"I had no idea that you were an artist," said Jesse.

"Oh, well. I, uh…haven't done much since I was a kid."

Jesse walked over to the painting on the easel and examined the woman's form emerging from the earth. "Is she submerged, like in the ground?"

"Sort of."

"What does that mean?"

"I'm not sure I know. Not yet."

I went to the door and opened it and waited until they were both out the door, then shut and locked it. I watched them through the window as they made their way to the van parked at the front curb. Jesse shot glances back at my house. A man in baggy khaki shorts carried a surfboard past the van. As he came closer, I recognized the dark, perfectly unkempt hair and the broad chest in the orange T-shirt. It was Coastal Eddy. Jesse noticed him, then stared at him with curiosity. Kip had packed it in and was ready to take off, but Jesse was still standing there when I opened the door and let Coastal Eddy in my house before there was even a knock.

"What's up?" Eddy said.

The banana-yellow surfboard came in with Eddy. I guess he didn't want anyone to steal it. I gaped at it as if it were the second coming of the Messiah. I closed the door behind him and looked out the peephole. Jesse peered at my house a little longer before he got in the van. Then unaccountably, the words to that Donovan song "There Is A Mountain" played over and over in my head. I guess it had something to do with the big yellow surfboard.

I didn't know what to think. I didn't know if I was happy to see Eddy or irritated by his arrogance. He had a weird effect on me. In a way, I had invited this visit by challenging him to find me with his investigating skills. I wanted to pick his brain and get a grip on him, find out what his take was. I decided, for the second time that day, to let things be revealed to me. Like I really had a choice anyway.

Pancho ran around in a circle, then jumped up and put his paws on Eddy's chest. I suppressed a nervous laugh, my right knee bent and my left hip shifted to one side. I found that my left hand had come to rest at my waist and my right hand floated up and touched the back of my neck. My eyes went down to the floor in embarrassment, then over to Eddy's big rubber sandals with cut tire treads for soles. Pancho panted happily, his expression one of expectation. I forced myself to look up at Eddy. His hair was wet. The ends were in curly points. He'd probably come from a morning of surfing. I resisted the urge to say *"Que hondas?"* and instead just stood there.

He patted the dog with big manly pats then stood before me beaming. I put out my hand to indicate he should have a seat. He placed his surfboard against the wall under the couch. Then he bounced down into the sofa, thrust out his long tanned legs, and crossed them. And made himself much more comfortable than I would have liked. Pancho sat down at his feet. It was quite the social day. My couch had not gotten so much action since I don't know when. I waited for Eddy to speak. He bounced a couple more times to get perfectly comfortable. He surveyed the room, reached into the pocket of his T-shirt, and pulled out the lighter that looks like the kind you take on a camping trip or into war or something.

"Got a cigarette?" he asked.

I rummaged around in my purse and came up with two cigarettes and he lit us up.

"Nice work," he said, meaning my mother's artwork.

I sighed, at a loss. Eddy popped up and crossed over to another canvas that I had placed so that it leaned against the entertainment center. It was a naked woman sitting on a huge golden ball. Her body was cast in partial shadow and her face was indistinct, multicolored. Huge curls of hair emanated out from her head in different colors. My mother had been preparing to add more gold accents to this piece. She had explained carefully how she would apply the gold and how that would give depth and change the piece from ordinary, which it wasn't, to extraordinary. Eddy considered the painting and looked at me curiously.

"Is this supposed to be you, like a self-portrait or something?"

"Oh, no. It was my mother's. She said that one was supposed to represent every woman."

"Every woman?"

"Right. Like all women in one image. I just received it, someone sent several of her unfinished paintings to me and I'm figuring out what I should do with them."

"The paint and brushes, too?"

"What?"

"The paint and brushes were your mother's as well?"

"Oh, yes."

"And the easel?"

"Uh-huh. That was hers. She died...when I was very young."

"Maybe someone thinks you should finish the paintings."

"Oh, I don't know."

He smiled at me like he had figured out a fun puzzle then sat back down on the couch.

I dashed into the kitchen, fetched an ashtray in the kitchen from under the sink, dashed back into the living room, and put it on the coffee table in front of Eddy, then flicked an ash into it. In that moment, I discovered that I was glad to see him.

"Did you hear about my latest win?" he asked.

I thought he might be talking about a surf contest. "No," I said. "Fill me in."

"The Ballona Wetlands."

"What about em?"

"It's only a few blocks from you; Don't you know what's been going on?"

I had heard that three billionaires were trying to put a new film studio there. Wildlife experts said it would destroy habitat for frogs, blue herons, egrets, and the like. But I hadn't kept up with it. I just figured that the money boys would win out. They usually do.

"Like I said, fill me in," I insisted.

"It's over."

"What, the frogs won?" I asked.

"Basically," he said with pride.

"And you're implying that you had something to do with that outcome?"

"It's easy to manipulate people when you know that their number one motivating force is greed."

"And what's your number one motivation?" I asked.

He took a deep drag on his cigarette, French-inhaled it, and gave me a long sybaritic look. I learned that word "sybaritic" from Gus.

I decided not to sit on the couch. Instead, I positioned myself on the edge of a wooden chair and smoked my cigarette.

"So, that's interesting she's alive, right?" he said changing the subject.

"Right. Do you know somebody by the name of Kunda?" I asked.

"Sure, everybody knows the Malibu Psychic."

"Have you ever gone to her?"

"Me?" He looked incredulous. "Nah, but I hear she's ninety-five percent accurate."

He rubbed his stomach and when he did so his T-shirt lifted to reveal his nice six-pack.

"I've already seen your abs. No need to show off."

"What? Oh, man. No. It's not like that."

"So, I take it you're not here to find out about Autumn's murderer since you know, for a fact, that she's alive."

"Did they do her death certificate?" he asked, smoke coming out of his nose like a dragon.

"No," I answered. "She left before the autopsy."

"Tell those guys to hold onto it, because from what I could see, she wasn't looking too good."

"You saw her?" He nodded. "Is she being drugged or poisoned, you think?"

"I'd say so, one way or another. She's not herself, put it like that."

"Where'd you see her?"

"On Melrose, but I didn't hang around to talk. I don't really like that jerk much."

"What jerk?"

"The Barb, he had her by the arm, dragging her around."

"I'd think a concerned guy like you would have wrestled her away from him, something along that line."

"I tried. She told me to fuck off. Believe me, she's not interested in being saved. There's more to the story than meets the eye. I have to admit I felt a little foolish."

"Do you have any idea where I can find her?"

"I don't know. This Barb guy, he's a punk, drug dealer, an asshole with big aspirations."

"Aspirations to what?"

"Hard to say exactly. He has movie and music connections, I think," he said.

"She never returned to her bungalow. We've been hoping she would. We followed up on The Barb but turns out he skipped out on his hotel bill. Do you know where they might be staying?"

"Don't know. Real winner, that guy."

"As opposed to you?" I asked and stubbed out my cigarette. I focused my eyes on the ashtray, making sure I had truly put it out.

"No, not me," he said, suddenly modest. "She liked me enough. I don't go really for models and actresses much. Don't have anything to say to them. I mean, it's like, uh, 'How was your audition honey? Did your glossies come out okay? What's the news from your agent?' or maybe 'How did your scene play in acting class?' That's about it."

"Sounds like you've been there before." I said.

"No way. I go more for the lady marine biologist or lady environmental lawyer or lady activist. I like having somebody I can talk to."

"That's a lot of ladies," I said.

"No, not at all." He got quiet, maybe rethinking it. "I did meet this one actress I liked okay. She was interested in saving the ocean, saving the whales, animal rights, gung ho. She wasn't bullshitting, either. She did eco fund-raisers and got people and a bunch of stars all riled up, started her own organization, even."

"And?"

"She married an actor. I think they're divorced now," he said with a smile. "How 'bout you?"

"What about me?"

"What kind of man do you like to talk to?"

He had me. "This conversation isn't so bad," I said.

My phone rang, crashing into my consciousness. I answered it reluctantly. It was Anthony on surveillance.

"Hey Joan, we got some information on Mason Jones."

"What?"

"He's been taking an acting class."

I glanced over at Eddy who met my gaze with concerned brown eyes. "And?"

"Last night, Mason walked one of the female students home."

"How old is she?"

"Seventeen."

"Give me names and addresses."

Eddy's face fell and he let out an exasperated rush of air. I took the information from surveillance and hung up the phone.

"I'm sorry, Eddy. I have to go. Listen, did you ever meet Dani? That friend of Autumn's?"

"Yeah. What's going on with her?"

"She's dead."

"Are you sure?"

"Look, I can't talk right now. Call me later, okay?"

Eddy stood up and pulled his surfboard from underneath the couch.

"And," I added, "anytime you want to tell me what your real story is and what exactly you want from me, I'd be interested to hear."

"Yeah, well. I might need more than ten minutes for that."

◀▐◀▐◀▐

I CAUGHT UP WITH Mason at his job in the parking lot at Costco. He was diligently stringing shopping carts together with his chain. His blond crewcut was wet with sweat as was his T-shirt. It was early in the week so his clothes were cleaner than last time I saw him. He wore a plastic name tag now that said "Mason" in red and white.

"Mason, how's it going?"

"Oh, shit. Now what?"

"Don't be like that Mason, you make me feel bad. Give me that handsome smile when I show up, be friendly."

"Where's your man friend?"

"You trying to insult me or something?"

"Fuck you, whaddya want?"

"What are you doing in an acting class, Mason? You recently become a thespian?"

"What's that? Some kind of pervert?"

"Funny you should mention that."

"No, there's nothing on me. I'm clean. Clean, you hear me? I got into acting in the slammer. We did some psychodrama stuff and I was pretty good. What, you think I should push around these shopping carts forever or something? I want to be somebody, make something of myself. What's wrong with that?"

"Everybody wants to be a movie star." I took out the flyers of the missing girls. "Recognize any of these?"

"Aw, fuck no."

"You didn't look, Mason. That's not very cooperative. I'll have to take you in for that."

"On what charge, not looking?"

"A prosecutor would call it obstruction of justice."

"Shit. There's no winning with you."

"Look at the pictures, Mason."

He did. His face became more concerned with each girl. He shook his head.

"I don't know them, man. I swear.

"You're not done yet, Mason."

"Goddammit. All right, I'm looking, I'm looking."

He went through them quickly and then stopped when he came to the black girl. He looked like he'd been cornered.

"I know her. Power of the ute, Vernice."

"Where from?"

"Acting class. She was pretty good. We did like a reversal on the Othello scene together. I played Desdemona, it was a trip."

"What's that mean, power of the ute?"

"Oh, she was always goin' on about how she had the power of beauty and booty and she gave it like a nickname—ute. She pronounced it like it was French or somethin'."

"Did you ever walk her home from class?"

"No, man. She didn't like me much."

"I don't know why not."

"Besides, she has her own car, a Jaguar, too, the bitch."

"You know, I don't really like it when men call young women bitches. It offends me. I'm concerned about this young lady."

"She missing?"

"She's missing, Mason. Funny coincidence, her being in your acting class."

"No, man. Don't say that."

"If you know where she is, tell me now, it will go better for you."

"I don't know shit. I'm clean, man, I'm telling you. I'll take a polygraph test, anything, please. I'm begging you. I'm begging you, man."

I believed him. "How did you find out about the class?"

"In the slammer, I met Johan Beaks when he came in on a drug charge."

"Who's Johan Beaks?'

"He's a famous soap star."

"Never heard of him."

"He was in the slammer wid me. We did the psycho drama shit together."

"Psycho drama shit?"

"Yeah, you know, workshops, like therapy. Johan said I had talent, charisma, and he told me about this acting class on the outside. This teacher he referred me to is some kind of acting guru, lots of stars took class from her. I'm telling you the truth, man. I swear."

"Who'd you walk home from class last night?"

"Huh?"

"The girl you walked home from acting class last night is too young for you, Mason."

"Oh, man. You're watching me? Shit."

"Every step you take."

"I won't even talk to her again. Okay? Not even a conversation. She was the one who asked me to walk her home."

"I bet she had to beg you."

"I won't do it again. I tell you that. No, no, uhn, uh."

◆◆◆

GUS WAS STILL IN court so it looked like I was on my own for the rest of the day. I grabbed a quick lunch at a Mexican fast-food joint and drove across the city toward tinsel town.

Hollyweird, they call it. Want to take a picture of the desolate and lonely? Grab your camera and drive down Hollywood Boulevard, stick your arm out the window and snap away. You don't even have to point the damn thing. Drug dealers, drug users, thieves, transvestites, hookers of every age, variety and specialty, the homeless, runaways, lunatics let out of asylums, crazed whacked-out murderers, perverts, you name it, it's all there. You could fill up a whole issue of an old *LIFE* magazine with the photos you got in the first pass. All that is smack in the middle of the specialty tourist shops with pictures of James Dean and Marilyn Monroe and coffee mugs that say I LOVE HOLLYWOOD. There's that old movie theatre with the hand and footprints of famous stars in cement. You can go there and see if your hands or feet match any of them.

I drove down Hollywood Boulevard and remembered the crime photos of all the butchered transvestites I had to study on the case I worked with Gilda. Nobody cares about these people. They are considered an infestation on the streets of Hollywood. That makes them easy targets. Like shooting fish in a barrel.

MASON'S ACTING TEACHER'S STUDIO was not on the boulevard but rather in the lovely Hollywood Hills, in a modern-looking building adjacent to her home. I figured she didn't realize she had a child molester enrolled in her prestigious acting class. A thin young man with spikey hair and John Lennon eyeglasses, her secretary, answered the door. He asked me to state my business, which I did as concisely as possible, mentioning Mason Jones but not his crimes. The guy left me standing at the door, I presumed to announce me. When he came back, he led me to Ms. Koch who was sitting beside a small running fountain in one corner of a large room. Her feet were propped up on a yellow ottoman and she had a script in her hand, which she placed beside her on the tapestry-covered couch. Ms. Koch was, in fact, the renowned acting guru, Melanie Koch, a spry older woman with silver-gray hair in a bun and gigantic thick black glasses that gave her severe look a slightly comedic slant.

"Mason is one of our most talented students," she insisted before I could even speak.

"How long has he been in class?"

"About three months."

"Did you ever see him hanging around before then?"

"No, we don't let people hang around. My students are carefully screened and most of them are referred. He came to two classes as an observer before he signed up."

"How did he find out about you?"

"He was referred to me by Johan Beaks."

"I'd be careful about anybody Johan refers to you in the future. He met Mason Jones in jail."

"I appreciate your advice, Detective."

"I should also mention that your student, Vernice, is missing."

"Oh, no. I'm sorry to hear that."

"Did Mason and Vernice get along?" I asked.

"Reasonably well. Mason is a bit of a scene stealer so they had some words about that, but that's par for the course in an acting class."

"Do you mind looking at some pictures of the other missing girls?"

"No, not at all."

I handed her the stack. She pushed her dark black glasses up her nose a bit. "Oh my, there's quite a few here."

"Yes, I'm sorry to say."

"This one, Katrice. She was my student for about two years. Exceptional. She's missing?"

"Yes, ma'am."

"That's terrible. I can't believe it. Often my students drop out without explanation, most of the time they come back after a little vacation. I had no idea that she was missing."

"Please keep looking, Ms. Koch."

Her hands trembled as she went through the rest of the flyers and picked out one more. Anne.

"She was my student, too."

"Do you know of any other connection that these three students, Vernice, Katrice, and Anne, share, other than being in your acting class?"

"Why, no. I don't really know much about their private lives. I mean, other than what they tell me in class, as it relates to scenes."

"Were there ever any altercations, arguments, anything at all that you can recall?"

"No, not really. We're a fairly lively bunch and often students become a bit histrionic. Oh, now that you mention it. I had this one student for a short time. She was a bit of a troublemaker. And all three of these missing girls got into a physical fight with her."

"Another student?"

"Yes, the girl wasn't very good, really. She was way over the top. She had a background in opera and therefore was laden with more than a few bad habits. A true prima donna, that one."

"A redhead?"

"Yes."

"Was her name Autumn Riley?"

"Yes, Autumn."

"How was she referred to you?"

"I believe her mother contacted me. The Manchesters are good friends of mine and gave Mrs. Riley my number."

"She took your class and had an altercation with these three missing girls?"

"Yes, they were doing a scene from *Dusa, Fish, Stas & Vi.* A dramatic piece, way too sophisticated for any of them, but it had roles for all four, you see. Autumn had convinced the other girls that they could pull it off. I don't remember how it all came about, but we had to tear them off each other during a rehearsal segment one evening."

"Was Mason Jones involved in this scene?"

"Oh, no. That was before Mason even enrolled."

⹋ ⹋ ⹋

I RETURNED TO THE office that evening and caught up on the paperwork. Gus was still in court. I like to make sure that my murder book is always up to date and already we had created quite a backlog. I find it meditative to collect all the information and put everything in perfect order. The office was quiet because of a crime scene downtown at the bus depot, so I had the place to myself. I got the updates, though. A homeless woman had snatched somebody's baby in the women's room. She'd held an opened cat food can against the baby's neck and was keeping the kid hostage until someone turned over her disability check. Apparently, there had been some clerical mistake and she hadn't received her benefits for six months and that's why she was out on the streets and not on her meds. Her appeals had been ignored until now. When they checked, it turned out the homeless woman was on disability for mental illness and, just like she said, they hadn't paid her for the last six months. Of course, the clerical staff found her files pretty quick today and delivered the check, all the last six months of her benefits, to the crime scene. I was relieved to get the final report that the baby and the homeless woman were unharmed during the incident.

When I got home, I could hardly move, I was so exhausted. I put some music on, Haydn's 103rd Drum Roll Symphony. I laid on my couch for just a second and passed all the way out. When I woke up from snoring so loud, I found I was drooling and had left a wet mark on the brown leather of the sofa. Pancho perked me up with a wagging tail and wet kisses.

The phone rang. I didn't intend to answer it, but then Coastal Eddy's voice filled my house.

"Joan, it's me, Eddy. I need to see you." He waited for a moment then said again, "I need to see you, Joan."

I picked up and told him to come over and to bring food.

Why had I done that? I didn't know. I had to eat, I supposed, and I'd been too tired to pick anything up on the way home. Pancho gave me an expectant bark so I fed him and put on some music, Hank Williams. I took a shower and for a brief time I let the music take me away and I wasn't in Los Angeles anymore. In my mind, I was back in the Ozarks and it was summertime. My grandmother was outside cutting the grass with a small push-mower. The blades spun round and round. My grandmother's strong arms and body weight worked to guide it around the corners of her garden. I think she was ninety-three years old the last time I watched her mow the lawn of her garden. I prayed that

I owned her strength, that it was somewhere in my DNA. If only I could access her mighty spirit and her genes at the same time, I'd be okay.

Eddy arrived that evening with white wine and Italian food. I had slipped on an oversize black turtleneck dress that came down to my knees. It was velvet and comfy and I hoped inviting. Pancho greeted Eddy with enthusiasm, his whole body shaking with joy. I took the wine and bag of food from Eddy so he could pet the dog with both hands.

"I think his name should be Demando instead of Pancho," I said. "I need to take him for a walk. You don't mind, do you?"

"No, of course not."

Eddy smiled, flashing bright whites. His eyes were soft and kind, his manner relaxed.

I reached for my Smith & Wesson, slipped it into the belt holster, and strapped that on around my waist.

"You're bringing your gun to walk the dog?"

"Uh, well. I was. Is that a problem?"

"Do you relate to the whole world with that gun in your belt?"

"Sort of."

"Why is that?"

"I dunno. Maybe it's because I'm a cop."

"How long you been carrying?"

"Since I was about ten."

"Jesus. Ten? Were you in a gang or something?"

"No. I'm from the Ozarks. We don't have gangs, okay? Or at least we didn't back then."

"Missouri or Arkansas?"

"Missouri."

"Humph. That's different."

"Different from what? All the other girls you've humped?"

"Whoa. Turn it down, will you? You're rough, you know that? Okay. Sure, bring your gun, I guess. If it makes you feel better. We might come across something you should kill."

"It's not like I want to kill things."

"What else do you do with a gun other than kill things, people mostly?"

"Well, you can coldcock someone."

"Hit them, you mean, with the gun."

"Right."

"That doesn't strike you as strange that you think like that?" he asked.

"Hey, this isn't the best neighborhood."

"Okay, whatever. Let's go." Eddy insisted on taking the leash. "You relax," he said, considerate as all hell. I liked it and maybe I softened a little.

The night was cool and quiet and I found it soothing. Pancho sniffed and peed and did his duty. Eddy explained that he had a Master of Science degree in marine biology and that he'd been living in Monterey until recently. It all sounded very civilized, nothing like my life and certainly not my past. I really couldn't comment without sounding sarcastic or stupid, so I just said "hmmm" and "oh" and let it go at that.

"How old were you when you shot your first gun?" he asked.

"Ten, like I said."

"Go on, tell me more."

"Let's see, I remember it well because things like guns are important to us mountain folk. My hair was long then, just like my mama's. And my father, who always treated me like a boy, something I took great pride in, took me out to the fields behind our house to fire a silvery-blue shotgun."

"Silvery blue?"

"Yes, it was well worn with a walnut stock that had an etched design on it and a switch to release the barrel."

"It was your dad's?"

"He had bought it for me, secondhand."

"Yes, go on, don't stop now."

"Well, my father showed me how to stand. Legs slightly apart." I demonstrated as if I held the gun in the stance. "I had been practicing with the shotgun under my father's guidance so I already knew how to handle it. I cracked it open and inserted the shells, then snapped the barrels shut, released the safety, snugged the butt of the stock firmly to my shoulder, aimed, and fired. It knocked me five feet back on my ass. I've owned a gun ever since, over twenty years now. 'Course, the Smith & Wesson I carry today is a lot handier than that old shotgun."

I patted my gun. Eddy shook his head.

We had made it back to my alley when I happened to look toward my house and I saw someone in the yard. I pulled out my gun and took off running, leaving Pancho and Eddy in a state of bewilderment. But the culprit spotted me and was already gone by the time I got there. Pursuit in the jungles of Venice at night is treacherous. Besides, more than 80 percent of people who run from the police get away. I let it slide because I was tired and hungry and I knew who it was anyways. Some nerve that guy had. My front door was wide open but other than that it didn't look like anything was disturbed. I heard Eddy and Pancho running toward the house and greeted them.

"What? What is it?" asked Eddy.

"Someone broke in; he took off running."

"What'd he look like?"

"It was a big guy with dark hair. I know who it was."

"Who?"

"The big bad bogey man. The one your parents tell scary stories about when you're a little kid. You better be good. You don't want the bogey man to get you. Hector. Hector Cardona. The guy I arrested at Addams's party."

I checked the door. Looked like a smooth job. He'd broken into houses before. In fact, I remembered that was why he was on probation. He'd jimmied the lock. No damage really, and nothing seemed to be missing. He didn't have much time. The thought that he had been watching the house bothered me. I was pissed.

"I take back everything I said about the gun," said Eddy.

"It's okay. I can understand how it might get wearing. You don't carry a gun, I take it."

"Nope, never have. Never will."

"How would you defend yourself if you ever...?"

"I take care of myself. You don't have to worry about me."

We calmed down and I served up the plates of the most delicious creamy pasta I had ever eaten. Eddy and I sat at the kitchen table and made small talk. Pancho was under the table at my feet. I found Coastal Eddy to be opinionated, political, and vigilant in his concern for the ocean and wildlife. In that moment, I understood Glenn Addams's appreciation for Autumn Riley's passion to save the environment. After dinner, we moved into the living room. Ever so often, I found myself looking out the windows and listening for sounds.

"That's all real interesting," I said to Eddy as I gave the scraps to Pancho. "Now, explain to me your connection to Autumn Riley."

"I met her at the beach, on the boardwalk, and invited her to a Save the Bay rally. She was spirited, an admirable person. Very engaging. I don't like what's happened to her."

"What did she do that was so engaging, exactly?"

"It's hard to say, really. When she spoke, it was with great vehemence and indignation. I shared her outrage and I could see others respond to her. You got the feeling that if she fought for something, she would accomplish it. I was looking forward to having her on the team. I knew she'd be an asset."

"And so then you also know Glenn Addams."

"Not well, he was friends with an actress I knew."

"Ginny Deavers? The star of his new movie?"

"Right. In fact, it was her who had invited him to the rally. Autumn and Addams hit it off right away and we didn't see much of either of them after that. I was invited to Autumn's party some time ago and though, no, its not my usual crowd, I went out of curiosity."

"And De Sade's Cage?"

"I went to the memorial and again, curious like you, I followed them over to the club."

"Eddy, all I ask is please don't hide anything from me and don't get in the way."

"I'm on your side, Joan. I am. I want to help. It's not the sort of thing I normally do, but…"

He fell silent and his eyes took in the stack of the porno promo photos from the Dani murder scene on the coffee table next to Dr. Blanchard's journal.

"What's all this?" he asked.

"Research, could be evidence, so don't touch it."

"And that?" He pointed at Dr. Blanchard's journal.

"The writings of some mad scientist in Haiti."

He nodded, his eyebrows furrowed. "That the doctor Dewey worked for in Haiti?"

"You know Dewey?"

"I know he worked for a pharmaceutical company in Haiti and that he's friends with The Barb."

"How exactly do you know all this?"

"I told you. I'm an investigator, Joan. I usually investigate environmental crimes. I was concerned about the disappearance of Autumn so I scratched around a bit."

"So tell me something."

"The same pharmaceutical company that hired Dr. Blanchard and, subsequently, Dewey? They're the same company that was doing new research and infected monkeys with the AIDS virus. An act of neglect allowed for the monkeys to escape. Then one bit a human."

"What qualifies as an act of neglect?"

"Some say it was accidental, that a door was left open. Evidence would indicate otherwise. Lucky for the pharmaceutical company, because then they had a whole population of people desperate for a cure to experiment their drugs on."

"If that were true, the pharmaceutical company responsible would have been indicted."

"Working on it."

"You aren't like a conspiracy person are you? I mean, that sounds pretty wild. I understood that monkeys have always had AIDS and that an unusual strain was transmitted to humans. I thought someone ate an infected monkey or something like that. Never heard this pharmaceutical company doing research theory before."

"Joan, you and I are charging up the same hill."

"I don't know about that. I don't do conspiracy theories. If you're going to make statements you better be able to back it up. No crazy paranoid talk is allowed in this house."

"You sound just like a despot."

"I'm just saying that you need some kind of proof if you want me to buy it. That's all."

"Proof is what I'm all about."

"Good, I like that. Me, I'm a homicide detective. It's really not political for me. It's personal."

"What I do is personal, too. People just don't know how personal it is."

"Okay, then. What do you want with me? You want to oversee the Autumn Riley investigation?"

"There's a lot I want with you." He smiled, but I didn't. "I'm concerned about Autumn Riley but I don't propose to oversee anything," he said with a much more serious tone. "I won't deny that I respect what you do. That's not a bad thing, is it?"

"No. I wouldn't say that was a bad thing necessarily."

"What happened with Dani, anyway?" he asked.

"Unfortunately she won't be getting up and walking away from her gurney at the morgue. Sadomasochistic theatrics and she's dead, really dead."

I showed him the picture of Dani, but then I regretted it immediately. It wasn't exactly romantic behavior. It was mean of me. Working homicide, you sometimes resent that people take what you do lightly. Eddy studied the picture.

"I'm sorry," he said as if she were someone I knew. In a way, she was. He handed the picture back to me in a tender, careful way.

"She wasn't nice," I said. "But she didn't deserve that." Something sank down from my stomach to my feet.

I went into the kitchen and dished out dessert: coffee ice cream sprinkled with pecans. Eddy followed me in and watched with tender eyes. I meant to dust the ice cream with powdered Dutch chocolate when Eddy took my hand, still holding a mound of the chocolate, and placed my fingers in his mouth. I caught my breath as a wave of pleasure flowed through my body. Chocolate dust spilled over his chin and my hands were dark brown where his mouth had been. He put his other arm around my waist and pulled me against him and I found myself melting into him. My body responded, feeling every muscle of his body. The intensity both ignited and frightened me. I pushed away from him with a moan. He pulled me back, kissed me full-mouthed. I tasted chocolate and felt his teeth, his tongue. He tightened his embrace. My hands were in his hair. I wrapped my legs around him and he bit my neck. Then my mouth was in his hair, the taste salty and fresh at the same time.

Sometimes death makes people want to affirm life with sex. It's a reaction that I'm familiar with. A large weight struck me from the side, paws and dog hair and a long wet tongue was lapping my face. We broke it up to give the dog its proper attention and we both laughed a nervous laugh. The tension went out of the moment like air out of a balloon.

"God, that dog is big," said Eddy.

"I know."

"How long you gonna have him, anyway?"

"Oh, I take him in tomorrow and LAPD will give him back to his family."

"That's good."

"Eddy, I'm glad we got together and all, but I really need to get some sleep."

"I understand. I hope you don't mind I kissed you."

"No, it was nice."

We walked to the door, Pancho trailing us every step and we all stood at the doorway for a moment.

"What I'd really like to do is get Tommy back to his family," I said.

"I know. If anybody could, it'd be you."

"Oh, Eddy." My eyes teared up. I was tired. He put his hand on my neck.

"Goodnight, Joan," he said and kissed me softly on the cheek.

After Eddy left, I double-checked the house to see if anything was missing or stolen in case I missed it the first time. I don't have many valuables in my place, just the usual television and CD player, but nothing I couldn't replace except, of course, now I had my mother's things. Hector had worked fast. It looked like nothing had been touched. Still, I wasn't going to let this slide. My space had been violated. I checked the bedroom.

The spot on my bed where I keep my Raggedy Ann doll was empty. Hector had stolen my Raggedy Ann.

CHAPTER FOURTEEN

I WAS UPSET ABOUT the doll, so I brewed chamomile tea to calm myself. I was sitting on the couch letting the tea steep when my eyes fell on the stacks of evidence on the coffee table and I decided to study the porno promo shots from the Dani crime scene. Pancho jumped up on the couch and curled up, as much as a big dog can, beside me. He'd be back with his family tomorrow. I patted his head and he licked my hand. As I went through the promo shots, one in particular drew me in. It was a full-color glossy of a woman that I recognized—Kunda, The Malibu Psychic. She had on a purple dog collar and held her hands up in front of her like they were paws. The bottom of the photo indicated the film was a Spike and Barb production.

I stood up. Pancho picked up on my change of energy and jumped off the couch in readiness. The promo shots slid to the floor and I bent over to pick them up. My chest welled with hope for a lead as I stacked them neatly and stared once more into those purple eyes.

I pulled on a pair of black jeans and grabbed my badge, holster, and gun. On the way out the door, I picked up Dani's photo and my cell phone.

"Pancho, you stay."

As I drove up Pacific Coast Highway, I dialed Gus. The ocean reflected a shining sliver of moon and there was hardly any traffic so I was making great time. Gus was asleep and I had awakened him.

"How was court?"

"That lousy bastard is going away for life."

"Good. Listen, I'm on my way to have a chat with the Malibu Psychic."

"Why the hell…"

"Kunda is in one of the promo shots doing doggie tricks."

"Say what?"

"Looks like it was a few years ago."

"Okay, and then what?"

"I'm gonna squeeze her like a lemon."

"Hmph, sounds good. Take it easy. Make sure she doesn't file a complaint. Keep me posted. In fact, call me when you're done. And when you do, don't tell me you did anything I'm not going to like."

Gus knows me like a brother and I love him for it.

⊪⊪⊪

I KNOCKED HARD THREE times. Kunda must have been up, because I heard her moving around as soon as I knocked. She had to come from the back and it took her a few seconds to open the door.

"Detective, what are you doing here?"

"I'd appreciate a moment of your time. I come to you with questions." My voice was strange in my ears. I was holding back, but my tone was forceful, insistent.

"Come in, come in. My, you dress different on your off time. I like that velvet-over-denim effect."

I entered the dimly lit room filled with pastel-colored chairs. Traces of incense still hung in the air.

"I'm not here to discuss fashion."

"No, of course not."

It was so dark in there that several people could have been hiding in the shadows.

"You kept some secrets from me, Kunda."

"What do you mean?"

"Turn up the lights, I can't see anything in here. I want to see your face."

"Okay, I have nothing to hide," she said as she adjusted the dimmer switch. A warm golden glow filled the room. She gave me a nervous smile. "What is it, Joan?"

Goddess posters stared at me, their eyes holding me responsible. Kunda was dressed in white silk pajamas. Her face was blank, no pretense, no otherworldly bullshit.

"I want you to tell me everything you know about our friend, Autumn, especially her relationship with The Barb and the dark world of S&M. Just tell me now, because I'm gonna find out anyway so please don't hold back even one detail."

"Oh, dear. I didn't realize."

"Get comfortable."

I pushed her down on the same pink chair she sat in the morning Gus and I first interviewed her. Her eyes took on a different look. No more pretense, no more airy-fairy. I paced back and forth to keep myself under control and even if she wasn't psychic she could've picked up on that.

"I don't know where to start. What do you want to know?"

I pulled out Dani's picture for the third time that day and flipped it down on Kunda's lap. It was strange how the ghastly photo looked against the pure white of Kunda's silk pajamas.

"That's Dani, she was Autumn's best friend. She's been murdered. We found this shot of you among her belongings."

I flipped the postcard-sized photo of Kunda in her purple dog collar on her lap as well.

"Oh no." She turned away from the photos as if from a harsh light.

"Oh yes. Why don't you start way back at the beginning so we don't get confused or miss any important details?"

"Okay. Please, take this back."

I snatched the photos off her lap and put them back in my jean pocket.

"Let's see, um, before I was a psychic I was an actress."

"What name did you use?"

"Laura Donate. I did a few B films but before that I did, uh, sort of, the first music video. Glenn Addams directed it and The Barb produced it."

"So, you know The Barb?" She nodded. "And you knew that he was involved with Autumn."

"No, I had no idea. I swear."

"Glenn Addams directed this music video? I thought he was a producer."

"Not too many people know about it because, well, it was an S&M band and Glenn went by Spike back then and that's what the credit says. It was, uh, sort of a subculture underground thing."

"A Spike and Barb production."

"Exactly."

"The Barb. How'd he get his nick name?"

"He was fond of tying girls up in barbed wire."

"Nice guy. What was the title?"

"Excuse me?"

"The film you did, what was the name of it?"

"*Dying Love.*"

"Where do people buy this film?"

"I'm sure Glenn Addams has bought the rights and taken it out of distribution by now. I didn't think the promo still existed. You couldn't really buy or rent it from the video stores."

"A snuff film."

She nodded. "But no one was really hurt," she said. "It was all drama. Makeup and special effects."

"Not one of your spiritual high points, I take it."

"No," she said in a hoarse whisper.

"What else?"

"That's all I know. I pretty much moved out of that orbit. I've evolved."

"Good for you. Who are some of the lower life forms still in it, besides The Barb?"

"Oh, I don't think The Barb does that sort of thing anymore. I'm pretty sure he wants to be on a higher level."

"Like his old partner, Spike, who is now the big producer Glenn Addams."

"Right. Um, there's this one guy, a video editor. He's older now, a big man, lots of health problems, corpulent, smokes, harmless really, but very much into all that, as I recall. A quiet, docile-type guy, but you know, there was that thing in his eyes. Gave me the shivers when he looked at me when ah... His name is Johnny Tyler."

"Do you have a phone number, address?"

"No, but you should be able to locate him in the North Hollywood white pages under Johnny XXX Tyler. He got a lot of business under that listing."

Johnny Tyler did indeed live in North Hollywood in what was once upon a time a nice neighborhood. The address was a thirties Spanish-style house that sat atop a hillock of dead grass and shrubs. I parked the Crown Vic right on the street from where it was clear that Mr. Tyler was obviously not someone who gave much thought to his landscape. Plant life was definitely on its own here. A steep flight of concrete steps went up to the wooden steps of a small covered porch. To the left of the porch was a large picture window with security bars and drawn sun-faded curtains. The bars struck me as a bit odd, since you would need an extension ladder to reach the window. A narrow, double-strip driveway ran up to a dilapidated wooden gate on the right side of the house. On the left side was a cinder-block privacy wall a few feet from the house. It was a quiet neighborhood where people mind their own business because it's the smart thing to do.

I needed to check in with Gus before I went in to question him. I had just gotten my phone out when a huge black SUV pulled up to the curb in front of the house. I waited to see if Mr. Tyler was about to have company when I immediately recognized the hulking form of Hector Cardona walking up the steps of the house. There was a skinny young girl with him. She had to be around twelve or thirteen and armed with an affected street-tough attitude. She walked as if her shoes were made of iron. In the porch light, her straggly pink hair looked electrified which went well with her electric-blue hip-huggers. A tiny red halter covered her flat chest. Though I was on a diagonal across the street, I scrunched down and dialed Gus as Hector went onto the porch and turned to the girl who was still clumping up the steps. He said something to her about moving her ass and then knocked on the door. I saw a movement in the curtains in the picture window and glimpsed a pale face.

Hector and the girl stood on the porch talking. He put his hand on the top of her head and she knocked it off though she probably didn't weigh much more than his arm. To my surprise, Hector left her there and went back to his SUV and took off, but not before I wrote down his license plate. The girl with pink hair stood on the porch and watched him leave. The door opened behind her and she went in. I didn't like that. I dialed Gus.

"I thought you were going to call me," Gus said. He was pissed.

"I'm calling you, I'm calling you. Listen, I'm in NoHo outside the residence of one Johnny Tyler. Hector Cardona just drove up and dropped off a young girl. She's got to be a minor. Could be street. This guy Tyler is in the sleaze business. Kunda turned me onto him."

"You're late on the draw, dammit. Now you've got to call the watch commander, you need backup to contain the area. Do you understand me, Joan?"

"Yes, sir."

"Hector's gone?"

"He dropped the girl off and split. She didn't offer any resistance. In fact, she could have left. But I'm telling you, she's a minor. Probably a runaway."

"Okay, tell the watch commander you have a possible kidnapping. Keep an eye on 'em. I'll be right there."

I gave Gus the address and called the watch commander with the situation and my location. I got out of the car, walked up the street, crossed to the house side, pausing behind a huge clump of pampas grass near the corner of the driveway. I was determined to have a look-see and was up the driveway before I had a chance to change my mind. The gate at the top was locked but was flimsy enough for me to slip through. There was a big boxy white van parked at the end of the driveway in front of a small garage that tilted to one side. The windows along this side of the house were covered with security bars like the front. The windows were too high for me to look through, but by standing precariously on the utility meters and holding on the security bars under the second window, I could see in.

The curtains were closed, but the window was open a few inches at the bottom. It was enough for me to squeeze my hand through the bars and open the curtains a couple of inches for my first unforgettable view of Johnny Tyler in a Barco lounger. Sweat darkened his Hawaiian-print shirt and his pants were pulled down to mid-thigh. He was casually masturbating. I couldn't see the screen of the large television in front of him, but the sounds emanating from it strongly suggested something of a prurient nature. The girl with the pink hair was sitting on the floor next to the chair and it took me a moment to realize that there was a rope around her neck. The fat man held the end of the rope and jerked in rhythm with his whack hand. Tears streamed down the girl's face as she fought to loosen the rope with her free hand. Her other hand was handcuffed to the metal bars that held up the leg rest on the Barco lounger. A blinding black red rage possessed me. I gripped the security bar as if to rip it from the side of the house.

I ran to the back door of the house, trembling with effort to keep control, to think clearly, to not make a mistake. I unholstered my gun. There was an enclosed storage area with an unlatched screen door. To my amazement, the back door was unlocked. I opened it cautiously and found myself in a kitchen that smelled like garbage. There were two doorways off of the kitchen. Through the one directly in front of me I could see a room with a dining table, and beyond that part of the living room and the front door. I opened the door to my right and checked out a bedroom. I crossed through. A door from there led to a bathroom. I listened at the door but could hear only the television and the caged drumbeat of my heart. Not another sound. He was alone.

Then I was in the living room moving fast from one end to the other, sighting down on Johnny Tyler.

"LAPD! Drop the rope!" I shouted. I pointed my gun at his pasty bloated face for emphasis. "Now!"

He did as he was told. The girl pulled the rope off and gasped for air.

"Where are the keys for the cuffs, you son of a bitch?"

Disassembled mannequins, the plastic body parts of women, were placed around the room and hung from the ceiling like human mobiles. Several half bodies leaned against the walls and sat in chairs. There were no faces. In fact, there weren't any heads at all. Just the plastic body parts. For some reason this affected me in a strange manner. I felt a slipping and sliding beneath me and the room closed in on me. I put my gun to Johnny's head. Johnny cringed but took the keys from his shirt pocket.

"Are you okay?" I asked the girl.

"Get me out of here," she wailed.

"Okay, take it easy. Everything's going to be okay." I moved around to be directly in front of Johnny. "Give her the keys," I ordered. "You so much as belch, you scum, and you're dead. Got it?"

He did. The girl frantically uncuffed herself, whimpering the whole time.

"You'll be okay," I reassured her. "Help is on the way. Wait over by the front door."

She ran out of the house like a shot. I was hoping she wouldn't go too far, but I had to scare the fat man first.

"You, down on the floor. Face down and pull your damn pants up! Now! Down! Put your hands behind your back."

He grunted like a hog as he did what he was told. I suddenly recognized him from somewhere.

"I'm not well," he whined. "Don't hurt me, I'm in fragile health."

I put a knee in his back and slapped the cuffs on. They were barely large enough for his wrists. It was then I found myself looking directly at the huge television screen in front of me. There was Dani. She was strapped to the same chair we found at the murder scene with gaffer's tape. Her arms were covered with cigarette burns. On screen, a big hand with a hammer took a swing at Dani and caught her on the cheek. It was disturbing how exact it was to what I had imagined. Then two huge hands, exactly the same as the ones I had just handcuffed, were around her neck. She struggled and died before my eyes. It was then that I smelled something rank, like bacon when it goes bad. Too late, I sensed a presence behind me, but before I could turn, the back of my head exploded with a fire and a bright light burst behind my eyeballs. Then there was only a brief gray static like when the television signs off, then black. There were sharp voices from far away at the end of a long inky black tunnel.

"Get the car!"

"No, I don't want to go out."

"Mary, we have to go out! We have to!"

CHAPTER FIFTEEN

I SURFACED FROM A deep-sea bed where grotesque skeletal fishes glowed and other various primal creatures meandered and swam around me. I heard a far-off groan. A groan that I realized was my own and the impossible pain rolling around in my head like a loose cannonball was because someone had a hold of my hair and was shaking my head like a rattle. They must have tired because they suddenly stopped and my head fell forward, my chin on my chest. I could smell cigarette smoke and as the darkness closed over me again I thought I could use one myself.

I came to again. This time my brain was working a little better. Through the pain throbbing in my head and jaw, my brain gave me a clear message not to move. Not to do so much as blink. Take inventory, it said. Someone still had a tight grip on my hair. A slimy liquid flowed from my open mouth and it tasted a lot like blood. Okay. I'd been roughed up. I was sitting on a seat, a back seat of a vehicle.

I listened to the wind around me and knew we were moving along at a pretty good clip. A freeway. An uncongested freeway. Judging by the creaks and wind rush, I was pretty sure that I was now in the back seat of the white van I had seen parked in Tyler's driveway. There had been somebody else there. And I had missed them. Damn, curses and double damn. I should have searched more carefully. Or maybe they came in afterwards. What did it matter? I knew I was in a world of trouble and it was not going to improve unless I did something. I hoped that I was not too badly damaged. They must have hustled me out of there fast, before backup or Gus arrived. Gus would be extremely disappointed to say the least.

I opened my eyes a slit. The front of my velvet turtleneck dress and the knees of my black jeans were covered with lines of blood and my hands were cuffed together on my lap. My own cuffs. A massive body pressed against my left side. It had to be Johnny. Smoking a cigarette. We hit a bump and I let my head loll a little, hoping to take a quick inventory. Johnny sat beside me with a cigarette between his lips staring right at me with a decidedly sinister look in his pale piggy eyes. He blew smoke in my face and I realized with a start that he had huge breasts. That hadn't registered on me before. He must be a hermaphrodite. His hair was much longer and he'd put on a blue denim shirt. I let my head fall forward but not before I looked at the driver and saw that it was also Johnny. Twins!

In that moment I remembered where I'd seen these faces before. They were the two lumps I'd noticed at the bar in De Sade's Cage. Right. Female Johnny was the one who had knocked out my lights in the bathroom. Female Johnny pressed herself against me and grabbed my hair, lifting my head. The bad bacon smell she gave off was intense and I thought I might vomit. "She's coming to," said Female Johnny.

"Good. It's no fun otherwise," said the male, adjusting the rearview mirror so he could get a look at me.

Still holding my hair, Female Johnny reached around with her other arm and clamped a massive hand covering my face and squeezed. I realized in an instant whose hands I'd seen around Dani's neck.

"You're a little old for the part," she said, "but we'll try to make you look as good as we can."

"Yeah, movie magic," Johnny said.

I took a dive emotionally, I mean, I had really messed up—and worse, I couldn't breathe. Was this part of their fun? I was going to have to pass on this party. I started to struggle against her and though I could raise my hands, I couldn't budge her. I soon discovered that my feet were bound together with silver gaffer's tape. She suddenly released my face and I gasped for air while she blew smoke in my face. Between exaggerated coughs, I noted that on the floor, beside Female Johnny's feet, next to a pair of bloody pliers, a claw hammer, a screwdriver, and a jar, was my badge. Next to that was my gun. That brightened my hopes considerably.

Female Johnny studied my face, her mouth twisted into a sneering grin.

214 E V A   M O N T E A L E G R E

"You're a disgusting mess, you know that, smart bitch?" She smiled and blew smoke in my face.

For some reason, maybe it was because of a concussion I was pretty certain I had, I thought odd thoughts. Like what if someone took a picture of this scene?

I imagined the shame I'd feel if the photo were in the newspaper. I was woozy and nauseous and had to fight against losing consciousness. I wondered when Female Johnny was going to burn me with the cigarette she was smoking. I tried to imagine different scenarios for retrieving my gun. On some deep level, I felt my body gathering its strength. Preparing.

It was then I noticed my mouth was filled with blood. It spilled out over my lips and onto my lap. I stared down at the red color in awe. I felt around inside my mouth with my tongue and discovered that my right wisdom tooth was missing. Christ. They had extracted my wisdom tooth while I was unconscious. I bet I could guess which one had done the dental work.

"Looking for this? A real beauty, this one. Long roots. You're an animal."

Female Johnny held a tooth, my tooth, between her forefinger and thumb. She was wearing a maniacal grin. My tooth was pink and a bit of gum tissue still clung to the broken root.

"Where's the girl?" I asked, the miracle of speech having returned.

"She didn't want to play anymore," said male Johnny in a pouty voice. "You scared her off."

"And so now," said sister dearest, "you're her—whatcha call it? Udderstudy?"

Female Johnny pointed to a small digital camcorder on the front seat. Maybe it was Dani's camcorder, the one that had never been found at the crime scene. Dani's torture as it had been depicted on Johnny's huge television screen flashed through my mind and an icy fear gripped my heart.

"We're gonna make you a star. Put your sweet ass on the Internet."

She blew more smoke in my face, then held her burning cigarette so close to my right eye that I felt the spot of heat on my eyeball. I focused on the yellow-brown camel on the cigarette paper and prayed that we didn't hit a bump. I wanted to close my eye but feared that my eyelash would catch. I slowly leaned my head onto the back seat, away from the cigarette. A deranged laugh started in the woman's soft belly, moved up through her chest, and came out her throat like the call of a rabid hyena. I tried hard not to show any emotion. When she laughed her fill at the idea of debasing me or torturing me, probably both, and distributing it on the Internet, she puffed on her cigarette some more and eyed me.

"Hey, don't I know you?" she asked.

"We've met."

"You're the hero dyke from the bathroom at De Sade's, right?"

"I'm not a dyke."

"You ain't lookin' like no hero, either."

She guffawed at her joke then reached for the jar that she held between her massive thighs. She held it in front of my face and rattled it. It was full of wisdom teeth. She twisted off the top and dropped mine in with the others.

There had to be two dozen teeth in that glass jar. One of them was more recent, like mine, with tissue still clinging to it; must have been Dani's. The look of deranged glee on Female Johnny's face filled me with repugnance. I felt nauseous. Bile rose up my throat. I let more blood flow out of my mouth onto my lap. I didn't want to swallow it and I had to make room for my tongue in there. I imagined myself diving to the floor, grabbing the gun, and shooting twisted sister. I began the slow maneuvering so that I could use my legs against the door of the van to propel me. It seemed like a way long shot, but it was the only chance I had.

"So, you guys brother and sister?" I asked in the way of conversation.

"Smart bitch, aren't you? If you're so fucking intell-agent, how come you're going to die? Huh, bitch?"

"Call me Joan. And you are?"

"Don't let her be so smug," said Johnny.

Female Johnny hoisted her massive body and a fresh wave of rancid body odor washed over me. I cannot convey the revulsion, nor the fear, that I felt when she bit my upper arm. I screamed and she stopped and promptly struck my face with her sledgehammer of a fist, which gave rise to another explosion of stars and meteors and ignited a special pain in my jaw where a tooth used to live.

"Don't be smart, bitch. It gets worse, not better. Got it?"

I got it, all right. The word "subhuman" took on new meaning for me.

"Okay, hold it down back there," Male Johnny said. "Don't get me excited when I'm trying to drive."

A safety-conscious psychopath. Interesting. The van was of the commercial variety; therefore there were no windows except for the back doors and in the front they were all tinted. All I could see was straight ahead through the front window. We were on a freeway going through desert, but nothing I saw struck me as familiar. I must have been out for hours. At that moment, a screeching siren came from my back pocket and the two ugly Johnnies froze. The siren was increasingly insistent.

Female Johnny leaned her hulk toward me again. I cringed as her probing fingers felt around in my pocket and came out with the phone and my keys.

"Look, the bitch is being called by three one oh, five six eight, three nine six seven," she said. "Who's that?"

"My partner."

"He's a little late, wouldn't you say?" Her maniacal laugh took over again. I didn't really relate to her humor.

Johnny looked into the rearview mirror like some kind of mad mesmerizer and said, "She didn't answer your question."

"I thought she was speaking rhetorically," Female Johnny said. "Smart cunt." She picked up a screwdriver and a hammer from the floor of the car. She clenched the screwdriver in her fist then cocked her arm back with menace.

"Now answer me, bitch!"

"Yes, he's late," I said calmly.

Female Johnny giggled for a long time then suddenly stopped and stared into my eyes. I stared back. "She's scared!" my tormentor hooted. "Maybe you are smart after all, honey. If ever there was time, this is it for shittin' your pants. Got that?"

"I got it."

The siren screeched again. She checked the number. Her eyes narrowed to slits.

From the front, Johnny said, "Kill it."

Mary put the phone on the floor, lifted the hammer, and swung it down, smashing it to smithereens.

"Those damn things can be so irritating." She kicked at the plastic shards.

"You can't possibly believe you can kill a cop, record it, webcast it, and think you're going to get away with it. They already know who you are and where you live. It's not going to work," I said.

"I suggest that you quit pretending that you have any measure of control," said Johnny. "Do you understand? Your laws don't apply here. Forget that."

"Hey, bitch. Did you know that the thighbone is the hardest bone to break in the human body?"

"No, I didn't."

"What do you think would happen if I hit your thigh as hard as I could with this hammer? Think I could break it?"

"Could you explain to me what the point is in this? I don't get it."

"She thinks we should explain ourselves to her," said Male Johnny. "She would like to know the point." He giggled, spurting a high creepy giggle like a deranged baby.

I eyed the jar of teeth. "Are the previous owners of all those teeth dead?"

"Your powers of deduction amaze the fuck out of me," Female Johnny barked. "Most of them were much younger than you. Let's see, you'll make the number twenty, even."

"In how many years?"

"No, fuck you," Female Johnny barked. "I asked you a question. I suggest you answer it at this time." She raised the hammer and snarled at me. "Think I can break your thighbone with this hammer?"

"I think you probably could."

"Let's just see about that, why don't we?"

"No, wait," said Johnny. "If you do that she won't be able to walk. Blindfold her and save that for later."

"Okay, fine," said Female Johnny and she pinched the inside of my upper arm and twisted. This time I refused to give her the satisfaction of showing my pain.

"Oh, she's a challenge, this one. She's going to be lots of fun," said Female Johnny.

My head ached and I wondered what I'd been hit with when she had surprised me from behind. The hammer? If so, it was lucky I wasn't already dead.

We left the freeway and began to drive into higher and greener country. I had to act soon, before we got to where we were going. I weighed the consequences of a possible car accident against being taken somewhere and bludgeoned to death, plus maybe even the honor of being tortured and having it recorded digitally for viewing in cyberspace. It was obvious to me that these two Johnnies were used to intimidating their captives into submission. I thought of their young victims and a new rage burned through my pain and weakness. Now was the time. Now. After one more moment of consideration, the car accident just seemed like the way to go. I didn't have much to work with seeing as my hands were handcuffed, but when did I ever let something like that stop me? I'd successfully twisted my body so that the soles of my feet were against the side of the van. I would have to shoot my body out straight and down, grab the gun, and turn before she could grab me. Maybe safety-first Johnny would stop the van. It seemed likely that I was going to die in a most unseemly fashion.

"You are a very bad impersonation of a human being and you really stink, you know that? I'm pretty sure I've met rabid dogs with better personalities. Didn't your mother teach you anything?"

It took a few seconds for the shock to give way to violence, but I was ready, and as she lunged for me, I invested everything I had and smashed my forehead into her nose. That stunned her. I was down on the floor, grabbed my gun, clicked off the safety and turned just as sis's knee crashed into my kidney. I managed to squeeze off a round into the tree trunk of a leg above that knee. The gunshot was as loud as an anti-aircraft gun inside the van.

"Pull over, you sick bastard, or your sister dies!"

"No!" said Male Johnny. "Please, no. Oh God, oh God, oh God."

"Stop the car or I'll kill her!" I shouted and punctuated my command with a hard jab of the gun barrel into her amazingly soft belly. "One wrong move and the gun goes off in your stomach."

"Shit," she whispered and grabbed at the gun. Her fingers pried at my hands like iron claws.

What could I do? I had to shoot her. I managed to pull the trigger and gut-shot her. A loud "oomph" escaped her, but her grip didn't falter. She'd hardly noticed. Blood oozed through her shirt. She managed to twist my hands so that the gun was pointed straight up.

"Stop this van!" I screamed. "Pull over!"

In our struggle for control, the gun went off again and fired through the roof. Johnny shouted something unintelligible from the front seat but kept driving. Another shot fired through the roof. Female Johnny was bending my arms back. I was giving every iota of strength I had, but I was losing control as the gun came down by the side of my head. Another shot went off and my ear went deaf except for an unbelievable ringing. This time it went out the front of the van which began to swerve from side to side.

"Pull over, now!" I screamed.

But the van was spinning out of control. There was a sharp jump as we hit the shoulder of the road and we plunged over the embankment, momentarily airborne. When the van hit, we were shoved up against the roof and the gun was knocked from my grasp. We bounced and bucked down into a ravine and came to a sudden stop against a tree. The side panel door had sprung open and I was looking out into the lovely green woods. The gun was at my feet, but before I could move, Female Johnny came over the back seat and made for my throat. I tried to stop her with my knees but the combination of her weight and strength was overwhelming. I managed somehow to get my hands between her arms and drove my knuckles into her larynx. Her lock on my throat continued. Just as her fingers were pressing down into my throat, I dug my thumbs into her eye sockets without mercy. I felt my face swell like a balloon. I was near passing out and grabbed with my fingers around her eyeballs when she backed off and my hands came away bloody. I grabbed my gun and flung myself out of the open door and rolled away as fast as I could. With one eye on the van, I worked on unwrapping the gaffer's tape around my ankles. I didn't know what happened to Johnny Tyler, but I knew the sister was still alive. I hoped the one bullet I had left in my gun would be enough to stop her if she should come at me. I didn't have long to worry when in the next moment, she charged out of the van like something out of a horror movie. I fired and hit her in the chest, but she kept coming at full charge. At the last instant, I curled into a ball and threw myself at her ankles. She went flying over me and out over the steep-sided ravine. I went to the edge and saw her sprawled out and unconscious. She was breathing. The van was spewing steamed heat and I hoped it wouldn't explode—or worse, catch on fire.

I looked up and saw a couple of lumberjack-looking guys standing up on the embankment.

"I'm a cop," I shouted. "Call nine-one-one. Tell them an officer needs assistance." I laughed in strange relief. What an understatement. Several more people gathered at the top of the hill looking down on us.

One of the lumberjack guys waved his cell phone at me. "I already called nine-one-one!" he shouted.

"Oh. Okay. Call three one oh, five six eight, three nine six seven!" I shouted back.

He looked surprised. "Say that again?"

I did. Plus, I told him to tell the detective that answers that Detective Lambert needs backup. I then asked if they would be good enough to get me out of there. There were very nice men. Very kind.

Once I was up on the road, I sat on the ground and allowed myself to have a little cry, I'm not ashamed to say. One of the men put his hand on my shoulder to comfort me. He didn't say anything, just kept his hand on my shoulder.

GUS WANTED TO TAKE me to the hospital, but I talked him into letting me go home instead. The Tylers were incapacitated but still alive. Gus was kind enough to take care of all that. He also arranged to have the guys drive my car from the Tylers' place to Parker Center so I'd be able to go right home once I got there. As Gus drove back to Parker Center, the night was quiet and everything; even the gray sedan seemed to be moving in slow motion. I recognized it as an aftereffect of a high adrenaline flush.

"When we got there and you weren't around, I knew there was a problem," Gus said. "I was damn worried; I don't mind telling you. You got a knack for getting right in the middle of some bad shit. Yes, you do. It's uncanny."

"At least we put an end to their tooth collection."

"There's that."

"Where's the girl?"

"What girl?"

"The one with the pink hair, the one Hector dropped off. Apparently, he's still providing runaways to the depraved."

"When we arrived, there was no girl with pink hair on the scene."

"Johnny was strangling her, Gus. That's why I went in. Exigent circumstances."

"I believe you, Joan, but there's no girl to verify your story."

"My story."

I fell silent. Twenty-one thousand kids went missing in this country a day. That's 750,000 a year. What was the chance that we'd ever find the girl with pink hair?

We came to a red light. It seemed to take several minutes before the car came to a stop. "There's the videotape," said Gus.

"Of Dani being killed?" I asked. He nodded.

"We can work that," he reassured me. "Are you sure you're okay?"

"Oh, yeah. Thanks, Gus."

The red light took eons to change to green.

I didn't let on that I'd been hit in the back of the head. I wasn't in a hurry to say that my concern for the girl with pink hair had caused an oversight on my part. That I let Female Johnny sneak up on me and knock my ass out. She had managed to get the upper hand on me twice now. Nor did I mention anything about the badge or the gun since, luckily, I had reclaimed them both. Of course, I'd have to explain some of these details in the report.

"Uh, Gus, I messed up... I, uh..."

"You're a good cop, Joan. A damn good cop. You just need reining in."

"Sounds like you're talking about a wild horse. You trying to break my spirit?" I gave him a weak smile.

"Not me. Nope. That would not be my intention."

"Gus, why are people so mean?"

"I don't know. Just crazy, I guess."

"Hector stole my doll."

"What'd you say?"

"Never mind."

"Joan, you look terrible, I really think you should go to the hospital."

"No way. I'm going home. I just need sleep."

⑈⑈⑈

THE JOHNNIES WERE BOOKED as John Tyler and Mary Tyler. They pled not guilty to all charges. The teeth, the videotape of Dani, the camcorder, and all their torture equipment were taken in as evidence. I had thankfully pulled my badge from between the seats before the lumberjacks helped me out of that ravine. I can't begin to tell you how relieved I was to have my gun and badge back. For as long as I lived, I would never forget my encounter with John and Mary Tyler.

I must have been in a daze when I got home because I don't remember it. In the morning, when I awoke, I didn't feel Pancho in the bed. I bolted upright and searched through my house. The dog was gone.

CHAPTER SIXTEEN

I CHARGED INTO THE captain's office. Satch was rearranging his workspace. This is not a good sign. Satch only moves things around in his office when he's upset. He was bending over to grab some books; his big body straightened when I came in. As I got closer, I could see on his computer screen that he was in the middle of typing up a press release for media relations and that he was sweating. I always feel concerned about his health when he sweats like that. Don't know why. I try to tell myself that it's only natural.

"May I speak with you, sir?"

Satch bent over and laid his hands flat on his desk and gave me his full attention.

"Yes, Joan?"

"First, I'd like to say that the dog is gone. Thought I'd tell you in person. Before I left the house last night, there was a prowler. It never occurred to me that he was after the dog." Satch gave me a pitying look.

"Any idea who would steal the dog?" he asked.

"No, but surveillance said Hector was hanging round my neighborhood at a coffee shop I go to. And the prowler was Hector."

"Surveillance failed you, wasn't your fault. They're scouring the city looking for your Hector right now."

"That's fine sir, but it doesn't help me…"

Satch put his hand up to stop me right there. "We're having trouble getting the Tylers to tell us where the bodies are. You think you could help with that?"

"Sure, what do you need?"

"Which one do you think would give it up?"

"Neither, but the woman, she and I had a thing. I might be able to get under her skin."

"Why don't you pay her a visit, say your farewell?"

"Yes, sir. I'd like to talk with her. I'll do it today."

"That would be good. You sure you're okay?"

"I'm cool. Don't worry 'bout me."

"We have one dead porno star, eighteen missing bodies, one missing woman, one missing boy, and now a missing dog. You're hip-deep in it, Joan."

"Yes, sir."

"I'll call Missings and explain about the dog. You think if we find Hector, we'll find the dog and the boy, right?"

"I do."

"I'll put all the resources I can on it. We have to figure out this mess and fast."

"I couldn't agree more, sir. I'll do everything I can. I put in a call to Presnell, the French language lady. She should be here soon."

Satch gave me a look. I didn't know what it meant. I got this odd feeling of disapproval.

"I want a written summary from you and Gus," he said.

"I'll get right on it."

He nodded and I was dismissed.

Gus came into Specials while I was writing up my notes for the murder book. When I told him about the dog being nabbed, it took the whistle right out of his walk.

"I have to go visit Mary Tyler and we have to use Tia, our waitress friend, as bait," I informed him.

"Whoa, hold on here," he protested.

"She's an obvious target, it's probably why The Barb and Autumn went to the diner and made a point of telling Tia about the photo shoot, then gave her a copy of Autumn's and Dani's raspberry photo." I was talking fast. "She's next anyway, Gus. Have her be informed and wired."

"She's been warned and I've got some people watching her. But forget about using her as bait. You don't look so good, Joan."

"So who cares? What did surveillance pick up on Hector Cardona?"

"Nothing, so far. He was clean, except for the steroids."

"Not if he stole that dog. We've got to use Tia as bait, we have no choice."

"It's not enough that you got kidnapped, no, you have to pull in some sweet young thing and put her up as a target?"

"I'm not the one targeting them, Gus. Come on. It's the best way to protect Tia. Is she working today?"

"Yes, but…"

"Lunch at the diner, it is."

"I don't believe you're thinking right, Joan. That traumatic experience must be affecting your judgment. You can just turn down the volume right now."

"Bonjour? Bonjour?" a voice came from the hallway.

"In here!" I yelled.

"What the…" asked Gus.

Nicole Presnell's high heels clicked suggestively when she walked in. She was a petite and feisty woman with tawny skin, a pointy feral look, and shapely legs in black stockings. She wore a blue skirted suit, which I'd bet a dollar to a broomstick was Chanel, and carried a slim black briefcase.

"'Ow is ever'buddy doing toe-day?"

"Great, Nicole. This is my partner, Gus."

Gus nodded in a gentlemanly fashion and pulled a chair out for her.

"Nice to meet youuu," she purred.

"And this is the nine-one-one tape." I shoved the recorder toward her and pressed play. "I'd like you to tell me if you can identify any regional accent in this voice."

Nicole immediately became business-like and listened to the tape several times. Finally, she looked up and pursed her lips in what I thought must be her version of a frown.

"Thees persan is not Texan. It's an Australian man. He is impersonating an American, using a voice, like, you know, ummmmm, Jean Wayne. Oui, that's eet, Jean Wayne." Gus and I exchanged looks.

"How do you know he's Australian?" asked Gus.

"You can tell by the emphasis on the words. It is the type of emphasis that an Australian would use." She played the tape again.

"It is not so obvious as he did a fairly good job, just barely discernible."

"Thanks, Nicole," I said, and whispered to Gus, "See?"

"Oh, you are so welcomed," she said and wrote out a bill for two hundred bucks.

"Excuse me," I said, "just give that to Gus. He'll make sure it gets paid, won't you Gus?"

"You bet," he agreed and engaged Nicole in private flirtation while I went to the ladies' room.

After I finished my business and was washing my hands in the washbasin, I took a look at myself in the bathroom mirror. Granted, the blinking florescent light was not so flattering, but I was not quite up to par. I had a partial black eye and some bruises on my face from the hard slaps and punches I took off Mary Tyler and I looked tired, worn. I felt the back of my head and found a big bumpy knot. Maybe I shouldn't have rushed back to work. Maybe I should have gone to the hospital as Gus suggested. But what was I gonna do? Get some rest? Lie in bed?

When I got back to my desk, Nicole Presnell was gone. Gus was sitting in my chair.

"Joan, don't get any funny ideas that you're going to run your program on this case. It's too dangerous to let you go off half-cocked."

"Okay." I said.

"Don't shine me on, here. I mean it. Plus, what's this with Mary Tyler?"

"Gus, please stop talking to me like I'm some dumb rookie. What do you want from me? I am a crime solver. I solve crimes." I pointed to my commendation, still on my desk, unframed. "Some people think I'm good at it. I do tend to get the bad guys."

"I just want to make sure they don't get you."

"Satch wants me to get a line on where the bodies are and I'm thinking my only chance is to irritate the hell out of Mary Tyler."

"I'm senior detective, he should've cleared it through me."

"Oh, okay. Satch glitched the protocol, so sue him."

The phone on my desk rang. Gus and I both stared at it. It rang again and I picked it up. Kunda's voice came through in a frantic rush. "Detective Lambert, please, I keep hearing music, loud horrible music. Then I see Autumn's face and she's dead. Dead! The music keeps crashing in my mind and there's screaming. Someone screaming and screaming, over and over again."

"Hello, Kunda, you're right on time. I'm starting to think maybe you really are psychic."

"What?"

"I'm glad you called, Gus and I want to ask you some more questions."

"Joan, her spirit is fading, fading. You have to save her."

"Yes, I'd like to do that. Kunda, can you meet with us in Beverly Hills for lunch? We would like to talk to you in person, okay? Do you know the diner over on Beverly? Say, about noon? See you then." I hung up.

"What are you doing?" Gus asked.

"I'm gonna need a new cell."

"Okay, here we go. This is the part where I kick your ass," Gus said, following right behind me.

We both walked at a fast clip down the hallway to the elevator. I pressed the down button.

"We're gonna find The Barb, Gus. The Barb. That's who it was on the phone and he must have thought he'd killed Autumn with an overdose and called nine-one-one. Plus, he's the one who picked up Autumn on Melrose. Coastal Eddy said they were together right in front of that store, Wacko, like Kunda said."

"And how'd he know?"

"He was there, he saw them. The Barb, Gus. We find him, we find Autumn. Simple."

The elevator arrived and we got in, interrupting a conversation between two secretaries. We nodded politely and they continued in lowered voices as did we.

"How's it this Coastal Eddy is always on the scene? What's up with that?" Gus asked.

"Eddy is an environmental activist, you know, and he enlisted Autumn in one of his organizations. That's where she met Addams. I think he felt responsible when the whole Autumn situation went down. Basically, Eddy is an ecoinvestigator."

"Eddy, huh? Has he investigated your eco?"

"What are you saying?"

"It's a question."

"You're not going to tell me to call Carl, are you?"

"No, I wasn't thinking about Carl."

"What are we talking about?"

"The fact that you were almost dead last night."

"Yeah," I said, "so what?"

The elevator landed, we exited and walked through Parker's lobby but continued in a conspiratorial whisper.

"I repeat, you were almost dead last night," said Gus

"Except luckily, I'm alive, unlike eighteen kids and one porno star."

"You're lucky, all right."

"Gus, Mason Jones is taking an acting class. It's the same acting class that three of the missing girls took, not to mention Autumn Riley. He met some soap star in jail, a Johan Beaks, who plugged Mason into this acting guru lady." We were about to walk out the entrance.

"Hold up," said Gus. I slowed, stopped, and turned to Gus. "Where did you get this information?"

"I went to see Mason Jones after Anthony in surveillance informed me about Mason taking the acting class. Then I went and interviewed the acting teacher."

"There's a connection between O'Malley's missing girls and Autumn Riley and you didn't bother to mention it to me?"

"I wrote down some notes for the murder book and I'm telling you now."

"Bullshit."

"Gus, come on, gimme a break."

"You need to make sure you don't dis me or I'll put your ass in a sling. I'm the D-three here. I'm your superior."

"Okay. I won't dis you. Come on, Gus. You know I respect you."

"Make sure you act like it. From now on, I want to know every goddam move you make, you hear me? You wouldn't even be on the job if it weren't for me. Shit. You think anybody else on this force wants to be your partner? You're a fucking nightmare."

"Okay, Gus. Can we go now?"

I pushed through the door, Gus right behind me. The heat of the day hit us like a furnace blast. I checked my watch. It was nine in the morning and already suffocating.

"Where to, may I ask?" Gus insisted.

"Beverly Hills. You heard me."

"I guess I still can't believe my ears. This Johan Beaks, you mentioned? He's in a drug rehab, up in the Malibu mountains. We should go see him."

"You know him?'

"I interviewed him last month while you were on sabbatical."

"Whadja interview him for?"

"Because of a dead girl found in the Hyperion sewage plant. Johan Beaks had plenty of good information. The girl was involved in a bad drug deal."

"This soap star had something to do with a dead girl found in the sewage?" Gus nodded. "That's disgusting."

"Anywhere you find a dead girl it's disgusting, Joan."

"I know, but God. Okay, well… Let's go talk to him."

We exited the building and walked down the wide sidewalk, two classic examples of hard-assed detectives outside Parker Center on a mean LA day. The smog was thick and the heat was hot. Traffic filled the streets and pedestrians in office-wear tromped on toward their offices with blank faces. I thought of that old movie, Metropolis, and decided that Gus and I were in the heart of some version of that. One thing the movie never depicted was the children, the young people victimized in such a society.

"You want to tell me your plan for Kunda?" asked Gus.

"Sure, I'd love to, only I don't have one."

"So, why is she meeting us in Bah?"

Gus uses this word, Bah. It's short for Beverly Hills. I think it's pretentious but I let it slide.

We were standing on the side of the building at the gray sedan that Gus drives, department issue, an obvious cop car, especially in gray. He unlocked the doors and we got in. It was even hotter in the car.

"Too bad we can't use that Kunda for a target," he snorted as he powered down the windows and put the air-conditioning on full blast.

"Really, huh?"

"What's her wise word for the day?" Gus asked.

"She says she sees a vision with loud music, Autumn appears, and she looks dead.'

"Maybe she's channeling MTV."

I had to laugh at that one. "Gus, really? MTV was million years ago."

He started the car and pulled out of the parking spot. "Don't fuck with me, Joan. I meant every word I said back there. Just keeping track of you is a full-time job. Can't do your job if your ass is dead, now can you? You're really pissing me off."

"Yes, sir. I'll do the right thing."

"Make sure that you do. I really feel for Carl right about now. You must have driven him completely crazy. Plus, he's so in love with you."

"Oh, no please. Let's not go there."

"Fine. So, you're going to tell Tia your great idea," Gus insisted.

"Okay, and then you'll tell her repeatedly that she doesn't have to do it. Am I right?"

"Something like that."

He pulled a cigarette out of his pocket.

"Give me one of those, goddammit," I said.

Gus grinned, handed me a smoke, and lit it with his ray gun lighter, smooth as a cat.

"Is surveillance still on Autumn's bungalow?" I asked.

"Nobody's gone in or out for a week now and we're gonna have to pull it, seeing as she isn't dead. But you'd think she'd want her clothes or something. And Hector really gave them the slip. They feel bad about the dog."

"Oh, well that's good, I have comfort in that, them feeling so bad."

Gus grunted.

"You got any more of those aspirins?" I asked.

Gus reached inside his breast pocket and handed me the little tin. Having a partner like Gus was one of the great things in my life. The tin had been refilled. I looked at the six pills and dumped them all into my mouth, then chewed. I had to force it down. Gus looked at me like I had swallowed a frog.

"I'm sorry I didn't tell you about that acting class thing," I said.

"It was a serious act of negligence on your part. You know better. We're partners, Joan. We're in it together. Always remember that I'm your superior. I'm responsible for you. I must know everything."

He reached in the back seat and came up with bottled water.

"You look like you need a drink."

I cracked open the water and drank. When I was done, the bottle was empty. Gus frowned and shook his head.

"Don't frown at me like that. Why did you give Carl the cell number?"

"He asked me for it."

"I gotta cut it off with him, Gus. I'm done."

"These things take time."

"His time is up."

"Did you even have coffee this morning?"

I shook my head. "Captain wants us to write up a full summary and have it on his desk ASAP."

"I bet he does."

"Someone stole the dog. It was Hector. Hector stole Pancho. I know it like I know my name."

"Yes, I know. I see it's got you upset. You tell the captain?"

I nodded.

"Yeah, well. This Hector is all over the place."

CHAPTER SEVENTEEN

THE DRUG REHAB WAS a gorgeous estate in the Malibu mountains. The air was scented with orange blossoms and jasmine. Birds of paradise sprouted up around a sign at the gated entrance that said, TRANSITIONS. We drove up a road with Jacaranda trees in full yellow bloom. It was like pulling into heaven. The Spanish colonial structure had a modern slant to it and it was vast. I followed Gus up the stairs to the front door in a state of wonder. He pressed a buzzer and a beautiful Latin woman answered the door. I recognized her as the daughter of a famous comedian well known for his drug problem. He had died from a drug overdose. We asked for Johan Beaks and she offered us a seat on one of several white Italian couches in a large living room. The floors were white marble with a coral vein running through it.

In the center of the room was a massive wood and beveled glass coffee table with big picture books. I read the titles out of standard curiosity. *Hollywood: The Pioneers*, *Pictorial History of the Silent Screen*, also *Film Directors*. As I sat there, I thought of a few nonfiction books on Hollywood that I'd like to write.

Before I had formulated catchy titles for each of my books, Johan Beaks appeared with a mug of coffee and a croissant. He put his goodies down on the glass coffee table. Johan had a certain aristocratic flair even though he was barefoot, wearing sweats and a Lakers T-shirt. I'd say he was in his late twenties. I figured he must play the rich guy in the soaps, a romantic lead. His blond streaks were swept back and held in place with gel.

"Hi Gus, who's your friend?"

I stood and shook his hand. "Joan Lambert," I said.

"Detective Joan Lambert, I take it."

"That's right."

He gave me the once-over.

"Hope the other guy looks worse. What can I do you for?"

"Did you know that Mason Jones is a child molester?"

Johan looked at me askance. I guess he thought my question was rude. I waited for his answer.

"Give me a moment to think about that. Let's get comfortable here. Take a load off. Wow, that's some question."

He sat down. Gus and I did the same. He took a bite of his croissant and a sip of his coffee while we waited for him to answer the question. His eyes continued to take me in as he dramatically swallowed and cleared his throat.

"Well, now. I understood that Mason was in prison for being with a girl that was underage. So, I guess the answer is yes."

Gus took over. "There's ten young women missing, Johan. Three of them are from the same acting class that you referred Mason Jones to."

"Ten missing young women? That's a lot." Gus nodded. "Who's missing from the acting class?"

I gave him the flyers of the three girls from the class.

"This is tragic, tragic. I can't believe it. I know these girls. They're like sisters. How can I help?"

"Here's the rest of the missing," I said. "Recognize any of these?"

He studied the flyers carefully.

"No. No, I only know the ones from class. Vernice, Katrice, and Anne. This is soooo tragic."

"How 'bout her?"

I gave him the picture of Autumn Riley.

"Oh yes, Autumn. She's missing, too? Oh, wait a minute. I heard something about her on the news. They thought she was dead, right? But then she wasn't or something like that?"

"Something like that," I said.

"And you think Mason Jones has done harm to these girls?"

"We're looking at everybody at this point."

"Not me, I hope. Well, first off, I haven't been around. I haven't even seen Mason because I've been here and I don't get to go out and party or anything. I can't even go to the grocery store. They're afraid I might down some cough medicine or drink rubbing alcohol. They're pretty strict about that. I know it looks cool here and all, but it's essentially a prison. They call it rehab, but believe me, it's a confinement situation. One false move and you're busted bad."

"Okay," I said. "It would seem you have a solid alibi. So, you referred Mason to this acting class because…"

"Oh, he's a real talent, the guy has got something, I'm telling you. But uh, let's see, in my opinion, whatever that's worth, Mason is a strong guy and all but…you think he did something to Autumn Riley? That cunt was a demon from hell. Okay? Let's not mince words here. I don't mean to offend you, Joan."

I didn't like the way he said my name.

"Not much could offend me at this point, Johan," I lied. "I'm just saying…if Mason was a predator like you're telling me? I don't think he would pick Autumn Riley out of the bunch to pick on. No way, Jose."

"And the other three?"

"The other girls are all brilliant, talented young women, as I'm sure you know. They come from good families, you know, they have maids, nannies and limos with chauffeurs and all that. Nobody is seriously doing drugs in that crowd. All those kinds of kids are already in here with me. The girls in acting class for the most part are all ambitious. They wear the latest designer clothes, are obsessed with diets and that whole scene, but they aren't the kind of kids that do heavy drugs or anything. Oh, I feel awful. I do hope I'm not talking about the dead or anything like that."

"I think I understand what you're saying," I said.

"Vernice, Anne, and Katrice don't hang with a bad crowd, right?"

"Right. It's not like that time, Gus, when you came and asked me about that one who ended up in the sewage system. Her, I could tell you something about because she went a lot of places nice girls don't go. I'm not saying that because these young girls come from good families it could never happen. I come from a good family, look at everything that's happened to me. What I mean is—the girls that you're asking me about? They're not the type. They aren't trampy enough, you see what I'm saying? And plenty are sluts, I'm here to tell you. But these particular girls? They probably date Phi Theta Kappa guys that their parents approve of, their high school sweetheart. Maybe their professor or an artist, that sort of thing. Really, though, I don't have the least clue about them except what I know from acting class."

Johan truly loved the sound of his own voice.

"Was Autumn Riley the type?" I asked. Johan looked at me and considered it.

"You mean was she a slut? Well, now, that's an interesting question. Autumn. Hmmmm. I think Autumn could be just about anything if it served her purposes."

"Do you think Autumn is capable of causing anyone harm?"

Gus looked at me, then to Johan for the answer.

"Capable? She could kill you with just her eyes. I'm absolutely convinced that Autumn Riley could murder a person with her bare hands."

⫯⫯⫯

THE DINER WHERE TIA worked was completely different at lunch hour compared to when Gus and I normally met there for breakfast. When we entered the barn-red diner, the place was buzzing with business chatter. Lawyers and upwardly mobile young professionals were everywhere; plus there was a sprinkling of creative types, writers, and musicians. You could tell by their clothing, snatches of conversation, the scripts and demo tapes on the tables. This was an ideal place for a power lunch that wouldn't break your piggy bank. People were hawking their wares, making connections, and schmoozing in mad desperation. I guess that was part of the attraction for the Autumn Riley clique of models and aspiring actresses. The red décor had to have been designed to create the high-energy feel of the place.

I had to admit, my thought processes were not crystal clear. My head was still foggy. My body ached and I yearned for sleep. We went toward Tia's section and we slid into the red leather booth. My latest close encounter with death made me no less sensitive to the loud clatter created by the busboys. The banging of dishes seemed to clang inside of my sensitive head.

When Tia approached our table, there was an urgency and intensity about her. Gus got a BLT and black water and her hand shook as she took the order. I wasn't hungry. I was tormented mightily from Mary Tyler's extraction of my wisdom tooth. I felt sick to my stomach and I considered that I might be suffering from an infection caused by her handiwork. Instead of food, I ordered two of the diner's mugs that they sell as souvenirs and a black coffee. Tia finished taking our order with a hard strike of the pencil on her pad. Then she reached into her apron pocket and pulled out a folded page from a magazine.

"Here!" she said tossing it on the table.

I unfolded the tattered page and saw a short music review with a photo of a singer named Zombita, her manager, and her agent. I looked back up at Tia. "What is it?" asked Gus.

"It's Autumn and The Barb with Caroline Johnson, her agent," said Tia.

I looked closer and read the caption more carefully.

Zombita and her manager, The Barb, with talent agent Caroline Johnson.

The photo spotlighted a young woman who looked amazingly like a cadaver. With a stretch of imagination, I could recognize Autumn Riley. Her beautiful red hair was matted and looked like she was going for a dreadlock style, if you could call it a style. She had on white face makeup and large black circles painted around her eyes. On one side, stood the Barb, in black T-shirt and jeans, his hair slicked down flat. He held her bare thin arm. On the other side, the agent, Caroline Johnson, stood wearing a big smile across her face. I read the blurb promoting the show:

An Operetta of death and destruction. ZOMBITA, the hottest new show at the AntiClub, was featured last night. Zombita's lyrics are fierce and her sound is outta this world! Zombita's manager, The Barb, has plans to showcase her talent at all the Los Angeles hotspots while top talent agent, Caroline Johnson, seeks movie deals and other venues. Caroline informed us that a CD is in the making, plus a music video will be released later this week. Pronounced dead two weeks ago by Los Angeles coroner's office, and the object of an intense homicide investigation by LAPD's most elite Homicide Special Section detectives, Zombita has somehow returned from the dead to kick ass.

The mention of LAPD burned me. I felt like I had a hot poker through my skull. We were being used as a tool in a publicity maneuver. It was while I was trying to recover from my shame that I noticed it—a worn Raggedy Ann doll clutched in Zombita's free hand. I said nothing, tried to pull it all together. I passed the magazine page to Gus. He looked at it carefully. For a moment, he allowed an uncertainty to pass over his face, and then it was gone.

"That's weird," was all I could say.

"Where'd you get this?" Gus asked Tia.

"I read it in *BAM Magazine*, about an hour ago. I was gonna call you on my lunch break but here you are. The mag just arrived this morning."

A middle-aged lady waved madly, trying to get Tia's attention.

"Hey, can I get some mustard over here?" she cried. Tia ignored the woman.

"I do remember something you might be interested in. Autumn was bragging one day about how she and some dude went down to Mexico and got this date rape drug."

"You mean Rohypnol?" I asked.

"Right. She was so excited—like a kid with the latest Playstation®. I was thinking it was bizarre, you know, a chick with some roofies. I mean, what was she going to do with them? So, I asked her, maybe I was a little outraged, and she just gave me this creepy smile."

"Waitress! Mustard, over here, please."

"Excuse me." Tia left to fetch mustard.

"Autumn gleeful about a date rape drug?" I asked.

"She bragged about it? Must be something bad wrong with that girl. Looks like Caroline Johnson got a second chance," said Gus.

"Not only that, but they're turning the homicide investigation into a publicity stunt." I was beside myself.

"Stars and their spin machines always do that. There's no such thing as bad publicity in that business."

"Jeez."

"Is that your Raggedy Ann doll she's got?" Gus asked. I had shown the doll to Gus ages ago and I wasn't surprised that he'd remembered it. The guy remembered everything. His mind was like one of his super gadgets.

"Sure looks like it," I said.

"You mentioned it last night. Dolls seem to be important to this strange clan," he said. "So, Hector stole Pancho and your Raggedy Ann doll."

"That seems to be the only explanation. Then he ran right over to the performance and gave Autumn the doll in time for the photo op. He could have picked up pink hair on the way back."

"Pink hair?"

"The twelve-year-old he delivered to the Tylers that disappeared as soon as I got her out of the cuffs."

"How could Hector do all those things so fast?" asked Gus.

"It doesn't take long to pick up a runaway. Not when you have a giant cozy SUV and can convince her she'll be connected to people in the movie and music industry."

"After he dropped off the girl, he must have gone back to your place to get the dog. So then, among others Hector is fetch and carry for...The Barb? What do you think he's going to do with the dog?" asked Gus.

"We never figured out what the dog was doing at Autumn's bungalow in the first place. It's got to have something to do with Tommy since he stole Pancho from my place."

"It's the hide-and-seek game, he wants us to connect the missing kid Tommy with Autumn and the Raggedy Ann Doll, it's gotta be something like that," said Gus.

"So...he's giving me a clue. Right, hide-and-seek. I challenged him on that."

Gus chewed on it. I could see the idea working on him.

"I'd say he's winning at this point," said Gus.

"Did you guys run Hector's plates?"

"Of course. It was an Echo Park address. I sent some guys over there and a Mexican family had recently moved in. Never heard of Hector."

Kunda entered the restaurant dressed in black silk; her hair was tightly curled and bounced around her head like something out of a Pre-Raphaelite painting. Her eyes searched over the crowd. When she spotted us, she came over directly. "What do you want to bet the music is loud and that Zombita does a lot of screaming?" I asked Gus.

"Yeah, Kunda could have read the same article herself this morning." Kunda arrived at our table, black silk floating behind her, and slid in next to Gus. I recognized her perfume of rose oil.

Tia quickly dropped off a BLT and two coffees. She raced away then came back with my coffee mugs tightly wrapped in brown paper, placed them inside yet another brown paper bag and handed them to me.

"You just can't get enough of this place, can you?" said Tia.

"Yeah, well, don't rub it in. Want something?" I asked Kunda. "My treat."

I sipped the hot coffee, careful to avoid the wound where my wisdom tooth used to be, and hot liquid slid down my throat like oil through a hot engine.

"Thank you, no. I'm not hungry. I have no appetite whatsoever."

"How 'bout some coffee?" prompted Gus.

"No, really. Nothing."

Tia spun away to her duties in the busy diner.

"So, uh, Kunda. It looks like you have a hundred-percent accuracy rate," I said.

Gus handed her the magazine clipping. Kunda looked at it and started taking deep breaths.

"So, that's it. That's why I had that vision. She certainly looks dead." She looked more closely at the photo. "She has a doll." Gus frowned at me before taking a big chomp out of his BLT. Kunda pointed to the doll with her long, manicured, and ornately ringed finger.

"I noticed," I said.

"And that's not all," said Kunda. She grew very somber, the oracle about to deliver bad news to the king.

"What else?" I asked.

"There's more girls."

Gus stopped for a moment mid-chew.

"You saw them in a vision, too?" I asked.

Kunda clutched a black stone at the end of a necklace and put her head down. When she came back up, there was a timbre in her voice full of dread and loathing.

"It's dark and wet. The wind howls. They're hungry, oh, so hungry. All they know is sleep. Only sleep," she paused.

"That's what I saw. It's real. Please believe me."

"That's not much to go on," I said.

Gus came in full force, "Look, Kunda. If you know something we want to hear it. Telling us your visions don't cut it. Whatever you know, come clean."

"I told you that I would help you and I will. I didn't know the extent that, uh, I didn't know... Listen, I'm telling you everything I've got!"

"The thing is, we appreciate your help, but we have to make a case. We need more than your visions to explain to our captain why we think there are, what did you say, more girls?"

She nodded.

"Okay, more girls being drugged? Held captive? Is that what you're trying to say?"

She nodded.

"And all we can tell the DA is, well, the wind howls. How can you expect us to work a case with such vague information?"

"If I knew more, I would give it to you, I swear! You think I want to carry this kind of karma on my head? The moment I get anything, I'll call you."

"But where are you getting this?" I asked.

"It just comes in. To tell you the truth, I wish it wouldn't sometimes."

Gus finished his BLT without comment. When Tia came back, we got the check and since Kunda didn't want anything we split. Outside the diner, Kunda clutched my arm. "I've never done anything like this before," she said. "I've never faced such evil."

Gus scowled.

"Thanks for your help," I said.

When she walked away, the wind blew up her black silk skirt. She had on black tights underneath and she didn't struggle with the wind, she just let her skirt blow. She looked like a big black flag flapping as she walked down Beverly Boulevard like Hell's own messenger.

"What do you think, Gus?"

"I think you'd have to be able to read her mind to know what's going on in there."

"She knows something," I said.

"What does she know? How? Does she really know it? Is it her intuition? Or is Autumn Riley calling her up for psychic advice? You see the problem here?"

"But she knows about the missing girls. Somethin' ain't right."

The bristles on my back were up.

"It would appear that Zombita is enjoying her new singing career."

"Yeah, not to mention, at our expense."

"About Tia," said Gus.

"I know, forget the bait idea," I said. "You got a phone number for Mrs. Riley on you?"

Gus gave me the number. I dialed it on my cell.

"Mrs. Riley, this is Detective Lambert."

"Hello."

"Have you had contact with your daughter recently?"

"Yes. I have."

"Did you call her or did she call you?"

"Why do you ask, Detective?"

"Do you know where she is?"

"I repeat; why do you ask?"

"Do you believe she's acting on her own behalf? I mean, of her own accord?"

"I'm not sure what you're asking. Can you give me some indication of what's going on? Has something happened recently that I should know about?"

I gave Gus a look expressing my frustration with the conversation.

"Yes, as a matter of fact, something unfortunate has occurred. Autumn's friend, Dani, was found murdered."

"Murdered? Are you sure?"

"Yes, ma'am."

"And you think Autumn had something to do with it?"

"No, ma'am. I wasn't thinking that exactly. There is a concern since the two were friends, and they moved in some of the same circles."

"I see," said Mrs. Riley.

She wasn't giving me any play and that really struck me as strange. Where were those concerned parents that organized to solve the mystery of their daughter's death? This was an iron door of unwillingness. How odd that she thought I suspected Autumn in regard to Dani's murder. Did Mrs. Riley have the same opinion of her daughter as the soap star, Johan Beaks?

"Another thing, Mrs. Riley."

"What's that?"

Though her voice was controlled and even, I felt a distinct note of apprehension.

"You mentioned that your daughter was using her credit cards for psychic readings. Can you tell me if she's had any readings lately?"

There was a pause. "What would that have to do with Dani's death?" Mrs. Riley was desperately hiding something.

"I don't know that there's any connection," I said, "but could I have your permission to check those charges?"

"I'm afraid I can't."

"You can't what?"

"I can't give you permission. I'm sure you know the law, Detective. That account is Autumn's and though we handle much of her financing, she is eighteen years old and an adult. Only she could grant you that."

"Of course. I was only hoping that the account was connected to you and your husband's and in that case, you could legally give me permission."

"I'm sorry, that's not the case."

"Are you still receiving the statements?"

"Uh, yes."

"Do you still open them and send them on to the accountant?"

Another pause.

"Ever notice what she's spending her money on?" I asked.

"Maybe."

"So, you could tell me, if you chose to."

"I could, if I understood why you think it will help in your investigation of Dani's death."

She was probably cursing herself for telling me about the credit charges for the psychic readings. Back then, Mrs. Riley believed her daughter was dead and she wanted to catch the murderer. And now, what did she believe?

"Mrs. Riley, maybe I'm asking the wrong questions here. Let's see...let me ask you something completely different. Was there ever an incident in Autumn's past that caused you and your husband to seek counseling or therapy for her?"

"It's a modern world, detective. Lots of parents seek counseling for their child at one point or another."

"That's true but that's not an answer to my question."

"I already explained to you that Autumn was an extremely intelligent child, with unusual needs. She required special attention." Her voice was a high-tension wire, crackling with nerves.

"My question is in regard to a particular incident. What happened exactly that caused you to seek counseling for Autumn?"

Gus was leaning into me now, as if he might be able to hear Mrs. Riley's answer. A dial tone hummed in my ear. She hung up on me. Or maybe it was my cell phone. It could have disconnected for no apparent reason. They do that sometimes, you know.

"What happened?" asked Gus.

"I think she hung up."

"Damn, you're smooth," said Gus. "It's scary."

A peculiar fear wrapped around my heart and consumed my entire chest.

"What's wrong?" asked Gus.

"I dunno. I'm not feeling too good."

"Oh." He gave me a worried glance.

"I've gotta go see Mary Tyler."

"Ach, that alone would make me feel like shit. I'm coming with."

"No way, Gus. You know how it is. She's not going to give anything up with you sitting there giving her the eagle eye."

CHAPTER EIGHTEEN

THE BUILDING WAS IMMENSE and yellow-brown, reflecting the sun's bright glare. Heat rippled off the concrete surrounding the prison. I'd been to this prison many times before, but never had it seemed so ominous and sad. I thought of all the lost souls sustained, kept in their prison cells, fed, managed, coerced, and controlled. What was the use? I was in a black mood. I don't like hellish hot days. Truth is, I've known some decent women who are ex-cons, and there have even been people on death row who were later found innocent and released. Mary Tyler was certainly not one of those. My job here was to get the location on the victims' bodies. I parked on the side of the building where there was some shade and kept my sunglasses on as I entered Sybil's House.

That's what the inmates call Sybil Brand Institute.

I had to go to the infirmary to see Mary Tyler as she was recuperating from the gunshot wounds, making this visit a hospital call. Apparently, the bullets hadn't struck a major vein or organ, so she was going to live. As investigating detective, I could set up the interview in a room and even be left alone with Mary Tyler. That meant an intimacy that could prove to be illuminating and possibly dangerous. I was counting on both, but I figured she wouldn't be up to much physical activity with her gunshot wounds and all. Heavy machinery clanked and growled and pounded against the head plates of my skull, making for a secure prison hospital and accenting my mood.

A psychology of evil provides a killer like Mary Tyler a unique ability to withstand ordinary investigative techniques because there is no empathy for other human beings. Any attempt to invoke sympathy for the victims or surviving families is a waste of time. I would have to appeal to her selfishness, to her ego. People like Mary are consumed with being in control. They need to dominate the way most people need to draw breath. I made sure I had a full pack of Camel cigarettes before I went in the room which was essentially a large steel cage with a midsized metal table between two metal chairs, all bolted to the concrete floor. There were also steel rings bolted to the floor to which the violent prisoners could be fettered. I sat on one of the metal chairs and waited for them to bring Mary in.

I was in my own thoughts and looked up when I heard her heavy shuffling walk. Her hair was greasy and she had on a short dress made from a blue cotton material. She didn't speak when the guard brought her in. Her hands were shackled together to a chain that ran to another chain shackle arrangement around her ankles. She walked with a slight limp in the leg where I'd shot her. There was a strange lumpiness to her stomach from the bandages. Her legs had layers of fat. The fat above her knee joints swelled out and over. There was a large white-and-beige bandage wrapped around one of her thighs. My first shot. She limped and winced with pain with each step. She could hide things in those folds of flesh if she wanted to. That might come in handy in prison. As she limped into the room, drag pulled her bad leg and she groaned her way to her chair, I tried to imagine her as a little girl dressed in a blue summer dress but was unsuccessful. Her ankles were swollen with gout. She was sporting the plastic flip-flops on her feet that they gave each new inmate and she smelled like bug spray. They must have shot her good with the lice hose when she was admitted. Her face was swollen and bruised around the eyes and I found I took some gratification in that. There was a patch over one eye and the other was bright red with hemorrhage.

"Take off the cuffs," I said to the guard.

"Are you sure, Ms. Lambert? This is some beast here." Yeah, don'cha know it.

"Yes, I'm sure. Leave her in the leg shackles. You can run the chain through the floor ring."

The guard reluctantly removed the cuffs without further question, then waited outside the cell with two other guards. Mary just stood there looking at me. Maybe she wanted to lunge at me and tear my throat out or something. She had been cheated out of my death.

"Have a seat, Mary."

"Why, thank you, I will," she said and dropped her heft onto the metal chair with yet another groan.

I let the silence speak for a while. Her rage built up without me saying a word. Her anger was a palpable thing that filled the room. It roared. I lit a cigarette.

"So, Mary, tell me where the bodies are." "Why? Why should I do that?"

"For the families, Mary." She laughed.

"Fuck the families."

"What happened to you to make you so mean? Huh, Mary? What happened to you that makes you think you have the right to cause others pain?"

"Nothing, that's what happened to me."

"Nothing?"

"Not a thing. But now—now, that I'm the big murderer, the kidnapper, the torturer, well, everybody wants to know my name. I'm going to be famous. I've got four lawyers competing for my case right now. One has already presented me with two different cable television offers and I haven't been in here for twenty-four hours yet. They want to know my side of the story. You want to know why I like to cause others pain? I'll tell you why. For those moments, those days, weeks, sometimes months that person is in my world, I have their undivided attention. If I fart, they're interested in it. Every move I make is extremely important to them. Together, me and that person, we're all about my next thought, my next whim. It means something to them whether I frown or smile. Hey, you know what? Right now, you're interested in me, aren't you? Tough bitch, smart bitch. You remember when you first saw me at the bar at De Sade's Cage? You looked at me like you were smelling shit. I remember that, when we were sitting at the bar, you looked at me like I was shit on your shoe. But, later, in the ladies' room, you had a very deep concern, you were very involved with me. Got your ass kicked, too! 'Course, that was nothin' compared to our little ride in the van. Now, that was an intimate experience. We know

now, don't we? But at first, at the bar, you couldn't even bring yourself to look at me. Now, I'm the fucking center of your life. Hmmph."

She put her nose up in the air in a freakish portrayal of a snooty celebrity.

"For the purpose of this conversation, I will need you to waive your right to an attorney or I won't be able to talk with you."

"I waive it for now, but later I might just take one of these lawyers up on his offer."

"Okay, but anything you say to me can and will be held against you. Is that understood?"

"Understood."

I offered her a cigarette, pulling it long for her out of the box. She snatched it and I lit it for her. She gave me a mean crooked smile for my gesture and took a long evil drag on the cigarette, making the end flare red.

"Let's see here," I said softly. "What can I offer you? Your life? Hmmm? Okay. Maybe if you help me locate the bodies and we blame the whole thing on your brother I can stop them from sticking you with the big needle. Do you want to live, Mary?"

"Not much."

"Your brother planned everything, didn't he? He was the director, and what were you? The one with the gaffer's tape." The put-down didn't really sit well with her. She sniffed and twisted her mouth into a sneer but didn't say anything. "Oh, but that's right, you were practically an actor in the films. Actually driving the action, so to speak. So you were talent after all. Then again, all we ever saw were your hands and they look an awful lot like Johnny's hands. In fact, it would probably be hard to prove otherwise."

"You want me to turn on Johnny? That's why you're here? There's not much point in that now, bitch."

"All right, you'll both get the needle." I stubbed out my cigarette and lit another one while I figured out another angle 'cuz this one was not working, not at all.

Mary's jaw dropped and her eyes narrowed as if she could see something in my brain. "Where you from? The South? Ain't no death penalty here in California."

She had me there. I was from Missouri, where I once feared my own death by lethal injection. Some said it was justifiable homicide, but there were others of a different opinion. Mary had discovered the most vulnerable and hidden aspect of my past. I had revealed it to her.

"Oh, now Mary, you know you can't count on that. As long as you're on death row, the laws can change and not to your favor. In fact, I happen to know that they're working on a newfangled death box, all fancy and efficient to put you completely out of your misery."

"What do I care? I hear you get treated much better on death row than you do with the lifers."

"Interesting to me that you're so well informed about that. Okay, you got me. If you don't care about living, I suppose there's nothing I can offer you. I'm at your mercy and I've seen what that's like."

"That's right."

I made a point of not looking at her—bowed my head in defeat.

"I bet you did all the digging," I said. "I bet Johnny didn't help at all."

"You think you're so smart. Know everything. You think I'll turn on Johnny? You're too late. You are too damn late. You can't begin to comprehend how little I care. You don't know shit." She hot-boxed the cigarette with a long drag and it burned down to the filter.

"Help me to understand then—feel free to correct me where I'm wrong. Let's see if I have this straight. You don't care about living, don't care if you are put to death. But it's a point of pride or something with you that you won't tell me where the bodies are? You say you don't give a damn about anything, but that's not true. Holding back that information is important to you. You see how I might be confused?"

"I could break your neck like a chicken."

I knew she wanted to hurt me. She was a great void, a black pit, empty without the pain of others to fill her. But she was used to doing things at Johnny's direction. "That's right, Mary, you could. So, why don'cha?"

She didn't say anything, just eyed my smokes.

"Here, have another cigarette."

I pushed the pack and lighter across the table to her. She took out a cigarette and lit it, gave me those pale pig eyes of hers. No, I'd seen pigs with more soul than her. I couldn't think of a creature low enough to compare to Mary Tyler. People are found of calling the Mary Tylers of the world animals, but animals would never do the things she had done. She drew the smoke into her lungs and narrowed her eyes at me.

"You know Mary, this conversation sucks. You're boring. You got some info? If not, I got things to do."

I stood up like I was about to leave and caught the brief flash of panic in her. For the tiniest instant a hurt peeked out of those stony eyes. She didn't want me to go, to reject her. I could feel it as strongly as I had felt the rage rise in her. Dear Lord, this creature was in mortal terror of rejection. The human soul is unfathomable in its agonies and twistings.

"See you in the death chamber, Mary. Guard!"

"They're off the fourteen, in Lancaster."

She said it quick; I barely heard it. The guard hurried toward me. I motioned for him to hold off and he did, but he stood attentively at the cage door, eyeing Mary like she might slip out of her leg shackles and kill me.

"Where?"

"In a field."

I sat back down. "Where's the field?"

"It's out at the end of this old highway nobody uses anymore. You could never find it on your own. They're all there. You happy now? You got what you wanted?"

"I wouldn't say that I was happy, no. What highway? What's the number?"

"I don't think it has a number, it's close to the Air Force Base."

"Twentynine Palms. Where those dried lakes are?"

"Exactly."

"That was smart. Who thought of that? You or Johnny?"

"I was stationed there a long time ago."

"You were in charge of the burials. That's vague, though, Mary. Out by the dried lakes? I could spend the rest of my life looking around out there and not find anything. I think you're lyin' to me."

"Try the south side of Jackrabbit Hill."

"I will. I'll try it." I leaned back in my chair like I was just getting relaxed. "How long have you been doing what Johnny said?"

"Always. I've always done what Johnny told me to."

"Where did you get the kids, how did you find them?"

"We had a supplier." ·

"Who?"

"I don't know. Johnny took care of that part."

"Did he ever say it was a street pimp, or anything like that?"

"He never said. They'd just show up at the place. Like the one with pink hair. Somebody sent them over."

"Did Johnny call someone on the phone?"

"Johnny is too smart for that."

"I don't know about that, Mary. He made mistakes. Dani was a mistake. That's how I found you."

"Well, that was because the supplier was trying to retire on us and we were desperate."

"The supplier stopped? After how many years?" Mary was reluctant to say. "After how many years?" I demanded.

She rolled her creepy eyes around the room. I wanted to scream at her, beat it out of her. But I couldn't go there. That's what she wanted, to have impact on me, to have control over me, get an emotional reaction.

"Okay," I said, "I got business that needs attending to."

Once again, I gathered the smokes and my lighter, stood up. The guard went to unlock the door.

"About ten years."

I stopped, gave the guard a signal to hold off. He gave me a frustrated look back. I turned to Mary, placing the cigarettes and the lighter back on the table.

"Why did the supplier stop?"

"I don't know. Johnny said the guy was making a career change."

"When did he stop?"

"Six months ago."

That was exactly when the young women started to disappear; Hector made a career change.

"And that's why you did Dani?"

"Johnny wanted one more and the supplier wouldn't fork one over. Then the supplier said, okay, he had one, but we had to go to her and that she was older than we liked."

I sat back down.

"Dani."

"Right. But Johnny liked her anyway because she looked like a boy. Johnny liked to do boys. I didn't want to go out of the house, but Johnny made me. He thought we could leave the body on the backlot, that it would mummify before anyone would find it."

"I see."

"Johnny told the supplier he had to come up with one more after Dani. After the pink one, we were going to be on our own."

"How much money did you pay for this service?"

"Ten years ago we paid two hundred bucks a kid. Over the years, the price went up to five hundred and then the last few were a thousand apiece."

"Did Johnny know the guy who delivered them? Was the guy who brought the girl with the pink hair your supplier?"

"I don't know. I didn't even see the guy, never did. I don't answer the door and I don't like to go out much."

"Why don't you like to go out?"

"I'm agoraphobic. Sure as hell, I leave the house and end up in this place."

"Well, now you don't have to worry about going out ever again."

"If I do get out of here, you're the first person I'm going to visit."

"That's a pretty feeble threat, Mary. Anything else you can tell me?"

"That's all for you today. Have to save something for the movie."

"Okay then. That's all you got for me? I guess I better go ask Johnny."

"It's too late." Her smile was a leer.

"What do you mean?"

"Johnny's dead."

"What?"

"He killed himself."

"I don't think so."

"Yeah, he's probably dead already by now."

I found myself fighting off an overwhelming feeling of gloom. We finally catch the person who can be held responsible and actually answer some of the questions we have and then he has to go and kill himself. It's so much better to be pissed off than depressed. "Why do you say that?" I asked.

"He can't handle jail. Not suited to it. He's too sensitive. Fragile. He's dead now. I know it. I can feel it. I had to talk him out of suicide all the time, practically every day. He was sick with liver disease and bad diabetes. He won't make it in jail. I won't be there to tell him not to do it. He was my twin, you know."

"What about you? You going to commit suicide?"

She shrugged. "I have to think about that."

The two of them could've offed themselves a long time ago and saved a lot of nice people unnecessary misery.

"Do people get high off that needle before they go?"

"I don't think so. I think it's merely relaxing."

"You could come back and interview me some more, you know," she said, "I could tell you details."

"Maybe I'll take you up on that. Right now, I need to know who your supplier was. It seems you can't help me with that. Thank you anyway, Mary. Goodbye."

"Yeah," she grunted. "Fuck you."

I reached for the cigarettes and lighter and felt the solid force of her body as she leapt at me. She caught a handful of my hair and pulled me straight down onto my back. I was flat on the table with the wind knocked out of me. I looked up at her enraged swollen face. She pulled me across the table and down at an angle; I was stunned, slow to react. I smelled hair burning. She'd lit my hair with the cigarette lighter! I felt my body going headfirst toward the floor. All I could think was: *No way am I going to let my head hit that floor.* Using all the momentum she had created plus my stomach muscles, I pulled my legs up and over, then kicked her hard with both of my feet in her face. The softness of her jowls felt strange under my shoes. She fell back against the wall. I put my hands down to stop my fall and did a backward walk over, back-kicking her on the way down, this time in the breast and then again, in the groin. The fact that her feet were shackled to the ground meant she couldn't hold her balance and she went down on her ass. I was on my feet and she was coming up fast.

The guards rushed in and beat Mary with their batons while I slapped my hands against the small fire in my hair. One of the guards zapped Mary with a stun gun. I was still patting my head and trying to pull myself together as they did everything they could to subdue her. I'm telling you, crazy people are unnaturally strong. I think it must have something to do with their adrenal glands. I snatched up my cigarettes and lighter from the floor and made my exit, leaving the sounds of Mary struggling with the guards behind me.

I called over to see how Johnny was doing in the men's facility. Mary was right. He'd hanged himself.

CHAPTER NINETEEN

Two hours later, Gus and I stood on a forlorn road in Lancaster, two hours northeast of Los Angeles. Lots of transplants from Oklahoma, Arkansas, and various parts of the Midwest, descendants of the dustbowl in the thirties. People like the Joads family in John Steinbeck's *The Grapes of Wrath*. There were no jackrabbits anywhere near Jackrabbit Hill and not much grass to speak of. Ominous dark clouds formed and moved across the gray sky and the smell of ozone in the air threatened rain. Jackrabbit Hill must have been man-made as it was the only hill for miles.

Dusk was about to fall and a heavy weariness overtook me.

A determined forensics group, men and women in blue plastic work-suits, was hard at work searching for eighteen graves. A photographer took photos of tire tracks and any other detail that looked promising. Two people dressed in the blue plastic were going over the area with metal detectors. A helicopter flew by overhead and I knew they were using thermal infrared photography to detect the heat of decomposing bodies. On the ground, a forensic archeologist probed the ground with a "tee" stick, a steel rod four to five feet long with a tee handle on one end and a sharp point on the other. Whenever she hit a soft spot, another forensic scientist would bring over a vapor detector to recognize body gases as a result of decomposition. So far they had located six graves.

"Only twelve more to go," I said. Gus merely shook his head.

A lizard appeared at my feet, looked up at me, obviously unused to humans. I stared back at it and the lizard scurried away. Probably got a bad vibe off me. I looked out at the expanding horizon.

Desert flatlands spread out as far as I could see. Where could a lizard hide in country like this?

He'd have to just dig a hole and hide, I guessed.

Mounds of dirt grew around us. Every four to six inches of dirt had to be sifted through screens in case there was any evidence. The botanist on the scene gave information on the vegetation, how long ago it had been damaged, what season of the year the ground had been disturbed. Each grave had a different history. I saw a rusty lunch box with Pebbles and Bamm-Bamm depicted on the front. In the hidden treasure of another was a pink three-ring binder. The child's name, Donna Jennings, was written in her own handwriting on the inside of the pink binder with blue magic marker. At another grave, laminated student identification showed a smiling young girl. It was too much to bear and it was easy to understand why people don't like to think about missing children. The detailed reality of their brutal deaths is horrific, the only blessing being that we'd be able to identify each victim. Despite what they say, ignorance is not bliss. Not for the victims nor their families and not for the future victims. Piles of bones began to appear next to the mounds of dirt. The dull white contrasted against the freshly dug earth. The small bones sang out a wail of accusation that pierced the shared consciousness of every detective and forensic worker there.

Eventually, all eighteen graves were located.

A crime scene artist sketched the story in detail with both plan and elevation views. Each was in a different stage of excavation. Though it was cool, he was sweating and his fingers were white with tension. I watched over his shoulder for a moment and when he looked up at me there was intensity in his eyes.

"Never did a gravesite quite like this," he said.

"Me either," I said.

My stomach twisted into a knot and I patted the guy on the back then walked over to where Gus was having a smoke outside the perimeter of the crime scene.

"Excellent work, Joan," said Gus.

"What would have been excellent? To save them. I find digging up the graves low on my list of accomplishments. They had a supplier, Gus."

"What?"

"The Tylers didn't drive around and abscond with kids. I mean, who would get into a car with them? They had them delivered. Hector dropped off that one so maybe it was him. Either that or he's just a deliveryman. Mary said the supplier quit on them and that was why they went for Dani. It was a definite break in the pattern."

"A supplier. A pimp, right?"

"I guess. Remember Gilda? With the long dress and long gloves like Rita Hayworth? She said something to me about the young ones getting killed. She meant the runaways working the streets. She even mentioned a mysterious graveyard and she said something about them getting set on fire. Apparently, it's like a legend, a spooky story they whisper to each other. People know about it."

"A subculture knows about it. Folks whose everyday life is a horror story. Bring her in, ask her if she recognizes any of the kids after forensics matches them to their missing files and verifies each with the odontologist. We'll see if we can find a pimp or something that connects them."

"Will do. Hector is definitely one connection. When we get back, let's go over the Tyler phone list again, huh? Mary said Johnny never called the supplier, but maybe she's wrong."

"How else would they communicate?"

"I don't know. You're the one who is up on those new tech things."

"They're already checking out the computer," said Gus. "Nothing so far. Maybe they just delivered the kids every once in a while, no schedule, and had a pick up for the cash. They could have had a meeting place."

"Could be. Maybe De Sade's Cage. The Barb took money from the Tylers that night I was there."

We were silent for a moment. Gus peered at the hole in my already short hair where Mary had set me on fire.

"So, what are you going to do about that hair?"

"I guess I'm gonna have to get a crew cut."

"People will think you're a butch."

"I don't care what people think."

"I had the impression it was terribly important to you."

"I'm over it."

Janice Worth, a forensic archeologist in her late forties, came over to us just then.

"I'm already recognizing a pattern of blunt force to the head and the femur bone in several of the bodies, probably with a hammer." She put her hand to her own head of short blond curls. I nodded and Gus looked at me. "Some bones display evidence of having been burned. Can't say yet if it was post mortem," she said. "The boys." She stood there looking at us after she said it.

"Thanks, Janice," I said.

"Oh, you're welcome." She was struggling to contain her emotions.

Gus put an arm around her shoulders and Janice sighed heavily.

I merely stood silently beside them, looking toward the rest of the toiling forensic team as they continued with their horrific task. A soft mist fell and became rain in a manner of seconds. We all leapt into urgent action to raise several tents in order to protect the graveyard and the precious bones of the unknown children we had unearthed. I was stung by the fact that our urgency and protection came too late. I let tears fall because in the rain they weren't so recognizable and I couldn't stop them if I had tried.

CHAPTER TWENTY

G ET OUT OF MY office with this shit," said Satch.
"No, sir. I really think we should get a search warrant on Autumn Riley's credit card."

"And do something about that hair, will ya? You look like a maniac."

"If you prefer, I could pull this Barb guy in."

Gus stood silently in the doorway. He looked down at the floor and did not argue on my behalf.

"You, of all people, should know better," said Satch. "After all that crap with you and Carl? Your first case back on the job and you want to play chicken. This is tough times for the police department, Joan. Goddammit. We're under a magnifying glass. Every single investigation is being watched. I can't okay this, and I won't. Just forget it."

"But Satch, she's not the same girl, I'm telling you. I know he's got her on drugs. She really looks like a zombie in this picture, like she's dead or something."

"That's not evidence of anything, it's a fashion statement."

"But what about their past history? The S&M music videos?"

"Put it together for me."

"Okay. Dani and Autumn both have a connection with The Barb, he got them the raspberry photo gig." Satch frowned. "It was a modeling gig. Red fibers from The Barb's motel room were found at the Autumn Riley crime scene and The Barb's hair matched the short blond hair from that same crime scene. Black hairs from a dog that went missing with a ten-year-old boy were also found there."

"It's not a crime scene anymore, Joan. Autumn Riley is alive and The Barb is her manager so his hair in her bungalow doesn't mean a damn thing. Your strongest case is the dog hairs, but how do they connect The Barb? They don't, do they? Everybody in the neighborhood said that dog was a stray. Autumn may have let the dog in her house when The Barb wasn't even there. You have no other evidence. The Barb being a slime ball is not enough, Joan. His influence over Autumn is not enough. Walk into MCA or Rhino Records, any of them! You'll see fifty success stories and the kids are all on drugs and look like they're dead. It's called Gothic or some shit, I don't know. So, she knew Dani, did a photo shoot with her. The Tylers went to De Sade's Cage same as The Barb. We can't go to the DA with that. You got no crime there. Give it up. You go near Autumn Riley or her manager and it will be a public relations fiasco. You might as well turn in your badge now."

"Satch, please. I'm telling you, I saw Hector bring that girl to the Tylers. Hector who hangs out at Hollywood parties, who stole the dog from my home, you don't see the connection to Tommy and all the missing girls?"

"I do, sort of. But where is the girl with the pink hair to corroborate? If we didn't have her on the Tyler video, you'd be in big trouble right now. You can't prove that Hector stole the dog, can you? Can you?"

I shook my head no.

"So, consider it an order, Joan. Forget The Barb and Autumn Riley for now. If you like, you can meet with the investigators on the case of the missing boy and get up to speed. Continue your work with Mark O'Malley on the missing girls. You did a good job with Mary Tyler. A fine day's work, but first go get some rest, you look like hell. Do something about that hair. You can't represent Special Section like that. People'll think you just escaped the asylum or something. Settle down, here."

"Just tell him," said Gus.

"Tell me what?" asked Satch.

"I talked with Mrs. Riley," I said.

"Oh, Jesus."

"She said she was in contact with Autumn but wouldn't tell me anything about Autumn's location, whether or not she thought Autumn was acting of her own accord, nothing."

"So what does that prove?"

"I got a hunch, you know, by the tone of her voice, and I asked her if there had ever been a significant event that caused them to seek counseling for Autumn Riley and she hung up on me."

"Are you crazy, Joan? Look, if you called my house and asked the same question about my son, I'd hang up on you, too."

"But, sir. There was also an incident with Autumn Riley in an acting class with three of the missing girls..."

"What?"

"Autumn knew three of the missing girls. They were all in an acting class."

"What kind of incident?"

"They got into a fight over some petty, egotistical thing."

"And that means what to you?"

"I suspect that Autumn may have had a hand in their disappearance."

"And you get that idea from what?"

I was tired and incoherent, not making a good case.

"Joan. Listen to me, you're losing your grip. Do what I say or you'll regret it. Your career is in danger and you can't see it. It's a goddam shame. Hell, I'm going to refer you for mandatory therapy if you don't shape up right now. A significant event. That's clever. Can't wait for the phone call I'm gonna get from the chief on that one. Gus, how can you let her go off like that? You're her senior. It's on you as her supervisor."

Gus raised an eyebrow but didn't argue.

I stood up to make one last point when Satch went gray, all white spots and static. My gray hands reached out towards Satch, then everything went black. When I came to, there was a circle of faces above me. I recognized Satch, Gus, and a couple guys from Robbery and more from Autos. They all had worried looks on their faces and I realized I was on the floor. The back of my head didn't feel so great.

"Get the paramedic," I heard Satch say. "She needs to go on medical leave, she has no business being here." Gus and the other guys agreed with Satch.

"Okay," I heard myself say, "you're right, I'll go home. Sorry, guys."

"You stay right there, don't even try to stand, just lie there," said Satch. "The paramedic will take you to the hospital and the doctor will tell you when you can go home. And listen to me carefully, Joan. Forget any case for now. Take care of yourself. You're no good to us on the floor."

"Yes, sir," I said. "Whatever you say."

After a gurney ride through the halls of Parker, during which I waved and cracked jokes, I got to go on an ambulance ride to USC. In a special area reserved for cops, I was given particular attention, and a dainty woman doctor ordered a CAT scan.

Finally, I found myself sitting in the doctor's office in a chair beside her desk. I looked at her certificate. Her name was Djiersinsky. She had an unhurried and warm disposition. She wore her hair in a feathery hip style that framed her face, which was remarkably youthful. I wondered what it was like to be her, so pretty and petite, living in her ordered world.

"The thing we are concerned about is a subdural hematoma," she said sweetly. "That doesn't seem likely after all this time, but we had to make sure. Your CAT scan looks good."

"Does that mean I'm okay?"

"You seem to be. Did you eat today?" Her voice had just the right combination of concern and disapproval. "I can get you some food from the kitchen, right now. What would you like?"

"No offense, Doc, but I prefer something other than hospital food. I'll get something to eat right away. Girl Scout's honor." I held up three fingers like a girl scout, hoping to win her over.

"You should rest, take it easy for at least a week, come in and see me before you go back to work. Okay?"

"You bet, I'll do that," I said.

She gave me some aspirins and water in a paper cup. I swallowed it all down as instructed. She smiled at me and wrote something down in my medical chart. *Patient is rough around the edges but obedient.*

"If you start getting dizzy or have severe headaches that won't go away, I want to see you immediately. Understand?"

"Right."

"I'll send in the paperwork to your department requiring you take the week off. You don't have to worry about that and I don't want you to work at home. No stress at all, understand? Just rest. And try to take it easy on your head."

"Sure, Doc, no blunt objects and no fires."

"Please."

"Listen, maybe you should write me a prescription so I can take some antibiotics or something."

"For what?"

I opened my mouth and showed her where Mary Tyler had pulled out my wisdom tooth."

"Good God. What happened?"

"Somebody took a souvenir."

"You need to have that taken care of by an oral surgeon."

"Can I pass on that for now? I just want to make sure it doesn't get infected."

"Only if you promise to go next week."

"Sure, I'll do as you say."

She wrote a prescription and eyed me suspiciously. "You should make an appointment for that right away," she said.

"I will, but maybe not today."

"I'll have the nurse fill the prescription for you. Do you have someone who can pick you up?"

She positioned her desk phone toward me. Our eyes met and after a fleeting moment of feeling sorry for myself I dialed and waited. The phone rang five times. I was about to hang up and call a taxi when Eddy answered, huffing and puffing.

"Hello?" he nearly bellowed.

"Hi, Eddy? Can you pick me up at the hospital? I've got a bump on my head and they say I can't drive home."

"Joan?"

"Yeah."

"Where are you?"

"USC, neuro something in Dr. Djiersinsky's office. Just go to emergency and ask for me, they'll tell you how to find me. Hurry, before they force-feed me hospital food."

"I'll be right there," he said and hung up.

CHAPTER TWENTY-ONE

WE WERE OUTSIDE ABBOT'S pizza on Abbot Kinney Boulevard, about three blocks from my house. It's a hot spot in the funky part of Venice. Merchants of cool hope to hook in the fresh-faced bored young people. Eddy went inside the New York-styled joint to order us pizza with chicken and spinach. I stayed behind in his car, one of those tiny insect-looking electric things. I got antsy and went next door to Abbot's Habit, a coffee bar. A sweet German girl named Casey owns the place. I entered, sat on a stool at the coffee bar, and took in the aroma of coffee beans from all over the world. The place was empty but someone was banging things around in back and I figured it was Casey. She came to the front carrying a tray of coffee cups. When she saw me, she looked startled, alarmed.

"Hey, Casey. Anybody been in looking for me?" I asked.

"Joan, Jesus... Are you okay?"

"I'm fine. Answer the question, will ya?"

"Oh, hmmmm, a big guy?"

"Real buff with long black hair?"

She nodded and wrinkled her nose at me. "Are you sure you're okay?"

"Did you tell him where I lived?"

"Hell no. But you know, I did catch him behind the counter, I thought he was ripping us off but he said he dropped some change and it rolled back here. There wasn't any money missing from the till when I checked it."

"Do you have my address written down somewhere, you know, for home deliveries?"

"Yes, it's here in this recipe box… Oh, was that what he was doing back here?"

"Is my address still in there?"

Casey checked her little file box under the letter L. My card wasn't in there.

"Oh, I'm sorry, Joan. He didn't hurt you, did he?"

"No, it's okay, really. Don't replace the card, okay? You know where I live, right?"

"Of course. I'm really sorry. Is he bothering you?"

"I'm gonna handle him." I started towards the door.

"Well, good luck. Feel better."

"Thanks."

I was back in the car and waiting before Eddy came back with the pizza.

"Popeye's special, just like you requested," Eddy said.

"Good."

"I'm glad you called me, Joan."

"Me, too," I said and let a silent moment go by. He was staring at me, sort of like he was in shock or something. I guess I looked really bad. "Can we go now?" I asked. "The pizza's getting cold."

He started the car, revved the engine such as it was, and took off through the streets of Venice headed for my place without my having to direct him. The pizza wafted a fragrance up my nose like in a cartoon and it smelled divine.

"Funny car. You're such the environmental activist."

"Yesssss, I am."

He looked at me as if he were prepared for an insult. He had parked and we both got out of the car and made our way into my tiny house.

"Is everything you do, like a political statement?" I asked.

"I try to live at one with my beliefs. Don't you?"

"Yeah, I try."

"Does it offend you that I'm not supporting Saudi Arabia's number one industry?"

"Not really. Are you Jewish?"

"No, I'm merely intelligent. You don't really think I should drive around in a gas-guzzling SUV like everybody else in LA, do you?"

"You're funny, you know that?"

"I'm so pleased you think so," he said, and he was smiling like he really was pleased.

I handed him the pizza while I got my keys and unlocked the door.

"I hope you're not some kind of anti-American," I said, my back to him.

"No, I love my country," he said as he leaned his chest into my back. I could feel his breath on my ear.

"Fiercely. I'm just anti-bullshit. Is that okay?"

"Sure, that works." I didn't let on what else was working.

We entered the front door of my house and we both went directly to the kitchen. I grabbed two twenty-four-ounce bottles of beer. Japanese. I like to keep a supply of the stuff. It goes great with pizza and chili.

"I'm not so sure such a large bottle of beer is good for a concussion, Joan."

"Concussion? It was probably low blood sugar."

"You got whacked on the head with a hammer."

"Who told you that?"

"Doesn't take a genius to figure it out."

"How did you know it was a hammer?"

"Okay, I read the file when the doc wasn't looking."

"Oh."

"Sorry. Just the way I am."

"I understand. Eddy, I'm drinkin' this beer and you're not going to stop me."

"All right, but don't die on me, okay?"

"It's a deal."

I took a bite out of my pizza, careful to chew only on the good side of my mouth, and slipped the rest of the pizza into the oven. Then we went into the living room where I put the DVD *Face/Off* with Nicolas Cage and John Travolta in the player. It's one of my favorites and I've watched it at least a dozen times. I think it's based on an old thirties movie I saw once as a kid on late-night television. I liked the old one, too, but don't remember the title.

I went into the bedroom, put on long-john pajamas, and got a blanket. When I came out, Eddy had taken a place on the leather couch and gotten comfortable. We sat there on the couch munching pizza, swilling beer, and generally having a good ol' time. Bit by bit we got closer and closer until finally I ended up falling asleep with my head in his lap, him stroking my hair, what was left of it. I woke up later to find Eddy gazing at me with what I took to be loving eyes.

"When are you going to finish your mother's paintings?"

I looked through hazy eyes at the paintings and sighed. "I don't know, when I get a free moment, maybe. Don't worry about it."

"Okay, fine with me. Why do you like this movie so damn much?" he asked.

"Because it's good," I said. "Hey, wake me up every once in a while to make sure I don't fall into a coma, all right?"

"I thought you said it was just low blood sugar."

"Just in case, okay?"

"You bet, babe."

I didn't see the end of the movie, but I know what happens. The good guy and the bad guy trade faces and go live in each other's worlds. Something about that was appealing to me. I was dreaming that I was both the bad and the good guy and had become completely confused when Eddy woke me up and walked me into the bedroom, put me to bed under the covers. He kissed my cheek and returned to the living room. I watched his form walk out of my bedroom and realized I had put my trust in a man I hardly knew. I was a regular Blanche DuBois. I immediately conked out.

I slept hard and woke up to a bright light. Someone held open one of my eyelids. Eddy. He was checking on me as I had requested, making sure I didn't slip into a coma or anything. I groaned in protest. He patted me on the cheek and disappeared. I fell back to sleep and dreamt that I was riding in a little yellow bumper car. My hair was long like my mother's and it was softly whipping around my head in a gentle breeze.

I was deep in sleep when I heard a loud bang that sounded like a ferocious wind had blown in my front door. I grabbed my gun from under my pillow and crept up to the bedroom doorway, gun first, to see Carl pointing his Berretta on Eddy. Eddy was standing in the middle of the living room clad only in jeans, holding his hands straight up.

I was relieved Eddy wasn't in his underwear or worse, naked.

"Carl? What are you doing?" I forced my voice to sound calm, matter-of-fact.

"Who is this guy?"

"He's my friend, he's watching out for me."

"That's my job."

"Once upon a time, Carl."

"I heard you were hurt and I came here and…and…"

Carl was looking at the paintings with a rather confused expression on his face. I moved from the doorway and into the living room.

"Get out, Carl. Go home, do you hear me? Go home."

My Smith & Wesson now pointed at his big-barreled chest.

"Who the fuck're you, anyway?" Carl asked Eddy.

"Nobody special."

"What kind of car is that you drive?" Eddy looked at me then back to Carl.

"It's electric."

I crossed the room and stood between Eddy and Carl so that Carl's Berretta was now pointed at my chest. I aimed right back at him smack dab between those sweet eyes of his. I was ready to shoot, at the same time praying to God I wouldn't have to.

"Carl, if you don't put down your weapon I'm going to shoot you dead. Do you understand?"

His face filled with shame; his body sagged in defeat. Without a word, he holstered the gun and walked out. I followed, my gun still steady on him. He turned back to me.

"Sorry about the door."

"Don't worry about it." The Smith & Wesson was now in his face. "Could've been worse."

He snorted. My gun still on him, he moved out the doorway and I followed him, my bare feet on the walkway, all the way to his car. He opened the car door, reached in, and pulled out a paper bag.

"Gus gave me these to bring to you. He said you forgot them in his car and he sort of suggested I use it as an excuse to come see you, to check on you. You know, a little surprise visit."

"Oh, I see." I recognized the brown bag wrapping from the breakfast place, my replacement diner mugs—a great irony, that.

"I just wasn't prepared for you to have company. It threw me off. I thought I could come and take care of you."

"Carl, you gotta get this: you can't take care of me anymore. Your chance for that is gone. You have to move on. It's different now. You have to accept that. Your job is to take care of Debbie now. Give her the surprises. I bet she digs that sort of thing."

My gun was still on him. He reached out with the brown package of diner mugs. I took it from him and held it against my chest.

"You don't have to keep pointing that gun at me, you know."

I put the gun down by my side. "I don't feel safe with you anymore. I don't trust you. And I won't. Not ever again. It's over, Carl."

"All right, Joan. I get it, I guess. Are those your paintings?"

"They're my mother's."

"Your mother's? You never told me she was an artist."

"You never asked."

"Where did those paintings come from?"

"My aunt sent them to me. I don't know why."

"Joanie, I need for us to be friends."

"I don't think I can do that. Trust is a big issue for me and that's been shot all to hell."

"You're the only one I can talk to."

"What's wrong with Debbie? She's a good woman, seems to have a fierce love thing going for you. I like that. You can trust that she has your back. I mean, it seems like a pretty good foundation for a relationship. A strong foothold to start with."

"But you and me, we have so much history together, Joan. How many times have we saved each other's lives? How many times have we done the right thing? How many bad guys have we put away? You can't even count 'em, that's how many. Too numerous to mention. That's how many."

Tears came out of his eyes. And before I knew it, my eyes were filled to the brim.

"Well, yeah, but things change, Carl. There's things about me you don't know. Secrets that I've kept from you about...about which... Look, you've done some things...that remind me of, um...things that are similar to some very bad history... Oh, please. Go now, Carl.

I'm tired, that's all the talking for today. Okay? I really don't feel all that great."

"Okay, I'm going to go now. Maybe I understand what you're trying to say. Maybe I don't, but even if we can't be together, I'd like for us to have coffee or even breakfast sometime."

"I don't know, Carl."

"Don't decide now. Just consider the possibility."

"Okay, I'll consider the possibility."

"Thank you, Joanie. Maybe one day I'll earn your trust back."

"Sometimes things just get destroyed, Carl, and there's no bringing them back."

He nodded. "Just consider the possibility."

"Right. I'll do that."

He got in his Mach I, pulled away, and roared down the alley. "She's A Brick House" blasted out of the car windows.

The alley pit bulls barked in retaliation and I stood there softly shaking my aching head.

I walked back into the house, my gun at my side, bag of mugs in my other hand.

Inside, Eddy had completely recovered and was grinning from ear to ear. He eyed the package clutched to my chest.

"You sure have a lot of visitors."

I put the bag of mugs down on the kitchen table with a thud. I looked around the room searching for a short explanation but didn't know where to begin and settled on, "Are you okay?"

"I'm fine. What about you?"

"I'm tired. I need some more sleep."

I walked back to the front door and tried to close it, but the wood holding the lock contraption in the doorframe was completely destroyed. Eddy came to my side and looked at the door.

"I'll guard the door, don't worry. You go on back to bed."

"Thanks. Sorry, about all this."

"Get some sleep."

⊪ ⊪ ⊪

THE NEXT MORNING, I woke to hear the shop sounds of Eddy fixing the front door. I felt amazingly refreshed and energetic. An unfamiliar feeling of hope filled my chest. I brushed my teeth and inspected the shocking wound in my mouth and popped one of my prescribed antibiotics. When the aroma of roasted coffee went up my nose and pleasantly tickled my brain, I figured Eddy must have prepared it and apparently he liked it strong. I followed the aroma into the kitchen.

"Look, we're alive!" Eddy said and poured me a cup of coffee in one of the two new diner mugs.

He sat down at my kitchen table still clad only in his jeans. Our fingers touched when he handed me my coffee, creating an electrifying response in my body. I tried not to let on, but I don't think I was successful.

"Thanks for fixing the door. I'm sorry about Carl."

"Don't apologize, I have a sneaking suspicion it's not your fault. I half don't blame the guy."

He grinned at me. I just looked at him with mild disbelief. I was impressed by how he handled Carl.

"Hey, did you know you have an opossum in your oak tree?"

"Oh, that's right. Was he friendly to you?"

"Not really. Mostly, he played dead."

"Well, don't feel bad. They do that, you know."

He grinned some more. I sipped coffee, wrapping my hands around the perfectly designed mug.

"Look," I said, "I need to go out for a while, make a few runs."

"For what?" he asked, "You've got me, I'll drive you anywhere you wanna go. I'm your vehicle, baby."

His masculine energy seemed to bounce off the walls of my kitchen. I was used to being alone in my home. His eyes bore through my resistance to him. He was the alpha male and his attraction toward me had not dimmed.

"How long is that gonna last?" I asked.

"Forever, if you want."

"Aw, come on."

"It's not like I have a job, Joan. I'm available, I just have to get my workout in and a rally here and there, some environmental espionage now and then."

"You're making fun of yourself."

"I have to do that sometimes," he said.

"Why?"

"Because otherwise things get to me."

Eddy stood up and came toward me and pulled me into him.

"You're taking advantage of me when I'm in a weakened state," I said.

"You're damn right, I am," he said, and he kissed me gently but it was good and I let him. It wasn't long before he led me back into my bedroom and I was out of my pajamas. He inspected the knife scars on my back and arm, tracing them with his fingers and then his lips. He took a good look at my head and face injuries and where Mary had burned my hair.

"That isn't looking so good."

"Don't hurt me," I said.

"That's a two-way street," he whispered in my ear.

I trembled when he caressed me, my body transforming into electricity with a kind voltage. I was an injured animal and Eddy held me in a manner more protective than a mother's. The caution between us made for a slow-rising orgasm that peaked in mountainous waves.

The afterglow encircled us like God's love. We lay in each other's arms, breathing each other's air, touching and gazing at each other. Tears streamed out my eyes but I made no crying sound. Eddy kissed me and kissed me.

"Why are you here?" I asked.

"Because you need someone, you need me."

"What do I need you for?"

"For a while," he said, making a joke. But I was serious.

"Is that all?" I asked. "You're just here for a while?"

"Joan, I'm staying with you, close as I can, until you tell me to go away. I might have to take care of some things, but I'm here for you. Understand?"

"Not really, but it sounds good," I said and kissed him.

I got slowly out of bed, felt more than a little stiff while Eddy pulled on his pants and followed me into the kitchen. We finished up the coffee, scrambled up some eggs and made buttered toast. I was washing the dishes, Eddy was drying, when we heard a loud squawking chorus.

"What's that?" Eddy asked. He went to the window and stood there. "Joan, come here," he said.

I moved up behind Eddy's muscular shoulder and peeked around him to see the sun shining part way into the kitchen and a whole flock of multicolored parrots sitting in my banana trees.

"Isn't that pretty?" he asked.

I laughed and hugged Eddy's torso. Tears of joy ran down my face and the squawking increased.

"Oh, Eddy."

God's noisy rainbows continued their serenade.

Eddy turned around and kissed my ear while I continued to watch in wonder. We stayed there like that until the parrots got interested in my birdbath and then we laughed at their funny antics. Then I kissed Eddy, my lips hungry, grateful for the love he had to offer.

"I'll have to point out parrots more often," he said.

He stroked my face and pulled me against him. We made love there in the kitchen.

A half hour later we were both in jeans, T-shirts, and tennies. Eddy assembled scissors, a comb, and a new disposable razor. He carefully trimmed my hair, his touch reminding me of my gramma.

"Where did you learn to cut hair?" I asked.

"In the Marines, the Fleet Marine Force."

"The Marines? You never mentioned that before."

"It wasn't my favorite time. Once I did six hundred haircuts in one day."

"Girls, too?"

"Yessss. Women, too."

The guy was so politically correct.

"Ohmigod, I'm a punker," I said when I looked in the mirror. "Is there some reason you didn't shave it all off?"

"You didn't have much to work with, but I was going for a certain look."

He grinned at me and I kissed him to let him know that I liked it.

"So where to?" he asked.

"Parker Center," I said.

"You're so in love with that place. It's distorted, you know. You can't save everybody. You can't right every wrong."

"Eddy, somebody has to mean it. You of all people, with all your Save the Bay and Save the World. You should understand. It takes more than the usual to fight the bad guys. You have to be a little bit crazy because they are. You can't be casual or nonchalant, just clock out at five and that's that."

"But you're only human."

"That's no excuse. I know, I know I'm only human but...don't tell anybody."

"Who'm I gonna tell?"

"I dunno. The press?" He laughed.

Eddy pulled on his leather jacket. I picked out a jean jacket from my closet and grabbed my gun, and we headed out the door. On the way, I asked him about a hundred questions. Was he was an only child? Yes. Were his parents alive? Yes. Was he popular in high school? Yes. Was he on the student council? Yes, the president, in fact. How old was he when he lost his virginity? Seventeen. Was it with an older woman? Yes. I had him pegged pretty good. Finally, he turned to me.

"What is this? An interrogation?"

"No, you can ask me things if you like."

"Okay, Detective, how old were you when you lost your virginity?"

"Fifteen."

"That's a little young."

I paused for a moment then said, "I thought so."

"Were you an only child?"

"Yes."

"Oh, we have that in common. Were you popular in school?"

"No."

"Are your parents still alive?"

"No."

"How old were you when they died?"

"Ten, when my mom died. Fourteen, when my grandmother died. Fifteen, when my father...died."

"I'm sorry. That must have been hard."

"It was very difficult."

Sort of an understatement, that.

"Where did you go, who took care of you?"

"I was sort of adopted by my juvenile officer."

"Juvenile officer? What did you do?"

"I…shot my father. Justifiable murder."

"What? No. Oh, I'm…so sorry."

"My father…he um…"

I couldn't speak. The words wouldn't come. For some reason I wanted to explain everything to Eddy, I wanted him to understand me, to know my darkest corner. Maybe if I blurted it all out, told him everything, he wouldn't make the mistakes that Carl made. I was willing to try that, but the words would not come. I looked at my hands as if I could find the answer there. For a moment I wondered what my life would be like if I had decided to be an artist or a healer, or even a chef, anything but a cop.

"It's okay, Joan." His kind brown eyes searched my face.

"Hey, be careful," I said with a false bravado. "You gotta keep your eyes on the road, or we'll have an accident. This ain't Monterey, ya know."

He looked back at the road and put his hand gently on my knee.

"Someone should have protected you, watched out for you."

"Who?" I said like a big hoot owl.

CHAPTER TWENTY-TWO

EDDY PULLED THE INSECT car into the parking lot at Parker Center. The guard eyed the car suspiciously and waved us in when he recognized me in the passenger seat.

"You're not going to make me wait out here forever, are you?" Eddy asked.

"I only need to run in and check on something," I said.

"Like what?"

"Like the records of each and every victim of the two Johnnies."

"The two who?"

"John and Mary Tyler, the brother and sister team who hit me in the head."

Eddy gave me a curious look before he spoke. "Why do I get the feeling you're doing something not quite right?"

"Because it takes one to know one?"

"Joan." His voice chastised me.

"It's just that I'm supposed to be resting. Medical leave and all that. My captain would be pissed and my partner probably wouldn't approve of me being up and about."

"I should stop you."

"You can't," I said. "Nobody can."

"Why do I believe that, I wonder?" He waved me on to do my bidding.

⦀⦀⦀

UPSTAIRS ON THE FIFTH floor I walked into a tiny yellow-painted room. It has always bothered me how small Missings is. There are only a few file cabinets and they cover the entire Los Angeles county. One of the reasons the different children involved in the Tyler case had never been connected is because so many children go missing every year and because juvenile files are kept separately in each district. It makes it that much more difficult to see a connection. On the Tyler case, the identifying objects found in the children's graves combined with the use of computers allowed for the correct missing file to be matched to the bones and dentures of each child and sent to Parker Center.

I talked the clerk, Debbie, Carl's new love, into giving me a copy of all the files, eighteen in all. She knew exactly where every piece of paper in that office was. Debbie was a beautiful and very earnest Korean woman with a slight build. Her shiny black hair was cut just below her chin. She was no dummy. Everyone was aware that she'd carried a major torch for Carl for years. With a circumspect look, she took me into the next office with the copier and gave me detailed instructions on the quirks of the copy machine. As she was leaving, she cut me a sideways look that could have been a warning but left without saying anything. There are usually several detectives sitting at their desks in that room, but at that time it was empty. I had an eight-inch stack of papers to copy. I was getting down to it when Debbie came back in the copy room. "You look terrible," she said.

I continued working and said, "I didn't know I was running for beauty queen. What's wrong, don'cha like my haircut?"

She ignored my humor. Hell, after what I'd been through it was appropriate to look like shit. And that wasn't even taking into account Carl blowing down my door in the middle of the night.

"Are you okay?" she insisted.

"I'm fine."

She stood there like a big ol' hawk eyeing me. I stopped working and faced her. Her black eyes were full of reproach.

"What is it?" I asked.

"Stay away from him," she said.

I didn't have to ask her who, I knew she meant Carl. "Don't worry," I said.

"Carl's got a new life."

"Okay, good."

"Don't call him, either. You'll just upset him, get him all worked up."

"I won't."

"He said you were going to call him."

"I was. But I won't now. Not if you don't want me to."

"He deserves to be loved and that's what I'm going to do."

"Great," I said. "I'm happy for him. For you, too. He's a good guy."

"I know that already. I don't need you to tell me."

"Fine."

There was a silence during which she eyed me some more as I continued with the copying. This must be why I hate girl talk.

"Heard you found the ones who killed all these missing kids," she said.

"Looks like." I was glad for the change of subject.

"What about the nine missing girls? The ones my friend, Detective Mark O'Malley, has been working on."

"There's exactly nine girls missing?"

"That's right. Nine girls."

Debbie always has her numbers perfect.

"I thought it was ten. I have ten flyers of missing girls, I'm sure of it."

"No, no. They're not really sure it is ten, see, the first one was eight months ago. The nine missing were in the last six months and they're more closely related. So, the nine are connected for sure and the first one is a question."

"How do you know all that?"

"Just because I'm a clerk doesn't mean I'm deaf. I overhear the detectives talking. Sometimes I even read the files. I might even notice something and bring it to the detective's attention. Imagine that. You're not the only one who cares about these people, you know."

"Okay. So, what about 'em?"

"Mark mentioned you were helping him with the case. Think you'll find them, too?"

"I don't know... I haven't had much time until just now. There does seem to be some connection between cases but it's a little shaky. Anyway, I hope so. I'd like to find them before they end up like these kids."

"They could still be alive."

"Could be." My mind was clicking away. I was elsewhere even though I was standing there talking to Debbie.

"You stay busy with your work and leave Carl be," I heard her say.

"You don't have to keep telling me that. I got it the first time."

"Just making sure."

She turned to walk away and then hesitated, turned back to me. I prepared myself for more admonitions. You'd think I was lurking in the bushes, trying to snatch back her man. She held her body straight as a board and her mouth was clamped tight in a thin line.

"Listen, congratulations and best of luck. Keep up the good work."

"Thanks, Debbie."

"You're welcome," she said and left me to my work.

I was on the basement floor when I stopped in at evidence on my way out and looked over the items collected from Autumn Riley's bungalow. I was supposed to sign an official document to take the garage door opener, but the evidence clerk was busy doing something, I didn't know what. I didn't want to keep Eddy waiting too long. That would be rude. I slipped the garage door opener into my jeans pocket and called out a bye to the clerk as I split. I got out of there as fast as I could, put my stack of papers in the back seat of Eddy's electric car, and let out a sigh. We pulled out of Parker Center with a wave to the guard.

Eddy didn't go straight to my place. Instead, he drove up the coast to Big Rock Beach. We got out and took a long walk on the sand, holding hands. I understood completely why Autumn longed for such a loving gesture. We climbed up and sat on the eponymous big rock and watched the emerald green waves roll in. "Thanks for bringing me here," I said.

"You need me. I'm someone who will take time out for love."

I sat there stunned and thankful at the same time.

"Did you say love?" I asked.

"Yes, I did, and I'm not taking it back. either."

"I wouldn't want you to."

"Wouldn't want me to what?"

"Take it back."

He circled my ear with his finger as if it were the most interesting thing he'd ever seen. How did he know that was my main erogenous zone? Then he kissed my ear and I kissed his neck. An unfamiliar happiness filled my chest.

On the way home, we stopped for fish and chips at this shack on Pacific Coast Highway and ordered fish sandwiches. We sat outside at a picnic table. The sun bounced golden on the ocean green and it seemed to go on forever. We munched on our sandwiches, smiling between bites. I thought about what Debbie, Carl's new girlfriend, had said. Nine girls. The number was suspiciously the same as the number of different nails bound together in Autumn's voodoo doll. What would Satch say if I tried that theory on him? God, he'd have a coronary. I needed more than a number. Eddy stopped still in the middle of his Ono sandwich.

"What's wrong?" I asked.

"There's something I need to know."

"So, ask."

He put down his food, wiped his hands with a paper napkin while I became increasingly wary of a question that would warrant so much preparation.

"When are you going to tell me what you're up to?" he asked.

"As soon as I know." I put down my sandwich, too, and took a sip of my beer. "What most people don't understand," I started, "is that good homicide investigation is hours and hours of a tedious, boring, skull-numbing search for a connection. What kind of connection? Nobody knows. It requires an amazing focus on the not-so-exciting. The only time it's not boring is when it's terrifying. You can know something, like maybe I know something right now, but it does you no damn good if you can't prove it. Horrible criminals can get off scot-free if you don't do every damn thing just right. And I still say you're taking advantage of me when I'm in a fragile state."

His hand reached out to my face and he touched my bruised eye with tenderness. I found his ways irresistible.

"You've always been in a fragile state," he said.

The funny thing was, in that moment, I realized it was true.

CHAPTER TWENTY-THREE

WE WERE TOOLING DOWN PCH and it was one of those perfect moments when you're glad to be alive, grateful your heart's beating and there's air to breathe. I looked over at the driver's seat where Eddy was earnestly at the helm and thought how strange it was that I was sitting beside him in his electric car. If someone had told me a month ago that I'd meet an environmentalist-slash-surfer who would break through my hard-assed shell and wiggle his way into my life, I would have laughed.

"You know where Autumn Riley's bungalow is?" I asked.

"Yes, I do."

"Go there."

"What? Why?"

"Just do it, please."

He shook his head and gave me concerned brown eyes, but I knew he would take me because he wouldn't want me going by myself, not with this big bump on my head. A person can sure get a lot of mileage out of an injury. Women especially, I think. Eddy shook his head again but made his way toward Autumn Riley's place.

We pulled up past the pepper trees and it brought back my first day back at work and the spell cast by the young dead beauty. I recalled the bold green gaze when I lifted her eyelid and how I'd held her cold hand and wished with all my might that she would breathe. And what do you know? She did. Autumn was not dead. Officially, I had no business here. I had to be extra careful, especially after Satch's harsh words of warning. Eddy waited in the car and I pulled out the garage door opener I'd confiscated from evidence and approached the house, trying to decide whether to commit the crime of breaking and entering or just go home and have fabulous sex.

There were no cars parked near the house.

Once inside the garage, I took a moment to check out the Audi T. I had never really inspected it because Gus said it was new and crime lab said there wasn't anything revealing in it. I looked at the mileage, still at an even thousand miles. Didn't Autumn even want her car? She must be crazy to leave behind such a cool ride. I moved into the kitchen and heard a noise from the back of the house, in the bedroom. I pulled out my gun.

"Crashing parties again, Detective?"

Glenn Addams appeared in the doorway. His green silk shirt was unbuttoned and his soft khaki pants were missing the belt. He didn't have shoes on.

"Didn't mean to interrupt anything," I said.

"Are you going to shoot me?" I put my gun away.

"Sorry to intrude. I didn't see a car parked outside. Didn't think anyone was here."

"I had a limo drop me."

"Oh. Is Autumn here? I'd like to talk to her."

I heard the car start in the garage and pull away with a screech.

"You just missed her."

"What'd she do? Climb out the bedroom window to avoid me? That seems like suspicious behavior."

"She had an appointment. You can talk to me if you like. Would you like a beer, some wine?" Glenn strode past me and into the kitchen.

Boy, was he cool and collected. Always good under pressure, this one.

"No thanks. Where is she staying? Not here obviously."

"I don't know, really. She called and I convinced her to meet me here. Things were going well until you arrived. But at least, now, we know what happened to the garage door opener," he said from the kitchen.

"Yes, right. I thought someone might be missing it." I pulled it out of my pocket and set it on the coffee table.

"Kind of you to bring it by."

"Think nothing of it. And if you need anything else, let me know and I'll see if I can't wrestle it from evidence for you. Or for Autumn, I should say."

"I should think all items would be returned at this point," said Addams as he came back into the living room with a glass of wine.

"I don't think so. Not quite yet."

"You don't have a warrant."

I shook my head. He sat on the maroon couch, the same one that Autumn was pronounced dead on, and sipped his wine.

"So, are you and Autumn Riley back together?" I asked.

"We were just talking about the possibility."

"In the bedroom?"

Glenn looked at the floor and made a snorting noise.

"You paid for that car?" I asked.

"Yes, I did, in fact."

"It's a nice ride. You gonna make her a movie star?"

"I don't think I have to answer these questions."

There was a knock on the front door. Addams got up to answer it. Wineglass still in hand, he greeted Eddy.

"Everything okay?" asked Eddy. "I saw Autumn take off in a hurry."

"It's fine," I said, moving toward the door to go.

"You two came together?" asked Addams. The question had an incredulous tone to it.

‖·‖·‖

WHEN EDDY AND I got back to my place, I had a seat at the kitchen table and inspected the files that matched the forensic finds from the graveyard. I discovered that there were five boys and thirteen girls. Forensic evidence indicated their deaths had occurred over the last ten years. The most recent over eight months ago, except, of course, for Dani. The Johnnies hadn't lied to me. Each body had been matched with a tooth in the jar. All the victims had been reported missing. Some of them had been runaways. Others had been walking home from school and disappeared.

One had gone to buy an ice cream cone and never returned.

I turned away from the files, overwrought with a pulsing anguish.

I called the number that Gilda had given me. Gus had told me, sometime before I passed out, to pull her in, to question her regarding the pimps for runaways. She knew the streets and would be reliable.

"Hello?"

"Gilda?"

"Yes?"

"This is Joan. Can you do me a big favor?"

"That the first thing out of your mouth? You want something from me?"

"Right."

"What?"

"How 'bout you come over to my house and look at these files I got here? You can tell me if any of the photos match some of the kids that were working the streets and disappeared."

"Oh, sure. That really sounds like fun. I want to do that."

"Come on, Gilda."

"When?"

"Now?"

"You always had nerve, you know that?'

"I know. Please?"

"My car's not working."

"I'll pay for the cab and make you dinner."

"You got any strong coffee over there?"

"That I got."

"What's the address?" I gave it to her. "Okay. You're paying for the cab return, too?" she asked.

"I said I was paying for the cab, didn't I?"

⼁⼁⼁

THE CORONER'S OFFICE PROVIDED an initial report on each of the Tylers' victims. The horrific, tortuous deaths made me edgy and impatient. Eddy opened a beer and set it on the table where I was working.

"Knock it off, now. That's enough," he said.

"I haven't even got started good."

"Have a beer," he said.

He strolled back to the couch and stretched out. I took a sip of beer and kept on working.

"Why are you going through all those files?" asked Eddy. I sighed. "You solved it," he insisted. "What is the point? Are you trying to drive yourself crazy? The case is over."

"I need to see if there was a pattern, or if there's any connection to Autumn."

"That's stretching it a bit."

"Well, Coastal, there's a boy out there somewhere, not to mention ten missing girls. I think a stretch might be in order."

"Okay, but the doc said to take it easy, no stress. You're putting in a full day, here."

"How do you know what the doctor said?"

"I told you, I read the file."

"Oh, right."

I heard a car idling in the alley. It was Gilda's cab. I paid the fare, forty bucks plus a five-dollar tip. The cab driver gave me a funny look. I guessed he was wondering what kind of trick I was. Gilda was wearing a black turtleneck and black hot-pants. Her legs were clad in black fishnets and short boots with fake fur and spiked heels. She wore a black beret set at a fashionable angle on her head.

"You're looking very European," I said.

"And hello to you, too."

She hesitated. I'm sure no cop had ever invited her into their home before. It wasn't usual procedure for me, either.

I opened the car door for her. She flicked her long legs out of the cab.

"This way," I said, stepping before her and opening my gate to allow her entrance.

"Sure, okay." Her walk, as always, was pronouncedly sensual. "Where'd you get that black eye?" she asked.

"Oh, I picked that up during a ride I unwittingly took in a white van."

"I got a piece of advice for you."

"What's that?"

"Don't ever get into a strange van, don't trust nobody who drives one of those things, and whatever you do in life, never ever get into a strange van. Especially not a white one."

"I'll have to remember that."

Gilda strolled right into my house. Her eyes got big when she got a load of Eddy. He rose to shake her hand and asked if he could get her anything.

"Coffee, please. Black."

Eddy poured her the coffee into one of the new white diner mugs. I thought for a moment of Carl's delivery of the mugs. I'd probably never be able to use them without remembering that whole scene. Gilda thanked Eddy graciously, eyed his butt, and looked at me, letting me know she approved. She sipped her coffee with a Cheshire grin on her face.

"Oh, I like that artwork! Who's the artist? Romeo, here?" It was interesting to me that she didn't imagine for a moment that the paintings were mine.

"No, it's my mother's art. She was working on these paintings when she died."

"Oh, how did she die?"

"Is it okay if we don't talk about it? I need to get this work done and I really can't rest until this case is, um…cleared."

Gilda and Eddy exchanged looks. I put on some classical music, Nocturne by Lieberman. It's sort of dark and moody.

I sat her down at the kitchen table and showed her the pictures. The first four she had never seen. The fifth one she inspected more closely than the others.

Eddy sat on the couch in the living room reading the paper but I was sure he heard every word we said.

"I knew this one, she was somethin'; smart thing. Called herself Posey."

"Her name was Sara Perkins," I said.

"She'll always be Posey, to me," said Gilda. "And, lord, she had a filthy mouth on her."

"She a runaway?" Gilda nodded. "Did she have a pimp?"

"H was her man."

"H?"

"Yeah, young guy went by H."

"Was he muscular with long black hair?" I asked.

"No, a chubby guy, no hair at all, he shaved his head."

"How long ago was this?"

"Six or seven years ago."

I checked the file and the matchup to the bones indicated the death of Sara Perkins was six years ago."

"Okay, keep looking."

Gilda went through the rest of the files and found three more matchups. Two more girls and one boy. Gilda said that they were also pimped by H.

I went through my photos and pulled out the recent one of Hector.

"Gilda, I want you to imagine that H has grown his hair long and been working out at the gym. Does he look like this?"

I showed her the picture.

"That's him."

"How did you know so quickly?"

"That slope eye."

It was true. Hector's smaller eye had a slightly downward slope to it.

"So, Hector pimped runaways. He was the supplier to the two Johnnies."

"To who?" asked Gilda.

"John and Mary Tyler."

"John and Mary Tyler. Are they the ones with the graveyard? The ones that set kids on fire?" asked Gilda.

"That's the ones."

"You found them?"

"Yes. Everything you said was true, the graveyard; them burning the victims…"

"Those two in prison?"

"One is. The other has already committed suicide."

"Which one's alive?"

"The woman, if you can call her that, the sister."

"Are they going to execute her?" asked Gilda, her voice rising with indignation.

"If I've got anything to do with it, yes," I said. Gilda nodded solemnly.

"I know how it is," said Gilda. "Most runaways come from elsewhere. Their families are in other states. Runaways don't pay taxes, don't vote, and they don't do nuthin' for your statistics."

"That's not how I feel about it, Gilda."

"I know. I see that. Okay. Now, you promised me dinner and ahm hungry." Gilda crossed her leg at the knee and swung her booted foot up and down to emphasize her point.

"Dinner's on its way," said Eddy as he grabbed his keys and made for the door. "Is Italian okay?"

"Sure, that'd be excellent," said Gilda, flashing him a big smile.

Once he was out the door, she giggled.

"Oh, girl. That man is fine. Feeeee-iiiine, do you hear me?"

"Yeah, I know."

"What you say his name was?"

"Coastal Eddy."

"What's his real name?"

"I don't know; he won't tell me. But it must be Italian cuz' that's all he eats."

We laughed and she gave me a big hug.

"Thanks for comin' over, Gilda," I said. "I really appreciate you for doing this."

"Oh, anytime."

"Do you mind if I make a few calls?" I asked.

"No, honey. Do your thing. Why is this music playing over and over?"

"I put it on repeat."

"A little dreary."

"I think it's beautiful. It honors these children. You and I are in the very important process of honoring these missing children that everyone has forgotten. Besides we might save one, or even many in the future."

"Okay."

"Besides, it helps me think. They have proven that classical music helps people think more efficiently." Gilda nodded at me and smiled.

〜〜〜

I CALLED INTERPOL AND asked them when Dewey and The Barb came into the country. The answer told me what I needed to know. Eight months ago. Mary Tyler had said the supplier had stopped service to the two Johnnies the last six months. That must have been when Hector hooked up solidly with Dewey and The Barb and made a career change. I made a call to the acting teacher, Ms. Koch. She informed me that Autumn enrolled in class six months ago, but she only stayed a month.

I made yet another call to check in with Interpol for the results of the more in-depth search I had requested on Dewey and The Barb. They had come up with some sketchy information on pharmaceutical shipments to a lab in Haiti. The lab, located in Gonaives, was the same lab mentioned in Dr. Blanchard's journal. Apparently, the truck bringing in lab supplies was looted. Dewey and The Barb were named as prime suspects but no actual case was built against them. The witnesses refused to testify against them.

Thereafter, nobody could bring anything into that town in Haiti. Not even the cocaine dealers. Ever since the success of their lab-supply attack, the people of the village would charge the suppliers, or smugglers in this case, and take the cocaine or whatever for their own. It set off a strange sort of revolution throughout Haiti and now the drug dealers were avoiding Haiti completely. It was a bitter justice though because the newly monied villagers apparently were as exploitive as their previous abusers. Child prostitution, ages twelve and under, was flourishing. You gotta wonder where it all ends.

Gilda listened in as I made all my calls. She "tsk, tsked" and shook her head. I shared with her some of my findings and she moaned with disapproval. At one point, she covered her face with her hands.

"What's the world coming to?" she asked.

CHAPTER TWENTY-FOUR

A FTER WE FINISHED OUR cannelloni, I got a cab for Gilda and sent her home. She made a point of inviting both Eddy and me over for dinner and a gaze at the stars. I was surprised when Eddy agreed. We stood in the alley and watched the cab take Gilda away from us.

"You don't have to hang around and take care of me," I said. As soon as I said it, I wondered why.

"It's not a problem. I'm on a hiatus right now. I've got the time. In a couple weeks I'm going to be busy."

"Busy where?"

"That's for me to know." That wasn't what I wanted to hear.

"What's your real name?" I asked.

"Same answer."

"You don't do anything illegal, do you?"

"Same answer."

"Do you hurt people? I'm a detective, I have to ask these things."

"My motto is: Get them where they live, find out their flaws and weaknesses, their crimes."

"So, I should figure that in a couple weeks, you might have to go save a whale?"

"More like a whole pod of them."

"A pod?"

"A school of fish, a pod of whales, a murder of crows."

We walked back into the house and I realized that I never wanted Eddy to leave my sight. I had some other ideas about what I wanted, but we sat on the couch and I listened to what he had to say instead.

My mind was racing around in my head, he went on and on—something to do with him not wanting to go out of town, but he absolutely had to. Then I finally tuned in.

"The Navy's intensive sonar tests in ocean waters is killing whales," Eddy continued. "The blasts are in excess of two hundred decibels. The whales are sound-sensitive and sound-dependent and the tests are killing them dead, there's no question. Last month, sixteen were beached."

"I'm so sorry, Eddy. But what are you going to do about it?"

"I don't know."

"Now, you sound like me. I guess I can relate."

"My style is different from yours."

"Yeah, how so?" I asked.

"Can't say, really."

"Do you have any felony convictions?"

"No, and wasn't planning on it."

"Good. Because I can't hang out with felons. So, when did you say you're going to disappear?"

"In about two weeks."

"When will you be back?"

"I don't know exactly, but I could keep in touch. I'll try to call you every day."

"I'd like that."

"Can I come back here?"

"Don't you have your own place?"

He laughed nervously. "Yes...I'd like to invite you to my place. When do you want to come?"

"After this case is over. Right now, it's best for me to stay on the home front."

"Okay, but what I'm trying to say is...when I get back..."

"Listen, you're invited here any time of day or night. I'll even make you a key. You are in." There, I had said it.

"I'm in?"

"Right."

"I'm in."

"Okay, I think I love you."

"You think?"

"Yes. I think so. I'll let you know when I'm absolutely sure, okay? It might help if I knew your real name."

He smiled and nodded and I thought his eyes were watery. I kissed him on the cheek.

"I gotta get back to work here," I said.

He nodded again and smiled some more. "I don't want to lose you," he said. "I want you in my life. I'm not like that guy, Carl. I won't ever do anything to make you afraid of me, or anything like that. I just want to be here for you." There was a pleading to his eyes.

"Don't worry, Eduardo. I'll eat my Wheaties, try to take care of my health, and if nobody kills me, I'll be around."

We laughed.

"Okay?" I asked.

He nodded.

"I have to make a phone call."

He nodded again.

I picked up the phone receiver on the table by my couch and dialed Kunda.

"Oh, Joan. I'm glad you phoned," she said. "I feel the truth is near."

"Is that intuition?" I asked with deep sarcasm. "Or firsthand knowledge?"

"The feeling is strong tonight. And it's up to you, all up to you. You are the center."

The woman was exasperating. Talking to her was like using a balloon for a punching bag. "Thanks, Kunda, I'll keep that in mind."

"My energy is with you, Joan."

"Well, let's hope your energy can get behind a few questions I have for you."

"I want to be of service."

"Can you tell me where I can find a guy named Hector? Hector Cardona. He's a big guy hooked on steroids, long black hair, ninja turtle tattoo on his forearm."

"No, I never met him."

"Do you know the whereabouts of The Barb or Dewey?"

"De Sade's Cage is all I can tell you. I have a feeling they may even be there this evening." She had a feeling.

"Tonight?" I asked.

"Yes," she said.

"Kunda, has Autumn been in touch with you lately, maybe for some psychic advice?"

"No, why do you ask?"

"Just a feeling." Hell, I could have them, too.

⁕⁕⁕

I REACHED FOR THE stack of files piled on my coffee table that Mark O'Malley had provided me on the ten missing girls. Mark had been on the case for eight months with no results. It must have been eating him up inside. His work had been thorough and I put on my memory cap and went through it.

The first one, Paige, was a tall brunette with coal-black eyes, winsome and charming, only eighteen. She was a folk and pop singer and had much recognition for her talents. Not only that, but she had exceptional athletic ability. She was a pole vaulter. When I was a kid, girls didn't pole vault. I had to admit I was impressed. I memorized every detail of her description. She reminded me of pictures I had seen of my mother at that age. Each file was a story with descriptions and personal notes, certain things to look for in order to ascertain identity. My focus and concentration were in an effort to emblazon each detail on my brain.

Several were cheerleaders and more than one was in the drama club, and three of them were singers. None of them were introverts. There was a mole here, a scar there, a tattoo, a birth defect, and a slight limp. It was imperative to discipline my brain in order to call up these details at will. I went over them several times, matching the first name with certain defining details. Suzy had the mole, Jeanette had the scar, Marissa had the tattoo, Judy had the birthmark, Brenda had the slight limp, Jennifer was tall, five foot nine. I repeated their names and their identifying traits over and over again. It's times like these that my memory serves me well. It's much better to have the information stored in your head than in a file. I imagined each girl standing in line with Autumn, waiting for their turn to try out at the pop star audition.

Then I went over the files that did not have any particular physical defining traits. I focused in on each photo, trying to find some aspect of their face that I could imprint on my mind so that I would recognize them if, or hopefully when, I saw them.

Vernice, the actress, she was the one Mason Jones had done the reversal Othello scene with. She had also been in that scene from the play, *Dusa, Fish, Stas & Vi*, with Autumn Riley and a couple of the other missing girls. Vernice was a young, petite, dark-skinned beauty who would be easy to recognize, and her eyes held a deep fire, though sometimes things like that changed once a person was abducted or abused for a length of time. But the heart shape of her face and her regal nose I committed to memory.

Anne, one of the other actresses, had also been involved in that altercation with Autumn in acting class. She had an olive complexion. I was struck by the way her small ears contrasted to her round moon face. Then again, the fullness of a face can change if a person isn't being fed properly or not eating because of anxiety. I focused in on her chin and the length of her neck.

Katrice, the other girl in the altercation, was the most nondescript of all the girls. She had an average all-American look with sandy-colored hair. A thousand teenagers at a thousand high schools looked just like her. Her parents had shared their daughter's diary and Mark O'Malley had copied it. I read the passage that Mark had mentioned but could see no real connection or clue in that. She had lyrics from songs throughout the diary and if any of them had any true significance, there would be no way to tell. Poor Mark was grasping at straws. 'Course, it wouldn't be the first time a determined detective had done that and more than once such long shots were exactly what put together a case. In fact, that was what I was counting on.

Though I was becoming increasingly convinced that this was no long shot.

I studied a photo of Katrice laughing with her friends. It looked like it had been taken at a birthday party. She had just blown out her candles. She had a dimple in only one of her cheeks. Her bright eyes haunted me. There were some handwritten notes that indicated that Katrice had gone missing with a friend and that the friend had resurfaced. I called

Mark O'Malley to ask him about that important detail because the notes looked like his handwriting. He wasn't in and I left a message.

I looked through the other details of each missing report. Clothing worn, personal habits, school, etc. There was nothing there that immediately jumped out at me. The jewelry indicated that Katrice, the girl with the laughing dimple, wore a pendant that her parents said she would never part with. It was made of pewter and dangled on a black string. The pewter had a simple symbol crudely carved into it. Sharp lines that meant nothing to me.

Vernice, the beautiful, spirited black girl, had an elephant hair bracelet from Africa. Anne, the one with the tiny ears and a moon face, wore a ring that her father had given her for her fifteenth birthday, a square gem, garnet, her birthstone. In the picture, it was elegant on her long, slender finger against her olive skin.

I recalled the ruby ring in Autumn's jewelry box. Maybe I was wrong and it wasn't a ruby. Maybe it was a garnet. The necklaces, bracelets, and rings in Autumn's jewelry box flashed before my eyes, including an elephant hair bracelet. I called Rose Torres.

"Rose, this is Joan."

"Are you okay? I heard you were out."

"I'm out but I'm in."

"What's that mean?"

"Never mind. Do you have the jewelry from the Autumn Riley bungalow?"

"It's in evidence."

"And the photo of the jewelry?"

"Filed."

"Can you email me a copy of the jewelry photo? You know, scan it or something."

"What do you think this is, Kinko's?"

"Rose, just email it to me, will ya?"

"Okay, but don't I have to find a special printer?"

"No, you don't. But you do need a scanner. Media Relations has one."

"Right. I think they do."

"Good. Do it now, okay?"

"Can't someone in your office do this?"

"Sure, if I asked them."

"I see. Aren't you supposed to be resting?"

"I can't rest."

"You got a complex, you know that?'

"Send me the email, Rose."

"You know I will."

I hung up with Rose, and Mark called. I asked him about the friend of Katrice and he hedged a little.

"Yeah, her name is Bujette, she's under psychiatric care and hasn't been able to give us anything." "I want to talk to her," I said.

"Her parents won't let you near her," he said.

"She's eighteen, I can talk to her without her parents."

"I'll give you the number to her doctor," said Mark. "I've already tried this and I did it all wrong, nearly got the department sued. But maybe you can get some action, being a woman and all."

He gave me the number and address of a chic private hospital in Marina Del Rey. A number of famous personalities were known to have fought addictions and dementia with some measure of success at this institution. "Do you want to come with?" I asked.

"No, I'd be a hindrance. They didn't respond to me and you might be able to slip in where I wasn't allowed."

He made a good point. I have a quality; people like to talk to me. Even before I was a cop I could sit down at a bar and by the end of the night three different people would have told me their darkest, most shameful secrets. I don't know why. Maybe it's because of my own shadowed past. It's like they choose me to share their demons with. Also, I've noticed that criminals tend to prefer to confess to a female cop over a male one. Probably has something to do with their mothers or something. 'Course, there's plenty who won't confess to anyone.

I said a prayer that Bujette would feel safe with me. I asked God to give her strength and me wisdom and gentleness. I hoped that if she could find her way to uncover one detail from her nightmare that she'd offer it to me.

CHAPTER TWENTY-FIVE

I APPROACHED A MODERN building of blue metal and glass, which vaguely reminded me of a huge whale, but maybe I just had whales on my mind. Coastal Eddy, savior to the whales. What could possibly be wrong with that? I entered the mouth of the whale, the famous clinic where the chic doctors took care of famous patients. Bujette's doctor, Dr. Filbert, a dweeby guy in his early thirties, was reluctant, to say the least. Since Bujette had turned eighteen, it was legal for me to question her without parental permission, but the doc didn't think it was such a good idea. He met me at the door of his pale green office and we talked there in the doorway. He didn't invite me in.

I thought that was incredibly rude and I wasn't feeling so diplomatic myself.

"I have to talk to her, Doc, that's all there is to it."

"You must understand, even under hypnosis, Bujette has not been able to remember anything." He spoke to me as if to a child.

"I do understand but I have to try, I have an obligation."

"I wish you could comprehend the depth of the trauma to Bujette."

"Maybe I do."

"It's complicated, but her complete inability to provide any information that could help her friend has endangered her already precarious mental state. A clinical depression ensued that led to suicide attempts on several occasions."

"I think I know how she feels," I said.

The doc looked confused. He blustered and finally indicated that I should enter his office and have a seat. He took a chair and crossed his legs.

"For example," he continued, "Bujette came in with a gorgeous head of curly blond hair, but because she felt that it had attracted their attackers, she insists on having her head shaved every day."

"Let me have a go at it. I promise to be gentle. We have some leads that may help us find Katrice."

"So pursue your leads."

"I need to speak with Bujette in order to do so properly."

"You can't guarantee that you'll catch these, these…"

"No, I can't but with a little more information I have a chance. Besides, Doc, there may be as many as nine other girls being held captive." That grabbed his attention. "We don't even know if they're dead or alive," I added.

"See? See there? That's exactly the kind of pressure I don't want her exposed to. I can barely stand the responsibility myself. I can't let you do this. You'll kill her."

"I don't have to tell her about the other girls to get the information I need, Doc. I get it, okay? I understand, she's fragile. Believe me, there's nothing in this world I want more than for Bujette to be a strong, happy person again. Trust me."

The doc didn't want to trust me, I could tell. I stared him down, holding him responsible with my eyes.

"I'll grant you one interview, but you must stop questioning her immediately if she has any negative reactions."

"What's a negative reaction mean, exactly?"

"If I see the signals, I'll let you know and you will stop."

"Okay."

"She's been doing well lately," he said. "We could jeopardize that."

"I understand, Doc. I don't want to harm her in any way."

⫶⫶⫶

BUJETTE SAT UP IN her bed with her arms wrapped around her knees, rocking back and forth. Though her hair was completely buzzed off, she was a beauty, as were all the girls who were missing. Bujette's perfect complexion was marred by a bright red scar near her ear and several puncture wounds on her neck. Her blue eyes took me in warily. I must have looked like a soul sister with my own hair much gone and the bruising still present around my eye and neck from my encounter with the Tylers. I stood at the end of her bed while the doctor introduced us.

"What happened to you?" she asked.

"Two people kidnapped me, knocked me unconscious with a hammer, and pulled out my wisdom tooth while I was conked out." Her eyes widened. "When I woke up," I continued, "they slapped me around for a while. Later, one of them tried to strangle me to death and set my hair on fire. It's been some week."

"They took out your wisdom tooth?"

I opened my mouth and showed her the wound. She peered in and made a face.

"Gross. You should get that sewn up or something."

"And how was your weekend?" I asked. She smiled.

"It's boring around here."

"Hey, sometimes boring is good, let me tell ya."

"Are you okay?" she asked.

I smiled at her concern for me. "I'm okay."

"What do you want?" she asked me.

"I want to find Katrice," I said.

"Katrice… She fought them, that's why I was able to get away. She fought and I ran. I should have helped her."

Dr. Filbert looked dismayed; apparently Bujette had never volunteered this information before. I was afraid he might stop me, but he gave me the slightest wave of the hand, urging me to continue.

"Maybe you can help her now. Who did she fight?" I asked.

"There were two of them. One was white and the other was black with snakes."

"Snakes?"

"He had these long snakes coming out of his head."

The doc put a hand to his mouth.

She meant dreadlocks, I guessed. That could have been Dewey or about a hundred thousand other men in Los Angeles.

"Did the man with snakes have a knot, a big bump, in his forehead?"

She nodded eagerly and looked over at the doc.

"Where exactly?"

She touched the center of her own forehead.

"Did either of them say anything that you can remember?"

"The one with snakes…"

"Yes?"

"He made strange moaning sounds. It was like he was putting a curse on us. It scared me so bad."

A chill went over my scalp and down my arms.

"If you saw these men again, could you identify them?"

She was still. Her eyes went up as if to plead to God and then the slightest nod of her head told me yes.

"Good. That would be real good. If we catch these men, we may be able to save Katrice. You'd like for us to do that, wouldn't you?"

"Yes. Please do that. Please catch them."

"What else did the men do?" I asked.

Her hand went to her throat and pain shot through her eyes.

"I'm sorry to remind you of those things, but it will help us if we know. Did one of them choke you?" A slight nod.

"Which one?"

"The white one."

"What did he choke you with, Bujette?"

She whispered something but I couldn't hear.

I moved around to the side of the bed to get closer to her. Dr. Filbert moved back from us and sat on a chair in the corner with a distressed look on his face. I didn't know if it was because of what she was saying or if it was because she was saying it to me and not him, but I didn't care. I had to reach inside this girl, to her pain, and get her to share it with me.

"I didn't hear you Bujette, what did he choke you with?"

"Barbed wire," she whispered, and a loud gulping sound burst from her throat. Tears streamed down her face and she sobbed in angry despair. I put my arms around her and we stayed like that, her crying and me holding her for half an hour.

⊪·⊪·⊪

ON THE DRIVE BACK, I put the case together in my mind. When I got home, Eddy was there, but I hardly said hello before I dialed Gus, explained to him what I thought was a strong connection between Autumn Riley, the missing boy, and the missing girls. With the dog hair and the missing girls' jewelry, not to mention the barbed wire, I thought we had something.

"You've been working this case without me, Joan."

"I'm reporting in. You're the one who told me to interview Gilda."

"You're on medical leave, you're supposed to be resting."

"Gus, I can't rest, okay?"

"So give me something good," said Gus.

"Mark's got the missing files and Rose has the photo of the jewelry. Compare them and you'll see a striking resemblance. And I'd bet my life that if the crime lab runs a DNA comparison between the nine strips of menstrual blood of the voodoo doll from the Autumn Riley crime scene, you'll find a match to the nine recently missing girls."

"I'll request the DNA test. You want to arrest The Barb and Dewey?"

"I don't know," I said.

"The goal is the girls."

"Right. I think they may still be alive. If we arrest those two bastards, it could put the girls in danger. And there's a strong possibility that the missing boy is with them."

"I'm with you there."

"Did surveillance ever pick up Hector again?" I asked.

"No"

"Those losers!"

"Take it easy."

"Too many are already doing that, it's crowded with take it easy."

"Come off the 'tude, will ya? Let's put it together."

"Okay, the missing girls are all beautiful, spirited girls. They're all, um, eighteen years old, same age as Autumn Riley. They're successful, popular, you know. They're not bookworms or members of the chess club, they're social creatures, trendy, uh, confident—adventurous, even. They're not runaways, but their parents' pride and joy. They're all sexy…"

"What? What is it?" Gus asked.

"What day is this?

"It's Thursday, Joan."

"Thursday is under-twenty-one night at De Sade's Cage. I just talked to Kunda. She said The Barb and Dewey were going to be at De Sade's Cage tonight and that something big was going down."

Gus was quiet as it sunk in.

"How does she know this?"

What do you mean, how does she know? She says she's psychic; I'm comin' with," I said.

"Okay, then. What time?"

"Early, eight. You know most kids that age have to go to school in the morning."

"I'll pick you up."

"Thanks, Gus."

"Just doing my job."

I hung up and Eddy gave me a serious look. "It's about to break?" he asked.

"One can only pray."

"I'd say you do a lot more than that."

Just then, the mail truck on my computer announced an arrival. I pulled up my browser and printed out the email from Rose. The photo of the jewelry was a perfect match to the descriptions in the files as well as my own memory.

My cell phone chirped. It was Anthony Sauri, surveillance.

"We got an update on Hector in Malibu Canyon. A sheriff's helicopter spotted an SUV with the license number you gave us. Could be foul play."

"What do you mean, foul play? Is he alive?"

"We've got a body down in the ravine. Might be Hector. Can't tell if he's dead or alive, but he's looking pretty bad from here."

"I'll be right there."

I called Gus back and told him to meet me. I drove up the winding Malibu Canyon road. Huge boulders of sandstone and blue sky betrayed the tone of my journey. I got there in time to see a fire department helicopter pulling a harnessed fireman and Hector in a rescue litter up from the precipitous cliffs of the green canyon.

I recognized upon sight that Hector had been brutalized by more than his fall into the ravine. There was a pattern of blue-black-and-purple chevron welts across his face, one arm hung separated from the shoulder, and it was clear that his right shin had a compound fracture. He was still alive when they released him from the cables and put him on the gurney. I went to his side. His smaller eye was swollen shut and blood dripped out both nostrils. Gus arrived just then and came over toward us.

"Hector, it's me, Joan Lambert."

"Joan."

"Right. Joan. Hector, please. Where are the girls? Where's Tommy? Where's the missing boy?"

"*Puma. Puma. Basura.*"

"He's speaking Spanish. What's *puma basura* mean?" I asked Gus.

"*Basura?* Dirt. It means dirt. *Puma?* That's a type of mountain lion."

"*Puma. Basura,*" repeated Hector. "Joan."

Hector reached out to me and he clutched my arm.

His Teenage Mutant Ninja Turtle tattoo was blood-streaked.

"*Lo siento,*" he said, and his head dropped to the side.

He went unconscious after that and the paramedics took him away.

"He's sorry," said Gus.

"Well, goddammit, he oughta be," I said, and a thousand tears welled up in me. A thousand tears for Hector, for every child he sold on the streets of Hollywood, for all runaways, for all the missing children, for abused children living in their own homes.

"I don't think he's gonna make it," said Gus.

Gus walked over to Hector's SUV parked dangerously close to the precipice. It looked like it could fall any moment into the deep cavernous canyon. I followed Gus over to the car. It was big, black, and ominous looking. On the shoulder of the road was a tire iron. Gus bent down to inspect it. It matched the chevron marks on Hector's face exactly. Just as I stepped toward Gus and the tire iron, I tripped on a rock and pitched forward. I was about to fall off the cliff when it was as if someone very strong grabbed me under my left arm, right below the shoulder, and saved me from going over the cliff. You know how an adult grabs a kid sometimes? Gus turned toward me with alarm and looked incredulous.

"Whoa nelly, you okay there? I thought we were gonna lose you just then."

"Yeah, I kinda had a misstep there." I looked around for my angel but saw none.

"Is it too optimistic to believe there might be fingerprints on the tire iron?" I asked trying to change the subject.

"You never know, in the heat of a moment, people sometimes lose their sense," said Gus, giving me a strange look.

"He was lured here so his body could be dumped," I said.

"Yes, but why leave the SUV sitting out here like a big sign?"

"Sloppy, maybe. Mafia used to dump bodies here. Once, an old rusted limo wasn't discovered here until decades after the crime."

Gus pulled out a cigarette, lit it. "So then the question is, why would The Barb do this to his own guy?"

"Who knows? Maybe it has something to do with Autumn Riley. Every damn thing seems to center around her."

"Hector was involved somehow with The Barb and Autumn Riley, he let you know that when he gave Autumn your doll, plus we know he supplied the Tylers," said Gus.

"But he was getting out of that according to Mary."

"So maybe The Barb got word about the Tyler case breaking and he knew Hector was their supplier?"

"The Barb would not have liked that," I said.

"I guess not. Hector's connection to the Tylers wouldn't be such good PR. It could ruin The Barb's new champagne career as Autumn's manager."

"What's *puma basura* mean, Gus?"

"Hell, I wish I knew. *Puma* is mountain lion and *basura* is dirt."

I stared at the SUV, not really seeing anything. And then I noticed the sticker. I moved closer to get a better look at it.

"What is it?" asked Gus.

It was a sticker for Topanga emergency access for this year.

"Only residents got these special stickers so they can be identified for access to their homes whenever there is a flood or fire," I said as a statement.

"That's right. Topanga, sanctuary for the rugged individualists and artists. Now, doctors and lawyers are populating the area. Guess no place is safe anymore."

"There's forest areas in Topanga still. It's considered remote from Los Angeles and it's not far from here, maybe about ten minutes."

"Hector's plates came up with an address in Echo Park," said Gus, "but he wasn't living there anymore."

We raced over mountain passages to the Topanga Town Council, which was essentially a log cabin set back in the woods next to a creek. An elderly woman answered the door. I recognized her. She was a respected character actress. She had long, curly white hair pulled back into a braid down to her waist and a twinkle to her blue eyes. She smiled easily and greeted us warmly. When I asked her for the address of Hector Cardona, an applicant for the Topanga emergency access sticker, her mouth formed into an "o" and her eyes went to the creek.

"I'm sorry, I can't help you. This year the creek was jammed up by debris and it rose all the way to my storage shed. All the files were destroyed. It was a terrible mess and…I don't have those records this year."

"Do you remember a Hector Cardona?"

"I sure don't. We organized a cleanup and the whole community came out to clear the creek so it won't happen again. Try me next year."

CHAPTER TWENTY-SIX

W E DROVE ACROSS TOWN to De Sade's Cage. The sun was setting and it warmed the back of my neck. I hardly noticed the traffic because the words *"puma basura"* kept repeating in my mind. Mountain lion dirt? Mountain lion grounds? I knew the land in Topanga and Malibu were considered to be sacred territory by the Chumash, an indigenous Native American tribe. Perhaps the girls and Tommy were being held in a cave in the mountains somewhere. We arrived at De Sade's Cage a few minutes before eight and entered.

The music coming out of the speakers was a horrible clash of electro-tech noise and shouts. The place was filling up quickly. Androgynous young men and women in overt sexual display crowded in, bringing an adolescent nervous energy with them. We sat at the bar and the bartender, the same guy I had questioned the night we arrested The Barb and Dewey, did a double take when he saw me. I walked over to him and I knew he had something for me. I only hoped I'd be able to hear what he had to say over the music.

"Hey, how are you?" he shouted.

"Great," I lied. People should know better than to ever ask how I am. "I see you're still here." He shrugged. "What's going on?" I asked.

"The girl you were asking about last time? She's performing here tonight."

"Autumn Riley?"

"She goes by Zombita now."

"Right, I heard that."

Gus and I looked at each other. I searched the room and a rising concern, a near hysteria, colored my perception of each and every young girl. Which one would be the next one on the list to be abducted, and for what purpose?

I went to the ladies' room several times in hopes of spotting Zombita backstage, but no luck. I bought cigarettes at the bar and went out back to have a smoke, thinking I might see her drive up.

A crowd of kids strolled in. I finished my cigarette and smashed the butt out with the heel of my boot. I was about to go back into the club when an all-terrain military vehicle that had been transformed into a limousine with tinted windows pulled into the parking lot. It was huge. I decided to have another smoke. The limo parked. Its tires were caked with dirt and the back had mud splattered across it.

The limo driver popped out in a tux and he opened the door. Next, skinny black-jeaned legs came out of the limo, topped by a silver jacket and bleach-blond hair. The Barb. The limo driver and The Barb turned to a woman who disembarked from the military vehicle. She moved slowly and was dressed in a low-cut black body stocking. Her body looked bony, like she had lost some weight, but it was Autumn Riley all right, aka: Zombita. She had pieces of chiffon-like gray-and-silver material tied around her arms and barbed wire wound around her waist, ankles, and wrists. Chills went up and down my body. A visceral desire to pull my gun, lunge forward, and rescue her from her captors rose up in me. I had to keep reminding myself that this was a career move for her. Autumn's face was painted white and gray with black circles drawn around her eyes. I was reminded of the moon goddess mask I'd seen in her bungalow. Her hair was woven into elaborate sexy dreadlocks in which several rags of silvery-gray material were tied. The Barb took her by the arm and led her toward the club entrance. She was clutching my Raggedy Ann doll.

One of the under-twenty-ones approached Zombita as she made her way into the club. The young girl looked like she was stoned; she stumbled a bit and blocked their entrance.

"Oh, hey," she said.

"Look out, will ya?" said The Barb.

"You're Zombita, right?" the girl asked.

"Yeah, she's Zombita," said The Barb.

"I hear your show is really incredible!" exclaimed the girl as she stumbled backward into the entrance, truly blocking them.

Autumn merely stood there with a vacant stare on her face. I couldn't tell if it was from drugs or part of her act. "You 'eard right, missy, and if you let us through, you might even get to see it," The Barb insisted. "We need to get by you, now."

"Oh, ahm sorry," she said and stood aside.

Autumn didn't pay the slightest attention to the exchange, just held onto that implacable stare out to the middle of nowhere. Once the girl was out of the way, Autumn dutifully entered the dark club, The Barb still clutching her arm.

I went out to the Humvee stretch and approached the driver. He was leaning on the hood, smoking a cigarette. He filled out his tux nicely, had peppered hair, and his skin appeared too perfect, like maybe he had on makeup.

"Hi," I said. "Aren't you an actor or something?"

"Oh, I used to be when I was younger and had time for that sort of thing."

"What did I see you in?" I asked.

"Maybe some equity waiver theater. I don't know. I did a few commercials, that's probably it."

"What's your name?"

"Larry Duvane."

"You always drive for Zombita?"

"Nah, this is the first time."

He dropped the cigarette, ground it out with his nice leather shoe, and shot me an uncomfortable look.

"Look, you better move on," he said. "These people asked me not to talk to anybody, you know."

I pulled out my badge and flashed him the silver and gold. He looked disappointed, hurt even.

"Where did you pick her up?" I asked. "It's important that you tell me quickly."

"Some weird place out in Topanga, far out and off the beaten path if you know what I mean. My worksheet didn't have an address and the road wasn't even paved. Doubt they have running water out there. Didn't see no phone lines or nothin'. Coyotes, saw a couple of those."

"Larry, could I have your work order, please?" I knew that limo drivers wrote up each job, listing names, phone numbers, exact times, etc. He reluctantly reached into his jacket pocket and pulled out the white sheet and handed it to me. The worksheet didn't have an address, just as Larry had said, but it did have a small printed map to the location.

"Open her up, will you?"

Larry opened the door of the limo and I had a look-see. The interior of the limousine was gray leather and featured an elaborate custom-made wet bar with cut crystal and several decanters. There were gray-and-black velvet pillows perfectly placed and a television that was playing music videos.

"They left the television on," I said.

"They requested it stay on the whole time."

"Why?"

"Zombita's first music video is going to be featured on *Hot Rock Stars* tonight. They're gonna come out and check every so often."

"It's a big night for them. A limo, *Hot Rock Stars* deals and everything."

"Big night."

"Don't mention that I asked you these questions, okay? It's a delicate situation we have here."

"One thing," Larry added. "Is that girl all right? Is she in danger?"

"I can't discuss it with you, Larry. Sorry. I'm keeping this map, you don't need it do you?"

"You can have it, there's another copy at the office."

I left Larry with a perplexed look on his face and walked back to the club. Inside, Gus was nowhere to be found. I had a seat and tried to figure where he'd gone off to. I took a good long look at the map, intending to commit it to memory.

At that moment, Glenn Addams made his entrance sans entourage. He scanned the room then sat at a table in the corner, alone. Gus approached from the back of the club. When he sat down, I gestured over to Addams and I watched as it registered with Gus.

"What's Addams doing here?" asked Gus.

"Maybe he's gonna catch a rising star. Where've you been?"

"I was listening to Jesse Cand interview Zombita."

"And?"

"Autumn Riley is dead, Zombita lives and she's a hot rock star."

"That'll make a nice headline," I said.

"Right. Wonder what PR genius thought that up."

"Gus, I got a question for you."

"Shoot," he said.

"What kind of road do you have, if it's not paved?"

"Dirt."

I pointed at the map.

Gus squinted trying to see, then read out loud, "Piuma Heights." Then he nodded seriously, taking in every detail.

"Piuma Heights is a dirt road," I said. *"Basura."*

"What is that?" asked Gus.

"It's a map I got from Zombita's limo driver."

The crowd shouted and hooted. The band came out on stage, women in black tights, black turtlenecks, and white painted faces, The Ghouls. Their music had a reggae-blues sound to it.

After a few tunes, Zombita appeared on stage in the midst of a smoke bomb. She walked stiff-legged through the smoke, arms straight out in front of her, like some bride of Frankenstein. The crowd screamed, hooted, and hollered. Zombita suddenly looked wild-eyed at the audience like a frightened animal, then approached the microphone as if she were hunting it. When she was on the mike, she opened her mouth as though to eat it but instead she sang, her voice low and sultry, her body a sinewy snake. The sound of her voice was a jeweled evening mist. Silver ripples of her sparkly bodysuit caught the stage lights and momentarily blinded the audience.

Autumn must have worked hard in preparation for this performance. It explained the Marlene Dietrich DVD that we had found at the crime scene. Autumn's act was a direct rip-off with a modern edge to it. She was a natural performer and quite good. Her songs were nearly all original, sexy and sometimes angry, violent. The range of her voice was awesome in its power and ability. Under different circumstances, I might have enjoyed the show.

A thought too horrible to contemplate had entered my consciousness. There it was in front of me and it chilled me to my core. My mind clicked with the images of the voodoo doll next to the jewelry on her dresser and the menstrual blood of nine young women. They had to have still been alive in order to create the voodoo doll. I thought of the Autumn her parents knew and that Eddy had found so charming. Was this Autumn, this Zombita, somebody else's work or her own? What was she? How much did Autumn, now a real-life zombie, believe in these things she seemed to have embraced? I thought of Dani and her gruesome death and the Tylers and their unholy activities. I went back in my mind to the first time I heard Autumn Riley's name. Such a strong name, a good family name. I recalled the chimerical quality of her bungalow on the beach and the sleeping beauty within, how I had held her hand in a distressing empathy. And now, I had before me a puzzle too horrible to contemplate that, if completed, would reveal a repulsive portrait of who and what Zombita was.

⋰ ⋰ ⋰

I WATCHED FROM THE shadows as Addams engaged The Barb in a short conversation. I followed them as they moved out the back door and climbed into the Humvee. Larry, the driver, stood outside the limo as the two men met within. He glanced at me and then pointedly ignored me, which was good. I was hoping the guy would be an ally, but you can never be too sure. The windows were tinted on the limo so I couldn't see any other interaction once Addams and The Barb were inside. By accident, I noticed Dewey get into a taxi and I thought that was very strange. Why would he leave this esteemed evening of events? Was he going back home?

I went back into the club, my anxiety level rising. Zombita was singing a spooky love ballad. It was a remake of an old Bessie Smith song. Something about her lover being buried in a graveyard and now she would always know where to find him. I listened to her voice, now a sinister haunting sound. More anger surged within me with every irony and rhyme. She finished the set and the crowd went crazy. I watched her cut off the stage, then through the backstage.

Then Gus signaled that it was time to move out. Our plan was to take a ride up to Piuma Heights and check out that dirt road.

CHAPTER TWENTY-SEVEN

W<small>E SPED THROUGH</small> H<small>OLLYWOOD</small> in a flash, zooming past all the tinsel, neon, and people of the night. We took La Cienega, the restaurant row of Los Angeles, and jumped on the Santa Monica freeway and were on Pacific Coast Highway in twenty minutes. There was traffic but it was moving fast.

Gus made a call to get some additional information on our destination. Came back that the Piuma Heights address was the home of an old man who had lived there since 1932.

"The guy must be ninety years old," I said.

"If he's still alive," said Gus.

Gus called Mark O'Malley and had him start the proceedings for a search warrant. In the meantime, we asked for backup. I took a pic of the limo driver's map and sent it on to Mark by text.

We followed Pacific Coast Highway along the beach. A sliver of moon shone down on the dark water. The sky was electric blue. A half hour later, we turned right on Rambla Pacifica and climbed up the Topanga mountainside. Ten minutes later, we took a secondary road that snaked ever higher up into the clouds.

An owl on a telephone wire took swooping flight as we passed. I could almost hear my gramma's voice telling me that an owl moving off into darkness was a sure sign that you were about to move into the unknown and mysterious. As we got closer, I realized what I already knew was plenty bad. I wouldn't like it to get much worse. What I would discover and the weight of the responsibility of it had me in its grip. I felt fear in my bones. Thoughts of the devil, quietly choosing victims to pull down to their deaths, filled my mind as we gazed into the black maw of that canyon.

We climbed up and up, wound round and round, until we hit Ridgeback Road where the map indicated to go left and follow the road to the top of the mountain. I peered at sleeping houses, a few with porch lights still on and cars parked askew on barely hewn driveways. Near the top of the mountain, the Piuma Heights road sign was lit up by our car beams. The map showed that we should pass that road and continue another winding seven hundred feet, then take a right.

Dread blossomed in my chest and I said a little prayer. When we took the right onto what looked like a fire road out through the heavy chaparral, a young coyote darted out in front of the car and we had to swerve not to hit it.

We drove onward to where the road ended. The car headlights fell on a rusty NO TRESPASSING sign that swung eerily from an old chain pulled across a poorly kept dirt road of washed-out sandstone. I looked into a canyon that went all the way down to the ocean. The wind was beating the chaparral. Trees and bushes appeared to frantically warn us.

"Canyons measureless to man down to a sunless sea," whispered Gus.

According to the map, the house we wanted was at the end of this gnarled dirt road. Gus parked the car behind a stand of tall pampas grass whipping in the wind.

We'd have to continue on foot. I estimated from the map that it was another two miles to the house, and we weren't talking about a neighborhood with streetlights. Except for the stars and the silver moon, the night was pitch black. Gus opened the trunk, got a flashlight, and put it into his back pocket. We moved on down the non-road to the sound of cicadas and furtive animal movements on either side.

There were such deep ruts in the road that we had to use the flashlight. Gus kept it as low and close to the ground as possible. We moved in a half circle around the mountain. A chorus of frogs sounded in the distance, growing louder and louder. In my youth, I often took walks at night. Thoughts of the Ozarks invaded my thoughts. The chorus of frogs came to a dead quiet when the flashlight beam bounced around onto mud, then water, and finally on Autumn's silver car, the Audi T. It was parked before a creek. She couldn't make it across in the car and had parked it there. The water was cold. Halfway across the creek, we were up to our knees in mud and water. A chill ran through my body and my stomach heaved. A faint but deadly fear revisited me.

"Joanie, are you okay?"

"Fine, let's just keep crossing."

A single frog croaked in encouragement. We managed to get across that damn creek, stream, whatever it was. I guess it wasn't just pomp that prompted them to rent the Humvee limo; they needed a military vehicle just to get in and out of this place without messing up their nice clothes. We were wet and cold and the wind wasn't kind to us. As soon as we were a few feet from the water, the frogs started back up in full chorus.

There certainly was a house somewhere nearby because a pipe ran along what had to be a rarely used road.

I was sure we'd approach a structure soon. After another quarter mile we came upon a foundation of large hewn stones. There was old broken pottery in different stages of development strewn around the structure of a small house. It was as if this were a dump for a potter's mistakes. The design of the building was old, like it had been built in the bootleg era. Gus flipped off the flashlight. A small florescent bulb hung from a wire in one room.

Gus and I moved up closer. We approached a window and peered in. Inside, we saw there was a short and roughly constructed doorway, with a rusty bar across it and a shiny new padlock on it. I figured it must lead to a cellar or a basement, which is highly unusual in earthquake-prone California.

We heard footsteps moving about inside, so Gus and I moved to each side of the window and pressed our backs against the rough stone. A shadow moved over the grass outside the window. Someone inside was obviously near the window, and from the sound of it, they unlocked the cellar door. Their footfalls went down the steps. When I thought it was safe, I took a peek to discover that it was Dewey disappearing down into the basement. I strained to see more when I heard a mewing sound and I guessed it was a cat. It seemed to be coming from behind us, but I couldn't locate the animal. There was a covered well with an old-fashioned lock on it, and the mewing had to be coming from there.

Maybe the cat had fallen in and couldn't get out. Or maybe someone had locked it in the well to be cruel. It was then I considered for a moment whether it was a cat mewing or a person, a woman, whimpering. I turned back and peered into the house. The shiny silver padlock dangled loosely from the hook on what I assumed was the basement door.

"What's going on?" whispered Gus.

"I don't know," I breathed. "It's Dewey. He just went down some steps. It's got to be a basement or something. I think I hear someone trapped in the well."

Gus looked over at the well. "Listened, but no mewing or whimpering came from the well."

"I heard it Gus, I'm sure of it."

He nodded. "If it's a basement, there's probably a window," said Gus as he started moving.

We felt our way around the building, being careful not to make any noise. We came across a huge vent coming out of the structure, even more unusual in California and especially for such a small structure. Several dozen propane tanks were lined up against the building and we scooted around them. There was a rusted military jeep, with no top, parked behind the house. It had to be fifty years old.

"When we get inside, we need the keys to that thing," Gus pointed at the jeep.

"You think it runs?"

Gus nodded. "There's fresh mud on the tires."

We continued to move around the building to a shining light that came from what had to be a basement window. On hands and knees, I bent down to carefully and quietly wipe away a small area of dust and cobwebs, being careful not to actually touch the window or make any movement that would be sighted from inside.

At that moment, the light went off. We froze and listened to the door being closed and padlocked. I waited a moment, stepped away from the window, and looked in.

Nothing but darkness.

Dewey had gone back upstairs and moved into what must have been the kitchen because he turned a faucet on and off and I heard the door to an icebox open and close. He rattled around in there for a while, then began a strange moaning sound that had a certain repeated rhythm to it like an incantation or a chant.

Gus went to work on the window with one of his gadget contraption things, a pocketknife with every kind of tool you can imagine.

"You got a glass cutter on that thing?" I asked.

Gus nodded, "But that ain't gonna get it."

The front door was thrown open and Dewey came out and shouted something out into the night. He did this repeatedly as if he were calling someone or something. I couldn't make out who or what.

Gus had some problems as the window was rusted and old. He'd have a hard time crawlin' in that window, but I could make it through, even with my hips, if he managed to get the window completely out of the frame. He was working it. Gus was sweating so much his collar was completely wet. His muscular arms and shoulders strained with the effort to control his movements and not make any sound. Finally, he managed it. When I bent down to enter, the rank stench that came out of that opening was disheartening. "Where's a gas mask when you need one?" Gus whispered.

"I'm going in," I whispered back.

Gus nodded solemnly and took out the flashlight.

He popped on a red plastic cover over the bulb so that when I used the flashlight it wouldn't dilate my eyes. My appreciation for his gadgets grew by the moment. I'd be able to continue to see in the dark after I used it. I tucked it into my back pocket.

I sat on my butt and stuck one leg in, then the other, and maneuvered around onto my stomach, twisting, inching my way through the window, trying not to crush my breasts.

I hung down the side of the wall from my fingers and my feet scrapped and slipped on slime. I heard Dewey walking across the floor above me and held my breath. I was stunned by the realization that the fear I felt was similar to when my father walked across the floor above me after he had killed my mother. An uncontrollable trembling came over me. I pushed it back, fighting it off, refusing its grip. I dropped to the ground, landed softly on my feet.

I stayed frozen there for a moment, listening. The air was thick with the smell of feces, urine, and mold. Upstairs, the footfalls moved to the living room area. I felt around in the darkness and put my hand against the damp wall and began to move, continuing to feel along the wall.

It was sweaty with a slimy moisture I couldn't identify. I gasped when something scurried over my feet. Two hands clasped my arm and I nearly screamed.

"Help," a voice whispered.

I pulled my flashlight out and flicked it on.

The face of Vernice, the black girl, was lit in red before me. Barbed wire was tied around her neck. Her eyes bulged in fear and desperation.

"Please, help," she whispered again. Her teeth chattered, creating an eerie percussion. Her body trembled and I thought my heart could not bear the weight that seemed to crush it.

CHAPTER TWENTY-EIGHT

A s I pointed the red beam on the rest of the room, I thought something was wrong with the bulb of my flashlight as it kept flickering. Then I realized the flashlight was fine—it was me that was shaking. I moved from bed to bed, almost unable to comprehend what I saw. I looked at the face of each sleeping young woman. Vernice was at my side, still clutching my arm. My heart beat against my chest. None of the young women were conscious except for Vernice. All had the cruel barbed wire wrapped around their necks. I recognized Suzy, the girl with the mole, and Jeanette, the one with the scar, Marissa, the one with the tattoo, Judy, the one with the birthmark, Jennifer, the tall one. Anne, with the olive complexion, was drooling.

Then finally I discovered Katrice, the one with a dimple when she smiled, but she wasn't smiling. I couldn't even be sure she was breathing. I touched her face but her skin was cold and clammy. I feared that she was near death, if not actually dead. Then I remembered Autumn and how well she had revived and I hoped the same would be true for Katrice. If, in fact, it was the same drug at work, for it was certain that they were all drugged. Katrice was more sunken down in the bed, almost as if she were in a shallow grave. I shone the flashlight under her bed and saw that the rusty wire webbing that was supposed to hold the mat in place sagged down. A rat dashed across the stone floor. I said their names over and over again. It was my mantra. My own protective chant.

I bumped into a huge propane gas tank. When I searched around the area with the flashlight, there was a large mass in the corner.

As I got closer I realized it was barbed wire. Anger flushed up the back of my head, but it was quickly replaced by horror when I realized that there were two thin red-and-black wires attached to the propane gas tank. Upon closer inspection, I saw that the tank was connected to a long pipe that also ran up and through the hole into what I guessed was the kitchen. The place was wired and the piping looked like the work of an advanced student of explosives. Neither Gus nor I had explosive training, and getting the bomb squad here in time was out of the question. Getting the victims out and safe was priority one.

An archway led into more darkness and I moved, pulling Vernice toward a smaller room with an even smaller wooden door. "I don't want to go in there," said Vernice.

"What's in there?" I asked. "Tell me."

She shook her head violently and let go of my arm. I found there was a rusty bar across the wooden door but no lock. I took the bar off and leaned it against the wall and gently opened the door. It creaked, so I moved it slowly. Once inside, I turned my flashlight onto the vent that led to this room and saw it was attached to a large kiln, which explained the pottery and at least one reason for the use of propane. I searched the rest of the room and found first a bucket, and then a boy, naked and huddled in the corner of the darkness behind it. His whole body trembled with fear.

"Hello," I said, my voice sounding strange and hollow. "My name is Joan and I'm going get you out of here."

He ducked his head between his knees. The trembling increased.

"I'm not here to hurt you. I'm here to help you. Understand?"

The boy ducked his head farther down and put his hands over his head.

"My name is Joan," I repeated. "What's your name?"

He lifted his head and peered at me, the trembling stopped.

"Tommy," he said.

Tommy, the missing boy.

"Okay, Tommy. We're getting out of here, okay?"

He looked doubtful. "They have guns," he said.

"We're going to trick them," I said. "We'll sneak out, okay?"

He thought about this, then nodded.

"Okay, let's go," I said.

I put out my hand. He grasped me with both his small cold hands. We walked together through the archway. As we turned around the corner, I bumped the bar I had placed there and it fell to the ground with a loud clang.

I heard Dewey's footsteps immediately. Vernice scuttled through the darkness to her bed.

"Tommy, go back and pretend I wasn't here, I'll come and get you, I promise."

He resisted, so I had to push him back into the dark room. My heart sunk as I closed the door and put the bar in place. I heard Dewey undo the padlock at the top of the stairs. I didn't have time to climb out the window so I had to disappear. I saw Gus place the window glass gently against the frame to disguise his handiwork. I crossed to the cots, found the one with Katrice, and lifted the mattress just enough to slide in underneath. The rusty wire webbing dug into the flesh all along my backside. I focused on not breathing. Dewey's footsteps came down the stairs and a bright light came on. Dewey immediately went into the smaller room where Tommy was. I could hear as the bar was removed and the door creaked open.

"Whas goin' on in here, boy?"

"Nothing."

"You tryin' to escape?"

"No."

"You better not be!"

I heard a struggle, then a slap, and something huge and fierce loomed up in me. I shot out from under that mattress and pulled the gun from my back holster. The smaller room was lit from a hanging light bulb just like the one with the girls. I heard Tommy whimper. A murderous bile came to my mouth.

Dewey's back was to me when I stepped into the room. Dewey had Tommy's head clasped in one hand with a tight grip on his hair. He was pulling the boy toward him. I placed my gun into the base of Dewey's skull.

"Don't move, Dewey. I wouldn't want to get your brains all over the place, the kid's already been through enough." Dewey was still. "Now, let go of the boy."

He did so, and Tommy scooted back to his corner and returned to his huddled position. I pressed the gun into Dewey's neck.

"What's going on here, Dewey? What's with all the spiritual preparations? Huh? You about to do a big ritual, sacrifice somebody?"

"No comment."

"You're not even going to brag about your fancy explosives?"

Dewey stared at the wall for an answer.

"Where's the trigger? Tell me and I'll say you cooperated."

Dewey laughed and shook his head.

"Man, you touch dese explosives to defuse them? We all dead. They'll blow, mon. The Barb got 'em rigged real tight. Don' even try. Ain't nuthin' goin' ta stop da fireworks."

"Okay. Fine. Tommy, I need you to help me, okay?"

Tommy lifted his head from between his knees where he was trying to hide.

"Will you please go get me a sheet off one of the beds?"

The kid just stared at me.

"Please do it now, Tommy. It's important."

He got up from the corner and went into the other room.

"Relax, Dewey, this won't hurt a bit." I coldcocked him in the head with my gun. He slumped forward and slid down the wall to the floor.

Tommy came back with a sheet and gave it to me. He stared at Dewey on the floor.

I tore the sheet in two. "Here, Tommy, wrap this around your body." The kid was anxious to cover himself.

I used the other half to tie Dewey's hands and feet together.

We exited the room. I closed the door and Tommy put the bar in place.

"Good job," I said.

"You have a gun, too."

"Yes, I do."

We went back into the room with all the young women lying in cots. I had to believe that wherever the trigger for the explosives was, it wasn't the way Dewey had just come or the front door that Dewey had opened when he called out.

Vernice grabbed my arm again. She, too, had torn a sheet and wrapped it around her body. The three of us went up the stairs to the cellar door. It opened easily since Dewey had left it unlocked. We moved quickly through the front room. I stopped only to pick up a set of keys from the coffee table. I noticed there was that same piping in the living room as in the basement leading up to the kitchen. I opened the front door, praying it wasn't attached to the trip.

Tommy and Vernice followed me outside where we saw Gus come from around the side of the house.

"Tommy, Vernice, this is Gus, he's going to help us."

"Hi, Tommy, Vernice."

I reported the situation inside to Gus.

Tommy stared up at us, expectant. He looked around as if he might make a run for it.

"I don't think we can wait to get the girls out of there," I said. "The Barb has the place rigged to blow."

Tommy looked back to the house as if considering it exploding.

"Is it high-tech or homemade stuff?" asked Gus.

"Homemade, but extensive. I think there's a pipe that goes to every room."

"Coming from the basement?"

"Yes."

"Okay, then that means the trip is somewhere else in the house. It could be by hand. Or it could go off when you open a door. It might be a motion detector."

"Or even on a timer for all we know," I added. "Since it didn't go off when we went through the window, we know that it's not that. You came out the front door so that's safe, too."

Gus looked at Vernice. "How come you're not knocked out like the others?" asked Gus.

"I spit it out from the beginning. I pretended to be asleep."

"Smart girl. Are you going to be able to help us?"

"I can help," said Vernice.

"I can't ask her to go back in there, Gus.

"We have to get them out," said Gus.

"I said I can help," insisted Vernice.

"Okay, you can help. Anyone else being held captive besides in the basement?" I asked.

"There's Paige," said Vernice. "She was the first one, she's in the well."

Of course, Paige, it was the first missing file, the pole vaulter. She had disappeared eight months ago, which made the full count of missing girls a total of ten.

"You got here just in time," Vernice continued. "They were going to sacrifice us at dawn, then blow the place."

"How do you know that?"

"I could hear them talking and planning, all three of them are totally wacked out."

"Where's the keys to the well?" I asked.

"The keys to the well are hanging on a hook in the kitchen. But I would get those girls out before you step in the kitchen, I'm pretty sure its rigged. The Barb is completely obsessed with the explosive stuff and I'd bet good money the trip is somewhere in the kitchen."

That must have been Paige mewing like a cat, trying to get my attention.

"Why is Paige in the well?" I asked. "Is she different somehow?"

"She tried to escape and didn't make it and so now, Autumn really hates her. Not that she loves any of us."

"Why does she have anything against any of you?"

"Something to do with a singing competition."

"The pop star audition?"

"Yeah, right."

"Is Paige conscious like you?"

"She was before she tried to escape. Now, I don't know."

⑊ ⑊ ⑊

WE HAD ALL MOVED inside to discuss an exact plan to remove the girls up the basement steps and out the front door since we knew that was clear of trips. We were down in the basement about to make the first move when the sound of tires on the muddy road and headlights approaching thwarted our plans. The Barb and Zombita arrived in the limo, driven by Larry. I pulled Tommy close to me and watched out the basement window with growing apprehension as The Barb and

Zombita appeared from the limo. I whispered to Tommy, reassuring him that we were going to be all right.

Music blasted from the limo. Zombita and The Barb both wavered, stumbled around, and finally moved toward the house. I assumed they were high.

"That was great, fuckin'-A great," roared The Barb. His words were slurred. "Looks like we got a movie deal."

"We don't have anything until we sign the contract," said Zombita. "You have to call Glenn first thing in the morning and request a written contract. I'll have my lawyer go over every detail. He can say anything. It's the contract that makes the deal."

"Wull, of course. I know that. Don't patronize me."

"I'm not. I'm just trying to make a point. You were excellent tonight. You were a real manager. But we have to finish up the details. We have to get it in writing."

She had my Raggedy Ann doll clasped in her hand.

Zombita and The Barb came inside, their footsteps just over our heads. I watched the limo driver make a U-turn in the grass.

"We need that limo," said Gus.

I slipped out the basement window and began running to cut Larry, the limo driver, off at the bend. As he came by me to pass, I leapt onto the sideboard on the driver's side and grabbed the door handle, pulled my gun and pointed it at him. He stopped the car and rolled down the window.

"What the fuck?" he said.

"You and this limo have just been commandeered."

"There's no pay for that, I take it."

"No. I need you to park here and be quiet. Don't play the radio, don't talk on the phone, keep all the lights off. Most importantly, don't leave. Got it?"

"What's goin' on?"

"I don't have time to explain. I have to go back and you better be here when I return or you'll have hell to pay, I promise you."

"Okay, I'll be here."

╫·╫·╫

WHEN I CRAWLED BACK into the basement, I told Gus where the limo was and gave him the keys to the jeep. The usual thing would be to neutralize the suspects. Normally, we would apprehend and arrest our criminals, then evacuate the hostages, but since the place was rigged and we had no clue where or how, our choices were greatly limited. The main objective was to get the girls out. Then we'd move in and make our arrests. Then only our own lives would be at stake, and that's not so uncommon in law enforcement.

"What about Paige?" I said. Gus shook his head.

"We have to get her out later."

I wanted to argue, but Gus was my supervisor and I knew he was right anyway. There was no way we could get Paige out of the well at that point without endangering the whole group. It was a major flaw in our plan.

There were more hoots and hollers from upstairs as Zombita and The Barb bumped around. I moved closer to where they were located in the kitchen and listened to their conversation.

"I'll call Caroline in the morning," said Autumn. "I'll have her discuss the contract in detail with Addams. It's more appropriate for the agent to do that anyway. You just concentrate on getting me more gigs."

"Sure, don't worry."

"Don't worry? Have you made contact with anyone at all in A&R? One person, even? A secretary?"

I tried to remember what A&R stood for. It had something to do with promoting musical artists or finding new talent.

"I'm way past that, babe. I got a call into John Lanster. We're having a fucking meeting next week. What do you think I am anyway, a bleedin' idiot? Hey, where's Dewey?"

"He's probably with one of the girls," said Autumn.

That must have seemed likely to The Barb because he didn't pursue it.

"Did you hear what I said about setting up more gigs?" she asked.

"Sure, of course, whatever you say. I'll do it. But we're plugging into the machine, babe. We don't have to do that. The Merchants of Cool are going to create a huge market explosion named Zombita and you're going to be the center of the universe, just like we planned."

Then he made grunting sounds like maybe they were having sex. A real Romeo, that guy. I walked back to Gus.

"What are they doing up there?" asked Gus.

"Coition," I whispered.

Gus gave me a double take.

"We have to make sure the girls are safe before we make an arrest," he said.

"Right. I know. That's not exactly an easy task."

"No kidding. If it's a hand trip and they discover us, or if we make the wrong move, we're fajitas."

"Why'd you have to say that? I'm never going to be able to eat those now."

"I'm thinking this is our window of opportunity," Gus said, and then he walked over to Tommy and put his hand on the kid's shoulder, bent over to give him instructions.

CHAPTER TWENTY-NINE

OUR ONLY REASONABLE CHOICE was to quietly move the girls out through the same basement window. I picked Jennifer, the tall one, first. Vernice and I were on basement duty. It wasn't easy. Jennifer's legs and arms dangled lifelessly and there is a good reason why they use that term "dead weight." A person who is unconscious is heavy and not at all cooperative. Finally, we coordinated our efforts. Vernice stood on a cot we pulled over to the window, while from outside Tommy reached through the window and guided her body to Gus, who lifted and pulled her through the window. Though it was not necessarily a smooth operation, we got her long body through that window and out of the basement. Gus carried her to the limo. Then I lifted Marissa, from her cot, then Judy, then Brenda. I lifted each girl, carried her to the window, and then Vernice and I, together, hefted each of them up and, carefully, so as not to bruise or scrape their soft flesh, through the window and out to Tommy and Gus. I was relieved that Zombita and The Barb were loaded out of their minds and busy having sex, as it would make them less perceptive to any slight noise we might make.

I kept my ears open for any sound at the basement door.

I'm not what you'd call a religious woman, but I have a direct line to God through my heart. Past rats and wet, sweating walls, I moved and I prayed for God's blessing. We had trouble with the last girl, Katrice. She was completely limp; her body was like a jellyfish, but somehow we got her out to Gus. Vernice scooted out the window like a pro. Finally, I pulled myself out of the basement, gulping the fresh air into my lungs, and was moving with Vernice and Tommy toward the limo when we heard sirens in the distance.

Gus set Katrice into a seat and Vernice belted her in.

Katrice's body slumped to one side like a rag doll. I felt something nudge me from behind. A nose in between my butt cheeks. It was Pancho, Tommy's dog. "Where'd he come from?" I asked Gus.

"He showed up right after we started pulling out the girls," said Gus.

Dawn was beginning to break. I looked at my watch. It was four forty-five in the morning.

"What about Zombita?" asked Larry.

"She's not the one who needs saving, pal," I said.

"Are you sure?"

"I made the same mistake, don't feel bad. Listen, Larry. I want you to go as fast as you can to the nearest hospital. Are we clear on that?"

"Clear."

"I want you to know that if these girls don't make it to the hospital for any reason, I'm going to hunt you down and kill you myself."

"Will you please stop threatening me? We're going to the hospital. I'm on your side. Don't worry."

"Okay, thanks Larry." I patted him hard on the back.

Vernice looked at me with serious eyes and said, "Paige."

"We'll get her. I promise." And I hoped it was true. Tommy held onto Pancho for dear life. "Thanks for your help, guys," I said. Tommy smiled.

"Thank you, lady," said Vernice.

I heard loud shouts coming from the house. It was The Barb's voice and then Dewey's. The Barb must have discovered Dewey in the kiln room and released him. I slammed the door of the limo shut.

Gus and I tore back to the house and the limo lurched away and down the road around the mountain. Just then, a high shriek came from my left. It sounded like some kind of demon. It was joined by another, and then another. Coyotes. Their voices lifted up in a terrifying chorus. Gus and I looked at each other and stood still as stone for a moment. I thought their eerie cries would never stop. We continued toward the house. The Barb was moving around inside and I could see him through the side window as we passed. He had a shotgun.

"WE HAVE TO GET Paige," I said.

"Right," said Gus.

The *WHACK, WHACK, WHACK* of a helicopter burst over the mountain.

"You get the keys to the well, hanging on that hook in the kitchen," said Gus.

"Sure, give me the easy stuff, why don'cha?"

"You're the agile one with all those fancy karate moves. Don't worry, got your back."

He shot out ahead of me and kicked in the front door. I followed right behind and we rushed in. Shots came from the hallway. I moved toward the kitchen, took a dive to avoid gunfire, did a forward roll, came up on my feet, and entered the kitchen running. The keys were hanging on a big hook attached to a roughly carved board that said "keys" on it. Wires went across the room and ceiling like some kind of mad rainbow spider web. I saw no trip connected to the key holder so I grabbed the keys. I jangled the keys so Gus could hear them. Footsteps pounded up the basement stairs and I could see a gigantic shadow of Dewey coming up the wall with a strange-looking gun in his hand. Gus ushered me out and I made for the door and out toward the well.

It was easy to pick out the right key for the lock as it was old and huge. I put the key in and with one loud click, the lock was loose. I pulled the rusty bars off and then the wooden cover to reveal Paige, naked, standing in water up to her waist. When she saw me, she cowered. Gunshots hit the side of the well and flew over my head and she winced.

"Come on, Paige. We're getting out of here. Now is the time."

I reached down to her and she stretched out to clasp my hand. Her grip was surprisingly strong. She grabbed my upper arm with her other hand, put her feet on the side of the well, and used her legs to make her way up. I leaned back, creating more weight, recalled her pole-vaulting career, and thanked God. She was out of that well in no time.

There were insect bites all over her upper body. Several more gunshots were exchanged and for a moment I thought Paige might jump back into the well. I spotted a small hill. It would work for temporary protection.

I grabbed Paige's hand and pulled her as I ran for the hill, counting on Gus to protect us. He was holding The Barb and Dewey back with return gunfire. We ran away from the house over toward the hill. Once we got started running good, I didn't have to pull Paige. She was out in front of me and we made it to the hill in no time.

I heard a *swoosh* sound. A searing pain burst in my right temple and my right hip. I knocked Paige to the ground when one of the windows exploded from the house and a burst of gunfire followed and we tumbled down behind the hill, safe from the gunfire for now. I reached to my temple and felt a small dart embedded in my skin. I pulled it out. I checked my hip and pulled out another dart.

"Joan, are you okay?" Gus shouted.

"I'm okay," I lied.

Colors began to swirl before my eyes and I realized I had been drugged. I fought to maintain.

"Look out for darts, Gus."

"What?!"

"Darts! Drug darts!"

Another *swoosh* and a dart buzzed by overhead. Gus shot back. I reached for my gun.

When I looked at Paige again, the face of my mother gave me a look of warning and my heart leapt to my throat. I told myself it was the drug. I heard running footsteps as The Barb ran to a back room, probably to get more ammo. I heard my father cursing, his fist pounding on the kitchen table. It frightened me to realize I was losing control of my mind and the drug was taking hold. I felt my legs turn to liquid but I willed them to move.

I got up and pulled Paige toward the jeep. She picked up the destination quickly and was out ahead of me again. I heard the pump of the shotgun and then gunfire from Gus. For a moment I recalled my first time shooting a shotgun and the next, I was running through the Ozark hills with my mother. Finally, Paige and I made it from the small hill to the jeep. She jumped in and hid on the floor.

"I'll be right back," I said and went back to the house for Gus.

I was dizzy and I felt like I was running through water. My legs were hot rubber. I had no bones. I fell twice before making it to the house and the second time I just wanted to stay down, right there on the ground, and go to sleep. For a moment, I lay there still. I swear I could hear the grass growing and I could smell the water from the well.

I crept up to the kitchen window and could see Autumn in the corner, her eyes like that of a wild animal. Then Dewey entered the kitchen and Autumn shot out from her corner and they started to argue. For a moment, I saw before me old stock footage of my parents arguing in the kitchen on the day my father killed my mother. But I forced myself to remember that it was Autumn and Dewey who were arguing now, not my parents. I saw that Autumn didn't want Dewey to go past her. She was a big red spider protecting a multicolored web of wires. Autumn didn't want them to set off the explosives. That was good. At least one of them was not so eager to die.

Dewey tried to push past Autumn and they began to struggle. I could see through the kitchen door that Gus was still trapped in the front room. I ran around the house. Once in front, I peered into the shot-out window and spotted The Barb taking aim at Gus. Then The Barb's face turned into my father's and I remember thinking, "Poor Gus, Daddy's trying to kill him with the shotgun." It's not your father, I thought. Don't be stupid, shoot him! Shoot him! I need a gun, I complained to myself, and then I noticed there was one in my hand. I took aim on my father though I knew it was The Barb. I squeezed off a round, shot my father, hitting him in the right arm, and he spun away with a screech.

Gus took that opportunity to go for the door. Dewey came out from the kitchen and I shot several times. Though my aim was no good, Gus was able to make it out the front door.

Everything became a blur and I could hear gunshots, but I had lost my sense of direction and couldn't judge where they were coming from. I knew Gus was going for the jeep. He kept calling my name. I started toward his voice but fell on the ground and couldn't get up. No matter how hard I tried I couldn't get back up on my feet, so I slithered across the ground like a snake. I could feel a soft breeze on my face and could actually hear the blades of grass rustling against each other, and then another sound came through, a sweet humming that I recognized with an intense clarity to be the harmony of all existence. Then I heard Gus screaming my name and I slithered toward his voice. Gunshots exploded in my brain, echoing with the sound of my name.

The next thing I remembered was Gus pulling me into the jeep. I was in the front seat. When I looked in the back, I saw my mother cowering on the floor.

Then my mind said, "That's Paige." Gus pulled off.

Autumn bolted from the house. She was a streak into the woods, the Raggedy Ann doll clutched in her fist. She transformed into a beast with horns. Fire shot out of her eyes. Zombita or Autumn, or whoever the hell she was, looked like the daughter of Satan. Her hair flowed out behind her, red snakes of Medusa. She moved like some supernatural creature, not human at all.

A strange feeling came over me, as if an invisible wave washed over me, and everything shifted into focus, making my vision crystal clear.

Dewey came running from the house with his dart gun; The Barb was right behind him with the shotgun. But we were pulling away, out of range for either of them. Then Dewey turned and ran back toward the house. The Barb shook his shotgun at us, then followed Dewey into the house as well.

"They're going to blow the house," I said. Gus looked at me. "Good thing we got everybody out," I said

"Yeah, good thing," said Gus. "There's Satch,"

I spotted two black SUVs coming around the bend ahead. I could see Satch in one of the 4x4s. He was talking on a handheld radio and directing with hand signals to the other 4x4 at the same time.

A loud explosion came from under the bowels of the earth and I turned to see the house shake. Hundred-foot flames of fire burst into the sky as we pulled away. Fear gripped my heart, but not because of the house. It was what the explosion signified. The beast was let loose into the atmosphere. Alarms went off in my mind and in my body.

"She's going for the car," I said.

"You think?" said Gus.

"Yes."

As we pulled around the bend, we saw Autumn break from the woods on the other side of the creek and jump into the Audi T. She took off, spewing dirt and mud.

"She's not going to make it," I said.

Gus looked at me for a second and then back to the road.

We splashed through the creek, and when we came around the next curve in the road, we were just in time to see the back end of the Audi T sailing over the side of the cliff.

And then I passed out.

〜〜〜

I WAS HOLDING MY mother's hand and she was smiling down at me, her face kind and loving. I woke with a start, realizing it was Eddy who was holding my hand. I was in a hospital bed and he was by my side. I mumbled something unintelligible and fell back into a vision of green rolling hills. When I woke again, Eddy was still holding my hand.

"Eduardo Sforza," he said.

"What?"

"When you woke up last time, you demanded to know my real name. It's Eduardo Sforza."

"Oh. That has a ring to it. Sounds like some Italian Baron or something."

"Duke," said Eddy.

"What?"

"Sforza was a Duke."

"Should I bow or something?"

"That won't be necessary. The castle is a rubble of stones these days. I'm pretty sure I'm the grandson of the bastard son of a bastard so we can forget the formalities."

"Good, glad to hear it."

"Are you okay, babe?"

"I think so."

There was a knock and Gus entered with a bouquet of daisies. Eddy let go of my hand so I could give Gus a hug.

"Are they dead, Gus?"

"They found identifiable pieces of The Barb, but nothing of Dewey yet."

"What about the old man? The owner of the house?"

"Buried in back. He was a potter, a hermit."

"And Autumn? Is she alive?"

"She was thrown from the car and knocked unconscious, but she's going to be okay. They have her secured at the UCLA medical center."

"How're Paige and the rest?"

"Everybody's fine."

"Katrice, too?" He nodded. "And Tommy?"

"He and Pancho are with their family. His parents asked for your phone number, so I gave it to them."

"Oh, that's nice. Thanks."

"There were a lot of happy reunions. You missed out on all the good stuff."

I laid there quietly for a moment to let it all sink in.

"Doc says you can go home," said Gus.

"Good. What was in that dart gun, anyway?" I asked.

"The lab evaluated it and found that it was a cocktail—part hallucinogen, part scopolamine, with a bit of belladonna thrown in for a smooth afterglow."

"That's a sophisticated brew," I said. "Sounds like a Dr. Sheffield recipe."

"The kind of thing you need a well-equipped lab for, not to mention an organic chemist," said Gus.

"It had a kick harder than Ozark moonshine, I tell you that."

Gus and Eddy chuckled. I smiled at them.

"What about Hector?" I asked.

"Well, Hector. He...he died last night around midnight."

"Oh."

The silence that filled the room was loud. Sun filtered through the blinds of the window.

Hector. I felt that somewhere in him I had caught a glimpse of his soul, but it had been too late to save it. The evil that he had assisted, had in fact perpetuated, had swallowed him whole.

"Look what I managed to find in the chaparral," said Gus.

He was holding my Raggedy Ann, a little worse for wear.

〰〰〰

EDDY DROVE ME HOME in his insect car. We rode in silence. The day was cool and cloudy. I found myself looking at the people in nearby cars. They appeared so calm and mundane. I couldn't begin to fathom their simple lives in comparison to mine. I rolled down my window. I could smell the ocean. I said a prayer thanking my mother and my grandmother. I felt their spirits were near. I thought of my father and all that he had taught me, how it served me still. I prayed that his spirit was at peace. I had never done that before. Then I asked my grandmother to collect all the souls of those children, those victims of the Tyler siblings, take them in her arms. I knew she would, and she would comfort them and heal them and guide them to safety, to the light, or however it works. Eddy looked over at me several times while I was deep in these thoughts, which were very much like prayers, but he didn't say anything. He's smart like that.

Once inside my own house, I took a bath and fell into bed. I was out by the time I hit the sheets. When I woke again, it was late afternoon. Eddy had tucked my Raggedy Ann doll under the covers next to me. I could hear him in the kitchen. He was humming and rattling pots and pans. Then I recognized the fragrance of fresh coffee and something baking in the oven. I tumbled out of bed and found Eddy in the kitchen covered with flour and beaming with pride.

"Fresh banana nut scones!" he announced.

We slathered them with butter and ate them while they were still hot from the oven. Funny, the way heaven can come to you.

"I didn't know you could bake," I said.

"What you don't know about me…"

"Yes, go on," I said.

"I can't think of anything clever. Sorry."

"It's okay. I probably wouldn't get it anyway. My head is still pretty thick."

Eddy had gotten the paper and it was spread out on the kitchen table. The headline read: TEN WOMEN, MISSING BOY AND DOG LIBERATED FROM TOMB.

"I don't think that was the kind of publicity Zombita was looking for," I said.

I heard the parrots squawking outside the window. I peered out and watched as they gathered in my banana trees. The big leaves bounced up and down under their weight.

The phone rang and I prepared myself for a barrage of media calls.

"Joan?" It was Tommy.

"Yes."

"My mother said I could call you."

"That's right, Tommy. You can call me anytime."

Eddy's eyes flicked over to me when he heard me say Tommy's name.

"I just wanted to say thank you," said Tommy.

"You're welcome, Tommy."

"Okay, I can't talk much. I have a lot of things to do."

"Yes, you have a whole life ahead of you."

"Bye, now."

"Bye, Tommy. Take care."

I hung up and looked at Eddy. "Kids say the damnedest things. He can't talk because has a lot of things to do."

"That's good."

I sat there in a state of joy, like it was the best thing anybody had ever said to me. That must have lasted about five minutes. The phone rang again; this time it was Gilda confirming dinner plans. Eddy agreed to go with me and we set a date for stargazing.

Then a not-so-pleasant thought occurred to me.

"You know I need to talk to Autumn Riley," I said.

"Why?"

"I need to hold her accountable."

"You don't," said Eddy.

"I do."

"She's going to claim Stockholm syndrome," he said. "She's going to say that The Barb drugged her and turned her into his personal slave."

"Nope, it doesn't ring true."

"Joan, she'll be a classic example. She's more legit than Patty Hearst. You're gonna have to live with it."

"Stop defending her."

"Joan, I would never presume to tell you what to do, but I feel it's important…"

"What is it with you men, anyway? What is it about that evil bitch that makes you all want to protect her?"

"You men? You just grouped me with all men."

"I'm sorry, wasn't that politically correct?"

"Stop it. Stop that right now. I don't want to protect her. It's you I'm concerned about."

"Who and what do you presume to protect me from?"

"Yourself," he whispered softly.

⊦⊩⊦⊩⊦⊩

I ARRIVED AT THE UCLA Medical Center and quickly learned Autumn's location. I shot like a bullet straight down the hall to Autumn's hospital room where two guards stood outside the door.

I walked into her room and found Autumn lying in the bed. Her face was washed clean of makeup. She had a deep gash on her forehead, a black eye, and what looked like a broken arm. I recalled the first time I saw her at the crime scene. Now, she looked at me with bloodshot eyes, then turned away.

"I need to ask you a few questions."

"Sorry about the doll. I didn't know it was yours."

"Why did you have it anyway?" I said to her back.

"Hector said if I kept it with me I'd be protected."

I paused for a moment, not quite sure which way to go.

"Did you feel you needed protection?" She nodded. "From what?" She turned to face me.

"I didn't mind getting high, but that time I, uh, woke up in the morgue, I don't know. Something wasn't quite right there. The Barb was trying to get over on me. I mean, that wasn't even necessary."

"I got the distinct impression that it was you running the show."

She looked at the floor.

"I was the talent, I was the creative element, but I really didn't understand how deeply disturbed The Barb and Dewey were. You can't possibly believe that I wanted to wake up in the morgue."

"I don't know. Maybe it was a publicity stunt."

"I suppose it's possible The Barb thought it'd be a good promo op, but he didn't clear it with me."

"We all thought you died."

"Yeah, so anyway."

She turned away from me again.

"You took the drug willingly?"

"Yes, it unleashed things in me," she said to the wall and sighed. "Creative things. I was soaring. You have no idea. It allowed me to be very creative."

"It allowed you to do things you wouldn't normally do?"

She propped herself up in the bed, trying to get comfortable, and now looked at me directly, committing to the conversation.

"Something like that. I became more realized, more potent somehow."

"Did Dewey indoctrinate you on the ways of voodoo?"

"No."

"No?"

"No."

She was lying to me; I knew it like I knew my name.

"What about Paige and the girls in the basement?"

"I don't know anything about that. I already told the cops. Never saw 'em."

"I think you did. I heard you tell The Barb that you thought Dewey was having sex with one of them. Plus, Vernice said you had a particular hatred for Paige."

"You heard wrong, detective. As far as Vernice...I don't know what's up with that."

"What about the boy?"

"What boy?"

"There was a boy down in the basement with the girls."

"You know, now that you mention it, I sort of remember one of The Barb's friends, Hector, saying something about a kid named

Tommy, that it was on the news or something? But I was out of it. I don't even remember what he said exactly."

"Never saw Tommy either?" She shook her head no. "You were staying there, right?"

"I was stoned, completely out of my mind, didn't know what was up half the time."

"You weren't too stoned to learn lyrics or dance routines. Not too stoned to record a CD. What about that?"

"Yes, but I was busy with that, focused. It's what I've always done, since I was a child. Look, what do you want from me? Maybe you saved my life, you got your doll back, now what?"

"I'm curious to know whether or not you believed that if you sacrificed nine, no, make that ten, beautiful and talented young women that it would help your musical career."

"I have no idea what you're talking about."

"How many of those girls did you compete against?"

"Excuse me?"

"You know, for the pop star audition or in acting class. Paige beat you out at that pop star audition, didn't she?"

"What? What pop star audition?"

"Your parents said you came to Los Angeles for a pop star competition but you didn't make the cut."

"They said that?" I nodded. "My parents have no clue, okay? I was working a record deal. Dani turned me onto The Barb. I wasn't thinking about a pop star audition. That's ridiculous."

"So, how did it work, Autumn? Did you point out the girls to Dewey and The Barb? Did you lure them into places where Hector could snatch them or what?"

"You're totally off. Leave me alone."

"I'm sorry, didn't you like that question?"

"Not much."

"Were you lovers with The Barb?" She was silent, looked at the floor again. "Don't like that question, either?"

Her bloodshot eyes met mine in defiance.

"I wouldn't say we were lovers."

"You had sex with him."

"Sometimes."

"Only when he promised to make you the center of a market explosion? What about Dani?"

"What about her?"

"Wasn't she your friend? Did you feel nothing when she was murdered?"

"Yeah, Dani. She was my best friend, ever."

"And?"

"I don't know what happened with that. The Barb was upset with her about something. He said Hector was going to take care of her. I thought he meant in a good way, connect her up with some money people or a modeling gig, something like that. I can't really remember. I was drugged, okay? You don't seem to get it. I guess you already have your mind made up."

"You want me to believe that The Barb was your Svengali?"

She smirked at that one.

"Who supplied you with the drug?"

Autumn sulked, pulled the covers up to her chin.

"I don't know, do your lab tests, figure it out. I'm tired. Leave me alone."

There were voices outside the room then the door opened and a burly suit, carrying a suitcase, walked in.

"Hi Autumn," said the big man.

"Lo," she said.

"Ms. Lambert?"

"Yes?"

"I'm Frederick Levy, Autumn's lawyer." He put his hand out. "I'm pleased to meet you."

I shook his hand and it wasn't a bad grip, fairly strong. His beard wrapped around his big face. I wondered if he was from St. Louis or Los Angeles.

"Do you also negotiate record deals, Mr. Levy?"

"Excuse me?"

"Don't answer her," said Autumn.

"Well, thank you for your legal advice," he said, smiling with great charm at Autumn. Then he turned to me.

"I'm trying to find out if Autumn knew anything about the drug," I said. "There haven't been any charges made against her so there's no need for alarm at this point."

Frederick scratched his beard, then showed me his teeth and turned to Autumn.

"Autumn, do you have any information on this drug matter?"

He was from St. Louis. No Los Angeles lawyer would have even used a pretense of cooperation.

Autumn vehemently shook her head no.

"Ms. Lambert, from now on I must ask you not to speak with my client, not without my presence."

"Okay."

He was from St. Louis, but he was in Los Angeles, now. "Autumn will help in any way she can in your investigation, but I understand the guilty parties in this are all dead."

"That's not entirely accurate. We've located the remains of The Barb but have yet to find any trace of Dewey."

A look of fear ran across Autumn's face. "Dewey is still alive?" she asked.

"We have every reason to believe so. He must have escaped into the mountains during the explosion." She considered this. "Someone supplied the drug," I said to Levy. "They had to get it from somebody. I'd like to know who."

"I see. If Autumn remembers anything, we'll call you first thing."

"I'd appreciate it," I said. "And Autumn will need to undergo some tests to see if the drug she was given is the same as the one used on the kidnap victims."

"We'll see about what Autumn needs," said Frederick Levy.

Autumn was staring at the end of her bed when I walked out. Once outside on the UCLA grounds, something jabbed at my brain. Like a stone in my shoe, I couldn't ignore it.

I called Gus and told him what was on my mind, but he insisted I join him at the LA County Museum for some exhibit. I said okay, but not with much enthusiasm.

"Meet me out front," he said.

When I got there, he was standing on the steps. Pink buttermilk clouds filled the blue sky over his head. I walked up to him and he grinned at me.

"What's so goddamn funny?" I asked.

"You're going to the museum with me. As you walk up these stairs, I want you to leave the world behind you and enter a different realm."

"I think I've spent plenty of time lately in a different realm, okay? It's not my first museum, Gus. Come off it."

It was a brisk trip up the stairs, Gus grinning all the way.

I patiently listened while Gus droned on about the Renaissance and then Latin Art, which included some souped-up cars with flames. I have to admit that I found the Goya intriguing. It underlined my desire to visit Spain. One day, I'm going to go. Then we came across something that looked vaguely familiar. It was a textured abstract painting with bright colors.

"What's that?" I asked.

"Oh, that's a Haitian artist," said Gus.

I walked up to the painting and looked at the caption. It was an unknown artist and the painting had been done on goatskin. Gus came up beside me.

"What is it?" he asked.

There was a white streak through bright colors of red, orange, and vibrant blue.

"Do you think that looks like lightning?" I asked. Gus pursed his lips and then turned to me.

"That's not really the question, is it?"

"No, the real question is—Where have we seen this before?"

CHAPTER THIRTY

WE DROVE OVER TO Dr. Sheffield's lab. The bored old lady receptionist took us down a hall. Dr. Sheffield wore rubber gloves and big safety goggles as he worked behind a glass wall. He looked up with dawning recognition as we approached. He stared at us blankly, eyed Gus, then nodded to the receptionist, so she left us there. We waited while he removed his gloves and goggles and came out of his glass box.

"You again," he said.

"Could we go into your office and get comfortable, have a nice conversation?" I asked.

"I'm busy. I have a lot of responsibility to attend to. In the future, an appointment would be prudent."

We followed him to his office and Gus spotted the painting behind Dr. Sheffield's desk. It was nearly an exact replica of the one at the museum. They could have been a set. Dr. Sheffield sat down at his desk. "Have you ever been to Haiti?" asked Gus.

"Why do you ask?"

Gus walked over to the painting. "Is that where you got this painting?"

"The painting is from Haiti. It was a gift to me."

"From Dr. Blanchard," I said as a statement.

"Yes."

"When I first came here, you didn't mention that you actually knew him. Why not?"

"It's not something I announce. But you seem to know already, so I'll tell you that I was his field researcher for two years. I was well out of there by the time of the incident. Is that what you are here about?"

"Can you tell us who would be able to supply a large amount of a drug, similar to the drug Dr. Blanchard used in Haiti?"

"No, I couldn't. I haven't been in that world for twelve years. What makes you think the case you're on now has anything to do with Dr. Blanchard?"

"Let me ask you another question. Do you know anyone by the name of The Barb or Dewey?"

Dr. Sheffield sighed and shook his head. He pushed his glasses down on his nose and squeezed the place between his eyes.

"There was a young man by the name of Dewey who worked for Dr. Blanchard in the lab, an assistant."

"And The Barb?"

"Never heard that name."

"Did Dr. Blanchard give you any other gifts? Maybe a journal with his formulas, a book of his potions?"

"No. And now, it is time for me to make a call. Excuse me. I will be with you in a moment."

He ushered us out. Gus and I stood outside the door of the doc's office and waited.

"Thanks for taking me to the museum," I said.

"I bet you lunch he's calling whoever financed this operation to get the name of a lawyer."

In two minutes, Dr. Blanchard opened the door and waved a piece of paper at us.

"Please feel free to call my lawyer if you have any further questions." He handed me the paper and closed the door on us.

"Lunch is on me," I said.

We went to Engine 52 for lunch, an old firehouse transformed into a classy restaurant. The fire pole is still there and sepia-stained pictures of all the firemen and the old fire engine built in 1941. It's a comfy but elegant place.

I ate my Mediterranean salad on the side of my mouth that still had all its teeth and gulped down a cup of coffee. Gus had meatloaf, which is his favorite.

"You want dessert?" asked Gus.

"No."

"Come on, you have to try the devastation cake."

"I think I've already had it."

"No, no. You'll love it."

"Sure, okay. Why not?"

We had our cake; it was delicious. We left the restaurant, drove over to Parker Center, and on the way Gus received a text with a file attached to it. I checked it out while he was driving.

"What's this?" I asked. "Says it's from Camarillo, the asylum."

"Oh, sorry. I didn't tell you. While you were out on medical leave, I found out Dewey has a cousin in Camarillo, murdered his wife. I followed up on it and one of the trustees had remembered a letter from Dewey and promised to text it to me."

"Amazing, really, but as your partner, I think you should keep me better informed."

"I'll work on it."

I read the letter out loud to Gus.

⫿⫿⫿

Dear Cousin,

I didn't know where you were until Bernie told me last week all about your wife and how you ended up in Camarillo. My heart was heavy with the bad news. If only we could go back to Haiti and start over again. So many of us have been splintered like wood for the fire. I am on my way to California and I will make a point to come visit you when I get there. I hope you are allowed visitors.

Mama made me go work for the doctors against my own will and good sense. I wanted to stay home and learn the old ways like her. I never liked those doctors. But she was convinced they had special magic and the secret to making money because they were from the United States. Everybody listened to my mother and so I did too. I wish I hadn't. In Haiti, I was my mother's son and the people loved me. Now, I have fled my village and can never return. Here, in New York, I am only another fool with no money or home. The funny thing is the man who brought me here believes I have the same power as my mother. My mother helped him once he says and he is indebted to me. He has taken an interest in spiritual things and he thinks I can help him. He is very ambitious and means for me to assist in his endeavors. What he doesn't know is that I am dead inside. I didn't learn the secrets from Mama like I wanted and now I have lost the spirits.

They don't talk to me anymore. I have offended them and I don't think I can get them to take me back. It is hard to convince the spirits because I don't even believe that I deserve their mercy. Mama is dead, as are many others, and though I didn't mean for any of it to happen, I feel I am to blame. Maybe Mama will explain to the spirits for me.

Pierre, why did you kill your wife? Was she cheating on you? I heard she was American. There are many beautiful women here but I don't seem to be able to befriend any. Maybe I will meet one in California. I don't know what will happen to me. This man I am working with has some crazy ideas and though I'd like to discourage him, I am afraid to alienate his good feelings toward me. In this world, a man must have at least one friend. Sometimes I think I should run off into the woods. But there are no good woods in America where a black man like me can live in peace. Perhaps if I disguised myself as that BEEEG FOOT THING. But then, can't you just see them coming after me with their cameras, inspecting my footprints? That would give me away for sure because my feet are too small. Maybe you should make some room for me in your asylum. I might end up there and at least I would have a safe roof over my head and get to see my cousin. I'll say a prayer for you but I warn you, no God or spirit listens to me.

Your cousin, Dewey

"You think Dewey is hiding out in the Malibu Mountains?" Gus asked.

"For all we know he's on a bus to New Orleans or Miami," I said. "Where he can just disappear."

"His description went out to all fifty-two states, so plenty of people will be looking for those dreadlocks and that knot in the middle of his forehead."

"Yep, there's that."

Dewey could make an interesting witness against Autumn Riley. That was for sure. Autumn and Dewey in a courtroom; I'd like to see that.

⚒ ⚒ ⚒

BACK AT THE OFFICE, we had to do yet more paperwork wrapping up the case and filling in the more recent details on Autumn and Dr. Sheffield. Gus added the letter from Dewey to his cousin to the murder book. I added the information from the coroner's office on the old man, the potter buried in the backyard. There was no next of kin. I didn't give any details regarding my Raggedy Ann, as I didn't think I could stand the harassment I'd receive if that ever got out. I did get plenty of congratulations and a big pat on the back from Satch. Then he called me into his office.

"Autumn Riley's parents were here; they were sorry to miss you."

"Oh, jeez, Cap'n. I would have liked to talk to them."

"Personally, I'm glad you didn't."

"I'm sure I wouldn't have been as diplomatic as you and the DA, but it would have been an enlightening encounter."

"The DA has worked out a deal. Autumn will go to an institution for deprogramming. It seems Autumn was unduly influenced by The Barb, manipulated with this powerful drug. He used it to control her. That was your original theory, right? The DA feels strongly that Autumn Riley is strictly a victim."

"What? The DA? Who? Which one?"

"Stephen Mollach."

"Stephen Mollach? Since when did he become an expert on these things? I'm going to call him myself and give him the blues, yes I am."

"Go right ahead, Joan. Waste your time if you like. Politics and justice don't mix, Satch. They don't go together. Autumn Riley is strictly a victim? Yeah, sure she is. You have proof different?"

"Paige and Vernice might have a different story." If only I could add the name Dewey to the list. I had this feeling that Dewey had the full story and that he just might want to tell it. Certainly, we'd have to offer him a deal.

"Legally, Autumn can't be held liable for acts done under the influence of The Barb and this drug."

"Don'cha think a jury should decide that? Satch, she locked Paige in a well. She had a personal vendetta against each of the girls, I'm sure."

"For what reason?"

"Well, I know that Paige, for one, beat Autumn out at the pop star audition. Several witnesses confirmed the confrontation in the acting class with Katrice, Anne, and Vernice. Tia, the waitress, said Autumn was bragging about acquiring scoring roofies down in Mexico. Plus, Vernice overheard Autumn planning the sacrifice of all the girls with The Barb and Dewey. I think that, in itself, qualifies as kidnap and attempted mass murder, don't you? Autumn is absolutely accountable for her actions. I know it."

"I need proof."

"Sure, no problem, as soon as I can get the psychic to turn."

"When's that?"

"When pigs fly out my ass."

"When pigs fly out your ass? Oh, that's a good one."

"It's not mine, I borrowed it."

"So, anyway, Autumn Riley's wrapped."

"Autumn Riley better make sure she pees straight because if I get even a…"

"Now, your Dr. Sheffield, you need to leave him alone, too. He's been cooperating since day one. When you first visited, he sent over some extremely helpful information to the coroner's office. Now, what do you want to do? Incriminate him with it?"

"But they had to get those drugs from somewhere. What? You think Dewey was able to brew them up all by himself or that he smuggled them into the country from his lab exploits in Haiti? Sheffield must know something."

"There's nothing on him. He's clean. His lawyer worked me over with a tractor this afternoon."

"With a tractor, Satch? Where'd you get that?"

"I got that one off you."

"Oh, you're just trying to smooth me over. Though it does sound like something I'd say. Jeez, you're killing me here."

And the conversation went on like that. To sum it up, I was told that I had been a good girl and to quit while I was ahead. Then Satch sent me home, said I looked beat. My head was pounding so I begged some aspirins off of Gus and downed them with water. I crushed the little Dixie cup in my hand and tossed it into my trash can and stared at it for a few moments, not thinking anything, just studying the little folds in the crunched paper of the cup. Probably a slight residual effect from the drug cocktail Dewey shot me with.

When I drove across town to my place, I stopped at a stand that makes keys and had an extra house key cut for Eddy. While I was waiting, I used my cell phone to call home. The answering machine answered and I told Eddy to pick up. He did.

"Do you want or need anything?" I asked like we were an old married couple. "I'm on my way home."

"No, but I'd like you to meet me at the Santa Monica Pier, in front of the carousel."

"Okay. Any particular reason?"

"Think of it as a date," he said.

I paused for a moment. "See you there."

I realized when I hung up that Eddy and I had never actually been on an honest-to-God date.

A half hour later, I stepped onto the historical Santa Monica Pier. When I walked across the wooden planks, the soles of my feet became suddenly very sensitive and it was as if I could feel each groove of the wood through my shoes.

I didn't see Eddy anywhere and I wasn't interested in the arcade or any of the other booths that attracted throngs of people every weekend. I stopped and stood outside the carousel as couples and families strolled by.

When a father and daughter walked by holding hands, I recalled my father giving me the gift of my Raggedy Ann doll and that got me thinking about Hector. He'd gone to a lot of trouble to make sure Autumn had my doll. I had to believe he wanted to tell me something. It was meant to be more than a taunt. He'd taken Pancho from my home but had not harmed the dog. Maybe an angel still had a hand in him. I could only guess that some place within him he still had a conscience and could know the pain of others. With his last spoken words, Hector had provided me the clue,

"Piuma," "basura," pointing me to the dirt road that I was able to recognize on the limousine driver's map. It was because of Hector that I was able to find the captives, to put it all together. He had enabled me to see the full picture so I could bring an end to it. Was it merely to get back at The Barb? I didn't think so, because he had been laying down tips, clues, from the beginning, starting with the Raggedy Ann

Doll. It was a game that he meant for me to win. Perhaps he had finally recognized what he had become. Or maybe it was some part of him that wanted it to be revealed. At any rate, it was Hector's last tortured words that led me down the trail, Piuma, the dirt road, to Tommy and the girls.

The carousel music drew me inside the glass-and-wood building of the permanent and famous carousel. It's the same carousel featured in the beginning of that movie, *The Sting*, and it's been in use since the 1930s. The flying horses and sleds with rococo ornamentation, their lights and music, were balm for a weary soul. The building that encases the carousel has large windows that allow passersby to look in. I sat down on one of the wooden benches to keep a lookout for Eddy. A clown walked by outside with a bouquet of colorful balloons and I watched his big red shoes *clomp, clomp* on the water-worn wood of the pier.

Children ran up to the carousel and climbed onto the bright horses, their parents often climbing onto a nearby one. It was uplifting to see their gleeful shining faces as the carousel started and the horses went up and down and around. I looked out the window for Eddy and caught my reflection in the glass. My face was encircled by the swirling colors of the carousel, the little horses with children going round and round my head. I was reminded of Epona, the goddess in Kunda's poster, and the vivid prism that encircled her pale face. I recalled the white colt in the background, as well as the skull of death. I turned back quickly to see the children and their joy, to hold death back from my mind, if only for a moment.

Eddy walked toward me. He stopped and talked to the clown and I watched as he bought a blue balloon. Eddy and the balloon made their way toward me and I smiled as he entered the carousel and sat beside me on the bench.

"The balloon is for you," he said.

"You hold it for me."

I put my arms around his middle and laid my head on his shoulder. I felt good, at one with the world. I decided that there wasn't anything at all wrong with Eddy. He wasn't too young or too anything. He was just right.

He gave me a hug and I went to sleep, dead away, right there on his shoulder. I hadn't realized I was so tired.

CHAPTER THIRTY-ONE

A FEW MONTHS WENT by. I was working a case in Koreatown that involved the murder of two slave labor immigrants, a brother and sister. I had spent the day interviewing people who thought it was clever to pretend they couldn't speak much English. To say I was frustrated wouldn't begin to describe it.

That week, as arresting officer, I had testified against Mary Tyler in the preliminary hearing. She had lost some weight but not her subtle charms, and I was thinking that the death penalty was going to be a no-brainer for the jury. Oh, but wait. No, not in California. I can't say if it's right or not to put someone to death, but I was pretty sure I wasn't going to lose any sleep over it. The Mary Tyler case had been a tough one in that so much was at stake and the details of the case were laced into the illusion of the silver screen. There had been several TV and cable movie versions of her story.

When it came to the case of the Korean brother and sister, I was in uncharted waters. Within the world of the garment industry, there's a subculture filled with languages, dealings, and personalities that I was not so familiar with and that worried me. I believe that one of the things that makes me unique as an investigator is the fact that, in addition to the foolproof methods of thorough investigation, I often go for the unusual approach that brings me into the case on a deeply personal level with those involved. I couldn't see how I was going to pull that off in the case with the brother and sister. I needed an in.

Gus came into Homicide and tossed a tabloid rag on my desk with Autumn Riley and Glenn Addams's picture splashed on the front. Bright red typeface announced their small secret wedding in Tuscany.

"Just thought I'd brighten up your day."

I picked up the paper and gazed at the figure of Autumn Riley in a pure white dress and a tiara.

"She looks just like an angel. Don't make me read it, okay? Just tell me what it says."

"They're doing a movie together."

"Oh, yeah? What kind of movie?"

"A thriller—storyline is of a rising pop star taken captive by a crazed manager."

"You've got to be kidding me."

"Nope."

"Isn't Hollywood a wonderful place? Speaking of which, I heard that Kunda is over at the police academy today. Is that right?"

"She's working with that bloodhound lady from Riverside."

"What's she doing?"

"Kunda, the psychic, is providing insights on what the dogs are feeling. It seems they've been traumatized by one of their assignments."

"You're lying."

"Nope. I swear it's true. It seems she has done extensive ESP work on animals and she's developed quite the reputation. Did you know that dogs are psychic, too?"

"This I got to see."

"I thought you would."

⁂

I FOUND KUNDA ON one of the park-like fields set aside for dog training. She was sitting on a low stone bench with three bloodhounds in front of her. One of the dogs had his big head on her lap. The other two sat like loyal disciples.

The dogs' handlers stood off to the side and showed me only a glancing interest. I wasn't certain it was Kunda until I came close enough to see her face well. I'd only seen her adorned in the flowing new age silks and Pre-Raphaelite hair arrangements. Today, she was dressed in brown suede pants and a white T-shirt and her hair was pulled back into a high ponytail. Her hand floated just above the hound's remarkably sad face. How had she convinced whomever she had convinced to give her this gig? Her eyes were closed and she was uttering an affirmation or something. Her voice was barely above a whisper. Maybe for the dog's sensitive ears. I wasn't sure what the etiquette was, so I just said hello and waited. The dogs all turned their sad eyes on me. They still had the scars from the homemade bomb that had killed one of them and two officers.

Kunda opened her big violet eyes and stared straight through me for a few seconds while she came back from wherever. The dog on her lap gave me a big huff as a hello. "Detective Lambert," she said. "I thought that it might be you. I see you're doing much better than the last time we met. Your aura has much greater clarity. I'm happy for you." She thought it might be me. You had to love this woman.

"Thanks," I said. "You look good yourself. A new style you got going here?"

"Not really. It's a little more conservative is all. I can fit in just about anywhere in order to do service. 'Course, there's some very rigid, closed beings around here…but I don't have to tell you, do I?"

"They're cops, Kunda."

"I suppose."

"So, are these guys going to be all right?"

"Definitely. They're very pure, very gentle spirits. I've been able to bring in the love, the healing love, of the spirits who passed on. They have kind, soothing messages to give those they've left behind and these gentle beings are responding very well, as you can see."

I wasn't sure if I could or not, but, if pressed, I'd have to say that the dogs did seem to adore her.

"Have you done this type of work before?"

"Sure, lots of times with dogs. But I also work with birds, cats. A fish once."

"A fish? No kidding."

She gave me that superior smile of hers and that tilt of her head.

"What has brought you to me? Is it a case? The brother and sister? I'm sensing you need help with that. I'm being well paid on this assignment but I'd be willing to work with you free of charge."

"I seem to remember you saying that before."

"And did I keep my promise?"

"Yes."

"And did the information I provided help you with your case?"

"Yes, as a matter of fact, it did."

"And that's why you're here, Joan. You need my help again."

"You think I want your advice?"

"I'm not offering advice exactly, more like assistance."

"No, Kunda, you've got it all wrong. I came here today because I couldn't believe that it was really you, doing this important work with the bloodhounds, and I had to see for myself. I'm very fond of them, by the way. So, please, do a good job."

"We never know where our paths lead, Detective. The important thing is to be open to traveling them with awareness. The wrong paths as well. There are always signs pointing the way. Closed doors are not always closed doors."

"Wish I knew what the hell you're talking about."

"I will always do a good job for you, Joan. I may have my flaws. I might have made mistakes in my past, but…"

"Yes, go on."

"It's foolish for you to turn away my help."

"So long, Kunda. Happy trails to you."

The goddess smiled, and the tilt of her head made its appearance again.

"What?" I asked.

"Nothing. It was nice of you to come by."

I nodded and walked away.

"There is one thing…I suppose it is a piece of advice. It's not coming through very clear, though. Maybe because you are not as receptive as the dogs."

I chuckled softly to myself, stopped, and turned back to her.

"Are you insulting me?"

"You should do the painting or finish the painting. Yes, that's it. Finish it. Are you in the middle of redecorating? Finish the painting… Oh, hey, do you do, like, ah, oil paintings?"

I tried not to clue her in, but my jaw may have dropped a bit when she said that, giving her the affirmation she was looking for. I didn't speak; I merely looked at her.

"Yes, that's it! You're an artist. Right."

"Maybe." I gave her a slight nod, tried again to make my exit outta there.

"Call me, Joan. I can help. I want to help."

I turned back to her one last time. One of the bloodhounds looked up at me.

"Ya know, I just might take you up on that."

A sincere grin took form on her face. Finally, I walked away from her. I could feel her bright smile shining on my back.

Behind me, one of the bloodhounds let out a soft mournful howl, and that set another softly howling, and then another joined the sad song. The collective refrain created a chorus that ushered me on my way.

ACKNOWLEDGMENTS

A SPECIAL ACKNOWLEDGMENT IS due to the detectives, all diligent men and women, of Pacific Homicide. Namely, Michael DiPasquale and Joe Lumbreras, who both gave me great insights to their work and the detailed picture of a crime.

I'd like to thank Pat Walsh and Tyson Cornell along with the gifted staff at Rare Bird Books.

I'm deeply grateful to Michael Connelly, who is quite the decent guy. He was generous to me and supported my process while writing this book. He also gave me sound advice about the publishing industry. Thank you, Michael, you are an inspiration and a friend.

ABOUT THE AUTHOR

EVA MONTEALEGRE CAME OF age on the historical showboat, *The River Queen*. Her father docked the old gambler's boat in St. Louis, Missouri, and transformed it into a renowned restaurant and nightclub. Her mother, a journalist for the respected *St. Lousian Magazine*, influenced Eva's ardent development as a researcher and writer from a young age. Eva grew up in an environment rich with the dramas of socialites, politicians, artists, and musicians.

Eva began writing professionally as the researcher for a small production company in Santa Monica, California. The position evolved into writer/producer and sometimes director on the project *The Shaping of America*, a series of historical spots on American history. Eva has an extensive interview and journalistic background and has worked for *Brentwood News* and *Venice Art Magazine* interviewing and reviewing the work of known personalities as illustrious as the beloved Dizzy Gillespie and the respected Chris Connelly, editor of *Premiere Magazine*.

Mixomatic, Eva's first short story, won Best Fiction award in *Direction* literary magazine. She has created a living anthology of short stories for the Internet. Eva has interviewed Michael Connelly, T. Jefferson Parker, Robert Eversz, Barbara Seranella, and other stellar mystery authors.

When working on her novels, Eva does firsthand research. She works closely with detectives in Los Angeles. She has also toured the coroner's office with the medical examiner. Eva has guest-lectured and taught writing to both children and adults; she has been on mystery panels and participates in mystery conventions.